KU-520-451

FROM TROPICAL
FLING TO FOREVER

NINA SINGH

To my dear friends and colleagues in the writing
community whom I didn't get to see in person this year.
I miss you all.

CHAPTER ONE

PERHAPS THE TWO-INCH heels might have been a bit much.

Victoria Preston stepped into the kitchen of the corner bakery she owned and operated. Removing an apron from the wall hook, she started to put it on, hoping her atypical attire didn't draw attention. No such luck. The other woman in the room immediately stopped what she was doing and took a good look.

"Wow, aren't you looking sharp! What's the occasion, Tori?"

Yep. She should have worn sensible sandals. No doubt she'd be having that very thought later again today after closing, when her feet were sore and achy.

Tori didn't quite meet her baker assistant's eyes as she answered. "No occasion. Just wanted to dress up a little today, that's all."

Shawna quirked an eyebrow and studied Tori from the rose-pink-painted nails in her open-toed heels to the loose bun atop her head. "Right."

Luckily, Shawna dropped the subject as she lifted a heavy bag of flour and poured what she needed into an industrial-size silver mixing bowl.

Not that Tori could blame the woman for noticing. Truth was, before discovering and reuniting with her long-lost, estranged twin sister not that long ago, Tori would have pegged herself as the last woman on earth to dress up for the sake of a man. She'd always preferred being less visible, didn't like to call attention to herself. But discovering the existence of her twin had led to Tori's reexamination of her life. Part of that scrutiny had included an undertaking to be bolder, more daring. Nothing like discovering an identical twin to make you contemplate your life's choices.

"Thanks for covering the early shift," Tori said to her most loyal employee, who also happened to be her dearest and most trusted friend since high school.

"You know I prefer it."

"And thank heavens for that." Tori was full of gratitude. She'd never been a morning person—definitely more of a night owl. Not a good trait for a bakery owner. It was the one aspect of her career choice she didn't love. Everything else about it, she absolutely adored. The creativity, the delicious aromas constantly surrounding her, the freedom to do her own thing. The excitement of not knowing who was going to walk through the front door from day to day yet also having regular customers she considered friends after these past three years.

"The muffins are in the oven, the bread is in the warmer and the scones are cooling on racks," Shawna informed her.

"You're too good to me. Gives me a chance to double-check inventory and figure out exactly what we need. There's a specialty order coming in later today." Her heart flipped in her chest as she thought of the customer placing that order. So foolish of her. The man probably didn't give her so much as a passing thought until he needed baked goods. While scarcely a day went by where she didn't think of him.

He'd called last night to announce he'd be arriving sometime after the lunch rush. He'd said no more than that.

Clayton Ramos. Most of the world referred to him as Clay.

How embarrassing that she'd felt the need to dress up just because he was coming. As if she wouldn't be covered in flour and chocolate syrup by midmorning anyway.

"What kind of specialty order?" Shawna asked, gazing at her intently. "The tall, dark and handsome kind?"

"I don't know what you could possibly mean."

Shawna laughed. "I mean that you don't typically dress up for a Tuesday spent baking and waiting on customers. Want to tell me about it?"

Her friend was far too observant. Tori should have known she wouldn't let the subject drop for long.

Tori put her hands on her hips. "If you must know, I'm meeting with a rather important client later." She motioned to the dress beneath her apron. "And it's hardly a ball gown."

"Which important client?" Shawna wanted to know, ignoring the latter comment.

Tori tried to feign indifference when she answered. "Mr. Ramos called last night to say he wanted to stop by to discuss an order."

"Oh really?"

"Yes."

"Funny, isn't it?" Shawna quipped, a mischievous hitch in her tone.

"What?"

"How Mr. Ramos's visit just happens to coincide with the same day you happen to run out of clean laundry and have to wear a silk wrap dress to work."

Tori didn't bother to suppress her chuckle. She should

have known better than to try to pull the wool over her best friend's eyes. Time to come clean.

She leaned her hip against the counter and faced her assistant. "Okay. Fine. I wanted to look my best for one of our more…exclusive clients. Is that so wrong?"

Shawna gave her a wink. "Now, was that so hard to admit? To your best friend?"

Sometimes Tori wished said best friend didn't know her quite so well. "Now, don't go reading into things. I just wanted to look a bit more professional. That's all."

"Sure." Shawna shrugged dismissively. "Let's go with that."

Tori ignored the gibe and began preparing the counter with an eye toward the clock. The hour before opening the bakery doors always seemed to move at lightning speed. Today was no exception.

"When is he due in?" Shawna asked.

"He wasn't very specific. Just said sometime in the afternoon, after the lunch rush."

"I wonder what he has in mind."

Tori had been speculating that question all night. Only one conclusion came to mind that made the most sense. "Maybe another wedding he needs a cake for. He does have another younger sister."

Shawna yelped an excited squeal. "Then that would make us one of the first few to know about a potential wedding. Like the last time."

"And we will be absolutely discreet. Like the last time," Tori echoed.

It had taken a good two months for the attention of various paparazzi and news outlets to settle down once the world had learned her bakery would be the pastry and cake provider for a wedding thrown by the one and only Clayton Ramos. Clayton was a celebrated architect to the stars and a globally sought-after bachelor.

The publicity had been great for business, of course. But the attention had often been nerve-racking, draining. Still, the attention had put Tori's Pastries on the map in a way that would be hard to duplicate.

Unlike Tori, Shawna had reveled in the spotlight, enjoyed every bit of the attention. She'd even gone out with a couple of the photographers and a blogger who'd showcased the bakery. No doubt she was excited at the prospect of it all happening again. Her next words confirmed it. "I wonder if the local news will want to run a spot on us this time, too. It's all so exciting."

Indeed. Tori had a feeling Clay's reappearance in her life would cause as much chaos and disruption as the last time.

One more disruption and Clay figured his focus would be completely shot for the day.

He really should call the bakery to reschedule. But he found he really didn't want to. For reasons he couldn't quite explain, he'd been looking forward to stopping in. It absolutely had nothing to do with the perky, cheerful owner with the sparkling green eyes and cute pert nose. No, that wasn't it at all.

Ha. He knew he was fooling himself. In truth, he was looking forward to seeing her—which made no sense whatsoever. He didn't even know her, despite the fact she'd made a handful of desserts and cakes for him over the past couple of years.

"Are you even listening, Clay?" his sister's voice demanded through the speaker of his cell phone. He hadn't even noticed she'd stopped talking.

Clay pinched the bridge of his nose. He'd obviously missed something in the conversation. Right on cue, the dramatics kicked in.

Gemma had always been the more theatrical of his two sisters. She was especially on edge now that she was due to be married in a few weeks.

Clay had been the only father figure his younger sisters had had since the three of them had barely said goodbye to their single-digit ages. Now, even as adults, the girls turned to him for solutions whenever anything went awry in their lives. He'd vowed long ago to always be there for them. And, so far, he'd managed to keep that vow. But heaven knew, it could all be so draining.

"Of course, I am," he answered.

"Do you think she'll say yes?" Gemma asked. "I really prefer her to anyone else. It is a big ask. It's not like we're simply asking her for a cake this time."

"I'm counting on it," he reassured her. After all, if the pretty baker didn't agree at first, he would simply negotiate until she did.

By the time he ended the call with his sister, he'd accepted that he was far too distracted to get any more work done in the office.

Though it was much too early for their scheduled meeting, he could use a strong cup of coffee like the brew served at the bakery. And a fresh, hot croissant would certainly hit the spot.

Why not? Decision made, Clay packed up his laptop and gathered his design tools. As he locked up behind him, he thought about his sister's question. Gemma was right. It was a fairly big ask that he was about to present to Ms. Victoria Preston. But he'd gotten pretty far in life by determining what he wanted and then doing whatever it took to go about getting it. He needed her services. He would get them.

He was about to make one Boston North End bakery owner an offer she couldn't refuse.

When her cell phone vibrated in her apron pocket, Tori didn't even have to look at the screen to know who was calling. Her intuition told her. Eloise termed it "twin sense." It still somewhat amazed Tori that up until a short while ago, she hadn't even known about the existence of her twin sister. Now, Eloise was an integral part of her entire being. Even when she traveled thousands of miles away to her home city of Sydney, Australia.

Pulling out the chair of the table she'd been wiping down in the dining area, she answered the video call.

Discovering Eloise's existence had been the shock of her life, but a part of Tori had always known. A part of her psyche had always reached out for something or someone, had known it was there for her to grasp.

"Hey, sis!" Eloise's smiling face greeted her from the small screen.

A surge of happiness flooded through Tori. Her twin never failed to lift her spirits. "Hey back."

"He'll be there later today then?" Eloise asked.

Tori used the phone grip on the back of her cell to prop it on the table.

"Why, whatever are you referring to?" She barely got the words out before she had to stifle a small giggle. She'd told Eloise about Clay's impending visit last night...when she'd called her sister right after hanging up with him.

Eloise wagged a finger. "Don't pretend you don't know what I'm talking about."

Tori had to laugh. "Okay. Sorry. Won't happen again."

"I would hope not. When is he due in?"

Tori glanced at the time above the screen. "In a few hours."

"You ready for him?"

Her heart leaped in her chest at the wording of her question. Maybe she'd divulged a bit too much about her feelings when she'd confided in her sister about him. "It's just a business meeting, Eloise. That's all."

"Doesn't have to be. I did some digging and looked him up after what you told me last night. That man is the straight-up definition of 'stone-melting hot.' I say you make a move."

Tori rolled her eyes. "You know me better than that, Eloise." How true. Her twin knew her better than anyone else on earth did—despite not having set eyes on each other until just a few weeks ago.

"She has your same exact face," an all too familiar voice said from over her shoulder. *His* voice. Tori didn't have to turn around to confirm that Clayton Ramos was standing right behind her.

Tori jumped out of her chair in shock, fire rushing to her cheeks in sheer embarrassment. Heavens, what if he'd heard? How utterly mortifying.

To her further horror, her leap had sent the chair careening backward. Tori reached out to try to catch it in a desperate attempt to keep it from crashing at his feet. Only, he did the same at the same time. The collision was unavoidable. As was the ensuing disaster that unfolded when Clay lost his grip on his extra-large cup of iced coffee, black. The cap flew off and the contents splashed like an upended bucket across his face and the front of his shirt.

From Tori's cell phone, Eloise's stunned voice echoed through the air. "Oh, Tori. Oh no."

Despite the words, Tori's "twin sense" told her that her sister was more than a little amused.

She quickly said goodbye and pocketed her phone.

Every eye in the bakery was on them, laser-focused on the bizarre scene that had just unfolded. Tori just wanted to disappear into thin air. For his part, Clay looked a bit shell-shocked as he studied the ever-growing splotch of dark brown spreading across his crisp white shirt.

You can dress a girl up...

"I'm so sorry!" Reaching for a handful of napkins from the dispenser on the table behind her, Tori tried to repair some of the damage, but all she managed was to further spread the blasted stain.

Shawna chose that moment to come out from the back. Taking in the disastrous scene, she clutched her hand to her chest. "Oh my, what happened?" Her voice shook ever so slightly.

Tori glanced over her shoulder to see her friend's lips quivering. Yep, she was definitely trying not to chuckle. How wonderful that Tori could be such a source of humor for two of the most important women in her life.

"I'll get a towel," Shawna declared, disappearing behind the swinging doors.

"Mr. Ramos, I'm so incredibly sorry," Tori repeated for the third time as she grabbed more napkins and continued the useless dabbing. "It's just, I didn't hear you approach from behind me, and our appointment isn't until much later. I didn't see you come in at all." Now she was just rambling.

He wrapped long fingers gently around her wrist. "Please stop. It's clearly not working."

He was certainly right about that. To make matters worse, there was the clear sound of snickering from more than one patron. Tori wanted to cry. Of all the ways she'd imagined their scheduled meeting would go, thoroughly humiliating herself had not been one of them.

"I'm so terr—"

He cut her off with an upheld palm. "Please. Don't apologize again."

She had to bite down on her lip to follow his direction.

"Besides," he added, "it was clearly my fault."

It was?

"I shouldn't have startled you. I'm the one who should be apologizing."

That was ridiculous. Only one of them was wearing a drenched and soggy shirt, for heaven's sake. The person with black iced coffee dripping down his shirtfront should most definitely not be the one to apologize. Still, Tori was at a loss for words. For him to try to take responsibility for something that was so clearly her doing, floored her.

Aside from her father and brothers, she hadn't really come across too many men who would do such a thing.

Shawna returned with a terry towel and tossed it to Tori. She held it out to him, but Clay didn't bother taking it. He just gave her a nod. What was the use? He was right; any attempt to blot the liquid was beyond pointless.

"So much for getting some work done." He cursed under his breath, adding some other muttered words she couldn't quite make out. Words that might have included "day from hell."

"I beg your pardon?" she asked.

"Nothing. I've just been having a bit of a vexing one."

"I'm so—" He cut her a sharp look and she stopped herself from apologizing yet again.

"Guess I have no choice but to head home and change. I'll come back for our meeting at the hour we scheduled. Not that I can spare the time today of all days."

"Don't leave."

He blinked at her then glanced down his chest. "Well, I can hardly sit here soaked to the skin." He leaned closer to her, as if to share a secret. "It's rather uncomfortable."

"I live in the apartment upstairs. I'll get you a shirt you can wear."

He studied her from head to toe and she felt a warmth creep into her cheeks. "Uh, thanks for the offer, but I'm guessing we're not the same size."

"Not my shirt."

His eyebrow shot up. "I don't think your boyfriend would appreciate—"

This time she cut him off. "Oh no! It's not like that."

"It isn't?"

Why had she suddenly lost the ability to communicate? The last thing Tori wanted was for Clay to think she was romantically attached to someone. And that was quite the acknowledgment, now that she thought about it.

Giving her head a shake, she tried to get her tongue to work properly. "I have two older brothers." Three, if she counted Josh. "I've confiscated more than my share of large T-shirts to sleep in."

Something flittered behind his eyes before he responded. "I see."

"Plus, I'm due to do a load of laundry. I'll just throw your shirt in, too, before any staining sets in. It will be washed and dry for you in a couple of hours."

"Huh." He seemed to consider it then nodded. "In that case, I think I will take you up on the offer."

Tori turned on her heel to head upstairs and retrieve the shirt. To her surprise, Clay followed her.

She'd fully intended to run down with a T-shirt and wait for him to change in the restroom so she could run back up to launder his shirt. But he clearly intended to follow her.

Of course, that made more sense—for him to just change in her apartment. So why was her pulse quickening at the thought of him being up there? She would look foolish and possibly offend him if she asked him not to follow her.

Had she even bothered to put away the breakfast dishes this morning? Or last night's dinner dishes, for that matter? Probably not. It had been a long, busy, and exhausting day at the bakery yesterday and she'd barely had the energy to kick her shoes off and scarf down a cheese croissant with a small salad. Though, in her defense, she hadn't been expecting *the* Clayton Ramos to be paying her a house visit.

Oh dear. What if he thought her a slob after seeing the state of her apartment? What if she'd never picked up the shoes she'd kicked off after arriving home? Or discarded the leftover ice cream carton? What if—?

She cut off the thought. Those days of being judged by a man were well past now. And she had no intention of going back to them.

"I appreciate this," Clay was saying behind her. "I'm already delayed on this next design, and phase two of the project is fast approaching."

"It's the least I can do. I feel terrible about what happened."

"Hey, don't worry about it, okay? It's not the first time I've had a drink spilled on me."

She stifled a chuckle. "Happens often, does it?"

"Let's just say that the last time someone threw an icy drink in my direction, I most determinedly deserved it."

Tori glanced back to find him flashing her a devilish grin that had her faltering a step.

By the time they walked through the storage room and up the back stairs to the front door of her second-floor apartment, Tori had somewhat convinced herself to calm down. Turning the unlocked knob, she stepped aside to let him enter ahead of her.

The calm faded as Clay immediately started to shrug out of his shirt.

He was clearly comfortable disrobing in ladies' apartments. Not surprising, based on his reputation as an international player. Who was the latest girlfriend rumored to be again? Oh yeah, the Austrian model. He'd been snapped walking out of her apartment building in the wee hours of the morning just last month.

Clay handed her the shirt and, for a moment, she couldn't move as she took it from his hand.

She was staring. Tori forced herself to look away. Not that it was easy. Sweet cupcakes, it was hard not to stare at him standing there in front of her all bare-chested. Golden-tanned. Chisel-muscled.

Stop it.

This was so not the time to be thinking along those lines.

"I'll get you that T-shirt," she managed to utter, hoping beyond hope she'd turned away before he'd noticed her ever-reddening cheeks.

Something told her it was wishful thinking.

How in the world had he ended up here?

Clay stood in the middle of the room, taking in his surroundings. Soft and rounded. Those two words described the space perfectly. A plush sofa sat in the center, atop an oval area rug that appeared to be hand woven. A large round mirror hung above an arched fireplace mantel. No sharp angles. His trained eye told him the circular theme had been deliberate. The occupant knew what she was doing when decorating this living space. These choices had been thought out and planned on a specific preference.

Victoria Preston did not like sharp edges.

He could hear her scrummaging around somewhere down the hallway. If someone had told him this morning that later that day he'd be waiting in Ms. Preston's charming apartment while shirtless and smelling of strong espresso…well, he wasn't sure what he would have thought.

But perhaps a better question was how had he forgotten her pretty eyes. Or the contrast the color of those eyes made with her spiky auburn hair…

Steady there, fella.

He really didn't need his thoughts to head in that direction. Tori, as everyone seemed to call her, was so not his usual type. She was too sweet, too unassuming. A woman like that didn't need the likes of him marring their well-planned, idyllic lives.

That's why it had made no sense earlier, the hollow feeling in his gut when he'd thought she'd be giving him a shirt that belonged to a boyfriend. Or the sense of relief he'd experienced once she'd corrected his assumption. For all he knew, she may very well have a significant other. Just one who didn't own apparel she found adequate as sleepwear. Women like Tori weren't often single. Not for long, anyway. Successful, smart, attractive—she could have her pick of men.

Really, it was none of his business at all.

He studied her apartment a little closer. It suited her. Tidy overall, aside from a couple of used dishes on the kitchen counter behind the living area. Not a speck of dust to be seen. Exactly the type of apartment he would have picked for her. Framed photographs littered almost every surface. Pictures filled with smiling faces against backdrops of scenic landscapes or charming rooms.

A raggedy, frayed and torn stuffed rabbit hugged a corner of the cream-colored couch. The thing had to be ancient.

Her place was cozy. Comfortable. Judging by the photos of her throughout the years, he could tell she'd live the kind of childhood he and his sisters had never experienced growing up.

A more recent photograph sitting on the circular marble coffee table in the center of the room caught his eye. Tori with another young woman who looked exactly like her. Only the hair was different. Whereas Tori wore hers short and spiky in an unconventional, rather modern style—he believed the kids would call it Goth—the other woman had wavier locks, a shade different.

She had a twin.

That explained what he'd seen on her phone screen earlier, what had led to the chain of events that had ultimately had him smelling like a coffee grinder.

Funny. He'd hired her more than once over the past three years—and they'd made plenty of small talk—but he didn't recall her ever mentioning a sister, much less a twin. Or maybe she had and he just hadn't been listening. How often in his life had he been told he was too distracted?

Always got your head in the clouds…always thinking you're better than everyone else.

Tori walked back into the room at that moment, dispelling the cruel memory. One of all too many.

She handed him a soft cotton T-shirt. Gray with bold blue FDNY letters across the front.

"Thanks. I take it one of your brothers is a fireman? In New York City?"

"An EMT."

"Ah." He took the shirt and pulled it over his head. A little snug, but it fit well enough. It smelled of Tori, a blend of berries and citrus and something appealingly spicy. Cinnamon maybe. Or cloves.

"Your shirt is already in the washer," she told him.

"Thanks." He pointed to the framed photo he'd been staring at when she'd walked in. "You never mentioned a sister."

She inhaled deeply. "That's because I didn't really know until recently that..." She looked down at her toes, grasping for words, it seemed. "It's actually a really long story, and I should probably get back downstairs. Shawna is by herself with cakes in the oven and customers waiting. We're a bit short-staffed until the afternoon."

"Of course," he responded immediately. "I didn't mean to hold you up. Or to pry." He felt compelled to add that last part because of the underlying tension in her tone.

"Oh, no. It's not that." She smiled and her whole face transformed, a brightness appearing behind her eyes. "I actually would like to tell you about it sometime. It's kind of a crazy tale."

"Then I'll look forward to hearing it. Consider me intrigued."

It surprised him just how much he meant that.

CHAPTER TWO

TORI FELT AN almost silly rush of relief once Clay put the T-shirt on. The man simply looked much too good topless. She gave herself a mental forehead thwack for acting like a schoolgirl with her first crush.

But was there really any harm in that? This was just some simple and innocent fantasizing on her part. Clay was ridiculously out of her league. He dated actresses and dancers, for heaven's sake. Plus, she presently had no desire or inclination to pursue any kind of romantic relationship. Not after she'd tried so hard to move on after her last one. Her only one.

She was finally at a point where she wasn't constantly looking over her shoulder or bracing herself for the next put-down.

Tori was perfectly content to live the single, unattached life for the moment. In fact, she'd never felt more at peace in years, not since that first date with Drew at the naïve and fresh age of seventeen.

Though it was hard to imagine turning a man like Clay down—if by some miracle he were even to ask her out.

And that was about as likely as bread rising without yeast.

Clay cleared his throat and she realized she'd drifted off into her own thoughts.

"I'll get your shirt back to you as soon as it's dry," she said and turned toward the door.

To her surprise, he stopped her with a hand on her forearm. The casual touch sent a tingle of electricity straight through to her chest. "If we could just have another minute…"

She blinked up at him.

"Since we happen to be here alone, I thought we could just discuss the matter I came here to see you about," he added.

Tori had to swallow the breath that had lodged in her throat. "Y-yes?"

"We were quite pleased with the cake you created for my sister Adria's wedding a couple of years back."

"Thank you."

"My other sister, Gemma, will also be getting married in a few weeks."

"I see. You want to discuss contracting for another cake then?"

"In a sense."

What in the world did that mean? And why would he want to have the conversation here in her apartment?

"Um, what dates were you thinking? And how many tiers?"

"The truth is, I don't really know," he said. "Gemma will have to tell you herself."

Clearly, Tori was missing something since it appeared his sister wouldn't even be joining them for the conversation. "I don't understand. You are here to hire me to make a cake, correct?"

"Sort of."

An uneasy feeling began to rise in her chest. Maybe he didn't want her at all for this gig. Maybe he was simply too nice and wanted to tell her she was being replaced face-to-face. "Sort of?"

"I wanted to meet with you because I'd like to speak to you about a job offer."

Tori blinked, trying to process the information. It didn't make any sense, so she stated the obvious. "I own my own business. I don't really need a job."

Clay pinched the bridge of his nose. "I'm sorry. I'm not really explaining this well. Maybe it would be clearer if I referred to it as a business opportunity."

Nope. Not clearer at all. No matter what he called it, she couldn't make sense of what was going on here.

"I think you might want to just come out and tell me exactly what this is all about, Clay."

"Right." He clasped his hands in front of him. "I'll preface it by saying I know how busy you are, how in demand your services are... So I know this might be asking a lot."

"Okay."

"My sister is having a destination wedding," he explained. "It's to take place over the span of five days on a small Bahamian island resort off the coast of Florida."

That made no sense. How was Tori supposed to get a cake delivered across land and sea to some island in the Bahamas? "And...?"

"And I'd like you to come along."

Tori gave her head a shake, as if to clear it. Had she heard him correctly? "Are you...asking me to your sister's wedding?"

As soon as the words left her mouth, Tori wanted to somehow suck them back in. Then she wanted to sink through the floor at the look of utter horror on Clay's face. She wouldn't forget that look for as long as she lived.

How breathtakingly humiliating. She'd gone and made the most embarrassing of assumptions: that he might actually be asking her to attend his sister's wedding as some kind of date.

Clearly, he'd had something else in mind.

"Gemma would like to bring along both a meal chef and a pastry chef to work the wedding," he quickly began to explain. "The latter being you."

Her mouth had gone dry but somehow Tori managed to answer. "I see."

"Gemma, my sister who's getting married," he added, abruptly blurting it out as if that fact hadn't already been made abundantly clear.

What a fool she was to even consider for a moment that he would ask her for anything even remotely personal.

Lifting her chin, Tori gave him the only answer she could if she had any hope of saving face. "I'm sorry, Clay. Thank you for the offer. But I'm afraid I can't take you up on it."

CHAPTER THREE

Three weeks later

WHAT IN THE world had she been thinking?

Tori adjusted her roomy bucket seat, tilted it slightly back and then turned to a fresh sheet on her sketch pad. She'd never been on a private jet before.

Clayton Ramos certainly knew how to drive a hard bargain. She had to give him that.

Who would have thought, after that afternoon in her apartment when Clay had made his offer, that she'd be southbound above the Atlantic on his private aircraft less than a month later? She'd resisted in the beginning. She really had. But he'd continually sweetened the deal to the point she'd have been a fool to turn it down. In the end, Tori had done what was best for the bakery. On top of the monetary incentive, she couldn't deny what the opportunity would do for her small shop. Tori's Pastries was managing quite well, if she did say so herself, but customers could be fickle.

Look at what had happened to her sister. A disgruntled and overly demanding influencer had almost destroyed Eloise's career as well as her reputation. Luckily, Josh and her sister had devised a rather unconventional plan to thwart the woman's cruel intentions. They'd had to go through the ruse of a relationship, but given it had led to a real wedding, everything had all worked out in the end.

The memory brought a smile to Tori's face.

But, fake relationship aside, the threat to Eloise's bridal dress design business had been much too real.

All it would take for something similar to happen to Tori would be one too many bad online reviews. She spent a fair amount of time monitoring such reviews. Luckily, most of what was written about her bakery was positive. But there were always the select few who found ways to criticize. The cupcakes were too sweet. The lines on weekends were too long. One customer had had the nerve to write that her red velvet cupcakes tasted like store-bought mix. It was her top-selling item, for heaven's sake!

Forgetting her sketch pad for the moment, Tori sighed softly to herself as she looked out the window. The rest of the wedding party had flown to Nassau earlier in the week and everyone was now waiting for Tori and Clay to arrive. Once they did, the group would all sail to the small island where the ceremony was to take place.

Clay, having had to stay behind for an important meeting, had suggested Tori travel with him since she hadn't been able to make the earlier flight.

Despite the size of the impressive plane, there was something quite intimate about being alone with Clay hundreds of feet up in the air. She glanced at him now.

As if sensing her gaze, he looked up and caught her eye. Tori resisted the urge to look away. It was much too late to pretend she hadn't been studying him.

He slowly shut his laptop and pushed back the tray table. Standing, he made his way toward her.

Taking the seat across from hers, he pointed to the graphic tee she was wearing. Imprinted with an image of a bowl of spaghetti, the italic lettering underneath read Vilardo's.

"That place isn't too far from your bakery. I've eaten there. Excellent restaurant."

She could only agree. "I like it a lot, too."

"It can be impossible to get a table some days."

"I've seen the line snake around the corner at times."

He nodded. "Worth the wait, though. The food is incomparable."

"It's often written up as one of the top five trattorias in Boston's North End."

He shook his head. "I'd say top three. The stuffed pasta shells are a work of art."

"I'll be sure to tell my mama you think so," she told him with a smile of pride.

"Your mama?"

"It's my parents' restaurant. My mother's maiden name is Vilardo."

Clay's eyes narrowed on her face. "Huh. Guess the food business runs in the blood."

This was the awkward part. Tori never knew how to respond to such comments. She usually brushed off the words with a polite smile or a deft change of subject. But this time felt different. For reasons she couldn't really articulate, she wanted Clay to know about this large part of her story. She even wanted to tell him about the utterly unbelievable way she'd found her sister. She had no idea why, but she found him easy to confide in. That was almost silly. She barely knew the man.

"Blood wouldn't really apply in my case," she told him.

He lifted an eyebrow in puzzlement. "Oh?"

"I was adopted as a toddler."

"Family doesn't always mean blood." He sounded like he was speaking from experience.

"Nurture versus nature, I suppose."

"Either way, your parents must be very proud of you."

Tori turned to look out the small window again. Outside, myriad thick, bouncy clouds littered the light blue sky. If only she could emphatically nod her head and agree with Clay's last statement. But she'd be lying. While it was true her parents were indeed very proud of her in many ways, they were also severely disappointed.

And there was no way she would be able to make them understand. Not without revealing a truth that would crush their spirits.

From where he stood, Tori wasn't looking all that great. Clay dropped the design specs he'd been reviewing and made his way over to where she sat portside. He couldn't seem to stay away from the woman; she pulled him like no one else he'd ever met.

"You're not getting seasick, are you?" he asked, sitting in the booth across from hers.

They'd landed at Nassau's Lynden Pindling International Airport about two hours ago. After clearing customs and meeting up with the rest of the wedding party, they'd immediately boarded a passenger catamaran to sail to their final destination.

Studying Tori now, he had no doubt her pallor was off.

"Maybe a little," she answered in a small voice. "Which makes no sense. I've been on plenty of boats on choppy Cape Cod waters."

"Though not after a long plane ride, I'm guessing."

She scoffed with a smile, looking out over the water. "A plane ride on a private jet is hardly something to complain about."

He shrugged. "It still makes for a long day of travel. And there was quite a bit of turbulence."

"Thanks for trying to make me feel like less of a wimp."

Wimp. Not a word he would ever use to describe her. Anyone who had opened their own business in a severely competitive field and was running it successfully almost entirely on her own was the antithesis of a wimp. "There're a couple of doctors and NPs among the guests on board. Would you like me to ask around to see if anyone might have something to help?"

Tori shook her head, the motion making her skin shade even greener. Even so, she still looked mind-scramblingly attractive. Funny. And why would his thoughts be going in that direction at such an inopportune time?

"I'll be fine," she said, turning her eyes toward the water once more. "I just need to sit here and focus on the horizon. That's supposed to help with mild motion sickness, isn't it?"

"I'll go get you a soda." He stood before she could protest and retrieved a ginger ale from the stocked bar set up for them.

He popped open the can and set it on the table in front of her.

"Thanks. Sorry to be a bother."

"You're hardly a bother, Tori. And I can't tell you how much I appreciate you coming along to do this for Gemma." He motioned to where his sister stood leaning against her groom. His other sister, Adria, was huddled with her young daughter over a tablet, watching a fairy-tale movie they'd downloaded before the trip.

"You and your siblings seem very close," Tori said, taking a small sip from the can.

"We're pretty much all we have."

She looked at him in question but he had no desire to get into the wreck that was his family history. "What about you?" he asked, changing the subject. "You have two older brothers, correct? Are you close with them?"

The truth was she adored them both. "They do their fair share of brotherly teasing. But yes, I would say we are close." Her gaze shifted back to the horizon. "I'm close with my sister, as well. We are twins, after all."

"That's right. She's the woman I saw on your phone screen that day." Tori'd spoken often of her brothers during their past interactions, but finding out she'd had a twin had come as a bit of a surprise to him. It was all very peculiar.

"Did you two play any twin pranks growing up? Switch spots in class to try to confuse people?"

Her smile faltered. "We didn't actually grow up together."

Peculiar indeed. She solved the mystery with her next words. "I mentioned that I was adopted as a toddler. As was she, but to a different family. I've been told it was a private adoption necessitated when my biological mother became ill. The agency decided it was best if we completely cut all ties and contact. Eloise and I had no say in the matter."

"Interesting," was all he could come up with to say. It appeared he wasn't the only one with an unconventional family dynamic.

"I found her completely by accident. Well, my friend Josh did, to be more accurate." An affectionate smile bloomed on her lips. "I've known him for as long as I can remember."

Clay's chest constricted at the way her face brightened when she'd mentioned the man's name. "Your friend Josh found your long-lost sister?"

She nodded, her smile widening. "He's something else. A true one in a million."

Quite the accolade, Clay thought. Who exactly was this guy? Every indication, from her expression to her tone of voice, hinted that he was much more than a friend.

Clay had no reason to want to question her about him, to find out exactly who this man was to her. Still, the tightening in his chest had yet to ease. Until he heard her next words.

"Eloise and Josh are married now. I was a bridesmaid."

A surge of relief Clay couldn't really explain flushed through him at the revelation. Tori and Josh were clearly no more than lifelong friends who now found themselves in-laws. Not that it was any of his business. The woman was simply here to bake, for goodness' sake. He shouldn't be interested in her life relationships.

Still, he couldn't help but feel moved by what she'd just told him. The discovery of a long-lost sibling as an adult wasn't a tale one heard every day.

"I've shocked you," Tori said with a smile after several moments of silence. She appeared to be feeling better. Some of the color had begun to appear on her cheeks and her lips weren't drawn quite so rigidly any longer.

"It's quite a story. I'm glad you and your sister found each other."

"Our connection was immediate. Now, it's like we were never apart. She's in the process of moving to Boston and opening another store."

There was no mistaking the pride in Tori's voice.

"What does she do?"

"She designs bridal dresses. For a very high-end clientele."

"Seems that's yet another connection. You do wedding cakes, she designs wedding dresses."

Tori ducked her head. "Not quite the same. I'm simply a baker. And you happen to be my only high-end client."

Clay was struck by the defeatism of her words. For such an accomplished woman, she seemed to have a warped sense of personal achievement at such a young age. "I get the feeling I'll be one of many. And I doubt it will take long."

Her eyes grew wide at the compliment. He'd clearly surprised her.

"Thank you for saying that." She lifted the now empty soda can. "And thank you for this. Seems to have done the trick."

"You're welcome. Glad to hear it."

He was also glad to have learned a bit more about the woman he was finding more and more fascinating with each passing moment.

"Do you play tennis?"

Shading her eyes from the sun, Tori looked up from her lounge chair where she'd been relaxing on the beach and sketching for the better part of an hour. It was their second day on the island and so far she'd baked a cupcake tower to follow this evening's dinner and was now stealing some time to work on the design of the wedding cake. So focused on the task, she hadn't noticed the shadow that fell over the paper until she heard the all too familiar voice.

"Sorry to interrupt," Clay said, pointing to her sketch. "But it's something of an emergency."

The slight tilt at the corners of his mouth told her the emergency couldn't be all that pressing.

"Beg your pardon?"

"I asked if you played. Tennis."

She thought she'd heard the rather random question

correctly. "I went to a summer camp every year until I turned thirteen. Tennis was part of the curriculum."

"Excellent." He reached for her hand. "I'll come with you as you get your sneakers."

Tori let him take her hand in his and slowly rose out of the chair. "I'm not quite sure I understand still."

"My sister and her groom have challenged me to a doubles match with a partner of my choice," he told her.

That didn't exactly explain why she was the choice in question. "And you're asking me?"

"Yes. And you're agreeing. Unless you really don't want to."

Tori was still processing what was happening. He took advantage of her hesitation. "Come on. It'll do you good to get some air and exercise. And you can help me beat those two. They've been talking smack all morning."

Everyone else must have turned him down. Why else would he be dragging the pastry chef along to play as his partner?

"But I didn't bring a racket or anything."

He shrugged. "The resort provides those."

"Was there no one else?"

He stopped walking and turned to her. "I'm starting to get the feeling you're not very enthusiastic to play with me."

The utter ridiculousness of the situation and the deadpan seriousness in his voice had Tori struggling to suppress a laugh. "It's not that. I'm just curious as to why you're asking the pastry chef when you have guests you can ask."

"I suppose I can go around the resort looking for someone. But it's going to get too hot to play in a bit. And here you are, right on the beach, sketching. Plus, you said you know how to play. It has to be fate, I'd say. Kismet even."

Well, when he put it that way. "I suppose that makes sense." Though she didn't quite know about the whole "fate" bit.

"Also, I'd like to play with you," he added with a devilish wink that had her knees growing weak.

"I guess it'd be nice to handle a racket again."

He didn't waste time waiting for a direct confirmation. "Let's go then."

In less than fifteen minutes, Tori, having changed into a shorts set and tennis shoes, found herself covering the deuce side.

Surprisingly, she and Clay appeared to make a good team. He seemed in tune with her play strategy and they did a good job with silent communication—understanding each other's hand gestures and unspoken plays. In no time, they had taken the lead and were able to maintain it for the match. Tori even managed to ace the groom, leading to the stroke that essentially won the set.

Before she knew what he was up to, Clay rushed over and lifted her up in the air, his arms tight around her middle. He swung her around with a resounding cheer.

Tori's pulse was pounding by the time he put her back on the ground. It was nothing more than a victory hug. But she couldn't deny the physical longing that had rushed through her when she'd found herself in Clay's arms.

Gemma and Tom approached from the other side of the net and Clay turned in their direction. If he was affected at all by their embrace, he certainly didn't show it. That only confirmed what she already knew. She had to fight her attraction to this man, for self-preservation.

"All right, big bro," Gemma said as the four of them

shook hands. "You two won fair and square. A deal is a deal. Drinks are on us. See you in the tavern in twenty?"

"Ha, ha. That's really funny considering it's an all-inclusive resort."

Gemma stuck her tongue out at him. "Yes, but I'll still pay dearly by having to listen to you brag about your win. Probably incessantly, until the end of time."

Clay chuckled. "There is that."

Bride and groom clasped hands as they walked away. "See you later, Tori," Gemma called over her shoulder. "Nice game."

Tori couldn't help but stare after them. They seemed so happy, so in love. She thought she'd had that once, but her relationship with Drew had only seemed ideal from the outside. That's why it had been so hard to explain to her family why she'd ultimately walked away. As much as she could explain, that is. She hadn't been able to bring herself to tell them the full extent of what had happened between her and her ex-boyfriend.

Her pride wouldn't allow it.

As a result, her friends and family all thought she was foolish for leaving a man that so many women would feel beyond fortunate to be with. Especially someone like her.

"Did you want to freshen up before heading over to the tavern?" Clay asked as they exited the court gates, pulling her out of her thoughts.

She knew should say no; turn him down flat. She was essentially his employee and fraternizing with the boss probably wasn't a good idea. "I should get back to sketching out the cake."

"Come on," he urged. "I can hardly take a victory lap without my play partner."

Tori faltered. One drink wouldn't hurt, would it? She really was rather thirsty after close to ninety minutes of hard play in the strong sun. And the bride and groom would be there. She might get some more ideas about exactly what they wanted. Details could make all the difference between a spectacular cake and a truly stunning one. Technically, it would even count as a business meeting with her main client.

"It won't take long," Clay assured her. "You can just help me gloat shamelessly about our victory and then we'll be on our way."

His persistence eroded her will to say no.

"Sure. Why not."

"I have to say—" he dramatically clasped a hand to his chest "—your lack of enthusiasm when it comes to spending time with me is a bit ego-crushing."

She had to laugh at that. If he only knew… "I apologize for my rudeness. I would love to join you for a drink with your sister and future brother-in-law." She bowed slightly for effect.

"That's more like it," he teased.

After Tori ran into a nearby restroom to throw some cold water on her sweaty face and tidy her frazzled hair, she met Clay where he waited at a high-top table in the far corner of the tavern.

She approached just as his phone dinged with a text.

"Good thing I didn't wait for them to order," he said as he read the message.

"What's going on?"

He held up the phone for her. "My sister informs me that they've run into a delay and are running late to meet us."

Tori could think of all sorts of reasons why a bride and groom might run into a delay after stopping in their hotel room. But she figured Clay probably didn't want to think about that, being the bride's brother and all.

A server appeared with a sweaty bottle of beer and a full, frosty glass of white wine.

"I figured you'd want something cold and ordered you a chardonnay. We can send it back if you'd like something else."

"This is perfect. Thank you." In fact, her mouth was watering for a taste of refreshment. It had gotten quite hot out there on the court. By the third game, she'd felt like a sweaty mess with frizzy, tangled hair.

Clay, by contrast, had managed to appear impeccable throughout the whole match, even with beads of sweat rolling down his cheeks and glistening along his arms.

Another text alert sounded on his phone and Tori could guess what it said.

Clay confirmed her assumptions. "Gemma again. They've decided to bag it altogether. They won't be joining us, after all."

He lifted his glass to her in a mini salute. "Looks like it's just you and me."

He noticed something that might be described as alarm flickered behind Tori's eyes. She recovered quickly, however, saying, "That's too bad. I wanted to talk to them some more about their cake."

Did that explain why she'd looked so alarmed when she'd heard Gemma and Tom wouldn't be joining them, after all? Or was it something else?

Clay couldn't deny there seemed to be an undercurrent between them. Almost like an ethereal crackling in the air. Was Tori aware of it, too? Maybe it was all in his head.

He studied her as she took a small sip of her wine. She was still flushed from their game. Already, her skin had developed a slight tan. Her lips were moist from the chilled wine.

Another thing he couldn't deny was how attracted he was to her. She possessed an underlying strength that seemed at odds with her sweet and soft demeanor. The contrast called to him in a way he couldn't recall ever experiencing before.

The problem was, he had no business thinking about any of this. And he'd certainly had no business pulling her into his arms and holding her close the way he had on the tennis court. Heaven help him, all he'd wanted to do after putting her back on her feet was to lift her chin, pull her face to his and take those tempting, full lips with his own. And he might have done just that if they'd been alone. Thank goodness they hadn't been.

He was much too damaged for a woman the likes of Victoria Preston. A fact he'd do well to remember.

Clay's musings were interrupted when the server reappeared by their side. He carried a wide, ceramic platter full of food that he placed between them on the table. "Cracked conch with various dipping sauces," he announced. "An island specialty. On the house for our esteemed guests."

The enticing aroma of the fried seafood had his stomach grumbling and he felt almost grateful for the distraction.

"That looks delicious," Tori told the waiter with a warm smile. "Thank you."

The man looked ready to melt at the smile she gave him.

Welcome to the club, buddy.

"I didn't think I was hungry until he brought this out." He motioned for her to go ahead. "Ladies first."

Tori gingerly lifted a small piece then dipped it into a

small cup of sauce. As she bit into it, her eyes grew wide and she let out a soft moan.

Clay had to grip the table to keep from reacting. "I take it it's good?"

"Heavenly. I'll have to see if I can wrangle the recipe to share with my mom. Wait till you try one!"

He almost didn't want to take any, just to watch her savor every last morsel. In the end, though, his stomach won out.

She was right. The conch melted in his mouth as a burst of flavor exploded on his tongue.

"Oh man. That is good." He pointed to the dipping sauce he'd just used. "You have to taste that one next."

Tori did as he suggested, her reaction instantaneous and just as visceral as the last time. Her eyelids lowered as her tongue darted out to lick her lower lip.

Sweet mercy.

He was going to have to look away. He might have to ask the waiter to turn the television on. Just so he had something else to focus on. Had any woman he'd ever encountered looked so sexy while she ate?

An image popped into his head before he could so much as stop it. He'd picked up a morsel of food and was feeding it to Tori. He could feel those luscious lips around his finger as she took in the bite—

Clay sucked in a breath.

A television wasn't going to help. He doubted even a cold shower might. Yet he still couldn't make himself look away. When she took another bite of food, a small drop of sauce landed on her chin, right below her lip. The gods were surely laughing at him with all the temptation they kept throwing his way.

He knew he shouldn't, but he couldn't seem to help himself. It was like asking him not to take his next breath. He leaned over to indicate the exact spot. "You, uh, missed your mouth with some of that."

"Huh?"

He lifted his hand to point out exactly where the sauce had dripped on her chin. Only he did more than point. His hand seemed to move on its own. Before he knew it, he was wiping the sauce away with his thumb. Her skin felt soft and smooth under his finger.

She gasped at his touch but made no move to shift away.

Another vision appeared in his mind. He was leaning closer, replacing his finger with his tongue. He imagined tasting her. He was sure she would taste of salt and sea and spice.

Man. This is bad. Totally wrong.

He couldn't be lusting after a friendly baker he'd only seen once or twice when an occasion called for it. What was the matter with him? He usually had a better hold on his libido.

He'd been without female companionship for too long. That's all this craziness was. But he couldn't seem to bring himself to move away, and his hand was still lingering on her face. Would it be so wrong to stroke her cheek? To gently grasp the tendril of hair that had fallen out of the elastic and tuck it back behind her ear?

Would he be able to stop himself once he started touching her, knowing it was the wrong thing to do? After all, he'd had to force himself to let her go after embracing her on the court.

It didn't help matters that Tori still hadn't made any kind of move to back away from his touch. Her breath warmed the skin of his hand. Her breathing had gone ragged and sharp.

A commotion from the direction of the doorway scattered his attention, breaking the moment. A gaggle of bikini-clad young women noisily entered the tavern and headed to the bar area. The disruption brought Clay to his senses. And not a moment too soon. He immediately dropped his hand and reached for another piece of conch.

Tori blinked twice and shifted in her chair to lean back.

He wasn't imagining it or reading into things. She was clearly as attracted to him as he was to her. And what was he to do with that information?

Of course, the only sane answer was to ignore it.

So that's what if felt like. To feel true desire, to tremble with temptation. To want a man as much as she wanted her next breath. Tori realized she'd never really experienced such a fierce longing for a man, despite having been in a years-long relationship.

In fact, she'd never experienced anything like this with Drew. Certainly not toward the end. No, she'd felt nothing then but trepidation and something akin to fear the more time they'd spent together. As each argument grew louder and scarier than the last... As each of his criticisms, on everything from her clothing to her hairstyle, became more and more insulting... He'd chipped away at her sense of self and security until desire was the last thing she felt toward the man.

No, she'd never felt for Drew what she was currently experiencing with Clay.

She sat stunned and disoriented at what had just transpired between them. For a moment there, she could have sworn that Clay was going to lean in and kiss her. And, heaven help her, she would have let him. More than that, she would have welcomed it.

She'd have kissed him back.

What would it feel like to kiss Clayton Ramos? As it was, the mere touch of his thumb on her chin had her quaking inside. Her face still felt hot, her cheeks burned. Her breath caught in her throat.

Snap out of it.

Regardless of what had just happened between them—or almost happened—she was here as Clay's employee. She couldn't let herself lose sight of that fact. They were in paradise. For a fantasy wedding, no less. The very atmosphere they found themselves in was ripe for tempting and romantic thoughts. A dangerous combination given how she'd harbored a crush on the man since first laying eyes on him.

But none of that was real. A reality she couldn't ignore, because reality would hit her soon enough, like immediately after she landed on US soil. Back in Boston, once all this was over, she'd return to a life of baking specialty cake orders and making cupcakes, along with occasionally working the random shift as needed at her family's restaurant. Without any certain knowledge of when she might even see Clay again. And he would probably forget her very existence until he needed another layered cake.

Tori refused to spend any time pining after a man she could never have. She wouldn't subject herself to a life committed to sitting by the phone waiting for a call that may never come.

And what would it do to her heart to see him with another woman? To watch him on various tabloid websites accompany someone else to the latest premiere?

She'd worked much too hard to build a life she found fulfilling and enjoyable. A life that merited her full focus. She owed herself that much.

Tori lifted her gaze upward to find him studying her face.

"Tori?" He said her name so softly, it bordered on a whisper. She knew full well the question he was asking. But she was nowhere near ready to answer it.

Making quick work of finishing the rest of her wine, she gave him a polite smile. "I really should get back to that sketch now."

Then, erring on the side of rudeness, she hopped off the stool and made herself walk away.

She heard him bite out a curse as she left.

CHAPTER FOUR

"THERE YOU ARE." Gemma's familiar voice sounded from behind her on the beach. Tori carefully placed the cupcake tower on the picnic table set up for desserts. The early evening sky was just starting to dim as a soft tropical wind breezed through the air.

Gemma reached her side. "Wow. That's a work of art."

"Thanks."

"I'm so tempted to just snare one of those right now rather than after dinner." She pointed to the middle layer. "Is that one key lime?"

"It is," Tori answered. "And I won't tell a soul should you have dessert before dinner."

Gemma giggled. "I'll be good. This time."

"Were you looking for me?"

"Yes. I wanted to make sure you knew to join us for dinner."

What a totally unexpected offer. Tori really had no intention of doing anything but hanging in her hotel room with a glass of wine and the paperback she'd picked up at the airport. She opened her mouth to argue but Gemma cut her off. "I insist."

It didn't seem right. She had no hope of avoiding Clay if she was to attend a beachside picnic dinner as if she were a regular guest. "Gemma, I couldn't impose that way."

Her eyebrows lifted. "Impose? We're tennis pals, remember. You just happen to be baking for me."

Tori couldn't help but be touched by her words. But there was still the question of Clay. She wasn't sure if she could act unaffected where he was concerned. Not after what had happened in the tavern after their tennis match. And the chances of avoiding him were probably slim to none at a beachside dinner.

Gemma threw down the proverbial gauntlet. "I'm the bride and what I say goes."

It was hard to argue that point.

About twenty minutes later, Tori found herself heading to the beach against her better judgment, in a red flowery summer dress and black canvas sandals. She'd packed exactly two dressy outfits, not really imagining she would need them, but was now glad she had.

Her heart nearly stopped when she saw him. Wearing loose cotton pants and a short-sleeved shirt unbuttoned at the neck, he exuded the perfect picture of a virile, handsome male. Walking from the direction of the residence cottages, she could tell even from this distance that his hair was wet, making it look a shade darker. It brought out the chocolate brown of his eyes.

A toddler in a white-lace dress darted out from nowhere and made a beeline for Clay. Tori watched with amusement as the tot wrapped herself around his shin. Without pause, he bent to retrieve her and swung her around in a circle. Tori could hear the little girl's giggles loud and clear despite the crashing of the waves behind her. Then, planting an affectionate kiss on her cheek, Clay set the toddler atop his shoulders.

"That's Lilly. Our niece." Gemma had come to stand beside her without Tori even noticing. No wonder, her gaze and focus had been completely on the man who so thoroughly seemed to demand her attention whenever he was present.

"She's almost three," Gemma said.

The pieces fell into place in Tori's mind. Lilly's mother had to be the other sister. Adria. The one whose wedding she'd created a cake for just about three years ago. Given the new information, she could definitely see the family resemblance. Lilly had the same nose and coloring of her mother's side of the family.

"She's absolutely adorable."

"And she knows it because we all spoil her rotten." Gemma pointed in her brother's direction. "Particularly that one there."

She so didn't need to be hearing about Clay as a doting uncle. Nor did she need to be seeing it firsthand. The picture was doing nothing to abate her patently inconvenient and ever-growing attraction.

Tori made herself look away and turn fully to face Gemma, to try to change the subject. As if she had any hope of getting her mind off of Clay Ramos in any way.

"The food looks divine." It smelled pretty good, too. Trays of barbecued meats, various pasta dishes and tropical salads with exotic fruits and vegetables had been set up on half a dozen wooden tables.

"So does your cupcake tower," Gemma said graciously. "You're very talented."

Tori had heard that before, but never tired of having clients remind her they thought so. "Thanks."

"For that matter, you're not a bad tennis player, either." She gave her a playful nudge. "Clay wouldn't have stood a chance at winning if it weren't for you. You should tell him I said so."

No part of that statement was true. Tori spread her

hands and shook her head. "Oh no. No way I'm getting in the middle of any kind of sibling rivalry."

Gemma chuckled. "Well, Tom and I have been thinking, and we've decided we'd like a rematch."

Tori laughed. "Is that so? I'll consider it. And Clay will have to agree, of course." That was a fib. Tori had no intention whatsoever of playing partner to Clay in any way, shape or form. Not again. Her psyche couldn't handle the proximity or the temptation.

"You and my brother make a good team," Gemma declared, taking her gently by the forearm. "Here, you can sit next to him at our table."

Tori Preston sure cleaned up well. Clay had to force himself not to stare outright as she walked with Gemma from the buffet area set up by the water.

Dressed in a loose-fitting, spaghetti-strapped red dress that brought out the bright color of her eyes and fell just above her knees, she looked like a vision straight out of the dreams of any red-blooded male. Including himself.

How had he not noticed how shapely her legs were before now? She looked the part of an innocent yet alluring seductress who had no idea just how seductive she was. He wasn't the only one who noticed. Glancing around the beach, Clay could see she was attracting all sorts of attention. More than one pair of male eyes followed her as the two women made their way over. His gut tautened in annoyance.

Funny, he'd never considered himself to be the jealous type before this very moment.

He set his niece on her feet on the sand and gave her a small tickle under her chin. The child ran back to her mother with a delightful squeal of laughter.

Tori smiled at Lilly as the little girl darted by and he

noticed that her hair seemed softer. She'd toned the spikes into delicate curls that framed her face.

And since when had he been the type to note changes in a woman's hairstyle? Tori Preston was bringing out a side of him he hardly recognized. A side he didn't want to examine too closely. Or even acknowledge.

He'd experienced firsthand the dire ramifications that could arise when lovesick souls followed their desires without regard to the end results. Without regard to the effect their actions would have on those around them.

He was smarter than that. He would never allow such basic needs or desires to change who he was at his core. Not like the parent who had utterly betrayed him and his siblings.

Clay pushed away the unpleasant wayward thoughts. This was to be a celebratory night, after all. He may as well try to enjoy it.

He hadn't expected to see Tori here, but her presence was a pleasant surprise. No offense to his lovely sister, but beachside dinner parties weren't exactly his kind of scene. But suddenly the hours ahead were looking quite a bit more promising.

At least he'd have someone engaging to talk to. Most of the guests were either Gemma's or Tom's friends. Other than immediate family and a handful of cousins he hadn't seen in ages, there was no one he would exactly call a friend or even an associate. And he was growing tired of small talk with people he didn't know from random strangers on the street.

In fact, the only person in attendance he'd directly invited was an officer of the charity Clay had founded—an outreach program for underprivileged kids in the Boston area.

"Look who I convinced to join us," Gemma said with a warm smile once they reached his side.

"Why, it's my lovely doubles partner. Has my sister informed you she's challenged us to a rematch?"

Tori laughed and the sound of it had his smile widening. He'd never been one to wax poetic, but she really did have a face that lit up whenever she smiled.

Oh man. Get a grip on yourself.

His sister was looking at him funny, the corners of her lips trembling ever so slightly. He didn't even want to know what she found so amusing. He'd have to be sure to set her straight if she was harboring any illusions that something might be brewing between him and the baker hired for her wedding.

Gemma should know him better than that.

Around them, several tiki torches were being lit one by one.

"That's our cue that all the food is out," Gemma informed them. "If you'll excuse me, I'll go let folks know they can begin eating. Clay, would you mind showing Tori to our table after you two get your plates?"

Subtle, she was not.

"Looks like you're stuck with me," he said with a wink when his sister left.

"And vice versa."

Tori appeared tense, less than comfortable. Was she thinking about their drink in the tavern earlier? Heaven knew he hadn't been able to get those moments out of his mind. But there was no reason they couldn't behave like mature adults. A few unguarded moments this afternoon didn't have to define or mar the rest of the evening. And the last thing he wanted was for Tori to be uncomfortable around him.

First, he had to somehow break the ice between them.

"I'm not all that hungry yet. Though I could use a drink. How about you?"

"That'd be nice. Thanks."

He took her gently by the elbow and led her to the poolside cabana bar several feet away. The evening's specialty drink was a coconut rum punch and Clay ordered one for each of them. The infinity pool was aglow with soft, neon lights from within. Several more tiki torches surrounded the area around the crystal-blue water.

After getting their drinks, he led her to a pair of poolside chaise longues.

"So what's the full story about your sister? How did you happen to just stumble upon a long-lost twin?" He paused. "I can't believe I just actually asked that question."

Tori's soft chuckle echoed slightly in the air. "It happens to be the truth."

"Please tell."

"My friend Josh—I told you about him on the boat ride to the island, remember?"

Clay remembered, all right. He remembered all too well the twinge of jealousy he'd felt until she'd clarified that they were nothing more than friends. "I do."

"Well, he came across a picture of a young woman who bore a striking resemblance to the sister of his two closest friends. Me." She pointed to her chest as if there was any doubt who she was referring to. "When he showed me the pic, it was like a missing piece of a puzzle fell into place. I suddenly had an answer to questions I didn't even realize were nagging at me."

Her eyes glittered with excitement as she continued. "Josh had a business trip planned to Australia—where she lived then—so I asked him to check her out. What happened next was straight out of a fairy tale. Eloise and

Josh fell madly in love and, after a few bumps in the road, decided they couldn't live without each other. They were recently married in a beautiful ceremony."

"Huh." That was all Clay could manage as a response. What a remarkable tale. The woman sitting before him was fascinating in myriad ways. He'd never met anyone like her.

Tori jutted her chin toward the crowded buffet. "I hope we're not being antisocial."

He shrugged. "It's hard to be social with people you haven't even met yet."

Both eyebrows quirked. "You don't know most of them?"

He shook his head. "Not really. Gemma and Tom created the guest list and picked the venue. In fact, I only invited one of the guests here. If we're not including you, that is."

"Just the one, huh?"

He nodded. "I mostly just write the checks."

She was silent, playing with her cardboard straw and swirling the ice at the bottom of her glass.

Clay felt compelled to explain. "My future brother-in-law is a graduate student with a boatload of student loans. He insists he'll pay me back as soon as he's solvent. I won't accept it, of course, but I appreciate his desire to do so. The man is a brilliant engineer and studying something I can't pronounce at MIT."

"Sounds like you're okay with the man your sister is about to bond herself with."

He chuckled. "Yeah. I guess I am. Don't understand why anyone would want to get married in the first place, but Tom's a good guy. He'll be a welcome addition to the family. Lord knows we need some good character to make up for—" He stopped. Tori was easy to talk to, and he was letting himself be carried away, but there was no use delving into the past. And he certainly didn't want to dampen the mood of the evening by rehashing all that unpleasantness. Nothing good ever came of looking backward, after all.

There really was no point in dredging up memories of how his life had been completely upended after the loss of his father. Or the way his mother had let him and his sisters down time after time.

All that was water under the bridge.

"I beg your pardon?" she asked after waiting several beats for him to continue.

"Never mind," he answered. "It's not important. You haven't tried it yet." He gestured to the glass she held.

Tori took a tentative sip of her drink. Her eyes widened. "Oh my."

He laughed at her reaction. "Good?"

"Dangerously good."

He chuckled. "Dangerous, huh?"

"Yes, tasty but strong. It would be much too easy to overindulge if not paying attention."

He got the impression she didn't indulge very often, didn't often let her guard down. It surprised him how badly he wanted to be the one to somehow change that about her.

But that was wishful thinking. The sweet, pretty pastry chef was off limits and out of his league.

So, he was something of a loner.

The revelation surprised Tori. All the parties he was photographed attending, all those high-society soirées with a beautiful woman draped on his arm—it all painted a much different picture than the man she was starting to get to know.

The fact that he was here solo was also pretty telling. Not that she had any business speculating about his personal life. Given his reputation as a ladies' man, it was more than clear where he stood on things such as marriage and commitment. Apparently, the only thing Clay was committed to was remaining a bachelor. And if that thought had her bemoaning reality, well then, that was her issue, wasn't it?

Polishing off the tropical drinks, they made their way over to the festivities and grabbed two plates of heaping food before heading for the table. Clay's being a bit more heaping than hers.

Tori was happy to see the cupcake tower almost empty. People were not waiting to finish their meal before grabbing their dessert.

In Clay's case, he wasn't even waiting to eat dessert. The first thing he bit into when he sat was her key lime concoction with citrus-cream filling. Closing his eyes, he took a deep breath. "You are a magician. This should be criminally banned it's so good."

The sheer enthusiasm of his compliment sent warmth through her body. She had to acknowledge she was actually having a really good time. It had been at least two years since she'd been at any kind of social event that didn't involve the bakery or her parents.

In fact, the last time she'd been at any kind of party had been with Drew. Toward the end, any time spent with him had felt obligatory and stressful. She'd been so afraid of saying or doing the wrong thing around him, she'd constantly walked on eggshells. It was so tense that, after a while, Tori had simply become accustomed to feeling coiled like a tight spring whenever they were together. She'd almost forgotten what if felt like to just enjoy herself. No small factor in all of this, she had to admit, was that Clay had a way of putting her at ease.

The coconut drink by the pool earlier also didn't hurt. Now, with a plate of delicious and exotic food in front of her, another tropical drink, and the rhythmic notes of calypso in the air, she felt more at ease then she had in months. Maybe even years.

Too bad it was all so temporary.

Thirty minutes after they'd taken their seats, Tom and Gemma stood and called for attention.

"All right, everyone, it's time for the entertainment portion of the evening," Tom announced. "First, we're starting off with some fun and games. Followed by a night of dancing with the island's most popular DJ."

Gemma took over. "And we're going to kick it off with some competitive fun. Grab a partner and join us by the water for a bag toss contest. There'll be prizes for the winners."

A split second of panic shot through Tori at the word "partner." The last thing she wanted was for Clay to feel obligated to spend the whole evening with her playing beach games. She turned to tell him so, but before she could so much as speak, he gently took her by the wrist and guided her up.

"Come on, I want one of those prizes."

Tori felt laughter bubble up her throat. "Do you even have any idea what the prizes are?"

He shook his head. "Not a clue."

"Then why the mad dash?"

He shrugged. "What can I say? I have a competitive streak."

She let him tug her toward the activity, unable to hold

her laughter. "Wait. There's something you should know before this goes any further."

"What's that?"

"I draw the line at three-legged races."

He scoffed. "No promises. I'll carry you if I have to."

The image that statement prompted sent a bolt of excitement through her chest and brought forth memories of the way he'd held her after they'd played tennis.

She absolutely could not go there. She'd spent most of the day trying to convince herself that her reaction had been nothing more than reflex and had no basis in anything authentic.

Clay was an attractive man oozing with sex appeal. And she'd simply had a natural reaction to being the target of his charms. Who could blame her?

Their opponents turned out to be Tom's college roommate and his fiancée—Steve and Brenda. They were an attractive couple who weren't exactly shying away from physical affection, their arms wrapped around each other's waists as they started to play. Tori felt a pang of longing that took her by surprise at the picture they presented.

"You go first, Tori," Clay prompted, distracting her from the disquieting thought and handing her a small beanbag.

Though she did her best, when she tossed it, the bag landed nowhere near the target hole. In fact, it landed perilously close to the water and was nearly swept away on a wave. Clay dashed to catch it just in time.

He groaned as he returned to stand next to her, and Tori's heart sank. It was just a silly game, but she remembered how Drew could become so disappointed with her at times. Even when it came to silly games. Nothing was lighthearted where Drew was concerned.

She swallowed and turned to apologize, to vow that she would try to do better with her next toss.

But Clay didn't look disappointed. He looked amused. And the grin he gave her had her heart jumping in her chest. "That was a bad toss, sweetheart," he told her, topping off the statement with a wink.

Tori felt the relief clear to her toes. She shrugged at him. "Oops."

In the end, they lost soundly, but they managed to win the next event, a couples' beach volleyball game. Their winnings consisted of a helium balloon and a bottle of chilled white wine, which Clay explained wasn't really any kind of prize at all, seeing as all food and beverage was already paid for.

By him.

Clay handed her the wine after the game. "This belongs to you," he said with an exaggerated bow.

"We won it together," she argued.

"That we did. But I insist you take it. A token symbolizing our triumph."

She thanked him and took the sweaty bottle. To think, she hadn't even wanted to be here tonight. But she couldn't recall the last time she'd enjoyed herself quite as much. It had been a while since she'd felt so relaxed and been able to just let go and play. She'd forgotten what it was like to be carefree. The fun-loving, lighthearted girl she'd once been had been slowly and determinedly crushed. And though she was working on it, rediscovering that girl was proving to be tougher than she would have liked. It was going to take some time and effort.

What better opportunity to do so than a night like tonight? She was in the Bahamas playing beach games!

Without anyone judging her, or making her feel less than. She could laugh as loud as she wanted, let her hair down and thoroughly enjoy herself. There was no one here to look down on her or to ridicule her for letting loose a little. It would be a wonder if she could even remember how after so many years of being stifled and put down.

A wave of bitterness threatened to wash over her when she thought of just how much of her natural personality she'd squelched all those years she'd been with Drew.

But bitterness wasn't going to restore what she'd lost during that time. And she'd vowed to do just that. To rediscover who she'd once been before the ill-fated relationship that had only managed to dampen her spirit and almost crush her soul. She owed it to that young woman she'd once been to try to bring her back. In full form. No, bitterness was the last thing she needed to be focused on right now.

So she focused on Clay instead.

"All these activities call for people partnering up. I bet you're sorry you didn't bring anyone along, aren't you?" she teased, her voice bubbling with laughter.

His eyes suddenly darkened and the air between them grew thick. "Actually, I think it might have been the best decision I've made in as long as I can remember."

Right then Tori realized that, for one of the very few times in her life, she knew exactly what she wanted, despite the fact that every sane sense she possessed was screaming to her that it was oh so wrong. She wanted Clay to kiss her. It didn't even matter that they were surrounded by others. It didn't matter that she knew no one here and barely knew the man himself. She wanted to feel his lips on hers.

And she wanted it with every fiber of her being.

* * *

How many times in the span of a day could a man feel an overwhelming desire to pull someone into his arms and kiss her senseless?

Clay could see in Tori's eyes that was also exactly what she wanted. It was clear as the full Bahamian moon above them.

Also clear was the fact that he had no business thinking such thoughts at all. Tori wasn't the type any decent man would entertain indulging in a fling with, knowing he would then walk away. And he simply didn't have it in him to offer anyone much more than that. His years simply trying to survive and ensuring that his sisters did so, as well, had taken too much out of him. There were days he barely felt like more than a shell.

Someone like that had no business even entertaining the idea of any kind of real relationship.

If only things were different. If reality wasn't what it was, he would be thanking his lucky stars that he'd run into Tori Preston and he'd be moving heaven and earth to be able to call himself her man. But his father's death served as a marker that delineated the before and after that defined Clay's life.

Maybe if his father had survived, Clay would have grown into the kind of man whose future included someone like Tori. But fate had thrown tragedy his way at such a young age.

So it made no sense that, instead of bidding her goodnight and walking away, he reached his hand out to her when the DJ started the first song.

"Dance with me?"

She hesitated just long enough that he thought she might turn him down. Part of him felt a flood of relief—

at least one of them was showing a lick of sense. A bigger part felt like someone might have kicked him in the teeth.

Finally, she slipped her palm into his and walked with him onto the makeshift dance area where several couples were already bouncing and swaying to the upbeat reggae tune.

"It's been a while since I've gone dancing," Tori whispered in his ear over the music. Like it was some sort of confession.

"Oh? Operating your own successful business must take a lot of your time."

She looked away but made no further comment. Was he imagining it or was there something in the way she was moving so stiffly, as if she were holding herself back?

It seemed uncharacteristic. She was the last woman he would have pegged as rigid or wooden in any sense.

It took some time, but Tori eventually seemed to loosen up.

And then he couldn't think at all. All he could do was stare openmouthed like some caveman at the way she began to move. Tori lifted both arms above her head and began swaying her hips in such an alluring tease, he felt his mouth go dry. Her expression went from guarded and cautious to one of near abandon. The transformation made Clay want to grab the nearest icy drink and pour it over his head to cool himself down. He tried to shift his gaze and somehow shut his mouth as she continued to move to the music. His efforts were futile. His fingers itched to reach for her, to pull her tempting, swaying hips up against him and move with her until they found a rhythm all their own.

Perhaps jumping in the pool would be more effective.

Two songs later, someone above must have finally

taken mercy on him. The next song was blessedly slow and he took her in his arms without thinking. His relief didn't last long, for now they were slow dancing. The touch of her soft, supple body up tight against his length was just further sweet agony.

He tried for conversation as a distraction.

"For someone who hasn't danced in a while, you sure don't seem to be at a loss for moves."

Her gasp was sudden and audible. She pulled back to look at him. Her eyes had grown wide with something akin to near panic. "I'm so sorry."

He blinked in confusion. "What in the world are you apologizing for? That was meant as a compliment."

"It was?"

How could she not see that?

She released a heavy breath. "So, I didn't embarrass you?"

Embarrassed? That was the last thing he'd been feeling while watching her dance.

In fact, he was certain he'd been the envy of most of the men present. Was he missing something?

"You most definitely didn't embarrass me. Not in any way, shape or form."

Her shoulders visibly slumped with relief. "I didn't?"

"Of course not. Why would you even think that?"

She chewed her bottom lip. "I've been told once or twice in the past that I can be a bit…unreserved at times. Particularly on the dance floor."

Huh. The thought wouldn't have crossed his mind. That would certainly explain why she hadn't been dancing in a while.

"Who in the world told you that?"

She looked away again. "Someone I was close to once. Not too long ago."

He put two and two together. "Boyfriend?"

She swallowed then nodded slowly. "An ex."

Silently, he pulled her back into his arms and began swaying with her once more.

Said ex-boyfriend had certainly done a number on her. Clay'd never had such an overwhelming rush of ire toward a faceless man he'd never met.

A frustrating jumble of emotions had his chest cramping. Rage that anyone had ever made her feel less in any way. Bafflement at the nameless former boyfriend who clearly hadn't appreciated what he'd had. And something else he couldn't quite name. Something he refused to acknowledge as protectiveness. Maybe the caveman description was more accurate than not.

Tori's eyes had grown shiny in moonlight. He lifted her chin, struggling for the right words. "I don't see how someone like you could ever be embarrassing, Tori. And certainly not for something as simple as enjoying yourself on the dance floor."

Her answer was to nestle closer against him as they continued to dance.

The next song was a faster, hip-hop beat but Clay didn't bother to alter his tempo. Tori made no move to, either.

What man in his right mind would want to stop her from doing what he'd just witnessed? Or want to try to tamp her joy or exuberance in any way?

He wanted so badly to find out.

Tori didn't know how much time had passed. Or how many romantically slow songs the DJ had even played up till now. She only knew it felt right to be held by Clay Ramos, to sway slowly in his arms. Time stood still when he held her. The rest of the world seemed to disappear.

He made her feel safe, coveted. Even as she'd told him about the uncomfortable experience she'd had with her ex-boyfriend.

But she didn't want to think about Drew. She didn't want to give him the power to mar this magical night any more than he already had. In fact, she regretted having mentioned him at all.

Clearly, she'd overreacted. But Clay's comment about her dancing had just sent a flood of insecurities gushing through her core and the old familiar serpent of self-doubt had slithered in. How many times had she been told that she was drawing too much attention? Doubt that Drew had been right all those times—that she could be too uninhibited at the wrong moment, that she was never serious enough—had resurfaced without warning. Clearly, Tori had more work to do rediscovering herself than she might have thought.

Until he'd explained, it hadn't even occurred to Tori that Clay may have been actually complimenting her on something she'd been told to rein in so often in the past.

A woman could get used to such compliments.

The now familiar aroma of Clay's aftershave settled around her, an enticing combination of sandalwood and mint. She might have to come up with a recipe inspired by those scents when she got back to Boston.

Not a good idea.

Because she'd be back in Boston soon enough. And then what? All of the magic she was experiencing right now would be nothing but a dream of memory. On second thought, the best thing for her to do once she returned to real life would be to forget about Clay altogether. His scent, his compliments, the warmth of his skin.

She'd be better off pretending he didn't even exist. The last thing she needed was to be reminded of the way

Clay had made her feel when he'd held her on a makeshift dance floor on a warm, breezy evening in the Bahamas one fairy-tale night.

No, far better for her to remind herself that this had just been some fantasy she may very well have made up. Then she could move on with her life, pretend none of it had ever really happened.

For the sake of her heart.

CHAPTER FIVE

TWO HOURS AFTER his first song, the DJ bade everyone a good night and started packing up. The activities over, the guests slowly started to disperse.

Tori felt a pang of disappointment. She didn't want the evening to end just yet. Though maybe it was a good thing. She hadn't intended to reveal quite so much of herself to Clay. On the dance floor, no less. In her defense, she found him easy to confide in, someone who listened without judgment. Aside from her sister, whom she'd only just found, Tori couldn't think of anyone else who had ever made her feel so understood when it came to her insecurities. Shawna was a dear friend, but often she could be too quick to try to offer advice or solutions when simply offering a shoulder to lean on would do.

Slowly, Clay released his hold around her and reluctantly she stepped away.

"Looks like the party's over." His voice sounded gravelly, forced. Would it be wishful thinking to imagine he wanted the night to continue, as well?

Tori couldn't remember a time she'd been so tempted by a man. And that said a lot about her previous relationship.

Stop it.

She really had no business comparing the two men.

Clay and Drew didn't have a thing in common. In fact, she couldn't really compare Clay to anyone. He really was a special kind of man. Gentle, kind, a good listener. Not to mention his professional success and his devotion to his sisters.

Almost too good to be true.

And perhaps he was. Tori couldn't discount the role that the sheer novelty of the situation might be playing on her perceptions overall. A tropical island, the romantic setting of a wedding, the way they kept being thrown together... It all made for a heady combination.

"Don't forget your trophy." He pointed to the wine bottle that sat at the nearest table. "I'll walk you back to your room."

"You don't need to bother."

"It's not a bother, Tori. In fact, it would be my pleasure."

Spoken like a true gentleman. Something she'd forgotten existed. It would take some getting used to. "In that case, I'd appreciate the company."

She picked up the wine bottle on their way toward the residence area.

"Do you mind if we walk along the beach? It's such a beautiful night," he asked, surprising her with the question.

She couldn't agree more. The moon had floated gradually higher above the clouds, casting a silvery glow on the white sand. In the distance, the water looked like an ocean of black ink. The horizon was the color of rich regal velvet. It would be a shame to head indoors now on such a night as this. Plus, she was all for prolonging the evening a little longer.

When they reached the water, she took her sandals off and gripped them in her free hand. He reached for them immediately. "Here, I'll carry those. You have enough of a load with that wine."

A gentleman in more ways than one. No wonder the ladies seemed to adore him, even the little ones. "Your niece is adorable, by the way," she said, recalling the little girl and how thrilled she'd seemed at the attention of her uncle.

His face visibly brightened at the mention of the little girl. "Thanks, it's been good to see Lilly again. It's been a while."

"Oh? Why's that?"

His smile faltered. "Adria and I have hit a bit of a rough patch due to a…disagreement, so to speak."

"I'm sorry to hear that. And at such a joyous time."

Tori wished she could soothe him somehow, just as he had managed to soothe her when she'd confided so much of herself as they'd danced.

The sheer dismay in his voice tugged at her heart. Whatever had happened between him and his sister, it was affecting him on a deep level.

He released a heavy sigh. "We'll get past it. It's just going to take some time."

A relatively high wave splashed at her shins, soaking the bottom of her dress. Tucking the bottle under her arm, she fashioned a makeshift knot of the wet fabric to keep the dampness off her skin. "Do you want to talk about it?" she asked, straightening.

The muscles around his jaw grew taut. "It was just a disagreement about the guest list." He paused then added, "More or less."

Tori had the impression it was probably more the former. "I thought you said you weren't really involved in who was invited."

He shrugged. "I wasn't, really. I just have a strong

opinion about one guest in particular. I didn't want her to have any part of this wedding celebration. Adria disagreed." He sounded utterly perplexed by the fact.

She wondered if he was speaking of an ex. Her guess would be that he'd dated someone his sister was friends with and it hadn't ended well. Jealousy prickled along her skin at the thought. But the theory made sense, didn't it? That would explain why he was here solo, why he'd bickered with his sister about one guest in particular.

"Wouldn't Gemma have the ultimate say?" she ventured. "It is her wedding, after all."

He shook his head. "She wanted nothing to do with the disagreement, and I can't blame her for wanting to stay out of it. She ordered Adria and me to work it out between us."

That clearly hadn't happened. Tori wondered if Adria had won out, if there was an ex-girlfriend of Clay's on the island. Perhaps Tori had even walked by her without having a clue as to who she was or what she might have meant to him before they'd broken up. The jealousy she didn't want to acknowledge ratcheted up several notches.

She wasn't going to ask him, refused to pry. Even though her curiosity was so strong, she could almost taste it in the back of her throat.

Turned out she didn't need to.

Clay huffed out a long sigh. "Adria wanted someone to attend who I no longer want to have any interaction with in this lifetime." Every muscle in Clay's body seemed to vibrate with tension and anger. Whoever he was referring to had clearly hurt him deeply and in a way that had left a lasting mark.

Tori held her breath, willing him to say more while at the same time afraid to hear there might be another woman on this very island who apparently had meant a great deal to him at some point in time.

He waited a beat before finally adding, "Our mother."

Tori bit back her gasp of surprise. Her guess hadn't even been close.

All this time, Tori had just figured Clay and his sisters had lost their parents. After all, there hadn't been a mother of the bride in attendance at any of the cake design or tasting visits for either Adria's or Gemma's wedding.

"My mother has been estranged from all of us for several years now," Clay explained, shedding some light on the mystery. "Adria suddenly wanted to see if she could change that. I don't."

"I see."

A slight chill had settled in the breezy air, though the water at her feet still felt balmy and warm. "What about your father?" Tori asked.

Clay's shoulders visibly slumped. "We lost him years ago. I was twelve."

Judging by the way the mere mention of his father completely deflated him, Tori had no doubt the two had been close. She couldn't imagine life without either of her parents. Even as an adult, the loss of her mother or father would completely shatter her. Her heart was breaking for the boy Clay must have been, trying to cope with so much grief at such a tender age. Just as he was about to enter the formative and angst-filled teen years. Heaven knew, her own teenage experience had held more drama than she would have cared for. But she'd had it easy compared to Clay and his sisters.

Nothing could parallel the loss of a beloved parent. "I'm so sorry, Clay."

"Thank you for saying that."

"Life can be so cruel and unfair sometimes."

He nodded and looked off into the horizon. "In a way, we lost my mother then, too. She became a completely different woman."

"People can be withdrawn or unavailable while dealing with their own grief." She recalled when her maternal grandmother had passed away. Her mom had rushed to Sicily to be by her side. Marissa had been a grief-stricken, unrecognizable version of herself upon her return and in the months that had followed.

"It was more than that," Clay continued. "Her entire personality changed."

Not for the better, it was clear. And from what she knew of Clay, Tori had no doubt he must have become the father figure in his younger sisters' lives. For a twelve-year-old to carry such a burden was sad enough in itself. To know that the remaining parent had somehow let them down, as well, just shattered her heart.

"As if my father was the sole source of the good within her." He added, "And with her sudden unexpected transformation, she brought an immeasurable amount of ugliness into our lives. Everything turned dark." He exhaled a ragged breath. "I just don't see how Adria can forget any of that. Or pretend it never happened."

Tori's curiosity was nearly palpable. What did he mean by brought ugliness and darkness into their lives? Had it been deliberate? If so, how could a mother do that to her children? But he clearly wasn't going to elaborate any further. Not yet, anyway. And she wasn't going to ask him to. He would tell her what he felt comfortable divulging.

Without giving herself a chance to think, she laid her hand on his forearm and leaned into his side. His response was to wrap his arm around her shoulders.

Wordlessly, they walked further along the beach. Tori searched for words of comfort, anything to tell him how much she felt for the child he must have been. But none came to mind. She couldn't pretend to understand. Though she'd always felt that there was something in her life just out of range, her childhood had been happy and full of love. She wasn't equipped with the words of understanding she so badly wanted to offer him.

"That's your building, isn't it?" Clay asked after several moments, awkwardly dropping his arm from around her shoulders. The loss of warmth where his skin had touched hers was downright striking. Somehow, over the span of such a short time, she'd grown used to his touch. Heaven help her.

Tori nodded and let him turn her away from the water, toward the path that led to the residences. Within moments, they were standing in front of the glass doors of her building.

A battle warred within her chest. She wanted to learn more about him and the boy he had been, to ask him to come upstairs.

But was asking him to join her the smart thing to do? He'd almost kissed her twice already. They'd never actually been alone in a room together. Was she prepared for how far things could potentially go when it was just the two of them within four walls?

No matter what she was beginning to feel for Clay, she was here as a professional. He was technically her boss. She couldn't act like some hormonal teenager unable to rein in her desires or her emotions.

Not to mention, she was still a mess emotionally from the disastrous breakup with Drew. She wasn't exactly sharply tuned to the opposite sex, completely unskilled in the laws of attraction and the methods of flirtation. There was a distinct possibility she was misreading things between them.

It was all so wrong. But, somehow, nothing had ever felt more right.

Some sympathetic spirit above must have taken pity on her to help her make a decision; a low rumble of thunder grumbled through the air. Almost immediately, fat raindrops began falling from the sky.

Clay looked up at the layer of clouds that had appeared above. "Great timing, I'd say. We got you here just in time."

"No so much for you. Aren't you on the other side of the resort?"

He chuckled. "It's okay. I won't melt."

Still, he grimaced as the rainfall intensified, accompanied by intermittent whipping winds.

"You could wait it out. I mean upstairs. With me." Why was she on the verge of stuttering incoherently? She was a grown, mature woman, for Pete's sake.

Clay merely quirked an eyebrow.

"Aren't tropical storms usually intense but quick? I'm sure it will stop in no time," she added. Tori wasn't certain who she was trying to convince, herself or Clay.

He tapped her nose playfully. "You sure you're not too tired? You were up at dawn baking cupcakes. And I'm guessing you have another early morning tomorrow."

"I'm sure. Besides, I find I'm still thirsty." She raised the wine bottle. "And we happen to have this perfectly good Sauvignon blanc."

He smiled at her, the tension in his face having completely dissipated since their walk on the beach.

"That's a tough invite to turn down."

"Then don't. Accept it. What do you say?"

"I say I'd be a fool to opt for making a mad dash

across the resort in pouring rain and hailing wind, when the other option is to share a bottle of wine with a pretty woman in a nice, comfortable hotel room."

The wise thing would have been to turn her down and just deal with the rain. He'd suffered worse things than a full drenching. Much worse.

But Tori's invitation proved too hard to resist. The way her eyes sparkled in the moonlight, how her hair curled gently around her face with the raindrops. One of her dress straps had fallen from her shoulder, exposing tanned golden skin his fingers itched to touch. She'd bunched up one side of the skirt of her dress, exposing a shapely leg.

It was all so beckoning.

A stronger man would have had the resolve to walk away, Clay thought as he followed her up the stone stairway and waited while she unlocked her door.

Light flooded the room as she flipped the switch and welcomed him inside.

Outside, the wind had grown harsher, driving the pounding rain almost horizontally now. "Thank you for sparing me from that," he said with gratitude, gesturing to the glass door of the balcony. Gentleman or not, he much preferred being indoors and relatively dry given what mother nature had on display at the moment.

"It's the least I can do. You wouldn't even be out this way if you hadn't walked me back. Now, to find a corkscrew." She walked over to the kitchenette where she began pulling open random drawers. All of which appeared empty.

"Here. I'll look for it. I'm sure you want to freshen up." After all, her dress had been partially soaked before the rain had even started.

"I think I'll take you up on that. I do appear to be somewhat damp."

As she headed to the adjacent bedroom, he took over the search for the opener. Locating it atop the mini fridge, he made quick work of removing the cork and poured the wine into two glasses.

Then he made his way to the sofa by the balcony and sat, watching the angry rain outside the window. The weather didn't seem to have calmed at all. Settling in the rather uncomfortable sofa, he waited for Tori to return.

And waited.

After about fifteen minutes, he walked over to knock on her door. No answer.

"Tori, the wine is poured."

Nothing.

Should he be concerned? "Can I come in?"

There was some sort of mumbled reply. He pushed the door slightly ajar and poked his head inside. The image he encountered made him smile. Tori was out cold, sprawled on top of her bed. One sandal lay at the foot of the bed, the other dangled from her other foot. She hadn't even had a chance to take off the wet dress.

He knew she was wiped, but hadn't realized it would catch up with her so fast.

"So tired," she said through a muffled yawn when he reached the side of the bed.

"I know, sweetheart. I'm just going to lift you for a second to get you under the covers, okay?"

"'Kay."

He did the best he could, wishing he could unburden her of the uncomfortable dress but unable to find a reasonable way to do so. When she was adequately tucked in, he switched off the light and gently shut the door behind him.

The wine bottle sat mostly full, the glasses untouched. Clay had zero interest in having any of it by himself.

He settled on the couch—half slouched, half sitting on the hard, scratchy cushions. Tori wouldn't mind if he just waited out the storm here. Then he'd be on his way.

Only, when he next opened his eyes, the digital clock atop the television screen said two thirty. He jolted upright in the darkness. He'd been asleep on Tori's couch until past two in the morning.

Through sleep-dazed grogginess, Clay realized the creaking of a door was what had awakened him.

"Clay?"

He heard Tori's voice in the darkness. "I'm here. Hope I didn't startle you. Didn't mean to crash on your couch."

"And I didn't mean to fall asleep on you."

He chuckled. "You had a long day yesterday. I'm surprised you held out as long as you did."

"You can't be comfortable on that sofa."

He wasn't going to lie to her. His body felt like it'd been stretched atop a bed of sharp-edged boulders. His lower back was screaming at him.

"My fault for falling asleep. I'll just head out."

"It's almost dawn. You should just stay here."

"I don't think my back can handle it, sweetheart."

"I meant on the bed."

He wasn't sure how to respond to that, so he stayed silent, waiting for her to continue. The last thing either of them needed was a misinterpretation of intentions.

"You know, just to sleep," she finally added.

Clay pondered the unexpected offer. His back really did hurt. And it looked dark and wet outside. He'd be a glutton for punishment if he turned her down.

He silently followed her into the bedroom and lay on the mattress as far as he could from the other side without toppling over. He could hear her breathe, feel her warmth. So he didn't let himself move so much as a muscle.

A night-light illuminated the dresser across the room and he was amused to see the tattered stuffed rabbit that he'd noticed in her apartment back in Boston. So she traveled with it.

How utterly adorable.

"Who was it, then?" Tori asked, her voice thick with drowsiness. He wondered for a moment if she was talking in her sleep. Her next words clarified. "Your one invite to the wedding."

He had to chuckle. He'd forgotten even mentioning that to her earlier this evening.

"Did you see the short, gray-haired woman with all the silver bracelets on her arm? I believe she was wearing a purple top."

"Mmm-hmm. The one that looked like she could be everyone's grandmother."

That was the perfect way to describe Gladys Thurman. "She's the one. She always wears at least a dozen silver bangles."

"Who is she?"

"Financial and operations director for Our New Start. It's a charity I run."

"You run a charity?"

"Figured I should. At least for a while. Since I founded it. Heard of it?"

She nodded. "Vaguely. You provide resources and youth centers for kids in homeless shelters throughout metro Boston."

"That's the one."

"You're quite an impressive man, Mr. Ramos."

Clay didn't know what to say to that, so he changed the subject. "Gladys is exactly what I'd imagine a charity representative would look li…ike." The last word came out on a rather large yawn.

Clay had a question of his own. "Tell me about this ex who didn't like you to dance," he found himself asking. He hadn't even realized he was going to bring up the subject.

He heard her sigh in the darkness. "It was more the way I danced. So he said, anyway. After he made a few too many comments, I became so self-conscious about it, I didn't even bother going anymore. Not even with girlfriends when he wasn't there." She took a deep breath. "It was just as well. He didn't really like hanging out with me when my girlfriends were around anyway."

The more she told him about this ex of hers, the more Clay was reminded of someone from his own life.

Someone who had nearly destroyed it.

He wanted to ask her about him, to find out more, but her breathing had evened to a slow and steady rhythm. If she wasn't already asleep, she certainly sounded close.

He'd learned so much about her tonight, but it would have to be enough for now. She was tired. And frankly, so was he. He found himself drifting off to sleep, as well.

All too soon, Tori's alarm went off and they both jolted upright and scrambled to get ready for the day. He did his best to freshen up before Tori jumped in the shower.

He was going to need a cold shower himself when he finally got back to his room. Lying next to her for hours, resisting the urge to reach out and touch her, had been nearly unbearable. Now, images of her under the spray of water, soaping up her skin…

He had to give his head a hard shake to clear the picture. By the time he stepped out of the building, the morning had turned bright and sunny. The chirping of birds rang through the air. He could hear the gentle crashing waves of the ocean in the distance.

A pair of joggers turned the corner along the pathway.

One of them glanced his way and did a double-take. She nudged her partner's arm until the man turned to look in his direction, as well.

Damn it.

The timing could not have been worse. His sister and Tom were early risers who liked to get a run in first thing in the morning.

The look of surprise on Gemma's face told him he'd have some explaining to do.

CHAPTER SIX

"YOU SHOULD PROBABLY know that my sister and her fiancé almost certainly believe that we've slept together."

Tori dropped the measuring cup full of sugar and swore at the mess that resulted on the previously pristine counter. A white cloud of powdered sugar hung in the air. She sneezed twice.

The batch of pie dough was ruined. She'd have to start all over again.

First things first, though.

"Come again?"

She couldn't have heard Clay correctly.

"Sorry. Didn't mean to startle you." He entered the kitchen and seemed to take stock of the mess he'd indirectly caused.

"What do you mean about your sister and Tom, exactly?"

He ducked his head with a sheepish set to his lips. "They saw me leaving your building."

She cupped a hand to her mouth. *Oh no.*

"You know, at dawn. After we'd been hanging out together the whole night before. Dancing, having cocktails," Clay added, as if she didn't know all that. As if she could have forgotten somehow. As if the whole evening and all that had happened afterward wasn't completely ingrained in her brain and would be for all time.

"Don't worry," he added, "I'll set them straight."

Somehow she didn't feel reassured.

This meant word would get out that she was sleeping with the boss. How utterly mortifying. Not that she had anything to be embarrassed about. She was a grown adult, after all. But the tabloid websites were constantly looking for juicy pieces about Clay and all it would take would be one wedding guest to be indiscreet once they returned Stateside.

Not the kind of attention Tori wanted as a professional business owner. Not to mention all the questions that would arise from friends and family. Questions she so didn't want to bother answering.

She would have to be so much more careful from now on. Should have never let her guard down in the first place.

But she'd already decided all that, hadn't she? This morning in the shower when she'd thought of how unaffected Clay had been even though they were merely inches apart atop the same bed. She'd been longing for his touch and he hadn't even so much as shifted near her.

Of course, he was solid and decent, the type of man who would never take advantage of circumstances. But he hadn't even showed the least bit of interest. While she'd been burning inside, yearning for him to touch her.

He could have asked.

Though, if he had, she had no earthly idea how she might have actually responded.

He gently took her by the upper arm and turned her to face him. "Hey, you're really upset about this, aren't you?"

"I'll be all right. Not upset so much as…"

"What?"

"I just feel embarrassed. I want Gemma and Tom to

think of me as a professional." More than that, she wanted Clay's family to like her, to respect her.

And now they thought she'd slept with their brother after spending one evening with him at a party.

Heaven help her, she very well might have if he'd even showed the slightest interest. Clearly, she'd read more into what had been happening between them than reality merited.

"Don't be embarrassed. I'll talk to them first chance I get. Tell them nothing happened."

"Thanks. I guess that's all that can be done."

"I tried calling Gemma, but didn't get an answer. I'll track her down."

"I appreciate that. Do you think she may have mentioned it to anyone else?"

His expression told her she wasn't going to like the answer to that question. "Almost certainly. My other sister."

Adria, of course. It was going to be mortifying seeing either one of his sisters again.

Adria. Who would most likely then tell her husband. Who would then tell another guest, and so on and so on... It was like a mortifying game of phone tree.

Tori rubbed her forehead as a slight ache settled behind her eyes.

"I'm really sorry about this, Tori."

"Don't apologize. You didn't do anything wrong." Not even in the least. She should have simply retired to her room after the meal was over. What business had she had mingling with actual wedding guests? This was all her fault.

The only reason she was there was as an employee. How could she have forgotten that for even a moment? Simply because Gemma had been gracious enough to invite her to dinner.

"Thanks. I appreciate that. I'm sorry, too."

His eyes narrowed on her. "I was the one who got caught sneaking out of your hotel room. What in the world are you apologizing for?"

"If I've caused you any awkwardness with your sister or if I've embarrassed you." She knew she was over-reacting—it wasn't as if she'd committed some kind of crime—but couldn't seem to help the sting of tears that suddenly burned behind her eyes. She couldn't imagine the way Clay's conversation with his sister might go.

He stepped closer to her. "Not this again. You said the same thing on the dance floor. It made no sense then, either." Clay raised her chin with his finger. "Hey. You did no such thing. It's just a silly misunderstanding and we'll set it straight."

"Thank you. I just don't like being the subject of gossip." Especially not with the type of crowd that was here at this wedding.

She'd been judged and found lacking often enough in the past.

Tori placed the tray of mini pastry crusts on the top rack of the oven and closed the door. She'd already whipped up the custard filling. The next step was to slice and glaze the tropical fruit that would serve as toppings on the tarts. But she couldn't bring herself to get started just yet. Usually, that was the piece of the fruit tart process she enjoyed the most. The sweet aroma of the fruit, the relaxing, repetitive motion of slicing. But today her heart wasn't in it. She needed a break.

This morning's conversation with Clay kept replaying over and over again in her mind. She wasn't looking forward to the next time she ran into the bride. Nor running into Clay again, for that matter.

She needed to vent, a shoulder to cry on. It would have to be a digital shoulder. Pulling out her cell phone, she clicked her sister's contact icon, not even caring about the time of day. Eloise was running back and forth from Sydney to Boston so often, Tori wasn't even sure where she might be at the moment. Her sister would have to forgive her for being awakened if that turned out to be the case.

"Tori!" Eloise immediately greeted, answering on the first ring. Simply hearing her voice had Tori's nerves soothing over. "I've been wondering when you'd call."

"Hey. Been meaning to. It's just been a little busy." And she'd been very preoccupied.

"So tell me, have you made your move on the hot architect yet?"

To her horror, Tori's bottom lip started to quiver. She was just such a conflicted mess where Clay was concerned. And her sister's comforting, familiar voice had served to flush all of it to the surface.

Eloise picked up on her distress. "What is it? Tell me."

"Nothing. I'm fine." But her voice was so shaky, Tori hardly sounded convincing.

Eloise's voice grew firmer over the speaker. "Has that man done something to upset you? I can be on the next—"

"No! No, Eloise, he hasn't done a thing." That was part of the problem, wasn't it? Clay hadn't so much as kissed her, while she was a quivering mess of feelings whenever they were together. How could she even know if those feelings were entirely one-sided?

"Promise?" Eloise asked.

"Yes. Cross my heart." Tori made an X motion over her heart, which made no sense. It wasn't as if they could see each other.

"Then what is it, sis?"

Her twin's gentle prodding seemed to open the floodgates.

In a jumble of words, Tori blurted out everything that had happened, her embarrassment of the morning, and how confused she was about all of it. When she finished, she used the bottom of her apron to dab at her eyes.

Eloise had remained silent, patiently listening the whole time. Finally, she cleared her throat. "Wow. That's a lot."

Tori nodded. "Yeah, it is, huh?"

"So what are you thinking?"

"I don't think I know what to think. It's just… I haven't felt this way about anyone ever." And that was astounding considering she'd had the same boyfriend since tenth grade until they'd broken up a couple years ago. Or until she'd broken up with him, to be more accurate.

"I see," Eloise said after a long pause.

"And I don't know what good can possibly come of it. We're from two very different worlds. I only see him when he has need of a bakery."

"So you're thinking about what's going to happen in the long term."

"Doesn't everyone?"

"Not all the time. Sometimes people throw caution to the wind. They just act spontaneously."

"I know. But it's not how I'm wired."

"Maybe you need to be rewired—by a gifted and qualified electrician."

Tori guffawed at the ridiculous metaphor, which, of course had been Eloise's intent.

"Seriously, Tori," her sister added. "Look how well things worked out for me and Josh when I finally decided to take a chance."

Tori tried not to scoff in dismissal. "It's hardly comparable, Eloise. You and Josh were the exception."

"I'd say your current scenario is pretty exceptional, as well. You're on a tropical island—a veritable paradise—far from home."

That was certainly the truth. "I suppose you might have a point."

Her sister chuckled softly. "Of course, I do. What better time to act a bit uncharacteristically?"

"Meaning?"

"Meaning don't look so deep into things. Don't overthink. Just see where things go and heed your heart about whether you'd like to follow or not."

Tori had to laugh at that. "Okay, you've moved from ridiculous metaphors to tired clichés. But I see your point. And I have to admit, you've given me a different perspective." She'd also managed to make her feel infinitely better.

"Hey, metaphors and clichés are what they are for a reason."

"I suppose that's true."

"So, will you try to throw some caution to the wind? And not be afraid to take a chance or two?"

Tori wasn't sure how to answer that. Not just yet. She decided to veer the subject back to Eloise's relationship instead. "So that's what you did with Josh, then? Took your chances?"

"Yes." The affection in her sister's voice for her new husband was clear as a bell, even over the phone. "You know I did. And he was absolutely worth it."

A smile spread over Tori's face. "Well, make sure you don't tell him that too often. Or he'll be even more insufferable," she joked.

Her sister chuckled. "I'll be sure."

Tori hung up after they chatted a few minutes longer, feeling much more lighthearted.

Without a doubt, her sister knew exactly what she spoke of on such matters. Eloise and Josh hadn't had the easiest time on their journey to happily-ever-after. Not that she and Clay were on any kind of romantic journey.

Was Eloise right? Was she just scared? She certainly had cause to be cautious, given the way things had gone with Drew—though Drew and Clay had absolutely nothing in common.

With a groan of frustration, Tori shook off the useless thoughts and went to replace her apron with a fresh one. Enough wasted time, she had to get started on that fruit. She couldn't avoid that part of the task any longer.

Like a lot of other things she wasn't going to be able to avoid.

"Are you certain you don't want to join us, Clay?" Gemma asked for the umpteenth time before boarding the van that would take the wedding party down to the retail area of the island. The planned excursion included a group shopping trip and outdoor beachside lunch. He had better things to do. He'd just wanted to catch his sister to explain about this morning before she and the others went on their touristy way.

He gave a mock shudder. "You know how much I loathe shopping."

Gemma laughed. "Okay. Guess we'll see you when we return." She turned back after stepping on the van's foot rail. "And apologies again for making assumptions about what I saw this morn—"

He held up a hand to stop her. "No need. I know how it must have looked."

He waved as the van drove away. Finally, some time

to himself, and there was plenty of work to catch up on. But he was having difficulty making himself head back to his room to fire up the laptop.

Tori was avoiding him.

He'd sent her several texts that, so far, had gone unanswered.

He had wanted so badly to pull her into his arms this morning in the kitchen, to comfort her. He'd had no idea she would be quite so bothered by Gemma and Tom's incorrect assumptions about what had happened between the two of them last night.

Maybe even telling her that they'd seen him leaving her building hadn't been such a great idea. Tori would have been none the wiser. And he'd managed to set the record straight with his sister easy enough.

But he'd never been a big fan of secrets. Too late to ponder that score, anyway. Cat out of the bag and all that.

Now, he was just trying to determine what he was going to do about it. He didn't want there to be any kind of new weird dynamic between them simply because they'd spent one night together where nothing had ever happened.

A glance at his watch told him it was almost noon. She would be breaking for lunch at some point. Maybe they could grab a bite together.

At the least, he wanted to ask about the day's dessert she'd been working on. The nutty, fruity smell in the air had had his mouth watering this morning. Maybe she could use a taste tester. Funny how he'd never particularly had a sweet tooth until he'd met Tori.

Armed with his excuse, he made his way to the building that housed the kitchen.

He found her with her back to the kitchen door, standing at the counter, stirring the contents of a bowl the size of a small tub. She was holding a container of salt in one hand.

He approached her from behind and was about to announce himself, to ask if it was a good time for her to get away, when Tori suddenly threw a pinch of salt over her shoulder. The seasoning hit him square in the face.

Just to be funny, Clay faked a sneeze.

Startled, she turned with a hand to her chest. "Clay! Sorry about that."

"Beats being doused with iced coffee."

She blinked in confusion until the puzzle piece fell in to place. "Oh. Like that day at the bakery. Seems like years ago."

"Do you often toss salt around?"

"I just throw a pinch over my shoulder whenever I use it." Ducking her head sheepishly, she gave him a small smile. "Bit of a superstition. Doing so is supposed to be good luck."

"Till someone gets salt in their eye."

Her giggle had him lighting up inside.

"What does a pastry chef use salt for, anyway?" he asked.

"Just to bind all the flavors of the fruit together before I pour the glaze over."

"Huh. Fascinating."

"Is there something you wanted, Clay?"

"As a matter of fact, I thought maybe you'd need a taste tester."

She laughed. "You did, did you? I have no shortage of volunteers for that."

"Hmm. Shame. Also, I wanted to see if you'd be up for a break. Maybe to grab a bite?"

Her mouth tightened. "With you?"

The way she asked dealt something of a bruise to his ego. "That was the general idea, yes."

"But I thought you were heading into town with the others."

He shook his head. "Nope. Not my kind of excursion. I hate shopping."

"Surprising, when you have two younger sisters."

"That's precisely why. Been there, done that often enough already."

"Makes sense, I suppose. My brothers always complained when they were dragged out for school clothes."

"Speaking of siblings, I sat Gemma down after breakfast and told her exactly what happened last night between us. Or didn't happen, to be more accurate."

Her eyes widened. "You did? And she believed you?"

He shrugged. "Sure. Why wouldn't she? I have no reason to lie to her."

"True."

"She said it wouldn't have bothered her, by the way."

"Huh," she chided, "you might have led with that, Clay. Considering I've been fretting about it all morning."

"I left you several texts and a couple of voice mails." He watched as she lifted a pitcher-size measuring cup of glaze and slowly poured it into the bowl of fruit. "So, what do you say?"

"About Gemma not caring if we are…?"

"What? No. I was asking what you thought about getting some lunch."

"Oh. That. Well, I need to finish this up." She motioned to the bowl.

"I can wait."

Tori bit her bottom her lip at the lower corner and he

had to make himself look away. She looked so utterly sexy when she did that.

"All right. I suppose I do need to eat at some point." As if on cue, he heard her stomach emit a low grumble.

"Again, you flatter me with your enthusiasm."

She took him by the shoulders and physically turned him the other way. "Right now, I have to get back to work. And you have to leave. Give me another hour or so."

"You got it." He let her give him a small shove toward the door. "I'm leaving."

"Yes, you are."

"You sure you don't need me to taste anything before I go?"

"Don't make me chase you out with the wooden spoon." Her warning fell flat thanks to the amused grin on her face.

Having lunch with Tori was a much better prospect than spending the day browsing trinkets and T-shirts. Even though he'd fully intended to utilize his free time on some much needed work—spending the afternoon being lazily unproductive was a foreign concept—he had no regrets about following this uncharacteristic whim in the least.

Then again, he was doing all sorts of uncharacteristic things on this trip. And the common denominator motivating those decisions appeared to be Tori Preston.

She drew him in like a magnet. The hours he spent alone while she'd been working seemed to drag on and on, and he often found himself counting the minutes until she'd be free.

But he wasn't smitten. Absolutely not. He was just trying to break the monotony. Just because he was so drawn to the woman didn't mean his life would be altered in any way. Back in the States, he would return to long work hours and the occasional social outing to appease the clients who insisted on inviting him to their various functions.

That was the life he was meant to live. A solitary, peaceful one. He deserved it after what he'd been through.

And that life left no room for any kind of complicated relationship. Not even with someone like Tori.

Especially not with someone like Tori.

CHAPTER SEVEN

HE TOOK HER to a cabana beachside restaurant, one recommended by almost everyone on staff at the resort. The gentle lapping of waves by their table and the warmth of the afternoon sun set a soothing atmosphere and made for a picture-perfect lunch date. Clay felt his relaxation gradually grow to the point where the ever-present knot in his neck muscles slowly started to ease.

The menu wasn't vast but everything on it sounded delicious. Tori ordered fish tacos while he opted for spicy jerk chicken. By the time their food arrived, he'd kicked off his shoes and had leaned back casually in his chair. For her part, Tori looked fairly relaxed herself.

He was glad he'd cleared the air with Gemma about what had happened.

The waitress stopped by to refresh their waters. "I heard there was a wedding taking place on the resort," she said while she poured. "Would you two be the happy couple then?"

Tori paused in the act of lifting her taco to her lips, her cheeks reddening. "Uh, no."

"My sister is getting married. I'm here to walk her down the aisle," he explained.

"Oh, sorry," the young woman said with a bright smile. "Honest mistake. You two look like a lovely couple." Again, she'd made the wrong assumption. Why did that seem to keep happening to the two of them?

Tori's cheeks grew redder as she took a small bite of her taco. She looked so cute when she was blushing. "Mmm…" she moaned as she chewed.

Clay felt the now familiar tightening in his gut. How had he not realized before how sexy a woman who really appreciated food could be? Tori had grown up in the restaurant business; she baked for a living. Food was a center theme in her life. He was finding that ridiculously seductive and attractive about her.

One thing was certain—if he continued to watch her eat, he was going to be much too focused on her to enjoy his own lunch.

The burn on his tongue from his spicy dish was a welcome distraction.

"So tell me…" Tori began, dabbing at her mouth with a napkin. "If shopping is not your thing, what kind of outing would you have preferred?"

He smiled at the question. "I don't know if I want to tell you."

Her eyes lit with merriment and curiosity. "Well, now you have to."

"You'll laugh at me. Then tell me that it's something a little boy would want to do."

She leaned closer to him over the table. "I have two older brothers. I happen to know firsthand that all men are true little boys at heart."

She was right. Only, he hadn't felt like a little boy in a long time. There'd been no opportunity to act boyish since his father had died. And especially not since his mother had remarried after his father's death.

It was why he'd been compelled to found and nurture a charity specifically focused on underprivileged youth.

Children who'd often not had the benefits and advantages of growing up in a stable and safe home. He could more than relate to those kids. His own family had been about as broken as could be if anyone had bothered to look under the surface of the façade.

He'd had to grow up quick. For his sisters' sake as well as his own. Maybe he'd tell Tori about it sometime… The thought took him by surprise. His past was not a subject he allowed himself to think about often, let alone discuss with others.

"I insist that you tell me," Tori ordered.

Clay did a double take. For a split second, he thought maybe she'd read his mind. But it occurred to him she was referring to the question she'd asked about his preferred outing.

"Fine then," he replied with feigned offense. "If you're going to get all bossy about it."

"Baby sisters have to be bossy sometimes."

That was certainly true, as he knew all too well. "Well, this island happens to be a maroon spot."

"A what? Like the color or something?"

She really was a delight. "No. Not the color. It was one of the islands that an unruly sailor who'd misbehaved was cast away on. It's said the famous pirate Killjoy Bob was deposited here after he tried a mutiny against his captain onboard his ship. They left him here to die with nothing but a half-empty bottle of rum."

She blinked at him, tilted her head. "Killjoy Bob?"

Clay could tell she was trying not to giggle. He crossed his arms in front of his chest. "Go ahead and laugh if you want. But there happens to be a whole pirate museum in downtown Nassau. Complete with a fake town and cruise tours aboard a pirate ship. You can even walk the plank if you'd like."

"Huh."

She leaned back in her chair and took another bite of her taco. "Again, I remind you that I have two brothers. Every time we went to the Cape, they made us do one of the many pirate tour attractions."

"Really?"

"Yep. In fact, they both mentor as Big Brothers. They take a group of kids every summer to the Cape and on one of those tours."

Her brothers sounded like fun, Clay mused, and like decent, honest men. Would they approve of him? he wondered. It was no secret he had a reputation as a hard-partying ladies' man who went through women like bar tabs. What brother would approve of someone like that for his baby sister?

Not that any of it made a whit of difference. He wouldn't be in Tori's life long enough for it to matter what her family believed of him. His spirits plummeting, he pushed the thoughts aside.

"Definitely," Tori answered. "Wait till I tell them I was on an authentic maroon island. They'll be so jealous." She threw her head back and laughed in a comically bad impression of some sort of movie villain.

"In that case, would you like to also tell them that you went to a real pirate museum?"

She set down her taco and focused an intense stare on his face. "Are you asking me?"

Looked like he was. "I was planning on going alone. No way I'm going to miss it. But I'd love the company."

The truth was, he hadn't really wanted to go by himself, not if there was a chance she might come with him. Despite what he'd just told her, he probably would have skipped it, hoped for another time.

Tori's answer brought an excited smile to his face.

"Now, why would I turn down the chance to tease my brothers about how I was at a pirate town in the Bahamas?"

"Is that a yes?"

"You bet it is. Of course, I'll come with you."

"Then finish up. I'll call the concierge to arrange transportation."

Tori gave him a dramatic salute. "Aye, aye, matey."

Don't look so deep into things. Don't overthink. Just see where things go and heed your heart about whether you'd like to follow or not...

Her sister's words echoed through Tori's head as she rushed back to the kitchen to leave detailed instructions about how the tarts should be set out tonight at dinner. She'd be too busy to do it herself as she'd be playing the part of a lady pirate.

If it wasn't for Eloise and their phone conversation earlier this morning, Tori was certain she'd have turned Clay down. She would have thought of an excuse and spent the day in her hotel room reading or mindlessly watching TV. Instead, she was going to follow her sister's advice. And she wasn't kidding about rubbing it in her brothers' faces that she'd be experiencing an authentic pirate adventure. That was just an added bonus, like icing on the cake.

She was so deep in thought about the afternoon that awaited her, she almost missed the recognizable figure seated at one of the dining tables outside the food services building. Tori focused on what she could see of the woman's face to be certain of who it was.

There was no doubt. It was Adria, Clay's other sister. She was sitting by herself, her head bent, and she appeared to be clutching her middle.

Tori hesitated, deliberating what to do. Clay had ordered a car and was probably waiting for her right this minute. On the other hand, Adria's entire demeanor looked as if she could use some kind of assistance.

There really was no decision to be made.

Tori approached the table and cleared her throat. "Hi, Adria."

Adria's head lifted ever so slowly. She just stared for a moment. Then her eyes seemed to clear with recognition.

"Tori, isn't it?" A shaky smile spread over her lips, her pallor the color of dewy damp grass on a New England morning. "You remember me then. You did the cake for my wedding, as well. Butter cream frosting. Marble sponge with seven tiers."

"A trophy," Tori supplied.

The woman's smile grew wider. "That's right. Somehow, you were able to craft it in the shape of a trophy."

"Your husband is a professional soccer player."

She nodded. "A striker for Madrid Royale. We didn't think you'd be able to do it. But you came through."

It had taken Tori weeks to try to figure it out. One of her most challenging creations. Most other cakes were... well, a piece of cake in comparison.

"You didn't go on the shopping excursion with the rest of the wedding group?" Tori asked. Why exactly was Adria here? And why did she look so unwell?

Adria visibly swallowed as if she'd just consumed something unsavory. "We came back early. I wasn't feeling well."

"Are you all right?"

"I'll be fine. Just the heat. And all the excitement. Enrique went to find me some crackers or something. Anything to help soothe a roiling stomach."

"Why don't we get you inside then?" Tori suggested. "Into the air-conditioning."

"You know, I think I'd like that." She pulled out her phone. "I'll just let Enrique know." After she fired off a text, they walked to the dining area of the main hall and Tori had her take a seat at the bar.

There were definitely some conclusions that could be drawn given the scenario before her. Adria still hadn't removed her left arm from where it rested on her stomach. She was clearly feeling nauseous. And she was holding her middle in a rather interesting way. Protectively.

Her years spent working in a restaurant, with a steady flow of female servers, Tori had encountered more than her fair share of pregnant colleagues. She'd be ready to bet money that Adria was expecting. Why she was keeping it a secret from everyone was a mystery however.

Tori was helping Adria get settled on a stool when her husband burst through the door. He was carrying Lilly in one arm and holding a grease-spotted paper bag in his other hand. Tall and lean, Enrique Maduro was the quintessential specimen of a Spanish heartthrob. Right now, however, he looked completely lost and panicked.

"I'm so sorry, *mi querida*," he addressed his wife. "All I could find was some popcorn." He gave Tori a distracted nod of acknowledgment.

Adria visibly shuddered and turned a deeper shade of green. Her eyes grew shiny with unshed tears.

Greasy popcorn for a queasy stomach was far less than ideal, even under the best of circumstances.

To make matters worse, Lilly had her head draped on her father's shoulder and was hiccupping loudly. Her cheeks were wet and stained with streaks of tears. It appeared she'd just completed the mother lode of toddler temper tantrums. Tori couldn't decide which of the haggard trio before her she felt sorrier for. They all looked completely miserable.

None of this would do at all.

Tori reintroduced herself to Enrique and gently took the bag of popcorn out of his hand. "Why don't you get Lilly back to your room? I'll make sure Adria gets something to eat that will calm her stomach."

One would think she'd just offered the man the key to eternal salvation. His look of relief was downright comical.

"Are you sure?" he asked.

Tori nodded. "Leave her to me."

He didn't argue. *"Gracias, señorita. Muchas gracias."*

With an affectionate kiss to the top of his wife's head, he bid Tori thanks once again, in English this time, then left.

Adria rested her head on the counter. "Just thinking about that popcorn makes me want to—"

Tori held her hand up to stop her from continuing. She could figure out the rest. It didn't help matters that the putrid aroma of burned grease still hovered in the air. She had to move quickly or Adria was sure to start to feel sicker. "There's a fresh baguette in the back that was baked just this morning. Loaded with a thick layer of sweet butter, it will make for a tasty, hearty toast. I'll also whip you up some scrambled eggs. Well done." Runny eggs would just make things worse. "The protein and the carbs mixed with a dose of fat should get you squared and feeling better in no time. And I'll pour you some ginger ale while you wait for the food."

It was Adria's turn to give her a grateful look. "You are a heaven-sent angel."

She shrugged. "Hardly. I just know when people need to be fed. I grew up working in my family's restaurant."

"Lucky for me you found me then."

Tori was spared the need to respond when Adria immediately followed her statement with a rather unexpected one. "So I hear you've been keeping my brother company these past couple of days."

Tori had to try hard not to betray any physical reaction to the mention of Clay. It wasn't easy. "We seem to be the only two people here unaccompanied."

Adria nodded. "I'm not sure why he came alone. But I'm glad he did."

It wouldn't do to read too much into that statement, tempting as it was to do so. "You are?"

"Yes. Some of the women he dates…" She let the sentence trail off.

Tori would ignore that. She didn't really want to think about the women Clay dated. Or who might be angry that she hadn't been invited to the wedding yet still awaited his return. That would be overanalyzing and she'd assured her twin that she was going to try to do as little of that as possible.

Easier said than done.

Pulling out a chilled can of soda from the industrial-size fridge, Tori set it in front of Adria after popping it open. "I'll get started on the food. It will just take a few minutes."

"You're very kind," she heard Adria say behind her as she pushed the kitchen door open.

When she returned with a full plate of hot food about ten minutes later, some of the natural color had returned to Adria's complexion. She was glad to see the ginger ale seemed to be doing the trick.

When Tori set the plate in front of her, Adria sighed. "So much better than greasy popcorn. Thank you."

"You're welcome."

"I feel strange eating when you're not having anything."

"I just finished lunch with—" She caught herself before his name dropped from her lips. Probably not a good idea to bring him up. But it was too late.

"My brother, I take it," Adria concluded with a knowing smile.

"Yes."

"It's good that you kept him company while the rest of us were out. He wanted to do something completely different as an excursion."

And not one of them had even entertained the idea.

"He told me," Tori said. "Pirate town."

Adria smiled around a forkful of food. "That's right. He's always loved pirates. Since he was a little boy."

"Then perhaps someone should have accommodated that one small interest of his?" Tori wanted to suck the words back as soon as she'd said them. None of this was really any of her concern. She certainly had no business second-guessing the bride's wishes let alone the wedding party's. Plus, in all fairness, Adria and Enrique had more pressing matters to deal with.

"I'm sorry, I shouldn't have said that."

Adria set her fork down. "No. You have every right to say what you think. Ironic that Clay finally has someone defending him for a change." Her voice trembled slightly as she spoke.

"I don't understand."

She gave her head a shake, as if she'd been the one to say too much this time. "Never mind. It's not important right now. And you happen to be right. We owe Clay a debt of gratitude that neither Gemma nor I will ever be able to repay. A debt that has nothing to do with him financially taking care of us. Or paying for elaborate weddings, by the way. We could have at least extended the courtesy of indulging him with something he wanted to do."

Tori waited for her to elaborate but it was as if Adria had read her mind. "You'll have to ask him about it yourself."

She could try. Something told her that asking Clay anything about his past would be fruitless, however. Plus, the whole conversation was starting to make her feel uncomfortable.

"You'll have to excuse me," she told Adria, perhaps a little too abruptly. "I have to go leave some instructions to the staff about tonight's dessert."

Adria was gone when Tori returned. She'd left her a little note on a napkin.

Feeling much better. Thank you for your kindness.
I'm guessing you've figured out my little secret.
Please be discreet and help me to keep it a while
longer.

She'd included a cell phone number.

Curiouser and curiouser, Tori thought as she folded the napkin and placed it in her pocket. It seemed the more she learned about Clay, the more mysterious he became.

What was taking her so long?

Clay stood leaning against the wall by the entrance of the resort trying not to count down the minutes until Tori showed up. Had they miscommunicated the meeting spot? That didn't seem likely. The plan had been pretty clear.

Had she changed her mind?

It would be unlike Tori to just have a sudden change of heart like that. And even more unlike her to not even let him know. Maybe she'd lost the connection on her cell phone.

He was beginning to panic when he finally saw her through the glass doors. A surge of relief flooded his chest. He'd been worried about her.

And worried that she might have decided to blow him off.

After all, it was rather silly when he thought about it. For a grown man to be excited about visiting a fake pirate town. Tori was probably just being polite, too embarrassed for him to up-front turn him down.

Nevertheless, now she was here and he was glad for it.

So he had no idea why he'd snapped at her when she reached him. "I was beginning to think I'd only imagined that you'd agreed to come."

She didn't take the bait. In fact, she looked rather distracted. "Sorry, I ran into someone."

"You couldn't stop chatting with this someone long enough to let me know?"

Her eyebrows drew together as she squinted at him in the sunlight. "My phone wasn't readily available. Are we going to go or not?"

Great. Now they were both annoyed. Should make for an enjoyable day then, with the two of them snapping at each other for no real reason. He was going to suggest that maybe they forget the whole thing but Tori was already walking down the wooden pathway that led to the catamaran.

Uttering a curse under his breath, he followed her.

By the time they arrived at the main island and reached the awaiting car, the tension between them had only grown thicker.

Their driver wordlessly started the engine and drove down the long driveway before pulling out onto the main road. An awkward silence ensued with only the vehicle's navigation system doing any talking.

They drove that way with neither saying a word for about seven minutes before Clay couldn't stand it any longer. "Look, I'm sorry if I sounded short with you back there. I was worried, that's all."

She tilted her head. "Thank you for the apology," she said simply, somewhat surprising him. Most of the women he dated prolonged his attempts at atonement. He'd been fully expecting to have to border on groveling to break the tension between them.

Then she surprised him even further with her next words. "And I'm sorry for making you worry," she added. "I should have found a way to let you know I was running late. It was unfair to you."

Her words echoed in his head. For the life of him, he couldn't remember receiving a genuine apology from someone in his lifetime. He was always expected to be the strong one. The rock.

Heaven knew, the one person on earth who was supposed to care for him and protect him had failed miserably. It would never occur to his mother to apologize for any of it. On the contrary, she refused to even acknowledge the neglect, would never take any responsibility for any wrongdoing.

"Apology accepted," he mumbled. But Tori had already turned to stare out her window at the passing scenery, unaware of the impact her words had delivered.

Finally, he eyed the specter of a large makeshift pirate's ship in the distance, complete with the skull and crossbone flags and willowy sails at full mast.

"Oh my God," Tori exclaimed next to him with clear glee.

"Impressive, huh?"

"It's even better than I had thought."

She really was excited to be here. Maybe even more than he was. He should have never doubted her.

The first exhibit took Tori's breath away, though to call it an exhibit was a discredit. They stepped into a moonlit night in the year 1716 on what appeared to be an authentic era dock. The sounds of lapping waves and roughhousing pirates in the distance added to the ambience. She could even smell the salty, fishy aroma of the ocean.

She couldn't help her squeal of delight. "I feel like Blackbeard is going to come walking out from behind that ship any second."

"With a yo-ho-ho and a bottle of rum."

She couldn't tell which one of them looked more entranced with the place. Oh yeah, her brothers were going to hear all about this museum.

Tori hadn't realized she'd said the last bit out loud. "You're gonna rub it in their faces huh?" Clay teased. "That you got to see this and they didn't?"

"Absolutely. Josh, too. He'll also be green with envy. Though I don't dare call it a museum or they'll stop listening."

Clay laughed as they walked further along the makeshift quayside in the shadow of a frigate. A drunken "pirate" lay sprawled on the ground in front of the pub. A loud argument could be heard from inside in clear pirate brogue.

"Want to board the ship?" Clay asked.

"You need to ask?"

They walked up the wooden ramp, which creaked loudly with each step. She could have sworn she felt the frigate rock as if it was really navigating ocean swells. An open treasure chest sat at the top of the ramp and there was a large map of the Bahamas on the wall.

It took a full hour to explore all of the attractions on the pirate ship alone. By the time they walked out of the museum, the afternoon had grown dark. Tori wore a felt pirate's tricorn adorned with a skull and crossbones in the front while Clay brandished an aluminum cutlass.

"I could use a drink," Clay announced, pointing to the pub next door.

"I'll find a table if you go to the bar."

He gave her a pirate's salute. "Anything for the fine young lady." His accent needed work.

"Why, thank you, guv'nor." Okay, so her accent wasn't all that much better.

Tori pulled her phone out as soon as she sat to take notes about everything they'd just experienced. She didn't want to miss any details when she told the three wannabe swashbucklers back home about any of this.

She had a full screen written by the time Clay arrived with two of the day's rum cocktail specials.

"That was a tour I'll never forget." And she had Clay to thank for it. Spending time on a makeshift pirate ship and walking through a replica eighteenth-century town was not something that would have even occurred to her.

"Same. Can't wait to do it again."

To her surprise, he reached across the table and took her hand in his. "Thanks for coming, Tori. Really."

An electric current ran up her arm and down her spine from the contact point. She would never get used to the way her body reacted whenever this man touched her.

She tried for a nonchalant shrug. "Sure. What are friends for?"

"Is that what we are, then?" he asked, his voice thick with heat and promise. "Just friends?"

He dropped her hand and pulled away before she could even think of a way to answer.

Tori took a sip of her drink, suddenly warm from the inside out. Though it tasted heavenly—a perfect combination of tart and fruity—the cocktail didn't do much to cool her down.

"So who'd you run into?" Clay was asking.

It took a moment to process what he meant.

"Before we left the resort," he added.

"Your sister, actually."

His eyebrows shot up. "How was Gemma back so fast? That shopping trip was supposed to take all day."

"Not Gemma. Adria."

A shadow crossed his face. "Oh. I'm guessing Enrique grew impatient and wanted to come back early. He enjoys such outings even less than I do."

Tori stayed silent, letting him run with his conclusion about Adria's early return. Trying to correct him could lead to a verbal land mine she didn't want to try to navigate. A slip-up would be all too easy.

"I haven't spoken to her in a few days," he said on a deep sigh. "Been meaning to rectify that. Just don't want to start an argument."

Tori knew she had to tread carefully. The last thing she wanted was to betray Adria's trust. Another woman's secret was not hers to tell, especially not one on that level of importance. Though maybe this rift between siblings could be faster healed if Clay knew. Still, it was not her place to decide.

"I would say it's worth a try. Risk of argument notwithstanding. Maybe you two just need an open and honest sit-down."

"And I should make the first move?"

She leaned further toward him. "Someone has to."

He rubbed his eyes and took a deep swallow of his drink. "I know you're right. Just putting it off."

He'd mentioned their mother had had something to do with whatever they were butting heads about. "I'm sure you both have valid viewpoints. Might be worth simply weighing those against each other."

He scoffed. "If only it were that simple. For some reason, Adria suddenly decided she'd like to contact our estranged mother. I can't begin to imagine why."

What exactly was the story there? The mother had never been involved in the previous wedding. And the woman certainly wasn't in attendance at this one.

"Adria found her on some social media site," Clay continued. "They've been messaging or whatever the kids call it."

"I see." Tori was beginning to see, indeed. She could think of more than one reason a woman experiencing an exhausting pregnancy might want to seek the comfort of a mother, estranged or not. Adria probably felt vulnerable and in need of nurturing. As considerate as Clay was as a brother, he wasn't exactly the nurturing type. And while Gemma and Adria seemed close, Gemma was on the brink of a whole new chapter in her own life. Which would no doubt mean less support and sisterly affection.

Though, judging by Clay's attitude, their mother clearly hadn't been all that loving.

"Hard to believe she even wanted to send her a last-minute invite to the wedding," Clay snapped through gritted teeth.

"And you refused."

He thrust his hand through his hair in frustration. "Not exactly. But something close to that."

"Oh?"

"I told her that if that woman attended, I certainly would not."

"Oh, Clay."

"I know it sounds extreme. Unreasonable. But, trust me, I have my reasons. That woman has no business re-entering our lives. Not for any reason."

Tori searched his face, silently willing him to continue. To just get it all out in the open, to maybe purge himself of the burden of it once and for all.

He finally began after several tense moments. "She remarried within a year after my father died," he told her. "And my stepfather was not a very nice man."

It was her turn to reach for him.

"In fact, he was skillfully cruel," Clay added.

"Your mother didn't stop it in time."

He grunted in disgust. "Worse. She pretended it wasn't even happening."

Clay's mouth had gone dry. Surprisingly, he looked down to find he'd already polished off his drink. Tori held firmly to his hand, her comfort and warmth spreading through him, right to his core.

Her eyes had grown shiny. But he didn't see any pity in their depths. That, he wouldn't have been able to bear. No, the only emotion he could sense was pure empathy.

"Tell me," she said on a shaky whisper.

The memories came roaring back like a tsunami of shame and anger. And hurt. Then the words just started to pour out.

"He loved to remind me that I was weak. I was never the sort of son he would have wanted."

"Weak? You were a child." Tori's voice shook with outrage on his behalf.

"A child who always had his head in a book. Or was sketching a picture or a design of some sort."

"And now you're a famous, accomplished architect. You must have had talent even at such a young age."

"He didn't see it as talent. He saw it as dreamy and worthless. At least I was able to keep him away from Gemma and Adria. That was all that mattered. The more he focused on what a disappointment I was, the less he was interested in the two of them."

She squeezed his hand. "You turned yourself into bait. To protect your sisters."

He shrugged. "What choice did I have? I could handle him. They wouldn't have been able to. He could be vicious."

"He was physical, wasn't he?"

"Yeah, but he was sneaky about it."

"Sneaky?"

"Yeah. A baseball would get misthrown and hit me in the chest. Somehow I wouldn't see his feet while running and trip over them. Things like that."

Now that he was saying the words out loud, the confusion and anger of those years threatened to bubble to the surface. Somehow focusing on Tori's face served as a buffer. "He just said it was proof I was not athletic and that my clumsiness was the reason any of it was happening."

"As though it was all your fault."

"Exactly. And my mom believed him. Because it was easier for her."

"I'm so sorry you had to go through that. No child deserves that."

He sneered. "If my mother thought so, she didn't bother to say it. Or do anything about it."

"You have every right not to want to forgive her."

Forgiveness had never even crossed his mind, not since he'd walked out of his mother's house for the final time years ago, taking both his sisters with him.

Why Adria felt the need to revisit any of the past was beyond his comprehension. She hadn't seemed to be able to give him any kind of answer when he'd asked. Yet somehow she was looking to open a sealed door that would let that past horror gush back into their lives. For no good reason that he could see.

Clay suddenly felt a heavy weariness settle over him. He hated that he was fighting with his sister. But her motives just didn't make any sense.

"Is that why you set up a charity for children?" Tori asked him now.

He shrugged. "I suppose it had a lot to do with it. My only escape growing up was a local teen center. It ran solely on donations and volunteers. The only peace I had was when I escaped there for a game of basketball or to just hang out. I guess I wanted to pay it forward."

"That was very noble, Clay. I hope you see that."

"I don't know about that." He stared at his empty glass. "Being able to do something for those kids benefits me as much as it benefits them."

Her eyes softened even as her grip on his hand tightened. "That says a lot about you. Tells me all I need to know about your character."

Clay wasn't sure what that meant. How could he explain to Tori that helping those kids helped him to recapture some of the innocence he'd abruptly lost when he'd had to grow so suddenly after his father's death.

Not that he needed to explain it. And he certainly didn't need to unburden himself this way to her. "We don't need to talk about any of this. It's all in the past.

What's done is done." He took his arm away, perhaps a little too forcefully. Tori slowly placed her hand back at her side.

"I could use another drink." Standing on shaky legs, Clay took his time walking over to the bar. He needed a moment, without Tori watching him with those kind, sympathetic eyes. Part of him felt rather relieved that she knew about that part of his life now. Another part felt shaky and vulnerable.

Is that what love is, then?

Whoa. What?

Clay froze in place. How had that word even come up? He really was a mess, throwing such loaded words around even silently. Yes, he and Tori appeared to be compatible in any number of ways. And clearly there was some sort of spark between them, a current of electricity. There was just so much about her he liked and admired. Her kindness. Her dedication when it came to her craft. The way her smile brightened a darkness within him that he'd never thought would see light.

But none of that meant love. He'd seen what love could be when his father was still alive. His parents had truly been happy together.

Clay had also seen what love was not. He'd seen how losing the man she'd adored had broken all that was decent within his mother. What his stepfather and she had shared was nothing more than an attachment to each other, a codependency that had led his sole remaining parent to neglect and betray the very same people she was supposed to cherish and protect.

Why would Clay risk leaving himself open to such vulnerability? Especially after what he'd overcome.

He and Tori weren't even dating, for Pete's sake.

They'd just been spending time together for a few days, not even that long.

Must have been something in that drink. He was going to switch to soda.

It was completely dark by the time they made it back to the resort and Clay walked her to her room.

Tori's heart still felt heavy thinking about their conversation at the bar. The things about his past that he'd confided in her would stay with Tori for the rest of her life. People could be so cruel. And those who were meant to protect the most vulnerable so often couldn't be bothered to do the right thing.

How little she'd known about him all this time. To think, she'd found him attractive before. To know now all that he'd overcome, and just how far he'd made it in life despite such punishing odds, added admiration to the myriad feelings she felt for Clay Ramos.

Including longing.

She couldn't deny it any longer. She yearned for him, wanted him with every cell in her body, down to her bones.

So what was she going to do about it?

"Thanks again for being my pirate playdate," he said with a smile that seemed less than heartfelt. No wonder. Their lighthearted afternoon had certainly grown heavy into the evening.

"You're welcome." She held up the silly pirate's hat. "Thank you for my souvenir."

"You're welcome. Have a good night." He saluted her with the fake cutlass before landing a soft peck on her cheek.

Tori's heart pounded in her chest as he made to leave.

He'd taken one step before she found her tongue. "Wait!" She hadn't meant for her voice to sound quite so urgent.

Clay turned, giving her an inquisitive look. "Something wrong?"

No. Yes. How was she going to articulate what she wanted? She had no experience with this. With Drew, he'd always been very clear about what he'd been after. Her desires and needs had always been afterthoughts.

She wasn't used to asking for what she wanted.

The truth was, she'd felt a kindred spirit when Clay had told her about his stepfather. In so many ways, she could relate to how he'd been mistreated by the bullying adult his mother had brought into their lives.

Unlike her, however, Clay hadn't chosen his tormentor. And he'd found a way to channel his turmoil into something productive and charitable. He'd found a way to help others, whereas Tori had barely been able to help herself.

Well, maybe this would be step one of that process.

"I'd like it if you would come in. Very much," she managed to blurt out.

Heat flooded his eyes and the muscle in his jaw clenched. "There's no storm tonight, sweetheart."

Aside from the proverbial storm raging within her. "I know. And I know what I'm asking."

"I'm not certain you do. Or if you've thought it through all the way."

Her heart plummeted to her toes. If this was his way of telling her he'd rather not be with her, she didn't think she would ever recover.

But she wasn't about to walk anything back. Much too late for that.

Her expression must have given away her thoughts.

"You can't think I don't want you," he said on a low growl. "You have to know better than that."

Relief and joy blended into a potpourri of emotion through her core. Her body was humming, her desire ratcheting up several notches at hearing that he did indeed want her, too. "Then what are we going to do about it, Clay?" The answer was oh so obvious as far as she was concerned.

"If this is some kind of pity—"

She physically clasped her hand over his mouth. "Please stop right there. Before you say something we're both going to end up regretting."

He gently pulled her hand from his lips. "I'm sorry. It's just been an intense couple of hours. I don't want there to be any misunderstandings between us."

"There won't be. I understand what I'm asking for."

He gently trailed a finger down her cheek then tucked a loose strand of her hair in place behind her hear. "Are you sure, Tori? Because I'm trying to be really up-front here. I can't be someone I'm not. And I can't give something I don't have to give."

"Then I'll take whatever you can give." She made sure to emphasize the last two words.

Dear heavens, who was this daring, unapologetic woman so blatantly stating what she was after? Tori didn't think she'd ever been so bold in the past, or could ever be so bold again.

And then she couldn't think at all. Clay's hand moved with lightning speed to grasp the back of her neck under her hair. He pulled her to him and took her mouth with his in a way that could only be described as savage. Demanding. Punishing. In all the best ways. She groaned under his mouth, let her hands roam across his chest and along his shoulders. Beneath his shirt, his skin felt like fire under her fingers. Her mind simply screamed for more.

He was pushing the door open behind her, half carrying her inside, their lips still fused together.

They didn't make it past the sofa until several hours later.

CHAPTER EIGHT

TORI DIDN'T HAVE to open her eyes to know that the bed was empty. She could feel his absence. Had he just up and left? It seemed implausible, after the night they'd shared, that he wouldn't so much as bid her good-bye before just taking off.

Memories flushed through her mind and she felt her cheeks burn. Clay had been arduous yet gentle. Demanding yet generous. Her body still tingled in response.

But now he was gone.

Forcing one eye open, she glanced around the room. Though his pants were nowhere to be seen, his shirt still lay where he'd haphazardly tossed it on the floor last night.

So he was here somewhere still, unless he'd dashed shirtless across the resort to his own room. Highly unlikely. Maybe he was getting a drink of water or something. She could use some herself. Embarrassingly enough, she found herself giggling. Maybe they could take up where they'd left off.

The sound of the balcony door opening then shutting again solved the mystery. He'd simply been out for some air.

He appeared in the doorway a moment later. "What's got you so amused this bright and early in the morning?"

"Is it that obvious?"

"Very."

"I was just remembering," she said with a coyness that surprised her. Even her voice sounded unfamiliar to her own ears.

He reached for her stuffed rabbit where it sat on the TV stand. "This thing's been staring at me. Rather accusingly, I might add. As if I took his spot last night."

Tori laughed. "I've had that for as long as I can remember."

He studied the worn and tattered outer material. The thing had been patched up more times than the scarecrow in that children's story. "I can tell. It's clearly seen better days. I saw it in your apartment back in Boston. So you travel with it, too, huh?"

She nodded. "It's the only thing I have of my biological mother. She gave Eloise and me identical stuffed rabbits before we were adopted out."

"Ah, so it's sentimental."

"Very." How odd that they were speaking about her stuffed rabbit when all she wanted to discuss was what they'd shared last night. Wasn't he feeling the slightest bit affected?

He walked over to the bed and handed her the toy, then gave her a tender peck on the cheek. Chaste. Innocent. Completely different than the way he'd kissed her last night.

It took all she had not to grab his arm and pull him down onto the mattress. Something told her it wouldn't be a good idea. That the reaction she'd receive wouldn't be entirely what she hoped for.

She propped her pillow and sat straight instead, the stuffed rabbit clutched snugly to her chest. "Were you just getting some air out there? On the balcony?"

"Actually I was just waiting for Gemma and Tom to come by on their morning run. We don't want a repeat of the last time I left your place in the morning. This time I don't think she'd quite believe it if I tried to tell her that nothing happened between us." With that, he picked his shirt up and began putting it on.

Tori reflexively tugged the sheet up higher over her breasts, suddenly feeling exposed.

"I've got something of a busy day," he told her, buttoning up.

Family events. And she certainly wasn't family. In fact, she wouldn't even know what to call herself as it pertained to Clay. She certainly wasn't his girlfriend.

She baked cakes for him.

"But I'll call you later," he said. "Maybe come by if you're up for it. No pressure, of course."

She could only nod, her tongue didn't seem to want to work. Just as well. Nothing she could have said would fit the current scenario.

He didn't want to be seen leaving her room. Plus, he wasn't even interested in seeing her again until later tonight. Why was she so unprepared for this? How had she not seen it coming? There was no excuse for such naïveté. Clay had felt vulnerable yesterday after their heartfelt conversation in the pub. He'd taken her up on her offer of a night of comfort. That's all their intimacy amounted to. Nothing more.

He couldn't have been more clear last night. And he couldn't be clearer now. To him, this was all nothing more than a meaningless fling.

Well, if that thought left a lump of disappointment lodged in her throat, she had no one but herself to blame. He had been up-front with her, after all.

His sister looked beat.

Clay supposed that wasn't surprising given that she

was the mom of a very energetic toddler. Still, Adria appeared as if she wanted to go to sleep right there on her lounge chair by the pool.

By contrast, her daughter didn't seem even remotely interested in napping. In fact, Lilly looked to be on the verge of a toddler tantrum. Growing impatient with having sunblock applied, she kept trying to slip out of her mother's arms.

He walked over to where they sat and crouched to his niece's level. "Hey, squirt, what seems to be the matter here?"

"No hat!" she yelled, and tried to yank her sunbonnet off her head. Apparently, her headwear was an issue as well as the dreaded sunscreen lotion.

"She's been in a mood all morning," Adria told him. "She's got me at my wit's end."

"Want Daddy!" Lilly demanded.

Uh-oh, Lilly's voice had risen a notch. The tantrum was looking inevitable.

"Daddy's on an important phone call, love," Adria told her daughter in a most soothing and calming voice. "Contract negotiations," she added for Clay's benefit.

He'd been out walking the resort to get some air, anything to try to clear his head, when Lilly's voice had carried across the patio. Not that his walk had been doing him any good anyway.

The way he'd left things with Tori this morning wasn't sitting well with him. She'd refused to meet his eyes as he'd walked out the door, had just clutched her toy rabbit tightly in her arms.

She'd looked so vulnerable, so damn hurt, that he'd almost turned around and crawled back under the covers with her. He'd so badly wanted to. But in the end, doing so would have only served as a temporary salve. Eventually, he would have to leave her bed, and leave her room. Just as, eventually, he would have to walk out of her life. For he would never be able to fit in to it. Tori's life was full of the love of a strong family and the challenge of a successful business. She didn't have room in it for a man like him. A man with a past that haunted him.

"Wanna swim!" Lilly shouted, breaking into his thoughts. She thrust a pudgy hand toward the pool "Wid Daddy."

Clay lifted the little girl in his arms and held her close to his face, her feet dangling playfully. His efforts got him a few solid kicks to the stomach. "Listen, squirt, your momma says Daddy's busy. How about if I take you in the pool instead?"

Her angry grimace immediately transformed into a wide grin. She clasped her hands on his cheeks. Clay decided he'd take that as a yes.

"Oh, Clay. Would you really do that?" Adria asked in a hopeful voice. "I could really use a break here."

He set his niece down on the concrete patio and fixed her bonnet.

"Sure. I'm not really doing anything right now."

As far as olive branches went, he figured it was a start. After the conversation at the pub yesterday, Tori's words about Adria in particular had rumbled around in his head. Tori was right. He should have probably listened better when Adria had first raised the subject of their mother. He was a mature, professional adult. The mere mention of his mother shouldn't have him seeing red and refusing to even hear his sister out. Ultimately, nothing Adria could say would ever change his mind about the family matriarch, but listening was free.

Tori. So much for clearing his head. Thoughts of her

had nagged at him all morning. He couldn't seem to get her out of his mind. Nor what they'd shared last night.

He had to come to terms with what had happened between them. He couldn't recall the last time a woman had gotten so deep under his skin.

"And where did you just drift off to?" Adria asked, pulling him back to the present.

"Just planning all the water games this little one and I are about the play," he lied. "Why don't you lay back and close your eyes for a bit?" She really did look tired. A bout of brotherly sympathy and concern settled in his chest.

They'd been through a lot together, the three of them. He couldn't ever forget that. He'd always feel responsible for her and Gemma on some deep level, no matter how old they got. Ingrained habits were hard to break.

His two sisters were the only family he really had. Plus the little one currently tugging at his hand, trying to drag him to the water. But she was a fairly new addition to the mix. And he would have yet another brother-in-law soon. Thankfully, they were both good men. But Clay wasn't at the point yet where he viewed either one as family. More like good friends or poker buddies, perhaps.

He was happy his sisters had found love and wanted to marry. He really was. The chances of him doing the same were slim to none. He'd already spent years feeling responsible for others, had finally reached a point in his life where he could focus on himself and his career goals.

It would be selfish of him to pull anyone else into his orbit when he had so little to offer. That's why he'd been absolutely straight with Tori last night. He could only hope she'd understood like she said she did.

A small hand smacked him on his knee. "Swim!"

Man, females could be so impatient.

Clay shrugged off his shirt, glad he'd thrown on nylon sports shorts this morning. He walked his niece to the edge of the pool and helped her navigate the steps.

Lilly held her arms up and pumped her legs.

"You want to be tossed, huh?"

"Up!"

And so began a marathon game of toss and catch until his upper arms started to ache. At least it looked like his sister was getting some R and R.

Tori's breath caught when she saw him.

Some unexplainable instinct had made her take the long way to her room after finishing the day's baking. She'd figured she'd take the scenic route that ran along the path leading to the infinity pool that served as the central landmark of the resort.

Clearly, said instinct wasn't of the self-preserving variety.

She couldn't help but stand and stare at the sight of Clay in the pool. Even the risk of being caught wasn't enough to make her turn around. She was mesmerized by the image he posed.

There he was, shirtless and tanned, playing with his niece. Something about seeing Clay swimming with the little girl, watching how affectionate and playful he was with her, had Tori's heart pounding in her chest. Pictures from the previous night flooded her mind. Her cheeks started to flame as a welcome warmth curled through her midsection.

Finally, she tore her gaze away and forced her jaw closed. It wasn't easy.

She'd almost made her getaway sight unseen when a familiar female voice called out her name. "Tori. Is that you?"

Clay's head snapped in her direction and a bolt of electricity shook her entire body when their eyes met. He almost missed catching his niece as she came down from the last toss, but managed to snatch her just in time. Tori uttered a mild curse. If she'd only stepped away a second sooner.

Maybe she could pretend she hadn't heard her name. But that was fruitless. Clay had locked eyes with her. In fact, he was staring at her now.

Adria sat up in her lounger and patted the chair next to her. "Come sit with us a bit. I just ordered a pitcher of lemonade."

Not exactly having a choice, Tori slowly made her way over.

"Again, Unca' Cway." Lilly's joyous shout echoed through the air.

"How are you feeling?" Tori asked, keeping her voice low, not that she could have been heard over toddler laughter and splashing water.

"More and more tired every day."

"Sorry to hear that. How about the nausea?"

"That can be kept at bay as long as I stay out of the heat." She pointed to the beach umbrella above her. "And if I make sure to eat."

"Is there anything I can bake for you?" Tori didn't envy the woman. A sweltering tropical island could only be so much fun while expecting. "Any cravings yet?"

Adria rested her hand on her middle. "Too many to mention, unfortunately."

"Please let me know if there's anything I can prepare for you."

Adria tilted her head, examining her. "Thank you. You really are a kind soul, aren't you?"

Tori shrugged. "I just happen to have an entire kitchen at my disposal."

Adria patted her knee. "I just may take you up on that. With Lilly, I only wanted savory dishes." She gave her belly a small affectionate rub. Tori didn't think Adria was even conscious of how often she touched her middle. "This one seems to have burdened me with a raving sweet tooth."

"It's a good thing your brother hired a baker then, I guess."

The woman chuckled melodically. "Good thing, indeed."

Adria was easy to talk to. Despite the disconcerting fact that Clay was so close and half undressed, chatting with his sister was starting to put Tori at ease. Heaven knew she could use it.

Judging by her next statement, Adria seemed to feel the same way. "You know, it's nice to be able to finally talk to somebody about all this. Besides Enrique."

"It must be hard to keep it completely close to your chest."

Adria shaded her eyes with the back of her hand. "Harder than I would have thought, to be honest." She sighed deeply. "You're wondering why I won't tell anyone."

The question had crossed her mind.

"It's simple, really," Adria continued. "This is Gemma's time. I don't want anything overshadowing her special day."

It was such a selfless motive. Tori's impression of the woman went up several pegs from an already pretty esteemed level. But her reasoning still didn't explain why she hadn't told those closest to her. Including her brother. Clay seemed like the type who could hold a secret.

"Do you mind if I'm honest about something else?" Adria asked.

"Of course. Please go ahead."

"I have to say, I had my suspicions, but there's really no doubt watching the two of you up close."

Tori gave her head a shake. "I don't understand."

"You've really got it bad." She motioned toward her brother. "The way you keep looking at him but pretend that you're not."

Tori felt heat rush into her face. "Oh no. It's not like that." Had Clay noticed her staring at him, too? She probably looked like a love-struck teenager gaping at the homecoming king.

Adria patted her knee again. "Of course it is."

Tori didn't bother to deny it. There'd be no point. She certainly didn't seem to be fooling the woman. Obviously, Tori wore her heart on her sleeve and her emotions on her face. "Is it that obvious?" she asked on a defeated sigh.

Adria's small laugh wasn't unkind. "Yes. For what it's worth, he keeps looking over here at you, too."

Probably just curious as to what she was talking to his sister about.

Tori ducked her head. How had she even gotten here? When had she fallen so hard? She could blame Eloise. All her talk about taking chances, how she would give Tori the wedding dress she'd be married in when it was her turn. Her sister had put dreamy ideas into her head, and look where she found herself. Hopelessly in love with a man she had no chance of a future with.

Adria gave her a conspiratorial wink. "Don't worry. I'll keep your secret just as well as you're keeping mine."

CHAPTER NINE

How DID A man look so sexy and tempting carrying a squirming, soaking wet toddler?

Tori's eyes were starting to ache from forcing them to look in any direction but where he stood. Clay hoisted his niece over his shoulder and climbed the steps out of the pool. Water gleamed like spun gold over his tanned skin. His hair was wet and fell in haphazard curls over his forehead.

She had to suck in a gasp of longing. Adria must have heard, as she could have sworn the woman chuckled under her breath.

"Hey," he said by way of greeting as he reached their side.

"Hey, yourself." Tori nearly groaned out loud. Way to come back with a witty response.

He flashed her that smile with a head tilt that always brought a flush to her skin. He slid on a pair of stylish sunglasses that made it difficult to gauge his expression. By contrast, he could no doubt read all the desire and longing swimming in her own eyes.

"Want to hand me that?" he said, pointing to something behind her.

For a second, Tori had no clue what he may be referring to. She glanced around. Did he want the lemonade pitcher?

Why was she suddenly such a frazzled mess around him?

The answer was obvious, of course. She'd spent the night in his arms, enjoying fully every pleasurable moment he gave her. Now, she couldn't deny just how much she wanted him to touch her that way again.

"The towel," he clarified.

"Oh! Of course. Here."

He had to be silently laughing at her. She didn't dare look in Adria's direction as she tossed him the towel. He expertly wrapped it around Lilly and began drying her off.

For a single bachelor who led a pretty busy life, he certainly seemed to know how to handle a toddler. Especially impressive considering he'd only been an uncle for under three years. And look how well he'd taken care of his sisters at such a high cost to himself. He'd essentially put himself in the line of fire to keep them safe.

She had no doubt in her mind, despite his nightmare of a childhood, that Clay would make an excellent father someday. Caring and attentive, he was beyond patient with Lilly.

Stop right this minute.

Thoughts like that were not going to lead anywhere good. The last thing she needed was to picture Clay as a father. To imagine dark-haired, olive-skinned little tykes who had their father's deep chocolate-brown eyes and perhaps her angular, dimpled chin.

Heavens. What in the world was wrong with her?

He'd offered her nothing more than a temporary physical fling. And here she was, fantasizing about having his babies. It was so uncharacteristic of her, it was totally disconcerting.

She looked up to find Adria studying her. "Are you all right, Tori? You've suddenly gone rather red."

"It is rather hot," Tori hedged. She wasn't overheated. She was blushing at the direction her wayward mind had just taken her.

Tori gave her head a shake to clear the useless images.

She could use a good dip in the pool herself. Though it probably wouldn't do much to cool her off.

She looked so cute when she was frazzled. Then again, Clay couldn't recall a time when she didn't look adorable. Even those times he'd seen her covered in sugar and flour, her apron stained.

Now, Tori seemed to be doing everything she could to avoid making eye contact with him. Was she thinking of all the ways he'd touched her last night? And all the ways she'd touched him? He, for one, hadn't been able to stop thinking about it.

She leaned over to address Lilly. "How was your swim?"

"Good," Lilly answered then stuck two fingers into her mouth.

"It wasn't so much a swim as an upper arm workout for her uncle," Adria quipped, handing her daughter a sippy cup full of lemonade.

Clay used the towel to try to dry himself off. It was hardly worth the effort, already soaked from Lilly's splashing. What he wanted to do, what he wouldn't have hesitated to do if his sister and niece weren't present, was to wrap the towel around Tori and use it to pull her to him. Then he would take her lips with his own…

But they weren't alone. Not to mention they were at the resort pool with several guests and workers meandering around.

"Cu'cake waydee!" Lilly announced, pointing to Tori with a toothless smile.

Tori's smile in return was brilliant and genuine. "That's right. I'm the cupcake lady."

Lilly nestled closer to her and tried to climb onto her lap. Tori didn't hesitate. Gently lifting the girl, she set her on her lap with an amused laugh. "I guess that makes me okay in your book, huh?"

Clay could hardly wait to take her into his own lap. She was pretty okay in his book, too. He sat next to them on the lounger. The smell of her coconut lotion and rose shampoo tickled his nostrils. He'd absorbed those scents so deeply last night.

Adria handed him a sweaty glass of lemonade and he took it gratefully, briefly considering dumping it over his head rather than drinking it. Lilly would sure get a kick out of it if he did that. But then he'd have to explain that he felt hot and bothered by the woman next to him—the cupcake lady herself. If he was smart, he would just get up and leave. He'd done his good deed by his sister. He could reward himself with a cold shower in his room.

Suddenly music filled the air and an exuberant resort employee jogged into the pool area. Wearing a bright yellow wig and enormous joke shop sunglasses, she asked the pool-goers, "Are you ready for a pool party?"

Lilly started clapping and scrambled to move off the lounger. "Yay!"

"It's kiddie dance time," Adria explained with a weary smile, slowly beginning to stand. Her voice said the last thing she was up for at the moment was play dancing by the pool to bouncy reggae versions of nursery songs.

Tori must have picked up on her lack of enthusiasm. "I can dance with her."

Adria's shoulders sagged with relief. "Oh, Tori. That would be fantastic. If you're sure you're up for it."

What was up with her? he wondered. She was usually much more energetic. Clay hardly recognized the sluggish, exhausted woman with the dark circles under her eyes.

"I would love to dance to 'Itsy Bitsy Spider' played on the steel drums with this young lady." Rising from the lounger, she took Lilly by the hand.

"Unca' Cway, too!" Lilly shouted and reached for his hand. Looked like he was on the hook.

With a resigned sigh, he let Lilly lead him and Tori to the other side of the pool where several other tots were already stomping tiny feet and pumping small arms.

Clay did his best version of the chicken dance then the electric slide. Judging by the way Tori laughed at him, his moves weren't impressing her. On the other hand, he couldn't stop watching her. Tori had a natural way to move to the music, her feet perfectly in sync with the beat. The pleasure on her face was captivating. Lilly's version of dancing was to run around the two of them while stomping her feet as hard as she could.

If someone had told him a week ago that he'd be dancing to kiddie reggae with the pretty baker from the North End by a pool while his niece ran around their legs, he might have wondered about their mental state.

The music outlasted Lilly's energy. Clay sensed the very moment she began to peter out and picked her up before she fell over from exhaustion.

Adria was already packing up when they walked back over to their chairs. "Thank you. Both of you." She threw the beach bag over her shoulder and took Lilly from Clay's arms. The child snuggled against her mother and fell asleep instantly on her shoulder.

"That had to be the most restful afternoon I've spent since we arrived here," Adria added in a soft whisper before walking away.

Again, it was fairly uncharacteristic of Adria to make such a statement. She was one of those people who was constantly on the move, with energy to spare. He would have to ask her exactly what was going on. There had to be something besides the recent strain on their relationship and all that was happening with Enrique's career prospects. Not to mention the whole chaos of the wedding.

But right now, his focus was solely honed on Tori. He was finally about to get her alone. He had no doubt she was thinking the same thing, and got all the confirmation he needed when she bit her lower lip, as she had a habit of doing.

No words needed to be said between them. Gently taking her hand, he silently led her from the pool area and along the path that led to his room.

When they finally reached the door and shut it behind them, it was a scramble to relieve her of her clothes.

"I thought I'd never get you to myself," he rasped against her cheek before trailing kisses along her neck and shoulder. Tori's response was a low-level groan that broke the last thread of his control.

Later, with her curled up against his side and the light breeze from an open window carrying the sound of the ocean through the air, he whispered softly in her ear. "Tori?"

"Yes?"

"I really love the way you dance."

"Even to kiddie reggae?"

"Absolutely."

She giggled softly, nestled closer against him. "Oh. Um…well, thanks, I guess."

"Any man who doesn't is a fool."

He hadn't meant to say that out loud.

* * *

She didn't think she was ever going to get enough of this man.

They'd opted for room service in Clay's room rather than venturing out again. That was fine with her. She could handle a few more stolen moments with Clay. Considering this was all so temporary, that it would end in just a couple short days, she would take what she could get.

The thought settled like a brick of disappointment in her stomach, so she pushed it away. For now, she would live in the moment. Enjoy the company of the man she'd somehow fallen head over heels in love with.

There was no denying that any longer.

Clay handed her a glass of wine and removed the covers from the plates on the serving trolley that had arrived only moments before. A hot curl of steam rose into the air along with the smell of lemon, exotic spices and roasted chicken.

"Hmm. A girl could get used to this," she said, unfolding a napkin onto her lap. Except that was a lie. She really couldn't get used to it, tempting as this was. At some point, she would be going back to reality. A reality that only held Clayton Ramos in her memories—until he called with an order.

Stop it already.

Why couldn't she just let go of all these pestering thoughts and enjoy herself? Live for the moment, like Eloise so often suggested?

"You spoil me," she added playfully. Her reward was a passionate kiss that almost had her suggesting they forget about the food.

"Anything for the cupcake lady," Clay teased.

The reminder of the afternoon with Lilly brought a

smile to her lips. "Your niece is absolutely adorable. But you know that, don't you?"

She wondered how he would feel when he finally learned that his uncle duties were about to double. Chances were strong that Tori wouldn't be in his life when the news was announced. Another pang of hurt tugged at her heart.

She couldn't seem to stop herself with the defeatist and depressing thoughts. Yet she couldn't help but consider how all this would affect the days to come. How exactly did one embrace carpe diem when they'd been living their whole lives with the complete opposite mindset until now?

"She is pretty cute," Clay said around a mouthful of food. "And she really seems to have taken a liking to you."

"That's because she associates me with small cakes and sugary frosting."

He shrugged. "Maybe. Or maybe she's a real good judge of character for a three-year-old."

It was silly to feel so touched by such an innocuous compliment. But Tori felt her chest swell just the same. "You're really good with her," she returned with a compliment of her own. It was the absolute truth. "Lilly's lucky to have an uncle like you."

"The kid could have done worse, I suppose. It's not like I have anyone else to spoil." He paused to sip his wine. "Or like I ever will."

She knew she shouldn't ask, knew without a doubt that she wasn't going to like the answer he would return. But she couldn't seem to help herself. "Does that mean you wouldn't ever want that for yourself? To be a parent." She swallowed, then added, "Or to be someone's husband?"

He visibly shuddered at the thought and Tori wanted to kick herself. She should have never even ventured down this path.

"Marriage and kids aren't for people like me," Clay told her.

She tried to sound unaffected by his answer, while inside she shook with hurt and disappointment, recalling how the conversation seemed to echo the very thoughts she'd had by the pool earlier.

Clay continued. "Marriage is for guys like Tom. Or Enrique. Guys who enjoyed the safety of stable homes. Guys who didn't have to grow up too soon." He poured more wine for both of them before adding, "A man like me is much better off sticking with uncle-hood."

Well, she'd asked the question and now she had her answer. Not that she spent her days pining for a future with the proverbial white picket fence, but she knew that at some point in her life she did want a family. A family like the one she'd grown up in, with loud meals and messy fights and tons of love and laughter.

She wanted what Adria had. She wanted a wedding like Gemma was about to enjoy, secure in the knowledge that she'd found a man who cherished her. A man who wanted to spend the rest of his life with her. She wanted what her sister had so recently found.

She also wanted Clay.

And all those things were mutually exclusive.

What did it matter? It wasn't as if she would be given any kind of choice in the matter. Clay hadn't so much as made one mention of how things between them might play out once they returned to the States.

In fact, he'd made it clear before they'd spent their first night together that what they had would be no more than physical. Not as far as he was concerned, anyway.

Suddenly, Tori found she no longer had an appetite. The roast chicken that had her stomach grumbling and her mouth watering just moments ago suddenly tasted like cardboard in her mouth. Even the sip of wine she'd just taken lodged like a slip of wet paper in her throat.

If Clay noticed the change in her demeanor, he didn't make any comment.

Or maybe he didn't care to notice.

It appeared neither one of them could sleep.

Clay watched silently as Tori left the bed and made her way to the balcony. Whatever was on her mind, she'd been tossing and turning since they'd retired at midnight. He debated leaving her to herself. She was probably just looking to clear her head.

But several minutes passed and his curiosity won out. At least, that's what he told himself.

The truth? He was trying to conveniently ignore the nagging feeling that his bed felt lonely without her in it.

And that wouldn't do at all. He just didn't know what he was going to do about it when the time came.

She started a little when he opened the door and joined her where she leaned against the balcony railing, staring out into the starlit sky.

"Do I snore or is something else keeping you from sleeping?" he asked, taking her in his arms from behind, her back against his chest. He couldn't seem to stop wanting to touch her.

She indulged him with a light chuckle, almost too low to hear over the gentle lapping of the waves in the distance. "Like a freight train."

If only he could somehow capture this moment, stop it in time. Everything was perfect as is.

Too bad the world had to keep turning.

"If I promise to be quiet, will you come back to bed?" he breathed against her ear.

"I lied. You do not snore. I was just admiring the night sky. So many stars shining like faraway diamonds."

"It's a beautiful sight." A poet, he wasn't. Nor was he the type to stand around admiring the stars above. But Tori was good at making him take note of things he normally wouldn't have.

"I love New England," she told him. "But the view here in the tropics is something out of a dream."

She continued. "My family owns a very small place on the beach. We go for a couple weeks every summer. Been doing so since I can remember, with my parents commuting to the restaurant on weekends."

Clay chuckled. "Weekends by the beach without parental supervision? I'm guessing you and your brothers got into all sorts of trouble."

She shook her head. "They co-own the house with my aunt and uncle. So adults were always present. Along with my four cousins. It gets crowded, but there's no shortage of fun. Even now that we're all adults ourselves."

"Sounds like a great way to spend summers." Not for the first time since meeting her, Clay pondered what it must have been like to belong to such a large family. To feel part of a tight-knit group that spent weekends on the beach together in a tiny house.

"Josh often came with us, too. Along with—"

She'd stopped midsentence, but he could guess who she'd been about to refer to.

"Ah, the ex." Without thought, he wrapped his arms snugly around her middle. The scent of her shampoo ticked his nose and he nuzzled her hair indulgently.

"Yes. Drew often came along with us."

Dislike and resentment for a man he'd never met and wouldn't recognize on the street swamped his gut. The thought of Tori with someone else left a bitter taste in his mouth. How utterly Neanderthal, but he couldn't help what he couldn't help.

"The funny thing is, I wasn't even the one who invited him along."

He pulled back in surprise. "You weren't?"

"No. I was actually looking for a few days apart. Summers seemed to be the only time that could happen."

"Then how was he there?"

She sighed, rubbed her forehead. He could feel her muscles stiffen under his touch. "My brother Ty invited him one year. And it seemed to become a tradition after that. They were all friends."

"Sounds like you two dated for a long time." A tendril of unease uncurled within him. He had to acknowledge it as jealousy.

"Since high school."

"High school sweethearts." The bitterness on his tongue grew stronger.

"Everyone thought I was crazy to break up with someone like him." Her voice sounded low and raspy. "But I knew I couldn't be who I was meant to be if I stayed."

"Meaning?"

She sighed. "Drew has a very strong personality. He didn't want me to go away to school. He didn't want me to spend my free time with anyone but him. I only had one good friend through school. Shawna was the only one who didn't care what Drew thought and stuck around." An affectionate tone slipped into her voice. "It all came to a head when I decided to open the bakery."

"How so?" Clay asked, though he figured he could guess. Men like her ex didn't often want to share their time. Especially when it came to pursuing their own dreams.

"He said I was foolish to even attempt it. That I was too young, too inexperienced. That I was doomed to fail. He told me he was doing me a favor in trying to discourage me."

"Yet you proved him wrong." Man, had she ever. A surge of pride shot through him, though it made no sense. He had no claim to her or to her professional success.

She turned her head to look at him over her shoulder. Even in the dark, he could see the brilliance of her smile. "I sure did, didn't I?"

Her earlier wording troubled him. "What did you mean when you said 'things came to a head'?"

Her chin lifted, set with strength and sheer grit as she settled back against his chest. "He never physically hurt me."

His vision grew dark at even the thought.

Tori gave her head a shake. "It's just… There was the time he pulled me away from the dance floor a little too abruptly at a party, his grip on my wrist a little tighter than usual. It happened after an argument we'd had. He'd said I was foolish for taking on so much debt with a business loan."

Clay's arms instinctively enveloped her as she continued. "I knew right then I had to walk away. Without looking back."

His response was to turn her in his arms and take her lips with his own, indulging in a kiss that had them both moaning out loud.

Clay lost sight of how long they stood out there, simply admiring the night. Even as the first early rays of dawn broke the sky, he was hesitant to let her go. Finally, after about Tori's third contagious yawn, he took her by the hand and led her back inside.

She fell asleep in his arms moments later. But sleep eluded him as he mulled over everything she'd told him about her former lover. The thought of any man treating her in any derogatory way made him want to punch a wall. He knew who he'd be thinking of as he threw that punch, too.

He'd never considered himself to be a violent man. Saints knew he'd been tempted often enough, especially as the years passed and he'd grown taller and gained some muscle. He'd managed to somehow always hold the anger at bay. But right at this moment, he couldn't say for certain what he might do if he ever crossed paths with Tori's former boyfriend.

The guy bore more than a striking resemblance to the man who had crashed into Clay's life without warning. Personality wise, at least. In Tori's description of her ex, Clay had detected several common characteristics—controlling, belittling, and demanding. A man who always had to have his own way.

A man just like the monster he'd had to grow up with.

Tori woke hours later in Clay's arms and allowed herself to simply feel his strength around her. The scents of sandalwood and mint that she was now so fond of flooded her nose and she breathed them in, deeply indulging in the familiarity.

She felt safe in his embrace, coveted.

She'd fallen asleep rather shaken. Divulging all she had about Drew had taken a lot out of her. As a result, her slumber had been restless and flitting.

"Bad dreams?" Clay asked softly in her ear. "You were tossing and turning a lot."

Now that he mentioned it, she realized a nightmare had indeed been what had roused her. "Yes. I'm sorry if I woke you."

He gently took her by the shoulder and rolled her over to face him. "Tell me what's up."

Tori nestled closer against his chest, allowing herself the full comfort of his warm embrace. "Just a lot of bad memories. Triggered by our conversation earlier."

"It might help to talk some more, then. I have wide shoulders, Tori. And when it comes to you, I'm all ears."

She took a deep breath. Maybe it *would* help to get it all off her chest finally. Her emotions were like a sea of violent waves when it came to her past relationship. And here was Clay, offering her a safe harbor. At least for a little while.

"He was my first boyfriend…" she began. "We were both juniors. I couldn't believe a boy would notice me. Let alone a boy like him."

"Big man on campus?"

"Complete with all the letters and captainships. While I was a bit of a loner."

He sniffed her hair. "I find that hard to believe, given what I know of you now."

"It's true. I never really felt comfortable in my own skin. Always felt like there was a piece of me missing." A chill ran down her spine. "I have to wonder now if it was some sixth sense telling me there was a sibling out there who could help me be complete."

"Oh, Tori."

"Everyone kept telling me how lucky I was. Especially all the girls who would have done anything to date him. And I believed them. I was too young to realize the effect the relationship was having on me."

"How so?"

Tori squeezed her eyes shut. "I started to change. Began dressing differently. I grew my hair long when I'd always preferred it short."

"I love your short, spiky hair."

"He said it didn't suit me."

Clay's entire body stiffened next to hers. "He was wrong."

"I know that now. But at the time I just wanted to please this boy who had miraculously chosen me. So I did what he told me."

"What else?" Clay prodded.

"He asked me to sign up for the same classes so that we could study together." She humphed a bitter laugh. "Free tutoring for him would be a more accurate way to describe it."

The memories came flashing back on a wave of regret. She'd lost so many days of her youth trying to accommodate someone else's wishes. But it could have been so much worse. She could consider herself lucky.

"By the time we graduated high school and attended college, he was fully ingrained in my life. My brothers and parents loved him. They only saw the friendly, charming side that he was so good at projecting. He could be quite clever." Her family still didn't understand why she'd turned her back on what they'd seen as an ideal life partner.

"What happened then? After you started university?"

"I was studying hospitality and restaurant management, but my heart wasn't in it. I love working for my parents at the trattoria. But it wasn't a lifelong goal. I started baking for fun. Then I took a baking class as an elective."

"And the rest is history."

She ran a finger up his chest and over his shoulder, just to be able to touch him, to feel his warmth on her fingertips. "It was the beginning of the end for me and Drew. He took it as a personal betrayal when I quit school to open up a bakery. I took out loans, both personal and business. He said no wife of his was going to go into debt and waste her talents. I knew right then without any doubt that I absolutely did not want to be his wife. And I told him as much."

Clay let out a low whistle.

"That's when his behavior started to grow more and more aggressive and hostile."

"So you got out."

"I had to. I would have lost myself if I'd stayed with him."

He pecked a kiss to the top of her head. "But you didn't stay with him. And look at all you've accomplished since. You're a household name in your field. You've put your heart and soul into a lifestyle that you love. You're the very definition of success, Tori. Despite how hard he tried to stop you."

Tori ducked her head under his chin and kissed the side of his neck. His pulse throbbed against her lips. When he spoke that way and held her tight in his arms, she could almost believe him.

CHAPTER TEN

The meringue was the key to the whole thing.

If the meringue was imperfect in any way, too soggy or too stiff, the whole thing would fall apart. Quite literally.

Tori bit her lip and focused on the job at hand. She had to get the consistency just right. The top layer of Gemma's cake was supposed to be a confectionary replica of the Leaning Tower of Pisa, the historic landmark in Italy where Gemma and Tom had taken their first vacation together.

She'd been having trouble concentrating all day. Clay was the one to blame for that. Tori couldn't seem to get him out of her mind. And she would tell him so as soon as she laid eyes on him again.

Focus.

The cake wasn't going to make itself.

It took her three more tries to get the consistency just right. Then she was on her way. By this time tomorrow, a masterpiece—if she did say so herself—of a wedding cake with five tiers topped by a molded sponge cake replica of an Italian landmark would be the centerpiece of a festive marital ceremony.

A ceremony she wasn't invited to.

Tori pushed the thought aside. She was here to do a

job, not attend a party. Regardless of what was happening between her and the bride's brother.

Not that she could define exactly what was happening between them. She'd never before shared with anyone the specifics about how Drew had treated her toward the end of their relationship. Not even Eloise. Clay had listened to her last night without any judgement. She hadn't realized exactly how much she'd needed that from someone. On a deep-seated level, she knew she had no blame for the way Drew had behaved toward her. But a tiny yet not silent part of her wondered how she'd ever let things get that far.

Why had she stayed? Even past the point where she'd known the relationship was hopeless, known that she hadn't loved Drew. And perhaps never had.

She'd been half afraid Clay would ask her that last night—if she'd loved Drew. Luckily he hadn't. She wasn't sure how she might have answered.

Hours later, Tori had all the pieces baked and cooling on various racks. All that was left was to assemble the cake, which could be done tomorrow morning.

And her job here would be done. Meaning her time here on the island was coming to an end, as well. She bit back a sob then silently reprimanded herself for being so foolish. She'd known what she was getting into. Clay had been nothing but straight with her from the beginning.

And she'd gone and fallen in love with him anyway.

As if her thoughts had prompted it, her cell phone pinged with a text message. Clay's profile appeared on the screen.

Where are you? Kitchen?

She answered then waited for the dancing dots to transform into words.

Is this a good time to stop by?

Yes. Timing couldn't be better, in fact.

Good. Have to ask you something. I need a favor.

???

Will explain when I get there.

Tori was about to put the phone back in her apron pocket when it pinged with yet another message. This one flooded her heart with warmth. And also with a heavy dose of sadness at what might have been if things had been different.

Miss you.

Yeah. Adria had been absolutely right yesterday by the pool. Tori did indeed have it bad.

The few minutes it took for Clay to arrive felt like eons. What kind of favor was he looking for exactly? Tori's curiosity heightened with each passing second until he finally showed up. He'd recently showered, she could tell. His hair was wet and combed back, his skin still damp and fresh.

Even casually dressed in plain khaki shorts and a fitted V-necked T-shirt, the man looked like he could walk down a runway in Milan. While here she was covered in flour and sugar and wearing a frumpy apron.

"What is that heavenly smell?" he asked, taking her by the hand and pulling her to him for a deep and lingering kiss that had her momentarily breathless.

She cleared her throat when she could find her voice again. "Well, it could be the meringue. Or the sponge candy used to make the tower. Or you might be referring to the buttercream frosting."

He flashed her a devilish grin. "Or it could be you."

The man certainly was a charmer. He grabbed her sketch pad from where it lay open on the counter and studied her drawing of the wedding cake.

"So this is the final plan, huh?"

She nodded.

"How in the world are you going to get it to stand upright, especially when the top is literally supposed to lean over?"

She pointed to the spots she'd drawn at strategic points on the pastry.

"Huh. This is a lot like architecture." He tapped her nose. "I make exactly those kinds of decisions when designing buildings. We have more in common than we even knew." He flashed her that dizzyingly handsome smile of his. "We'd make a great team."

He had to stop saying those things to her. Every such comment made her long for the future they might have had. For what could be between them if only he were open enough to consider it.

But Clay had decided long ago that he was going to close himself off. And Tori didn't have it in her to twist herself into some kind of pretzel to accommodate a man who was supposed to love her and accept her as she was.

Been there, done that.

She pulled the sketch pad back and closed it, perhaps

a little too abruptly. "Yes. Well, let's hope it works. It's never a certainty."

He blinked at her in question. "I have no doubt that it will. I have faith in your abilities."

Yet more compliments. "So, what's this favor you need?"

"I've been asked to babysit again. Lilly needs someone to accompany her to an activity."

"Is Adria not feeling well?" She'd been meaning to check on his sister but time had gotten away from her. Poor thing really seemed to be having a tough first trimester.

"Yeah. I'm wondering if she picked up a bug or something on the way here. Everyone else seems to be doing fine, though."

Tori made sure to remain silent.

"And Enrique is stuck on another phone call with his agent and his club. Sounds like negotiations aren't going very well."

"That's too bad." One more thing for Adria to have to deal with. She'd be sure to give her a call as soon as she had a moment.

"I'd rather have some help with this one. Not sure I trust myself to take it on alone. And I guess they've already paid for it and have talked it up to Lilly. They don't want to let her down."

Whatever he was referring to sounded like a bit more than an afternoon of face painting or craft of some sort. "What kind of activity are we talking about here?"

He leaned in closer to her over the counter. "Tell me, how do you feel about dolphins?"

She looked pretty darn sexy in a wet suit.

Clay had been nervous back there for a while when it

looked like Tori might not want to join them. She'd certainly taken long enough to answer. In the end, much to his relief, she'd finally agreed. Clay hadn't exactly been looking forward to wrangling his toddler niece by himself in a small cay with oversize fish circling them, trained or not.

Admit it, a little voice goaded in his head. *You just wanted her here.*

"I've never been swimming with dolphins before," Tori said next to him in the aquatics hut slash gift store. Souvenirs like stuffed dolphins and sea turtle keychains surrounded them.

The animal trainer was given instructions about exactly what to expect and all the safety precautions to be adhered to once everyone was in the water.

Lilly made it hard to pay attention. She'd made it a game to demand going from Tori's lap back to his repeatedly. Not to mention how distracted he was by Tori's enticing curves in that suit. Finally, Tori gently started to stroke the little girl's hair, which somehow soothed her enough to settle down.

About twenty minutes later, they followed the pleasant young aquatics trainer, Liv, to a small cay with crystal-blue water.

Liv blew her whistle and they waited for the show to start. And waited. Nothing seemed to be happening.

"Sometimes they take their time," Liv told them rather apologetically.

Remarkably, Lilly noticed it before either of them. She pointed a wet finger toward the water. "Fish."

Sure enough, the water rippled several feet in front of them as a silvery gray fin glided along the surface. Suddenly, a dolphin's head popped up so close Clay could reach out and touch it. Lilly clapped with glee from where

Tori still held her on one hip. For her part, Tori looked pretty entranced herself.

He'd be hard pressed to decide which of them seemed more excited, in fact. Both Tori and his niece had matching expressions of wonder. Not everyone could be patient when it came to unruly, energetic toddlers.

Tori was beyond good with Lilly.

Yeah, he was really glad she hadn't turned him down.

Tori held Lilly cozily in her arms as they watched the dolphins play in the water. When the trainer blew her whistle and twirled her hand, they spun around upright in the water then landed with a splash. Lilly erupted in excited laughter every time they were doused with spray.

Now, Liv was pumping her hand up and down in the air. The dolphins started bobbing in and out of the water in response.

"This is quite a show," Clay said, a smile of utter joy on his face. He looked boyish and carefree. Tori had to wonder how many days during his childhood he could recall as totally untroubled.

How many days had he been able to spend riding a bike or tossing a ball or just lazily wasting the hours? Instead of mourning the loss of his father and dodging a bully.

"Ah, one of the dolphins has decided to leave us," Liv told them, her accent charming. "We never force the dolphins to do anything. They come if they please and stay for as long as they please."

Liv turned to Lilly after reaching for something in one of the pockets on her utility belt. "This one must be hungry." She pointed to the remaining dolphin. "I'm guessing that's why she didn't follow her friend when he swam off. Would you like to help your mommy feed her?"

"Oh, I'm not—"

But the young woman wasn't listening. Handing Tori and Lilly a small bait fish of some kind, she instructed, "Hold your hand out like this."

To Tori's delight, the remaining dolphin swam up slowly and gently took the offering from her hand.

"She likes you," Liv said and then turned to face Clay. "Would you like to feed her, too?"

Clay shook his head with a wide smile. "No, that's okay. I think my two ladies here have it under control."

Tori didn't even allow herself to lament on that statement. *His ladies.* She'd rather focus on the delightful scene in front of her.

"She wants to be petted," Liv explained. "It's why she's staying so close to you."

Tori gingerly reached out her hand, still balancing Lilly on her hip. Ever so softly, she touched the surface of the animal's back. Its skin felt like wet velvet, and it made no move to swim away.

"She really likes you!" Liv exclaimed, handing her another fish. This time, Tori took Lilly's hand in hers when she extended the treat to the dolphin. The child squealed in delight when the fish took the food and flung its head back.

Lilly suddenly threw her arms around Tori's neck and gave a squeeze. "Wiwwy wikes Towi, too."

It took a moment to figure out what the little girl had just said. When she did, Tori's heart felt like it had swollen to twice its size. *Lilly likes Tori, too.*

She nuzzled the top of the toddler's head with her cheek, and gave her a small kiss on the top of her wet curls. "I like you, too, sweetheart. Very much."

Heaven help her, she'd somehow grown attached to his niece as well as to the man himself.

CHAPTER ELEVEN

"WHO'S UP FOR some ice cream?" Clay asked from above her head where Tori sat drying Lilly off and getting her dressed.

She'd been tending to the little girl while Clay had gone off to buy half the gift shop, it seemed. He could barely hold all the packages in both arms. It was clear he liked to spoil the little girl, but all the purchases seemed a bit excessive.

"Who is that all for? Seems too much for one little girl."

He blinked at her. "I founded and help run Our New Start, remember? I figured the kids might get a kick out of some of these. I plan to ship them out tomorrow."

Tori didn't know whether to laugh or cry. At every turn, she seemed to experience something new or to find out something more that pulled her further toward the wonder that was Clay Ramos. Not only had he founded the charity, he was hands on enough to purchase toys for it. Just one more layer of frosting on the cake.

How in the world would she ever go about forgetting him?

"So how about it?" he addressed Lilly. "You up for some chocolate-chip ice cream with fudge on top?"

"Yay!"

* * *

Fifteen minutes later, they sat at a picnic table by the resort's ice cream parlor. A ground-level fountain intermittently shot out streams of neon-colored water a few feet away. Lilly was transfixed as she watched it, jumping into Tori's arms every time the water erupted into the air.

She was also covered from head to toe in sticky, gooey ice cream. Adria hadn't seemed the type to fret over such things. And her uncle certainly didn't seem concerned about the messy state of his niece.

Tori looked up to find two familiar faces approaching them. "Aun' Geya!" Lilly yelled, squirming to free herself.

"That's right. It's Aunt Gemma." Gemma walked over to the toddler and picked her up to give her a tight hug. "I'd kiss you but I don't like chocolate ice cream," she told her.

Tom and Clay did some kind of masculine handshake by way of greeting.

"How about I take this little rug rat off your hands and get her cleaned up?"

Tori looked up to find Gemma actually addressing her with the question. "Uh, I guess it's up to Clay."

"What do say, big bro? Had enough of this little bossy tyrant yet?"

"I suppose so."

"You need a bath." Before walking away, Gemma suddenly turned. "I can't wait to see that cake, Tori."

"Come by tomorrow before you start getting ready, if you'd like. I'll have it all assembled and chilling in the refrigerator."

Gemma shook her head. "Nope, I'd rather see it when it's unveiled at the wedding. You can witness firsthand my awed impression of your creation."

That sounded as though Gemma expected her to be there. Had she missed something? She certainly didn't recall receiving any kind of invite.

This was certainly awkward. "Oh. I, uh, didn't realize I was supposed to be in attendance."

Gemma's eyes narrowed and her jaw actually dropped. "Of course you're going to be there, Tori. At the wedding as well as the rehearsal dinner, in fact. As a guest of the bride herself. I insist. The only reason I didn't say anything was that I figured my clueless sibling here would have taken care of inviting you himself already." She rolled her eyes in Clay's direction then turned to Tori once more. "Wait till you see my dress."

Okay. So she wasn't expected to be at the wedding as some kind of employee then. Tori snuck a glance at Clay.

He didn't look up from his sundae.

If the past few moments had been awkward, things didn't get any better after Gemma and Tom walked away, Lilly in tow.

Tori continued spooning her cup of Rocky Road but wasn't really tasting it.

Clay didn't seem to be in any kind of hurry to talk, either.

Did he even want her at the wedding? The silence between them right now seemed to indicate the answer to that was a resounding no.

"Hope Adria's feeling better," she began, just to get some conversation flowing.

"I'm sure she's fine. I'll check on her before I head back to the room."

"Please give her my best."

"Sure."

"She certainly seems to have a lot on her mind on top of having to keep up with an active toddler. Between her husband's contract dealings, the excitement of her sister's wedding, and renewed contact with her estranged mother…"

Tori wasn't even sure why she brought up that last topic. Just that she really didn't think the situation involving their mother was helping matters as far as Adria's stress level was concerned. If there was any chance that his sister might feel better physically if the issue were somehow addressed, wasn't it worth pursuing?

The shadow that fell over Clay's face said he clearly felt differently.

His voice was cold and harsh when he spoke. "I don't see how that's a matter that you and I need to be discussing in any way."

Tori felt the chill of his words travel through her ears, down her spine, right clear to her toes.

In other words, it was none of her business. She'd clearly overstepped.

So she was good enough to share his bed, but apparently he drew the line at family events or even speaking of matters that concerned his family. A compelling urge to throw her now melted ice cream into his face nearly overwhelmed her good sense. Somehow she resisted, instead gripping the stem of the sundae glass so firmly her knuckles began to hurt. There was no use in sitting there, steaming with anger and feeling upset. And hurt.

"It's been a long day," she announced as she stood. "Thanks for taking me along on the dolphin adventure."

He gave a brisk nod of his head. "Sure thing. Hope you can get some rest."

He made no move to stop her from leaving.

What had just happened?

The mood of the afternoon had turned so quickly. Clay rose from the picnic table with a curse. The dolphin swim had been one of the most entertaining experiences of his life. Tori's face as she'd held Lilly in her arms to feed the dolphins would be an image ingrained in his mind forever. He hadn't been able to wait to get her alone to tell her just how tempting she'd looked in that wet suit.

But as soon as Tom and Gemma had showed up, an unsettling feeling had risen in his chest.

Gemma had invited her to the wedding… Lilly had treated her like a beloved aunt she'd known her whole life… And it sounded like Adria had confided in her, at least on some level.

He had to take stock of it all. Having Tori in their lives was a temporary state of affairs. Did his sisters not see that?

What exactly did they think was going to happen? That they would all get together once in a while and just include Tori in the plans? Invite her to family gatherings and barbecues?

Tori inquiring about Adria reconnecting with their estranged mother had completely caught him off guard. He had no intention of getting into all that with anyone. Not even Tori. He was still hoping Adria would drop the whole thing altogether. How could she not see how futile and damaging her quest was? Already it was leading to all sorts of conflicts and frazzled nerves.

Women. He'd probably never understand them.

One thing he did understand—in just a few short days, Tori had somehow become entrenched in all their lives. Not just his.

Somehow it had happened when he hadn't been paying attention.

But the way he'd snapped at her had been uncalled for. Gemma was right. He did want her at the wedding. He should have been the one to ask her.

He'd held back, procrastinated. For reasons that had nothing to do with Tori and everything to do with him. *It's not you, it's me.*

The classic line of doomed relationships. Only in this case, it happened to be the truth.

By the time he got to his hotel room, Clay was feeling all the worse for snapping at Tori the way he had. Not like it was her fault she had the kind of personality that drew people to her and then made them want to stick around. Look at what had happened to him after spending such a short amount of time with her.

And therein was the problem, wasn't it?

The only person he was really annoyed with was himself. He'd fallen for her—which was completely not right. He had nothing to offer a woman like Tori. He had no intention of settling down or attaching himself to any one person. Not in the foreseeable future. Probably not ever.

Whereas everything Tori was, down to her very fiber, revolved around family and love, and the way she bonded so easily with those around her. She'd already been badly burned in the relationship department. He wouldn't be the bastard that did anything to further hurt her the way her previous boyfriend had.

He rubbed his forehead and cursed some more. *This.* This was exactly what he'd wanted to avoid. He'd experienced firsthand the dire ramifications that could arise when lovesick souls followed their desires without regard to the end results. Without regard to the effect their actions would have on those around them.

Entanglements and careless affairs only led to unneeded complications. Yet somehow she'd gotten under his skin when he hadn't been paying attention. He was a mess of emotions right now—anger, confusion and disappointment, mostly with himself for allowing things to get this far.

Tori deserved stability. She deserved commitment. And she deserved better than the likes of what he could offer her. She deserved someone who would be there for her, through thick and thin. Good times and bad. He just didn't have it in him to risk any more of the bad in his life.

Hell, he couldn't even be sure what city he'd be in from week to week. In fact, there was even now a project in Amsterdam that he'd been offered and had yet to formally reply to. A brand-new modern art museum.

Not that he had any intention of accepting. It would be a long-term contract, keeping him out of the States for the next several months. Maybe up to a year or more, depending on the progress.

His mind was running in circles and he had to find some kind of outlet. Pacing around the room like a caged animal only served to further frustrate him, spiking his blood pressure sky-high.

Getting out of here would be good start. The air might do him good. Throwing on a fresh pair of shorts and an athletic T-shirt, he grabbed his running shoes from the closet.

The day was already scorching hot when he got to the beach—probably too hot to run—but he wanted the punishment.

As grueling as it was, Clay pushed himself to run harder and faster, willing the strenuous exercise to somehow put his thoughts straight. The heat was bearable if he stopped to splash some ocean water on his face and neck. Finally, the endorphins started to kick in, a sense of calm and clarity gradually settling over his nerves, helping to finally start clearing his head.

He'd been running about half a mile when the realization hit him like an ocean wave. As the blood pounded through his system and his mind slowly began to clear, the answer became more and more obvious. Now that he really thought about it, he'd be a fool to turn down the Amsterdam offer. What if nothing like that ever came his way again?

The more his feet pounded the sand, the clearer everything became. His life in the States would be waiting for him as soon as he was ready to return. Sure, he'd miss seeing his sisters, and not being able to see Lilly once or twice a week would leave a hole in his life. But it was temporary. Plus, he'd visit every chance he could.

As for anyone else? Well, there really wasn't anyone else, was there? Not really. He had no business thinking of Tori as a permanent fixture in his life. Better to make a clean break, mostly for her sake. And here was one more way to do exactly that.

Pulling out his cell phone, he called up the email with the offer he'd archived, then started typing out a reply he had no idea he'd even been considering just a few short hours ago.

Why not? He had nothing to lose.

He ignored the faint voice in his head that tried to argue that very point.

When Tori wanted to relax back home, or when she wanted to try to take her mind off of things after a stressful day, she soothed herself by testing new recipes. Or sometimes she'd bake one of the specialty pastries she knew by heart. The orderly sequence of steps and the precise measuring of the needed ingredients always served to settle her nerves and soothe her spirit.

She didn't have that option now. As much as she had

access to the resort's kitchen, she couldn't very well just pop in there for her own personal use and start tossing ingredients together.

But she did have the option of a world-class spa located right on the premises. Additionally, she could think of one other person on the island who would benefit from a spa treatment, as well.

Picking up the phone, she dialed the number Adria had written on the napkin that first day.

Three hours later, she and Adria were walking out with fresh manicures, painted toenails and massage-loosened limbs.

"Oh, Tori. Thank you so much for suggesting that. I really needed it."

"Me, too. I'm glad you were able to come along."

"You really are too good to me, you know. You feed me when I'm nauseous, invite me to a luxurious spa day and you help my brother babysit my child. You're almost too good to be true."

At the mention of Clay, all of Tori's tenseness seemed to surge right back into her muscles. Not that she'd been able to take her mind off him for long. Even under the expert hand of the masseuse, she'd had to remind herself to breathe out the tension.

He hadn't contacted her since their ice cream date with Lilly earlier. What in the world had made her bring up Adria and his mother? She should have known better.

While his sister had done more than her share of talking as they'd had their nails and toes painted, a good portion of the conversation had been dedicated to how she'd found her mother through a popular website. Adria knew her brother was against any contact with their surviving parent, apparently even her husband had reservations.

Though the siblings were close, Tori had the impression there weren't too many heart-to-heart conversations among the Ramos clan.

"It was nice to have someone to talk to," Adria said, echoing Tori's thoughts and confirming her suspicions as they casually strolled along the concrete pathway to the residential cottages.

"I'm glad I could lend an ear."

She suddenly stopped and placed a hand on Tori's forearm. A sheen of tears appeared in her eyes. "Am I being selfish, Tori? Enrique's parents passed in a plane accident before we met. Is it so wrong for me to want my children to have at least one grandparent in their lives? Flawed as she may be."

Tori wished so badly to somehow comfort the poor woman. She had no idea what she would do in a similar situation.

"No. Not from where I'm standing. People do change. You deserve the chance to find out once and for all if your mother has." She covered Adria's hand with her own where it rested on her arm.

That's how Clay found them when he turned the corner around the spa building.

Tori commanded her jaw not to drop open at the sight of him. His golden skin glistened with sweat, chest heaving with the exertion of exercise, his T-shirt soaked. He appeared to have been running.

Maybe he'd felt the need to let off a little steam the same way she'd needed a release of tension.

"What are you two up to?" he asked, stopping in front of them. He bent with his hands on his knees to suck in some air. Even in his current state, he looked devastatingly handsome. Her heart was never going to recover having to get over a man like this.

"Just a bit of a girls' outing," his sister answered. "But

I'm afraid I have to get going. Lilly's probably wondering where Mama is." She patted her brother's cheek affectionately. "I'll leave you two to yourselves."

He pointed to her feet after his sister walked away, his breathing somewhat back to normal. "Nice color toes."

"Thanks. Adria and I just enjoyed a mani-pedi followed by a full body massage."

"You two seem to have really hit it off."

She shrugged. "Just figured she could use some pampering, that's all. I imagine being the mother of a toddler doesn't often leave much time for luxury." Not to mention being pregnant and exhausted, but her lips were sealed on that score. Keeping Adria's secret solely to herself was rather nerve-racking. What if she let it slip? She had enough on her hands with one Ramos cross with her at the moment.

She would apologize. There was no way around it. In her sympathy for Adria, she'd overstepped her bounds with Clay. If it would lessen some of this newfound tension between them, she'd be happy to issue a mea culpa.

"Do you want to sit together at the rehearsal dinner?" She'd blurted out the question before she could give herself time to think.

They only had a little time left here together on the island. She didn't want to spend it at odds with each other. Back in Boston, she knew Clay would be prepared to walk away from her and what they'd shared on the island.

"Yeah. Sure," he answered simply, wiping the sweat off his forehead with the back of his hand. As if she'd asked him if he wanted extra toppings on his pizza. "I should probably shower first."

"Yes. I'd appreciate it if you did."

That tease finally cracked a smile out of him, albeit a small one. "All right. Meet you back here around seven?"

So polite, so unaffected, so very casual. Clay was very deliberately putting distance between them. Any woman would have been able to sense it. "That sounds good," she answered then forced a fake smile.

Unlike last night, it was clear they wouldn't be enjoying a private room-service dinner in his room.

CHAPTER TWELVE

THE MASSIVE FIREPIT in the middle of the barbecue food court had been lit for the evening. The aroma of the burned wood, combined with the various scents of the myriad delicacies cooking around them, made for a pleasantly appetizing atmosphere.

In addition to her heaving plate of plantains and exotic fried greens, Tori was fully prepared to eat crow.

"Keeping it light this evening?" Clay asked as they took their seats among the rest of the rehearsal dinner guests at a wood table by the crackling fire.

The truth was, her stomach felt a little off, twisted with apprehension. She so missed the easy camaraderie they'd once had.

"Saving room for dessert. Looks like there's a chocolate tower being set up close to the beach. Along with a champagne fountain."

"We should check it out." He took in a forkful of pulled barbecue beef.

"I'd like that."

She waited until they'd both finished eating before breaching the proverbial elephant in the room. "Look, Clay, I want to tell you that I'm sorry. I didn't mean to overstep that way I did earlier. It's really none of my concern."

He sighed deeply and rubbed his forehead. "Thank you for saying that. And I apologize, too. I had no right to snap at you the way I did."

He looked so disappointed in himself that she felt compelled to defend him. "You didn't really snap."

"Yes, I did. And I have no excuse for it. Just been wound up a little tight lately. Which makes no sense considering I'm in paradise and in the company of a beautiful woman whose company I thoroughly enjoy."

Tori felt like the anvil had been removed from her shoulders. Her stomach muscles slowly unclenched. She hated being on the receiving end of his coldness. Even for the briefest period of time following their adventure with the dolphins in the cay.

"So, truce then?" She reached a hand toward him.

He took it but not to shake. Instead he gently pulled her close to give her a brief kiss on the lips. He tasted of slow-cooked beef, exotic spices and cold beer. As far as peace offerings went, Tori figured she could have done worse.

"How about we toast this new truce of ours with a glass of champagne and some chocolate?" Clay asked as he helped her out of her chair once the speeches had concluded.

"Best offer I've had all day."

Clay went to procure their flutes of bubbly while Tori prepared a tray of assorted fruit dipped in chocolate. Everything from luscious strawberries to thick bananas to plump cherries. She added some biscuits to round out the flavors.

They eschewed the crowds by the dessert table and took their bounty to an open cabana by the water. He pulled her down to lie beside him in the cushioned lounge chair.

A girl could get used to this.

She had no idea she was about to doze off until the flute fell from her hand to land with a thud on the sand under their lounger.

"Here, I'll get it." He reached over to grab it and his shirt rode up, revealing his lower back.

There was no mistaking the angry-looking scar above his left hipbone. Tori couldn't hide her gasp of horror.

He knew immediately that she'd seen it. He straightened and pulled her closer. "It's no big deal. Happened a long time ago."

"How did I not notice it when we… Can I ask how you got it?" She didn't want a repeat of earlier when she'd overstepped, but her heart was breaking for him. She desperately wanted to learn that maybe her horrible suspicions about how he'd gotten such a nasty wound were wrong.

He shrugged. "Courtesy of my bas—" He bit off the curse.

Tori's eyes burned with the hot sting of tears. She remained completely still in his arms, completely silent, giving him the choice as to how much he wanted to divulge. Rage and sorrow launched a war in her chest when he finally began to speak.

"I was about fourteen. He didn't like the way Adria baited a fishing line, started to get very angry. I went over and made sure to mess it up even worse. Somehow the pole found my skin." He scoffed. "None of us even wanted to go fishing. My mother made us, to try to get us to somehow bond with him. As if it was even possible."

"Oh, Clay." From everything he had shared so far, she'd known that it was bad. But what she was hearing now was the stuff of nightmares. "I'm so very sorry. What you must have endured."

"Like I said, it's all in the past. What matters is that it's over. He's long gone. And that I ensured he never, ever, laid a hand on either Gemma or Adria."

"Would he really have tried anything with either of them?" When she thought about the utter horror of what she was actually asking, she shuddered.

"Wasn't gonna take the risk."

So he'd done what he'd had to do.

"I didn't sleep well at night for many years. Always had one eye open and my ears alert," he continued.

"Were there no adults around who could help?"

"Not when she was always sticking up for him. Everyone just took their word for it whenever something went down."

His resistance to Adria's idea about reuniting with their mother made all the sense in the world now. He'd spent the better part of his childhood shielding his younger sisters from a monster and bearing the brunt of the abuse solely on his own.

All to protect them.

In many ways, he must have taken Adria's sudden interest in her mother to be nothing less than a betrayal. It didn't help that he had no clue that her newfound desire stemmed from the impending arrival of a new baby.

Her heart ached for both of them. And for Gemma, too.

The conversation had gotten too heavy and taken a turn he hadn't intended. He was usually more evasive whenever someone asked him about that scar. He usually did a better job at keeping it hidden. As well as any of the others.

Normally, he was better at finding ways to answer without really answering.

But he found he didn't want to lie to Tori. So he'd told her the whole ugly truth.

She was trying hard to hide it, but there was no doubt she was crying. He hated that she was hurting on his behalf. But confiding in her had felt surprisingly cathartic. He'd never told a soul about the fishing pole incident. And he and his sisters didn't talk about their shared past. All three considered the latter part of their childhood to be better off forgotten, each building their own sturdy walls to block out the most painful memories.

But Tori had somehow broken through his walls when he hadn't expected it. Gathering her closer in his embrace, he simply held her while they watched the sun set on the horizon over the crystal-blue water.

Now that he'd made his decision about the job offer, he felt a sense of peace and purpose. He'd make it public in due time. But for now, he just wanted to enjoy one more night in Tori's company, simply talking to her and just being with her. Probably for one final time.

The night grew darker and colder, the champagne and treats long consumed.

Finally, he gently lifted her and half carried her to his room, where they fell asleep in each other's arms. It was perhaps the most restful night he'd spent in as long as he could remember.

Too bad it would never happen again.

All eyes were on the gorgeous bride as she approached her eagerly awaiting groom. Except for Tori's. Tori's gaze was solely focused on the man walking the bride down the aisle.

Clay was dressed in casual khaki pants and a Hawaiian shirt as per the tropical theme of the ceremony. He looked so rakishly handsome that Tori felt her breath catch. She hadn't seen him since this morning, when she'd woken in his arms after falling asleep on his bed the night before.

Then she'd been a flurry of activity all day, making sure the cake was still holding and refrigerated correctly. Afterward, she'd had to get dressed. Now that she was seeing him again, it occurred to her how empty the day had seemed without him. Not that a minute had gone by when she hadn't thought of him or wondered what he was up to.

Gemma was beaming as she approached her intended. Tom clutched his chest as she neared the pulpit on her brother's arm, his expression full of love and affection. The scene brought forth memories of her own sister's wedding where she'd been a bridesmaid. Josh and Eloise had looked equally as enamored with each other.

A pang of longing shot through her chest. Josh had surprised Eloise with a romantic proposal after sweeping her off her feet. Gemma and Tom had fallen in love after traveling through Italy together. Would she ever have that? Would a man ever commit himself to her that way? Her eyes automatically found him and she had to tear her gaze away before they filled with tears.

Clay gave his sister an affectionate pat on the arm as they stopped beside Tom. Then he stepped to the side, his hands clasped in front of him while the officiant began the process of transforming Gemma and Tom into husband and wife.

Though she felt ridiculous, Tori couldn't help the emotional tears that started rolling down her cheeks; she just couldn't hold them at bay any longer. Clay and his sisters had been through so much yet all three of them had become successful, loving, compassionate people. People she'd grown to care so much for in such a short period of time.

Somehow she was supposed to turn around and shut off all those feelings like some kind of light switch now that the week was coming to an end. Even the tender, amorous feelings she had developed for Clay.

There was no way she would be able to do that. Particularly not when it came to Clay. She'd fallen so hard in love with him that a piece of her heart would always belong to Clayton Ramos for as long as she lived.

"Gemma, you may now kiss your husband. And Tom, you may kiss your wife."

An uproarious cheer erupted from the wedding party and the steel drum band waiting in the wings began to play. Dancing commenced right away. As she hoped he would, Tori found Clay heading in her direction.

"You look beautiful," he told her when he reached her side.

She gave a playful bow. "I'm just glad this isn't a formal attire wedding. I didn't pack anything that would have suited."

His gaze assessed her from head to toe and she felt heat rush to her cheeks then travel down her entire body. "I'd say that dress suits you just fine."

Would he be taking it off her later? Something told her that was not meant to be, and a wave of sadness washed over her before she shook it off. "Thanks, you're looking pretty dapper yourself."

"The cake looks amazing. You did a fantastic job."

"This will be a first for me. I've actually never seen one of my cakes get smashed in anyone's face before."

He chuckled softly but it sounded forced. Alarm bells began ringing in her head. Something was off. Clay was back to the aloof, distant version of himself. She wasn't sure what to make of it.

He extended his hand to her. "Walk with me."

They strolled further along the beach, the music and chatter of the party growing softer and lower behind them with each step.

"Something going on?" she asked when she couldn't stand it any longer.

"I'm not sure how long the party will go—I'm guessing till the early morning hours—but I'm going to make it an early night and head to my room right after the cake is cut."

And he wasn't telling her that because he wanted to invite her to go up with him. She would be naïve to think that. Everything from Clay's body stance to the tone of his voice told her so.

"I see."

"I'll be flying back to Logan first thing after breakfast tomorrow."

Tori's breath hitched in her throat. This was really happening. He really was saying goodbye. Tori wanted the sea behind her to rise and carry her away so she didn't have to listen to any more of this. She bit down on her lip to keep if from trembling.

"I haven't even told my sisters yet. I'll let them know as soon as they stop dancing long enough."

"Why the sudden rush?"

"There's a matter I have to tend to in Boston."

"I'm sorry to hear that." She knew she was making a mistake, but the next words she uttered seemed to spill out of her mouth before she could stop them. "Maybe once I get back to Boston I'll get in touch…"

The grimace on his face told her more than any words could. She felt a shattering sensation in the vicinity of her heart.

"I won't be there for long, Tori."

She swallowed. "Why's that?"

"I've accepted an assignment in Amsterdam. I'll be there for the next year or so."

For a split second, Tori wondered if she'd heard him correctly.

"You what?"

"I've accepted a job overseas."

Where was this coming from? He'd completely blindsided her. "You didn't say anything." She was surprised her mouth worked and that she could even get the words out.

"It came about rather suddenly."

"So suddenly you didn't even think to mention it before this?"

He merely nodded. She knew then that there was nothing more to say. How naïve she'd been, how utterly clueless. That he could so easily turn away from her with such finality. As far as Clay was concerned, she'd served her purpose and he was ready to leave behind everything they'd shared together.

She'd move on from this. She'd somehow find a way to get past it. It would take time and it would hurt. But she'd dusted herself off before and built a life for herself that she could be proud of. That's what she had to focus on now. She couldn't let old doubts and insecurities come crashing back in just because she'd misread Clay so thoroughly.

She would find a way to heal.

It took everything she had to continue standing upright, to keep her knees from giving out underneath her. His rejection was complete. When she could finally get her legs to move, she turned and walked away.

CHAPTER THIRTEEN

THE CAKE WAS a big hit. As dawn approached and the last tiki torch extinguished, and the handful of revelers finally drunkenly stumbled away, the cake had proven to be one of the evening's highlights. Tori had done an outstanding job. He'd never doubted it, of course.

She'd also done an amazing job of avoiding him all night. Not that he could really blame her. He'd been pretty straightforward. But what point would there have been in delaying the inevitable?

By the time he'd walked to his room, they hadn't shared so much as a wave goodbye.

Clay snapped his travel case closed and ran through a mental checklist to ensure he had everything. He felt disoriented and out of sorts. Insomnia had plagued him when he'd tried to catch at least a couple hours of sleep. The bed felt empty. His soul felt cold. But he'd done what needed to be done.

Better for Tori to go live the rest of her life believing that he was an uncaring bastard. And the next time he needed to hire a talented baker...well, he would have to cross that proverbial bridge when it appeared.

A knock on the door snapped him alert. The car service was early.

But it wasn't a driver standing across the threshold when he opened the door.

His sisters stood there, glaring at him. Adria wore a rigid frown. Gemma, disheveled and drowsy, looked like she was ready to feed him to the wolves.

They walked past him into the room. "Come in," he said sarcastically with a flourish of his hand. Whatever was going on with them, he really didn't have time for it.

"Have a seat, big brother." Gemma pulled him over to the sofa and physically pushed him down by his shoulders. For someone with such a slight build, she was surprisingly strong.

"Can I help you two? What are you doing here?" He pointed at Gemma. "You just got married a few hours ago."

"I know. But we need to chat," Gemma began. "And considering last night was my wedding night, I have to warn you, I'm not big on patience right now."

So they weren't taking the news very well, then.

"That was quite a bombshell you dropped on us last night," Gemma charged while Adria nodded her agreement. "Didn't see that coming at all."

If they only knew.

"I apologize for that," he said, meaning it wholeheartedly. He really was sorry about the way it had all come about. But now that his decision had been made, he didn't want to dally. There was no point delaying the inevitable.

"You're just going to move across the globe?" Gemma blustered.

"For the better part of the year?" Adria added.

"I'll visit often," he reassured them. "And you can all come visit me. Lilly will get a kick out of the canals and we can take her to a tulip field."

"Somehow I think she'd prefer to have her uncle in town for her next birthday."

Clay sighed, striving for patience. "It's done, ladies. And the sooner I get back to Boston, the sooner I can wrap things up and prep for this new role." It made no sense to stick around some island in the Bahamas when he was about to start a whole new chapter of his life.

"Is that why you're leaving? So you can wrap up and prep?"

That sounded like a trick question. What choice did he have but to walk into the trap? "Why else?"

"Because it looks an awful lot like you're just simply running away."

He scoffed. "What would I be running from?"

Adria stepped around the couch, her hands on her hips. "The question is more like *who* you're running away from, I'd say."

"That's ridiculous. I'm making a career decision that feels right for this point in my life. That's all there is to it." The words sounded hollow even to his own ears. He certainly didn't seem to be convincing either one of his perturbed siblings. He felt compelled to explain further given their disbelieving expressions. "You two are both hitched now. You have your own lives. It's about time I started living mine."

"Kind of sudden, don't you think?"

"I can be impulsive like everyone else."

Adria actually laughed out loud at that. "You've never been impulsive a day in your life."

"I'm turning over a new leaf." That was a rather lame statement and the expression on both their faces told him they thought so, too.

"You're just turning over," Gemma said. "And giving up before you have a chance to fail."

He had no response. On some level, he knew her point was valid, knew that's what he'd been doing. But the underlying issues remained unchanged. "I'm no good for her. I can't be what she needs."

He couldn't even tell which one of them sucked in a breath first. "You don't mean that," Gemma told him. "You've just spent so much of your life looking over your shoulder that now you're afraid to look forward."

Adria nodded. "Take the chance, Clay. She's worth it. You know she is."

Gemma walked over and took both his hands in her small ones. "That man took away a lot of your childhood. He took away our mother. Don't let him take away your shot at happiness."

He absorbed Gemma's words as they permeated his soul. They were both right. He'd been such a fool. But what was done was done.

"Look, there's only so much I can do now. The wheels have been set in motion. I've accepted the offer and booked a flight."

"Huh. I always thought my big brother could do anything." Adria's voice dripped with mock surprise.

He ran his hand through his hair. Maybe they had a point. He at least owed Tori more of a conversation after all they'd shared together. "I'll go talk to her now. She's probably up."

"Too late," Gemma quipped with no small amount of derision.

"What? Why?"

"She's back in Boston. She took a red-eye last night. She's already gone."

"I could have done this cake in my sleep."

Tori set the simple sheet cake on the counter and grabbed a box from the cabinet below to begin packaging it. Hard to believe it had already been a week and a half since she'd returned from her fateful trip to the Bahamas. She wished she could say things were beginning to return to normal. But normal wasn't what she wanted.

The problem was, she wanted what she couldn't have.

"It's what the customer ordered," Shawna replied. "Who are we to tell him it's boring."

Boring certainly was an apt description. Single-layer marble cake with buttercream frosting. Not even a request for fruit filling. "Are you sure we took down the order right? He didn't even ask for some kind of custom-made figurine? Not even a flower?" Flowers made her think of tulips. Tulips made her think of Amsterdam. And that made her think of Clay.

Almost everything made her think of Clay. If anything, she should be thanking her lucky stars that one of her cake orders was this simple. It had been hard to concentrate on much since she'd returned.

Had he left yet? Was he even now riding a canal boat down one of Amsterdam's waterways? How easily had he moved on?

Did he even think of her?

"The client's exact words were, 'I just need a plain old cake that'll feed about twenty,'" Shawna said as she pulled a batch of homemade brownies from the oven.

"Huh. He could have gone to a grocery store for this."

Shawna shrugged. "He could have. But he wanted an authentic Tori Preston creation."

Tori rolled her eyes. "I would hardly call this a creation."

She carefully lifted the cake and placed it in the box then folded and taped up the sides. "In any case, it's ready for the delivery service."

Shawna swiveled in her direction. "Oh, bad news on that front. They said they're not available today."

"What? That's never happened before. Did they give you any kind of explanation?"

"Some kind of emergency. Luckily that's the only order that needs to get out this afternoon."

"Well, how are we supposed to get it there?"

"Guess we have to deliver it ourselves."

"That's just great. Not like we have a bakery to run."

"Do you mind doing it, Tori? My back's been acting up and I don't think I have it in me to handle that drive sitting so long."

"Long drive? Where is it going?"

"Hyannis. Near the docks."

The Cape? She had to make her own delivery and it was all the way to the Cape.

Tori sighed, resigned to the circumstances. Maybe a long drive wouldn't be such a bad thing. It would give her some time to come to terms with all she'd have to accept about her life now that she'd had a chance to finally experience true love only to lose it within a span of mere days. It was so much worse to know exactly what you were missing out on.

"All right. Guess I'll be on my way."

She could have sworn she heard Shawna giggle as she walked out the kitchen door.

An hour and a half later, Tori parked and pulled her delivery out of the specialty cooler, rechecking the address. Something wasn't quite right. When Shawna had said the docks, Tori had assumed the destination would be one of the houses across the water or a restaurant or café near the port authority.

But the number didn't match any of the buildings. Could it be a dock number? Was this cake supposed to go on a boat?

Strange detail to leave out of the delivery instructions.

She had taken several steps, studying slip numbers, when it came into view. The *Ocean Nomad*. A children's cruise boat. Or more accurately, a modern-day replica pirate ship.

Her pulse pounded through her veins as a strange kind of hope blossomed in her chest.

Clay leaned over the railing of the replica frigate and watched as Tori approached. For several moments, he simply allowed himself to take in the sight of her.

A physical ache tugged at his heart. He'd missed her.

The days spent without her had been miserable and lonely. He'd been a fool to think he'd be able to spend his life without her in it. He'd barely survived less than two weeks apart. Even before Gemma and Adria had barreled into his room that morning, his regret had started to ignite like the beginning spark of a wildfire.

He couldn't let the past rob him of his opportunity for a bright and love-filled future. It was high time he told all that to Tori.

The look of confusion on her face just made her look all the more fetching. She held the cake box precariously as she glanced around, trying to determine where to go.

Clay's pulse beat hard through his veins, his muscles taut. It shocked him to realize he was nervous.

What if it all goes wrong? What if she isn't ready to forgive me?

It would no doubt serve him right. He'd been a downright bastard to her the night of the wedding. All because she'd exposed a vulnerability in him he hadn't wanted to acknowledge.

So he'd pushed her away and might very well have lost

the one woman who could serve as a light for the darkness he'd lived through.

Hopefully, he wouldn't be wearing that cake she carried by the time this was over.

Only one way to find out. Uttering a silent prayer, he cupped his hands around his lips and called out to her.

A hauntingly familiar voice sounded through the air.

"Ahoy there, matey."

Tori turned so fast on her heel she almost dropped the cake box.

Standing on the deck, beneath a black-and-white skull and crossbones flag, was Clay.

She knew she wasn't imagining things. It was really him. Flesh and blood, and wearing a silly pirate's hat. The one she'd left behind at the resort in her haste to leave. The toy cutlass hung loosely in his belt.

The mystery of it all slowly began to unravel. Shawna had to have been in on it, which explained the giggle Tori had heard on her way out.

Her jaw agape, Tori could only watch as Clay lowered the wooden ramp and walked down to where she stood frozen in shock.

"Clay?"

"Hey, sweetheart."

"Hey, yourself." Again with the witty conversation, just like back in the Bahamas by the pool. She had to cut herself some slack, though. She was lucky she could find any words at all.

He chuckled, wandering closer until she could see the golden specks of his eyes. He sported a smattering of dark stubble, adding an authenticity to the pirate getup. It was all so ridiculous and fantastic and hard to believe.

She'd missed him so much, her body ached with the urge to touch him. But she seemed unable to move a muscle.

"I thought you were in Amsterdam."

"Couldn't bring myself to go."

"You couldn't?"

He shook his head. "No. Not worth what I might be leaving behind. My life is here. My family's here. By the way, did you know I'll be getting another little niece or nephew soon?"

She had to come clean on that score. "I actually did know that."

He smiled that handsome smile of his, the one that made her insides go squishy. The smile she hadn't been able to get out of her mind when she lay awake at night missing him with every fiber of her being.

"I kind of figured you might have," he said, tapping her nose playfully. "And then there's the most important thing I didn't want to leave behind."

"What's that?"

"The woman I love."

"Oh, Clay."

"I behaved mutinously. Please forgive me."

It was so very tempting to simply throw herself into his arms. Her body ached to be held in his embrace, she longed to thrust her fingers through his hair and to pull his face to hers for a deep and lingering kiss. But she couldn't make it that easy on him. He owed her more than that. He'd delivered quite a blow to her heart and to her spirit when he'd walked away from her so easily.

"It's not that simple…" she began. "I'm afraid I might need some convincing. How do I know you won't be tempted by another job offer at some point?"

He shook his head slowly. "I'm not going anywhere unless you agree to come with me. You have my word."

She sucked in a breath. She believed him; sincerity rang true and clear in his voice. "I have half a mind to throw this at you, you know." With one hand, she raised the box that held the cake.

He chuckled and took hold of her free hand. "I figured as much. It's why I ordered such a plain one."

She resisted the urge to laugh. "You're going to have to make it up to me somehow, Clay. The way you tried to run off before you came to your senses…"

He lifted her chin, his gaze focused fully on her face. "I know, sweetheart. I vow to do just that. As long as it takes."

Tori felt her already flimsy resolve slowly start to drain away. How was she supposed to stand firm when he looked at her like that?

Maybe she was weak, but she wanted him too much to pretend anymore. She longed for him to hold her, to kiss her. She needed his touch as much as her next breath.

"Okay," she said with a sniffle.

"You have every right to tell me to go walk the plank. But I'm asking instead if you'll walk to me down the aisle." Before she could process exactly what was happening, he pulled out a small velvet box.

"Victoria Preston, will you do me the honor of marrying me?"

The cake didn't stand a chance. It slipped right out of her hand as she threw her arms around him.

"Yes!" she called out with all the jubilation and joy flooding through her heart. "I would follow you across the seas, my love."

EPILOGUE

VILARDO'S TRATTORIA WAS closed for the evening, a rare occurrence for a Saturday during the height of summer. There was a good and happy reason for the closure, though—a private event that just happened to be the wedding ceremony of the proprietors' only daughter.

It wasn't a large gathering by many standards. But everyone Tori loved and cared about was in attendance. Most of them currently on the dance floor. Including Clay, who had Lilly on his shoulders as he danced across from Tori's mom. The man apparently had impressive balancing skills. Rhythm? Not so much. Tori would have be sure to tease him about that later when they were finally alone.

"I told you the dress was lucky."

Tori tore her gaze away from the man she loved—who, as of three hours ago, now happened to be her husband—at the sound of her sister's voice.

Eloise had helped her with every detail of her wedding day. Tori didn't know what she would have done without her.

"I think you're the actual good luck charm," she told her twin, running her hand over the silky material. Eloise had gifted Tori the dress after her own wedding, with instructions to go after the man of her dreams. "The dress is just an added bonus."

Eloise didn't get a chance to answer. Her husband swooped up behind her and spun her around with a mischievous grin until she started dancing with him. Josh had gotten even more playful since becoming a husband. He and Eloise were made for each other.

Just as Clay was made for her.

Tori watched as he gently set his niece down and bowed to her mother before turning away. Their eyes met over the crowd of dancers and the love that shone in his nearly knocked the breath out of her. How had she gotten so fortunate?

He approached her now from across the dance floor doing a silly version of the electric slide. Taking her by the waist, he dipped her and wiggled his eyebrows.

"Dance with me," he said with a laugh as he brought her back to him.

She answered by pressing herself against his length and swaying slowly to the music despite the fast tempo of the song.

"I love the way you dance," he whispered in her ear.

"Even to kiddie reggae?" she asked.

He chuckled at the reminder of the time they'd "danced" together by the pool all those weeks ago in the Bahamas. "As long as you're in my arms."

Tears of joy filled her eyes. Everyone around them may as well have disappeared. Even the sound of the loud music seemed to dull in her ears. Her focus narrowed completely on the man she'd be spending the rest of her life with.

"There's nowhere else I'd rather be."

* * * * *

THE LAST ONE HOME

CHRISTINE RIMMER

For MSR, always.

Chapter One

"We never see the bears, Ian. I think we should." Abby Haralson gazed up at Ian McNeill with a bright smile on her wide-eyed, lightly freckled face. The kid had been wrapping him around her pinkie finger for nine years now—ever since the age of two, when her mother, Ella, brought her to work for the first time. That day, Abby had climbed into his lap without being invited and then refused to get down.

He'd been nineteen then, working summers and part-time during the school year while he earned his degree, determined to master every job at Patch&Pebble, the toy company he would someday inherit from the woman who had saved him and claimed him as her son.

On that first day he met toddler Abby, she'd turned those big brown eyes on him, same as now. She'd smiled so sweetly—and peed on his brand-new suit.

As for the bears, no. Just no. "Not today, Abby."

"Well, Ian, then when?" She fluttered her eyelashes, her smile turning wistful. No doubt about it, Abby was destined to break a whole bunch of hearts.

"I don't know. One of these days." He and Abby had their things they did together—Yankees and Knicks games, in the good seats, down close to the action. He took her to her favorite Disney movies now and then, to see *Frozen* and *The Lion King* on Broadway, and he attended her dance recitals. A couple of times a year, on days like today when the weather was right, when he could get away and she didn't have school, they spent an afternoon in Central Park, including a visit to the zoo. Never once in all those years had they gone to see the bears.

And Ian had no intention of going to see them now.

"Ian." Abby pinched up her mouth at him. "It's like Nike. You need to just do it. You'll be surprised. It's going to be fine. Betty and Veronica are *really* friendly grizzly bears. We read about them in class.

They are *so* friendly that, for their own safety, Betty had to be removed from Montana and Veronica had to be taken out of Yellowstone—so Ian, come on. Don't you want to see the *friendly* bears?"

No, Ian did not.

But there was just something about Abby. She could make him do what she wanted him to do using only her big eyes and that angelic smile. Now, she kept both trained on him expectantly as she waited for him to say yes. He almost said it.

But bears?

Not going to happen.

Ian frankly acknowledged his fear of bears— even ones safely locked in fancy outdoor cages. Maybe someday he'd deal with that fear. Not today, though.

"What about the seals?" he suggested. "You love the seals."

Abby planted her legs apart and braced her fists on her hips, adorably adamant. "Betty and Veronica can't hurt you, Ian. They're in a special bear habitat and they can't get near the people."

"I'm aware of that."

"Ian." She pulled out all the stops, folding her arms, sticking out her chin and puffing up her chest. "You really need to face your fears."

Bemused by her absolute unwillingness to let it go, he stared down at her as she gave him a bullet-point rundown of a story she'd read during library time about a Midwestern farmer's daughter who faced her deepest fear and jumped out of a hayloft.

"How'd that work out for her?"

Abby wrinkled her freckled nose at him. "Okay, she broke her leg. But it was *character building*, and that's what matters."

Ian bit the inside of his lip to keep from grinning. Abby could be so stern and earnest. "I'm not *that* afraid of bears," he lied. "Have you forgotten? *Patch* is a bear." Patch was one of the two all-time top-selling toys manufactured by his company.

Abby scoffed. "Patch is a *stuffie*."

"And stuffed bears are my favorite kind."

"But why don't you like *real* bears?" As she asked the question, her glance shifted to the faded white scar that ran upward diagonally from his left temple, barely skirting his eye, to the center of his forehead. Once she'd compared it to Harry Potter's lightning-bolt scar, though Ian's scar was ragged, uneven and not the least photogenic.

"Abby, you already know why I avoid real bears." She'd known how he got that scar since the age of eight, when she'd coaxed him into telling her how it happened—or at least, as much as he remembered of how it happened.

"Oh, Ian…" A mournful sigh escaped her. "Betty and Veronica won't hurt you."

"Betty and Veronica are *bears*. That's all I need to know—and how about the flamingos?" he offered hopefully. "Let's head over there."

Abby slowly shook her head. "There is nothing to worry about. I *promise* you. I'll be right there with you, Ian." And she slipped her hand in his.

That did it. He couldn't deny her. Besides, her reasoning rang true; they were just bears in the zoo. Bears in a special habitat, walled off from the humans. Nice bears. Friendly ones—according to Abby, anyway. How bad could it be?

Five minutes later, Ian stood next to Abby at the shatterproof viewing screen above the grizzly habitat and stared down at the two giant bears below.

Surprisingly, nothing happened. He didn't find himself paralyzed with terror. No flashing visions assailed him. He had zero urge to run away screaming.

"See?" Abby nudged him with her elbow. He could hear the grin in her voice. "You're just fine."

"It appears so." *At least, for the moment.*

The horror might still kick in.

But he watched the bears a little longer, and still it didn't.

He heard himself chuckle. They were enormous, those two bears. And playful. They snuffled and shuffled and slid around in the water, climbing out onto the rocks, rolling in again.

As for Ian, he felt relaxed and amused, not the least panicked. He had to hand it to the kid. Turning to meet her eyes, he said, "You're right, Abby. I should have let you drag me here years ago."

"Yes, you should have." Her smile had turned smug. Abby loved being right.

He shifted his attention back through the viewing screen, smiling at his own fears just as Betty threw back her enormous furry head and let out a roar that showed way too many long, sharp teeth.

It happened right then.

Like a stop-motion movie, the images began. They flashed and vanished in front of his eyes. Strobing and pulsing, they filled his head, each more terrifying than the one before it.

They flipped by faster and faster.

He was thrown back in time, only a boy and scared out of his mind.

Shadows on snow, blood on the white. Angry growls, long, piercing claws reaching for him, sharp teeth coming at him...

His vision zeroed to a tiny circle in the center of an endless night—no stars, no moon—nothing to light the unremitting dark.

As he sank to the ground, from somewhere far away, he could hear Abby screaming. He needed to comfort her, to promise her that it was all in his mind, that everything would be all right.

But he couldn't move. He stared up at a pinprick of blue sky surrounded by darkness.

And everything went black.

Chapter Two

In the blackness, something different happened.

He was still just a kid, but not terrified, not alone. He tagged after an older boy along a snowy path. Somehow, he knew that the older boy was his brother, Matt.

Matt turned to him and ordered him to go back to the others.

His boy self insisted, "Mom said I could come with you," and he kept following, chattering away about how he thought the huskies that pulled their sled were so cool, with their weird, bright blue eyes. "I want a husky, Matt. I'm asking Mom for one when we get home."

Matt turned on him again, glaring. "Just shut up, will you, Finnegan? Just. Please. Stop. Talking."

He stared up at his brother and did what Matt said, pressing his lips together so no words could get out. Matt made a sound of disgust low in his throat, turned back around and started walking again.

His boy self kept quiet after that. He trudged along through the snow behind his grumpy big brother, thinking that Matt was a dick and wishing he had the nerve to say the bad word out loud. He even practiced it, mouthing the accusation— You're a dick, Matt—but not giving it sound.

A few minutes went by. He started to find it difficult to keep being mad at Matt. Being mad was hard, and it didn't feel good. He let his anger go and opened his mouth to say more about getting a husky when he spotted movement from the corner of his eye.

Blinking, he swung his head that way and saw it was a chipmunk, only white—a white chipmunk. "Wow," he whispered to himself. "Just, wow."

The chipmunk had pale tan stripes and a fluffy white tail. Its white fur made it difficult to spot against the snow. It got up on its rear legs, sniffed the air—and then darted off toward a tangle of bare bushes.

Fascinated, he took off in pursuit of the cute little creature, veering away from Matt to give chase as it raced across the snow—and wait.

What was that?

It sounded like crying...

The sound brought the darkness back, the snowy world zeroing down to a pinprick of brightness.

Ian blinked and stared up at the girl bending over him. "Abby?"

She sobbed, "Ian! Oh, Ian, I'm so, so sorry..."

His vision still blurry, his mind a gray fog, he tried to reach up, to soothe her, but his arms wouldn't move.

Someone pushed her back.

Abby disappeared from his line of sight. Now he frowned up at the tired face of a concerned-looking dark-haired woman. She wore a blue uniform with *FDNY* over the left pocket and *EMT* above the right. He managed to form two words. "I'm fine..."

The woman shook her head and spoke to him. He heard nothing but a flood of garbled sounds until the last word. "...hospital."

"Hospital? I don't need to go to any hospital—Abby!" He called for her. Somewhere nearby, he could hear her, still crying. He struggled again to free his arms, to kick his legs, which wouldn't move, either. As he struggled, he tried to reassure her, shouting, "I'm fine, Abby! Abby, don't cry…" He looked up at the EMT and said in a pleading voice, "Really, I'm all right…" He glanced down at himself and put it together: strapped to a gurney. When had that happened?

"Ian!" Abby called from behind another blue uniform. "I'll go with you…"

Yes. If they were taking him anywhere, Abby had damn well better come, too. "Let her come in the ambulance," he said to the woman bending over him. "She's only eleven. You can't leave her here."

The woman only patted his shoulder gently and spoke in a coaxing tone. "Don't worry. You're going to be fine."

As they loaded him into the red-and-white vehicle, he kept saying, "No!" and kept calling for Abby.

Finally the woman said what he needed to hear. "She's coming. Stop struggling. She'll ride along."

And then he was in the small, enclosed space—with Abby beside him, her eyes red from crying, but her expression calm and determined. "It's okay," she promised him, patting his shoulder with one hand and holding up her jewel-bedecked pink phone with the other. "I'm here, Ian. Right here with you. I've called Mom. She's meeting us at Manhattan General…"

"Good…" Abby needed her mom, and he needed Ella, too. His longtime friend and, for the last four years, chief operating officer at Patch&Pebble, Ella had a way about her. Calm and no-nonsense, she took every crisis in stride.

Abby sniffled—but bravely. "You're going to be fine."

"Of course I am. I'm sorry I scared you."

She patted his shoulder again. "I feel so *terrible*. I shouldn't have—"

"Honey, you need to sit," the EMT cut in. Gently, she guided Abby to a bench by the doors. "Buckle up," the woman said.

Then she took Abby's place at his side.

Hours later, the doctors at Manhattan General had asked him an endless array of repetitive questions, run a battery of tests, contacted his own doctor to confer on his condition and concluded exactly what Ian had expected they would. After he'd explained what little he knew of his childhood before his adoptive mother had brought him to America, the hospital's medical team deduced that the incident was a flashback to past trauma. They advised therapy.

He replied that he'd *had* therapy, a lot of it. Glynis McNeill, the only mother he'd ever known, had adopted him at the estimated age of ten from an orphanage in Krasnoyarsk, Russia. She'd named him Ian, after her deceased father, and given him her last name.

More important, Glynis had lavished time and attention on him. Fifty years old and unmarried when she adopted him, his mother got him plastic surgery for the worst of his scars and therapy for his PTSD. Until a few hours ago, his early childhood had remained mostly a blank. What memories he did have were of the orphanage, a hospital and random, bloody flashes of the bear attacking him.

And now, he had the new memory of a brother named Matt, a walk in the snow and a white rodent with pale tan stripes leading him off into the woods.

"You're right," he told the doctors. "I survived a bear attack when I was a child. The incident today was a flashback and it's over and I'm fine. I'll be even better once you let me go home."

Dr. Cummings, who seemed to be in charge of his care today, wanted to know if he had a therapist he saw regularly.

"Not for several years. I had a therapist starting when I was ten or so until I was in my midteens."

Dr. Cummings frowned. "I strongly advise

that you talk to a therapist now about this. It's possible that the incident today will have an ongoing effect—more suppressed memories could surface, and any number of emotional reactions could occur that you will need help processing. Not to mention headaches and the like. You can contact your regular doctor for a referral, or we can provide you one today."

"I'll handle it." And *not* by seeing a shrink. If more memories surfaced, so be it. As for any processing, he could manage that fine on his own.

"Good enough." Dr. Cummings dipped his head in a nod.

After the tests and consultations, Ian ended up in a curtained-off ER bed. Ella and Abby settled into the chairs on either side of him as they waited for someone to come in and release him.

When he asked for his phone, Ella produced it from the plastic bag of his clothes and belongings. He checked messages, replying to one from his girlfriend, Lucinda.

The minute Lucinda learned he'd spent most of the afternoon in the hospital, she shot him a reply:

Why didn't you SAY something, Ian?

I'm fine, really.

Did it even occur to you that I might want to be there for you?

It's not necessary.

Yes, it is. I'm on my way.

You do not need to come. I mean it, there's no big deal.

But Lucinda wasn't having that. I'm coming over there.

He shook his head at his phone. He'd just about reached that point with her, the one he always got to with the women he dated—the point where he faced the fact that it didn't work and it wouldn't work—and the time had come for Lucinda and him to part ways.

With a weary huff of breath, Ian set the phone on the bed tray. "You two should just go," he advised Ella and Abby. "I'll call the car service when they finally get around to letting me out of here. It will be fine."

Abby stuck out her chin at him. "No way am I leaving you."

Ella shook her head and pinned him with those eyes that were even bigger and darker brown than her daughter's. "I've called Philip." Philip was

Ella's ex-husband, Abby's father. "He'll take Abby and I'll stick around."

"Mom!" Abby made three full syllables out of the word. "I'm not leaving Ian." Her sweet face crumpled. "And I'll never make anyone face their fears again." She would be bursting into tears any minute now if he didn't do something.

He held out a hand. "Come here."

She put her soft fingers in his and grumbled, "What?"

"You did nothing wrong and, as you can see, I'm okay. A hundred tests they did on me. If there was anything that wrong with me, they wouldn't be planning on sending me home."

"Oh, Ian! I was so wrong. I've *traumatized* you."

"No, you haven't."

"I *have*. You've come through so much and I've only made it worse. You could be scarred emotionally—I mean, even more than before—for the rest of your life. I'll never forgive myself..." She threw herself on him.

He gathered her in as Ella looked on patiently. "It's okay, Abby." She smelled of red licorice, dust and something faintly floral, and that made him smile. "There's nothing to blame yourself for. Whatever happened to me when I was younger than you are, I got through it and ended up safe and sound right here in New York. Now I'm living the good life, going to Knicks games with you." He stroked her light brown hair. "It really is okay."

"I just think I need to stay."

Ella spoke up then. "It's no problem. *I'll* stay. You have tap class."

Abby pulled out of his hold and whirled to face her mother. "I can skip. It's only for fun and enrichment, like you always say." Three years ago, Abby had started taking acting and dance classes, planning a Broadway career. Since then, she'd changed her lifetime ambition to becoming a children's book author, but she still enjoyed the dancing. "I just don't feel so fun right now. Enrichment can wait."

"What's this about skipping your dance class?" Philip Haralson, tall and thin with the same light brown hair as his daughter, stood in the gap between the privacy curtains.

Five minutes later, still reluctant and more than a little bit sulky, Abby followed her dad out.

That left just Ian and Ella.

The room fell silent—a relaxed, companionable silence.

Ian knew he should insist that Ella leave, too. But Ell had a way about her, both steady and calm. He liked sitting quietly with her. He also enjoyed talking with her. He liked the way her mind worked, her savvy ideas, her dry sense of humor, her reasonable, no-nonsense approach to life. Ella would call him on his crap, and yet somehow when she did, it never felt like she judged him—more like she held him to account, kept him honest.

Looking at her gave him pleasure, too. He liked her wavy, seal-brown hair and those steady dark eyes. It felt good to have her there.

Bald truth: he didn't want her to go.

Another half hour went by. They laughed together about how the doctor would probably never come. Ian would be stuck here in an ER cubicle at Manhattan General for the rest of his life.

He'd just decided to confide in her, to share the new memory that had come to him right after the grueling flashback at the zoo, when he glanced over and saw Lucinda standing in the gap between the curtains. She had a dangerous expression on her gorgeous face—like someone had just insulted her and she couldn't wait to start ranting in retaliation.

Ian tried to head her off. "Sweetheart, come on over here and—"

"Don't you 'sweetheart' me." She sent a withering glare at Ella and then swung her gaze back on him. "You called *her* and then took *hours* to even answer my text?"

He started to tell her to knock off the attitude.

But Ella spoke first. "He didn't call me," she said, her voice kind and reasonable, which was way more than Lucinda deserved. "He was with Abby, at the park. When he passed out, *Abby* called me."

Lucinda swung her glittering green eyes his way again. "It's worse than a stepchild," she muttered, "you and that kid. It's over, Ian. I'm out of here." With a shake of her tumbling blond curls, she spun on her red-soled, sky-high heel and vanished from sight.

Ella drew a slow breath. "I'll talk to her."

"Let her go," he commanded.

Ella pointed at him. "Stay. There." She raced after Lucinda.

Ella caught up with Ian's girlfriend at the elevator. "Come on, Lucinda." She pitched her voice low, making it just between the two of them. No, she didn't especially care for Lucinda, who wore her drama-queen ways as a badge of honor, but she also didn't want to be the reason for Ian's breakup with the woman.

"Please, Lucinda. Don't go running off angry…"

The woman whirled on her. Getting right up in Ella's face, she whisper-shouted, "Forget it. I've had enough. I'm done with Ian. As for you, everyone knows you're in love with him. It's pathetic. You need to get a life."

The elevator doors parted. Lucinda got on the empty car. Ella stood there with her mouth hanging open as the doors slid shut on Ian's angry girlfriend—correction. *Ex*-girlfriend, apparently.

When Ella got back to Ian's cubicle, she found him standing in the split between the curtains waiting for her, his big arms crossed over his broad chest, his muscular, hairy legs sticking out below his hospital gown, wearing those silly nonskid socks the hospital had given him. Was he naked under that gown? Probably. It tied down the back. He must have hesitated to set off after her and give the nurses a view of his bare ass.

When she reached him, he demanded, "What did she say?"

Ella ordered her heart rate to slow and her palms to stop sweating. "Nothing important—oh, she might have mentioned again that she's through with you."

He dared to smirk. "What do you know? Something Lucinda and I can agree on."

Ella drew a slower breath. At least he hadn't demanded that she tell him everything the woman had said.

And as for the demise of his relationship with Lucinda, *quelle surprise*. Ian had never been the kind of guy who got married and settled down. He dated exclusively, but none of them lasted. With Ian, it was a revolving door of beautiful women.

Lucinda, apparently, had reached her expiration date on the Ian McNeill relationship wheel.

Ella tried. She tried so hard.

But that night, the next day and the day after that, she couldn't make herself stop obsessing over what Lucinda had said.

It's not true, no way, she kept reassuring herself. *It can't be true. It's ridiculous. Me and Ian? Uh-uh. Impossible...*

By Friday, four days after the incident, she still hadn't stopped fixating on Lucinda's whispered taunt. That day, she left the office at a little before noon to meet her longtime friend Marisol Hardy, whose daughter, Charlotte, was Abby's bestie. Ella and Marisol had met in childbirth class, and now their daughters took hip-hop and tap together. Marisol knew Ian casually. She'd dropped in at the office more than once over the years, and Ian always showed up at the girls' dance recitals.

Bottom line, Marisol would put Ella's mind at ease. They would laugh together over the mere idea that Ella might have a thing for her boss and longtime friend—let alone have fallen in love with the man.

That Friday, they met for lunch at Telegraphe Café, midway between their two apartments in Chelsea. Once they were settled at a small table with tall iced teas and caprese salads, Ella told Marisol what had happened at the hospital that Monday, concluding with Lucinda's preposterous parting shot.

"I mean, where in the world could she have come up with that one?" Ella demanded. "Ian's my friend and I love him dearly, but you know how he is, ten dates maximum—more likely five or six—and the woman is outta there. I want real, lasting love, and Ian is not the kind of guy to pin any hopes on. A woman who falls for him is just begging for heartbreak."

Ella paused to nibble a bite of bread, tossing the crust down in disgust. "Let alone, he's my boss. *And* two years younger than me. How many ways is he all wrong for me?" She picked up her fork, speared a bite of her salad and stuck it in her mouth. Once she'd finished chewing and swallowing, she concluded with, "No. Just no." And then indulged in a sip of iced tea while she waited for her friend to start laughing.

But Marisol didn't laugh. In fact, she winced.

Ella put her glass down and demanded, "What was that? Did you just *wince* at me?" Marisol, clearly uncomfortable, guided a corkscrew of rust-brown hair behind her ear and sagged against the banquette cushion. "You did, then?" Ella's voice sounded plaintive to her own ears. "You *winced* at me."

"What do you want me to tell you?"

Ella knew then that she should just leave it alone. But somehow, she couldn't. "I want the truth, of course."

Marisol gave her the side-eye and then let out a tired little sigh. "You *are* in love with Ian," she said softly. "You have been for years."

Like an acid bath, her friend's words washed over her, burning. She ate another bite of salad and followed that up with a second sip of tea. "Why did you have to tell me that?"

"Um, you asked?"

With her fork, Ella nudged a bit of mozzarella off a tomato slice. "Point taken—and you know what? Let's not talk about it anymore."

"Ella…"

"No, really. I mean it. We need to leave the subject of Ian McNeill far behind."

Marisol reached across the table, caught the back of Ella's hand briefly and gave it a squeeze. "Okay."

Ella's friend was as good as her word. They left it at that.

But Ella didn't really leave it. For the rest of the

day, she thought about Ian constantly, swinging from absolute denial to a sense of growing horror that she might have somehow, impossibly, fallen in love with her commitment-averse friend and boss.

At least Ian was out of the office that afternoon. She didn't have to see him or speak with him.

Still, her misery and confusion only got worse.

After school that day, Abby went to her dad's for the weekend. She forgot her retainer and sent Ella a text as she was leaving the office asking if maybe, *please* she might run the device over to Philip's.

It wasn't a big deal. Philip and his family lived just around the corner from Ella. As soon as she got home, Ella grabbed the retainer case from the night table by Abby's bed and went on over there.

Philip answered the door. "Ella." He gave her a warm smile of welcome. "Come on in."

"Thanks, I have to run." She held out the retainer case. "Just here to drop off the usual."

Philip studied her face and frowned. "What's the matter?"

"Nothing."

He stepped out into the hallway with her and pulled the door shut behind him, raising his index and middle finger and aiming them both at the space just over her nose. "You've got the lines between your eyes." He'd always claimed she scrunched her eyebrows together when something was bothering her.

Yeah, her ex knew far too much about her. The same age and the same grade through school, they'd been best friends since they were nine, when Ella's parents had died in a boating accident and her aunt Clara in New York City had taken her in. The Haralson family had lived in the same building as her aunt.

No, she'd never fallen in love with Philip, nor he with her. It was friendship between them, pure and strong and simple, always had been. They'd had a lot in common, Ella and Philip. Both shy and semi-invisible at school, they'd sworn to be besties forever.

And at the age of eighteen, they'd hatched a scheme to experiment with sex together—in order that when they finally did fall in love, they would know what they were doing in bed.

A slipup on the contraception front had resulted in Abby. Under pressure from Philip's parents, whom Ella had always adored, they'd caved. She and Philip got married right after graduation from high school, while secretly vowing to each other that they would divorce as soon as they both finished college. And they'd kept that vow, too, splitting up as planned, much to the disappointment of the elder Haralsons.

Philip had found his true love, Chloe, a year later. Now, he and Chloe had two adorable little girls, Zoe and Leah. Some people had all the luck.

Philip narrowed his eyes at her. It was his *I can see inside your head* look. "Talk to me."

"Philip, I'm fine."

"Something's bothering you."

"I have to get going…"

"Wait." He blinked and loomed closer. "Now I get it. You've met someone."

"Stop." He really was a sweetheart, and he wanted her to find her true love as much as she did. But she refused to get into this with him. In fact, she felt minimally grateful Philip had no clue that her "someone" might be Ian, of all people. "There's no one, I promise you," she insisted, trying hard to believe it. And then she went up on tiptoe and brushed a kiss on his cheek. "Gotta go. Hugs to Chloe and the girls. Tell our daughter I love her, and I'll see her Monday after work."

She turned and got out of there before he could say another word.

Down the street, she got takeout from her favorite falafel place and carried the food back to her too-quiet apartment, where her mind would not stop arguing with itself over the scary possibility that the man she wanted might actually be Ian.

Oh, dear God. What if it *was* Ian? What if she did love him?

What if Ian was her "one"?

That man would never commit. In the past, she'd always found it thoroughly annoying when Philip quizzed her on her love life—or lack thereof.

Now, though? Downright depressing.

Oh, God. Please, no.

She couldn't be in love with Ian. She *wouldn't* be in love with Ian.

Denial. Definitely. Denial was the only way to go.

Monday, at the office, she managed pretty well. She dealt with Ian the same way she always did, with the usual wry humor, honesty and friendly respect. They were a great team. He ran the business, and she backed him up and communicated his decisions to their employees. In meetings, she spoke up when she felt that he or their CFO, David Karnavan, were on the wrong track. Both men took her seriously.

That day, she behaved as though nothing had changed. It worked. No one seemed to suspect she might be freaking out internally. Most important, she felt certain that Ian didn't have a clue as to the chaos in her head and her heart.

However...

It did seem to her that, since that awful day

when he'd ended up in the ER and she'd found out what she never wanted to know from his now ex-girlfriend…

Well, looking back, it seemed to Ella that from that day on, something strange was going on with Ian, too.

He seemed preoccupied, like something bothered him, nagged at him. Whatever troubled him, he hid it well in meetings. But sometimes she would see him in his corner office alone, staring off into the middle distance.

After a couple more days of that strangeness, she asked him outright if anything was wrong.

He put on a puzzled expression. "No idea what you're talking about, Ell. I'm good. Nothing out of the ordinary going on."

She would have pressed him a little, but he started in about her upcoming trip to the factory in Minneapolis. Six years ago, when Glynis was still at the helm, they'd moved production to the Twin Cities to keep costs down. Now Ella flew out there at least twice a month to check in with the design, development and manufacturing teams.

By the time they'd talked through Ian's questions for the design team, the workday had ended. She went home more certain than ever that something weighed on his mind.

Eventually, he *would* tell her. Her supposed

hopeless love for him aside, she knew him. Though he rarely trusted anyone, he did trust her. He would bust himself to her eventually.

Thursday, she flew to Minneapolis, returning after seven on Friday night. From the airport, she went straight home.

Early Saturday, she picked up Abby at Philip's. They shopped for groceries, after which they cleaned the apartment they both loved. It had gorgeous old pine floors, an original fireplace and a view of the Empire State Building—if you stood in the living area window just so. The thousand-square-foot two-bedroom co-op had cost Ella a lot. And it was worth every penny, too.

Around five, Abby went back to Philip's for pizza and a family movie night.

At a little after six, Ella settled on the sofa with the remote. She was scrolling the Netflix options when someone buzzed from downstairs. She got up and answered.

It was Ian. "You busy?"

Chapter Three

Despite her annoying hyperawareness of him lately, Ella smiled to herself. *About time*, she thought. Whatever he had on his mind, she would do her best to help him get to the bottom of it.

She buzzed him up and then waited in her open doorway for him to appear.

He came around the corner from the elevator. The sight of him made her heart ache—and not because of her own confusion over her feelings for him.

No. She ached for his sake alone. His thick, dark blond hair, cut long on top and close at the sides, looked kind of scrambled. He must have been shoving his fingers in it. His blue eyes had shadows under them, and his beard scruff seemed a little longer than usual.

Her friend was a mess, and she wanted to help.

Marching right up to her, he muttered, "Don't look at me like that."

"Like what?"

He scowled. "Where's Abby?"

"At her dad's."

"Good. She doesn't need to hear this crap."

What crap? she almost demanded. But no. Better to let him open up about the problem in his own good time.

They regarded each other. After several seconds, he demanded, "You gonna let me in?"

She moved aside and gestured him forward with a wave of her hand. "Coffee?"

"Got anything stronger?"

She followed him down the narrow entry hallway to the living area, where he dropped to the sofa with an audible sigh, as though he carried the weight of the world on those broad shoulders.

She offered, "Vodka? White wine?"

"The vodka. Just ice."

"Lime?"

"Perfect."

She poured one for herself, too, and joined him on the sofa.

He took the drink and sipped. "It's good."

"You're welcome. So, what's going on?"

He leaned forward, braced his elbows on his spread knees, the glass dangling between them in both hands, and stared down into the clear liquid as though the answers to deep questions lurked between the chunks of crushed ice. "I need to talk."

"Yeah, I figured."

He slanted her a wry glance. "Sorry about the other day. I was still hoping... I don't know. That if I stayed in denial long enough, the whole thing would just go away."

She had to hold back a laugh. After all, she felt the same—about the grim possibility that she loved him in a way destined to end badly for her. She prompted, "But it *didn't* go away..."

He nodded, head down again, eyes focused on the glass between his hands. "I mean, you asked me, the other day. And I lied and said there was nothing. But then I kept thinking that I really do need to talk to someone, and I don't even want to get going with a therapist again." He turned those blue eyes directly on her. "I just need to talk it out with a friend."

She resisted the urge to put her hand on his knee. After what Lucinda had said, well, it just felt wrong to touch him, like she'd be indulging her secret, unacceptable desires.

God. This was awful. It shouldn't be happening, these feelings she suddenly realized she had for this man. He had his problems—with getting close, with commitment. And yet he'd always been good to her, *there* for her. He treated her daughter like a princess. They all—at work, Philip and Chloe, everyone in their circle of colleagues, family and friends—jokingly called Ian "Abby's second dad."

But it wasn't a joke, not really. Whatever happened, Ian would make sure that Abby had whatever she needed to get a great start in life.

"Just tell me," Ella said softly. "Just get it out."

He shook his head. "You should probably suggest that I pull it together and then send me home."

Enough. She was so done with waiting for him to open up. Time to give him a push in the right direction. "Stop it. You're here. You didn't come just so I could tell you to get over it and go away. I mean it, Ian. Talk."

He took another sip of his drink, a big one, no doubt to brace himself, and then he said, "Since that day at the zoo, I've been remembering."

At his gruffly spoken words, the breath seemed to flee her body. All these years he'd lived in the dark when it came to his early childhood. She dragged in a giant gulp of air. "About your life before the bear attack?"

"Yeah."

"Tell me. Everything."

He started talking about Russia, the stuff she already knew from bits of information he and Glynis had shared with her over the years. He spoke of the hospital where he woke in pain, covered in bandages, not knowing his own name, with everyone speaking a language he didn't understand.

"And the orphanage…" His voice trailed off. "I've always remembered way too much about my life there, too…"

He'd told her a few years ago that the other children were hardened, either completely withdrawn or dangerous, that the women who cared for them had grim faces, with too many kids to look after and no time to give comfort or hugs. He'd learned quickly that drawing the attention of those women would only earn him a slap and a harsh reprimand—or worse.

On the sofa, Ian had fallen silent. Again, Ella found herself holding her breath. He remained quiet. She drew in air and let it out slowly and recalled the old story, of how, at the orphanage, they'd given him the name Nicolas Ivanov, but he'd refused to answer to it—refused to speak at all. Even later, after he'd picked up enough Russian to communicate if he'd wanted to, he'd felt safer just letting them all believe he was mute.

Ian told more of the story Ella already knew. "Then Glynis showed up to find a child to adopt."

Glynis had looked at the boy they called Nicolas, and he'd gazed back at her and he'd *known* that she was good, that she was kind. And then he'd heard her speak and he knew he had to find a way to go home with her, that he was an American—though from what part of the country or who his people were, he had no clue. He'd felt bleakly certain that she wouldn't take him, that she would want a baby, as everyone did, a pretty, pure, happy little baby.

"No would want some scarred-up kid who never said a word to anyone." He knocked back another big gulp of his drink. "But she looked at me and I stared at her and I saw in her eyes then that she felt what I felt." Both he and Glynis had described their first eye contact as a connection, an understanding. "And I knew with zero doubt that she would do it, take *me* with her instead of the baby she'd come for…" He seemed to run out of words.

"She was one of a kind, your mother." Glynis, who'd been raised in the foster care system after her only parent, her father, had died, never let her tough start in life get her down. Always upbeat and ready to take on the world, Glynis had fallen from a ladder trying to change a lightbulb in her Upper East Side brownstone. She'd hit her head and died instantly. That was a little over a year ago now.

She'd left her adopted son everything she owned, including the toy business she'd loved.

Ian nodded, eyes vacant, gaze fixed on the hallway. "I miss her."

"Me, too." Ella waited. He continued to stare blankly down the hallway for several long seconds. Carefully, she prompted, "But about your life before that, here in the States?"

"Yeah. About who I was before..." His burnished eyebrows scrunched together. He downed the rest of his drink and held out the glass. "Just one more?"

She traded him for hers, which she'd yet to taste.

"Thanks." He held the fresh drink between his big, long-fingered hands, as if just the feel of the cold glass steadied him. "Okay, so within a few days of losing it at the zoo, I'd remembered a bunch of random stuff about my family here in the US, that their last name was Bravo, that we lived in some little town on the Oregon coast called Valentine Bay."

Sudden tears blurred her vision—for him, for the childhood he'd lost. For the family he would finally have a chance to reconnect with, at last, after all this time. "Ian. That's amazing. That's so big."

"Big." He scoffed. "Too bad I'm not coping very well."

"Of course you are. I mean, you're dealing

with it. Don't be hard on yourself. Give yourself a break. You're talking about it, you're facing it. And you have to do that in your own time and your own way."

He turned his gaze to her then. A ghost of a smile haunted his gorgeous mouth, with its full bottom lip and distinct cupid's bow. "You're a good friend, Ell. Steady. Solid."

Steady and solid. He meant it as compliment, though she couldn't help hearing it as something else altogether. *Steady and solid*, huh? He might as well just call her dull and dependable.

"Yeah, I'm a rock, all right."

"True that." He sent her a wry smile.

She reminded herself that she needed to keep her own inner turmoil out of this. Right now, her focus belonged on what he needed as her friend.

Ian set his half-finished second drink on the coffee table and folded his hands between his spread knees. "So anyway, I spent a whole night, dusk till dawn last week, scouring the internet for whatever I could find about the Bravo family of Valentine Bay. And then I took what I'd remembered and what I'd learned online to a private investigator. Yesterday, the PI sent me a big file packed with more than I could ever want to know about my lost family and the boy I used to be."

Rising, he went to the window next to the sofa.

He knew where to stand for the view of the Art Deco skyscraper with the giant antenna on top. As he stared at the marvel of twentieth-century architecture, he rattled off facts.

"My name was Finnegan Bravo—called Finn. I was sixth-born of nine children—five boys, four girls. My parents apparently had a thing for world travel and died in a tsunami on a trip to Thailand two years after I disappeared. I vanished in Siberia near the city of Irkutsk when I was eight." His gaze shifted to her briefly.

And then he stared out the window some more. "Irkutsk, by the way, is almost seven hundred miles from Krasnoyarsk, where I woke up in the hospital God only knows how long after I wandered away from my family. And how I traveled all that distance? I don't have a clue. There was an extensive search for the lost Finn Bravo, though, and a large reward offered to anyone who found me. My ending up so far from where I was last seen explains why nobody ever turned me in to collect the money."

She reminded him, "Plus, you never spoke until after Glynis brought you to New York. The Russians really had no way of knowing who you were or where you'd come from."

"Right. I had no idea who I was, either. And I trusted no one." Shoving his hands in the pockets of his dark-wash Italian-made jeans, he turned from the window to meet her eyes, that beautiful, rueful smile flickering across his face again. "I stole your drink, didn't I? Sorry."

"No problem. I know where to get more." She picked up the glass from the coffee table and held it out to him.

He took it, had another sip. "I can't stop thinking about flying out there to Oregon, about meeting them—at the same time, though, I just can't see myself doing that."

Ella couldn't let that go. "You need to do it."

"Ell." He said her name—the nickname only he ever called her—so tenderly. *Friendship*, she reminded herself sternly. *That's what we have. That's who we are together.* He chided, "You don't get to decide if I meet them or not."

"I know, but Ian. Consider the possibilities. You have brothers and sisters. You have *family*. A big family." What she wouldn't give for a big family. When her mom and dad died, there had only been her dad's much-older sister, Aunt Clara, between Ella and the foster care system. A good person who did her duty by Ella and stepped up as Ella's guardian, Aunt Clara had avoided strong emotions and steered clear of physical contact. With Aunt Clara, hugs were rare. That first year with her aunt, Ella had cried in her room alone a lot. She would have given just about anything to have had a brother or sister to hold on to.

"I don't know them," Ian insisted. "Glynis was my mom. She was enough."

Ella wanted to shake him. "Ian, love…*expands*. You won't love Glynis less if you meet your birth family—and okay, maybe you won't even like them when you meet them. But maybe you will. And they'll *know* things about the boy you were once. They're your history, just waiting out there in Oregon for you to discover them."

Was she pushing too hard? Definitely. She really did want him to do this his own way. But when she thought about him *not* meeting his lost family, well, that just felt so wrong. He *had* to go.

She pushed some more. "You need to meet them, to get to know them…"

He gazed down at her indulgently, the way he looked at Abby sometimes, like she was just so cute, so amusing in her youth and innocence. "May I remind you that I passed out just from watching a couple of frolicking grizzly bears from thirty feet away through a shatterproof protective viewing screen?"

"You're not going pass out when you meet your brothers and sisters."

"You can't be sure of that."

For a moment, they just looked at each other. It was, essentially, a face-off. A stare-down.

He broke the silence. "Hard fact. I'm not doing that alone."

She got it then. "You want me to go with you. That's why you're here. To get me to go with you." She laughed, but her throat felt tight with feelings she refused to examine too closely.

He handed her drink back. "Will you? Ell, I need a friend for this."

"Of course you do." Lucinda's cruel taunt echoed through her mind... *Everyone knows you're in love with him. It's pathetic.*

He'd said it himself. He needed a *friend*. And she hardly understood her own heart at this point. Flying off to the West Coast with him? Probably not the best choice for her emotional well-being right now.

But it wasn't about her. It was about Ian and what she would give to see that he got what he needed.

A lot. She would give a lot.

She brought the glass to her lips and drank the rest. "Of course I'll go."

"Thank you." Ian felt grateful for a friend like Ella, who didn't so much as hesitate when he'd asked her to help him meet the family he wasn't even sure he wanted to know.

"When do we leave?" she asked brightly, so obviously eager and ready to reunite him with a bunch of people he felt nothing for.

"Soon. I'm thinking Thursday, returning the following Monday. I want to get in and get out." The whole thing made him edgy—unnerved. He agreed with Ella that he needed to do it, but that didn't mean he had to like it.

"Abby will want to go," she said, after which they shook their heads simultaneously and said "No" at the same time.

Ella added, "You're right that we have no idea how things will shake out when we get there. *I* think it will be great, and if it is, maybe one of these days you'll want to fly her out there with you."

"Maybe." He could not see that ever happening but saw no need to make a point of it. Right now, he just wanted to get the whole thing over with.

She grinned at him. "You look so uncomfortable."

"Yeah, well. It's not what I would call a pleasure trip."

"True." Ella shrugged. "So then, as for Abby, I'll tell her what's going on, that you've remembered enough about your birth family to pay them a visit. Is that okay?"

"That'll work."

"She can stay with her dad and she has school anyway, so we don't have to get too specific with her about why she can't come with."

"Good plan."

Ella wiggled her empty glass. "Another drink?"

"Better not."

She set the glass next to his on the coffee table. "Ian, it's going to work out. You'll be glad you went." Her dark eyes gleamed, and her pretty, soft mouth had curved in a happy smile. She seemed excited about the whole thing. He wished he could share her enthusiasm for meeting a bunch of strangers in the interest of reforging family bonds.

"I hope so." He tried not to sound as full of doubt and discomfort as he felt.

Abby called him Sunday morning. "Ian! You've been remembering…" She sounded thrilled at the very idea. "I should come over. I know you need to talk about it."

No, he didn't. "Can't, sorry. Got a busy Sunday lined up." It was true, more or less. He planned to spend several hours at the office that day, getting ahead of the workload in preparation for taking three weekdays off.

"Mom says I can't go to Oregon with you." Abby used her pouty voice.

"School is important."

"Yeah, right—and I guess this means making you face your fears wasn't *all* bad, after all?" Now she sounded equal parts hesitant and hopeful.

He wondered if anything good could possibly come from meeting relatives he hadn't seen since he was someone else entirely. But Abby needed reassurance about the incident at the zoo. He put on his best imitation of a happy voice and gave it to her. "You're right. It was a good thing. Thanks for, uh, giving me a nudge in the right direction."

"I still feel bad about it."

"Don't."

"That day, when your eyes rolled back, and you crumpled to the ground? I couldn't stop screaming. I thought, maybe, you were never going to wake up."

"Well, I did wake up, and I'm good as new." And Abby Haralson would never feel guilty or unhappy—not if he could do anything about it. "Stop blaming yourself. It all turned out fine."

She blew out a heavy breath. "I guess you really are okay."

"I am, I promise you."

"And you'll get to meet your family finally, after all this time."

"Yay."

She laughed. "Oh, Ian. Sometimes you're such a Grumpy Gus."

He made a grumpy sound, just to prove her right.

She started in about the book she was reading and then moved on to a story she'd begun writing in which a girl very much like her discovered she could time travel and saved the world by changing history. He praised her storytelling skills and admired her vivid imagination.

When they said goodbye twenty minutes later, she sounded happy and upbeat. He might only be her second dad, but he congratulated himself on doing a decent job of lifting her spirits and banishing the last of her guilt over what had happened at the zoo.

First thing Monday, he had Audrey, his assistant, book him and Ella flights to and from Portland, Oregon. A rental car would be waiting at PDX and Ian would drive them the rest of the way to the little town on the Pacific up near the border with Washington State. Audrey had them staying at a hotel right there in town.

How bad could it be? he kept asking himself bleakly. Five days out of his life to meet a bunch of people he'd had no memory of until a couple of weeks ago—five days, two of which would be for travel.

He could do this. And then he could say he'd met his birth family.

Ella strolled into his office at nine thirty Monday morning, dropped into the chair opposite his desk and sipped from the Black Fox Coffee Company to-go cup she'd carried in with her. "So. Did that investigator you hired give you phone numbers?" He must have looked confused, because she clarified, "Phone numbers for any of your brothers and sisters?"

He guessed where she was leading him, and he didn't plan to go there. But still, he answered honestly, "Yeah."

She took a slow sip of coffee. "Then you'll call them, let them know you're coming?"

"I'll call them when we get there."

Ella became very still. He tried not to smile. He knew that look on her face. She thought he should contact them beforehand but also knew that once he'd made up his mind about something, he rarely changed course.

"Ian." She spoke in a solemn yet coaxing voice. "It seems only fair to give them a heads-up. Look at it from their point of view. It's going to be a shock, to say the least. A little warning wouldn't hurt."

She was right—as usual.

Didn't matter. He would face the Bravos in Oregon and not until then. "Ell. I don't want to call ahead."

"Why not?"

"I see no need to drag it out."

"What if you can't reach any of them when we get there?"

"I have eight siblings—all but two of them married, all of them living either in that little town or close by. Odds are someone will be available when I decide to get in touch."

"But—" He cut her off with a shake of his head and, finally, she accepted his decision. "Well, then. Guess you're not calling ahead." She rose and turned for the door.

"See you at ten," he said gently to her retreating back.

"I know when the morning meeting is, Ian," she replied downright snippily without pausing or glancing back.

Snippy was good. Snippy meant she wouldn't be getting on him again about calling ahead, and that worked for him.

More than once that week, Ella considered backing out of the Portland trip. Being Ian's best buddy and emotional support for five days seemed like such a bad idea for her right now.

She had her own issues lately—issues that mostly consisted of the need to constantly deny the remote possibility that his most recent ex-girlfriend had been right, that Ella had made the giant mistake of falling for the ultimate unavailable man. All that denial took a whole bunch of effort already, when she only had to deal with him at work. She didn't need five days of constant proximity to the guy messing with her focus on pretending that bitch Lucinda didn't know her ass from up.

But every time she convinced herself that she needed to march into Ian's office and let him know she'd changed her mind about going with him, well, she just couldn't do it.

He could be a jerk. But he was *her* jerk—in a friends-only way. It mattered, that a woman stuck by a friend.

Thus, on Thursday at nine in the morning, they boarded their flight to Oregon. The first-class seats were roomy and comfortable, the brunch delicious. Ian seemed preoccupied and reluctant to chat.

Fine with her. She put on her sleep mask and adjusted her seat.

When she woke, Ian had his black-rimmed glasses on and his laptop opened—working, as usual.

He glanced over at her and gave her his beautiful smile—the real one that he saved for the small group of people who had his trust. She didn't get that smile often. Nobody did—except Abby, of course.

Ella basked in that smile, though the voice in her head that lately sounded like Lucinda taunted, *Give it up, fool. He doesn't do lasting relationships and a fling with him is a bad, bad idea.*

Not that Ian would want a fling with Ella, anyway. He considered her a good friend and colleague. She was no Lucinda. She lacked the bombshell packaging *and* the disposability. No way he would sacrifice her true value to him for something as easy to get as sex.

"Sleep well?" he asked.

"I did, thanks." Had she drooled on herself? She made a quick inventory. No spots on her shirt, nothing on her face. Wrinkling her nose at him, she asked, "Did I snore?"

"Not a peep." He leaned a little closer. She got a whiff of that expensive cologne he wore that smelled of grass and deep woods, all cool and somehow soothing. "Want some champagne?"

She shook her head. "Too dehydrating on a flight. But maybe with dinner."

"You're so well behaved." He still leaned into her, his elbow on the wide, padded armrest between their seats. She could see the silvery rays fanning out from his pupils through the blue irises. And she felt better about everything. What did Lucinda know, anyway—or Marisol, for that matter?

Ella loved Ian, yeah. As a dear friend. Nothing else going on here. Tagging along for moral support as he reunited with his birth family would be good for him and a nice change of pace for her.

"On second thought," she said, "bring on the bubbly."

Did she get a little tipsy before they touched down in Portland? Maybe.

Ian enjoyed a single scotch rocks while she sipped her champagne, and they whispered together about Abby's next dance recital and the new stuffed toy, Woodrow the warthog, that Patch&Pebble would be launching in time for the holiday market.

They landed in Portland right on time. Forty-five minutes later, they headed for Valentine Bay in the Lexus SUV Audrey had rented for them.

The drive took an hour and a half. At a little before five, they checked into the Isabel Inn, a gorgeous, shingled New England–style hotel a short walk from the ocean in Valentine Bay. Audrey had booked them a two-bedroom suite, with a large, beautifully furnished deck that faced the

Pacific and offered access directly to the beach. The hotel also boasted a dining room where the chef prepared well-reviewed seasonal fare. They had dinner reservations for six thirty.

Before retreating to her own room to settle in, Ella tried again to convince Ian he ought to give one of the Bravos a call.

"It's a big deal, Ian, your showing up here in Oregon. Your family deserves a heads-up."

He stood at the end of the sand-colored sofa, next to the coffee table stacked with large, beautifully illustrated books about the Oregon coast and graced with a white orchid soaring out of a tea-green pot on a slender, curving stem. He had the remote in hand, his eyes on the flat screen over the fireplace as he flipped through channels. "Tomorrow."

"Ian, I just think—"

"Stop." He sent her that look, the one that said no way would she get him to do that and she'd better give it up now.

"All righty, then." She flicked him a wave over her shoulder and marched through the door to her room, pulling it closed behind her—quietly, too, though the urge to give it a nice, hard slam vibrated through her, making her clench her teeth and growl low in her throat.

* * *

Ian turned off the flat screen and tossed the remote on the sofa.

Maybe Ella had a point. He probably should call. The PI he'd hired had reported that, over the years, the Bravos had put feelers out everywhere for him. They'd tried to find him.

And they never would have. Not without him remembering them first. Whatever series of circumstances had carried him from that snowy path near Irkutsk to a hospital hundreds of miles away had severed the connection between Finn Bravo and the boy who became Nicolas Ivanov and, finally, Ian McNeill. His refusal to speak for all that time hadn't helped, either.

The Bravos must think him dead by now. Showing up on their doorstep out of the blue might cause someone to suffer a heart attack.

A call first would help ease the way.

Ian slid his phone from his pocket and brought up his contacts list. He'd entered all the Bravo family phone numbers the PI had sent him. Daniel was the eldest brother, so he would probably be the top choice to try first. Ian stared at the screen, his thumb hovering over the phone icon next to Daniel Bravo's name.

"No." He dropped the phone on a book of landscape photographs, grabbed his laptop and went to his room, where he tossed the computer on the bed, kicked off his shoes, threw his jacket on a chair and flopped down on the mattress.

After ten minutes of staring at the ceiling, wondering why he'd let himself become a total wreck over this situation, he sat up, grabbed the laptop and emailed some questions to David, his CFO. After reading through David's response, he shut the device and flopped to his back again.

The ceiling hadn't changed one bit since the last time he stared at it.

Eventually, he got up and padded back into the living area. Scooping up his phone, he keyed in his PIN and stared at Daniel Bravo's name some more.

It had started to rain.

Dropping the phone, he went to the glass door that looked out on the deck, with the beach and the ocean beyond. For a while he stared at the misty sky, at the gulls dipping and soaring over the water, the waves rolling in, leading edges laced with foam.

No, he wasn't calling Daniel Bravo. Tomorrow, he would show up. If some brother or sister fell over dead from the shock, well, then he would have that on his conscience. They would all get through it, somehow.

He just needed to stop thinking about it, stop second-guessing his choices. And Ella needed to stop pressuring him to do what he didn't intend to do.

Out there beyond the deck, on the beach midway to the water's edge, a man and a woman strolled along, holding hands. The breeze blew their hair back, away from their faces. As he watched, the woman laughed, tossing her head, exposing the sleek column of her long neck.

She reminded him of Ella, somehow—the wavy dark hair falling below her shoulders, the slim, leggy body. Had he been too hard on Ella about the phone call?

Probably—okay, yeah. He had.

She'd come all this way to help him get through this grueling meeting-the-lost-family thing. He shouldn't treat her cruelly because she encouraged him to show consideration for the siblings he hadn't seen for twenty years.

And no. That didn't mean he would call ahead and give his lost family fair warning. He wouldn't. He just couldn't deal with any of that right now. Tonight, he needed to relax and get his bearings, get his head in the right space for whatever would go down tomorrow.

But he *would* apologize to Ella for being a jackass.

Before he could think of all the reasons he ought to just leave the poor woman alone until it was time to head over to the dining room for dinner, he spun away from the view of the beach, marched to her door and turned the knob. She hadn't locked it, so he pushed it open.

And found her standing by the bed in a black satin thong and bra to match.

Chapter Four

"Ian!" Ella said his name on a gasp, her coffee-colored eyes wide and startled.

He blinked. "Uh. Sorry. It was open."

With a scowl that hinted she just might punch him in the face, she marched toward him.

Really, his good friend was hot—all lean and smooth and tight, with small, high breasts. Willowy. Yeah. That was the word. She had legs that didn't quit and long, graceful arms.

She walked right up to him. "Did you want something, Ian?"

Did he want something? Right at this moment, he could get ideas. "Er, just wanted you to know.

I get it. I was a douche to you about the whole calling-ahead thing and I'm sorry for that."

"You're sorry." She spoke with zero inflection.

It took a whole lot of effort, but he resisted the temptation to let his gaze meander down her sleek, pretty body and slowly back up again. "I am sorry. Very."

"So then, you *will* call one of your brothers now?"

It took him a second or two to respond to her question. She must have showered. She smelled so good—sweet and a little bit spicy. The urge to sneak a quick glance at all that smoothness lower down kept distracting him. But somehow, he kept his focus locked on her face. "No. Not calling tonight."

"If not tonight, when?"

"I never said I would call ahead."

"Ah. So nothing has changed, then?"

"No. It's only, I'm sorry for being an ass to you about it. That's all."

"Step back, Ian."

"Huh?"

She waited. It took about three seconds for his brain to catch up with his ears. When that happened, he stepped back into the living area of the suite.

"One more thing," she said.

"Of course."

"I know Glynis taught you not to barge into other people's rooms without knocking."

"She did, yes." He felt really guilty, like a kid caught with a mouthful of cookies and crumbs on his shirt. "I'm sorry about that, too—about barging in on you like this. I should have knocked."

"Yes, you should. Do so in the future."

"Definitely. I will."

She gave the door a push, and it closed in his face.

He stood there, staring at the shut door for several long seconds, feeling so strange—aroused, addle-headed and embarrassed, too.

Finally, with a slow, deep breath, he squared his shoulders and turned for his bedroom suite, where he showered and changed into casual gray pants and a white button-up, rolling the sleeves to the elbows and skipping a jacket. The Oregon coast hardly seemed a place where a guy needed a jacket to get seated for dinner.

As he put on his socks and shoes, he tried to clear his mind of troubling thoughts, yet he felt a hum of anticipation. Images of Ella in her little black thong kept popping into his brain. That buzz of heat under his skin wouldn't quite go away.

Not only did he seem to have a sudden case of unforeseen lust for his dear friend and COO, but he hardly knew what to expect when she emerged to go to dinner.

She might still be pissed at him—justifiably so.

But he needn't have worried. At six fifteen, she breezed into the shared room of the suite looking great, wearing a short black dress scattered with white flowers and black ankle boots, the dark silk of her hair falling in soft waves over her shoulders.

She seemed completely relaxed and not the least annoyed with him. And hadn't he always loved that about her? Ella made her point and moved on. She never let weird feelings linger.

As soon as Ian gave her a smile, Ella felt better about everything.

Apparently, he'd gotten past her reaction to him bursting in on her earlier. She'd worried a little that he might hold a grudge for the way she'd scolded him. Really, she shouldn't have been so hard on him. It was painfully clear to her that the prospect of meeting his family again after all this time had stressed him out in a big way.

She needed to keep firmly in mind that she'd come on this trip to support Ian, to help him keep some semblance of emotional equilibrium. He'd never excelled at dealing with his feelings. This situation had to be hell for him.

Yeah, it had shocked her to glance over and see

him framed in the open doorway, gaping at her in her underwear—of course, he'd gaped. He had his mind on tomorrow. Walking in on a friend with most of her clothes off had made him understandably uncomfortable.

She shouldn't have snapped at him.

And she refused to feel hurt that he could not have cared less about getting an eyeful of her in her skimpy undies.

Because no matter what anybody said, Ella was not in love with Ian. No way.

"You get a chance to talk to Abby?" he asked.

"Yeah. Just briefly. She sends her love and she got an A on her math test."

"Like mother, like daughter."

She grinned. "Brains do run in the family."

"Ready?" he asked, his gaze warm on her. Sometimes he looked at her as though he liked what he saw.

But why wouldn't he? They were friends. He liked *her*.

And she needed to quit second-guessing his every random glance in her direction.

She nodded. "I'm starved."

He offered his arm, and she took it.

Round in structure, with a cone-shaped red-cedar ceiling, the dining room at the center of the Isabel Inn had the same feel as the rest of the hotel—casually elegant and cozy. Ella and Ian split a bottle of local wine and both chose Dungeness crab Caesar salad, with rack of lamb for the main course.

Ian kept the talk light and she went along with that, letting the evening serve as a distraction from any worries he might have about tomorrow. She didn't mention the Bravos and neither did he.

Outside, the sky remained layered in clouds, though the rain had stopped. After the meal, they detoured to the suite to get jackets. Leaving their shoes behind on the deck, they went down two sets of steps to the beach, where they strolled barefoot in the sand. The sun sent fingers of orange spreading over the sky as it slipped below the horizon way out there on the ocean.

"I could learn to like it here," she said as they stood side by side a few feet from the incoming waves, watching the sky slowly darken.

He made a sound of agreement low in his throat, his gaze on the horizon. "It's a good place to be a kid—safe," he said quietly. "Lots of time on the beach in the summers. We had a big house on a hill—Rhinehart Hill. And us kids had the run of it. A big backyard, with a swing set and tall trees all around. I remember my mom used to..." He blinked several times in rapid succession.

She didn't know what to say, what to do in this

moment. Beg him to go on? Pretend he hadn't said anything?

The memories he'd just shared sounded lovely. Nothing traumatic. A happy family in which the children felt safe and loved—but how horrible for a little boy to have been torn from his good life so completely, to find himself lost in a strange land, attacked and brutalized by a wild animal, waking up in a hospital where the people spoke words he didn't understand.

He was watching her now, his mouth set, his eyes impossible to read.

"Don't stop," she said hopefully. Now that he'd turned to her, it felt wrong not to encourage his good memories. "Your mom used to…?"

His brows cinched together. "Nah."

Please… She almost kept after him. But if he didn't want to go on about it, well, right now she felt wrong pushing him.

"Come on, let's go back." He offered his big hand. She looked down at it, a little bit stunned. Nine years she'd known this man, worked alongside him, called him her friend, trusted her daughter to his care on a regular basis.

And yet she couldn't recall ever holding his hand—not that it was a big deal, a little hand-holding. Between friends.

She slipped her fingers in his. His warm, strong grip felt good.

Maybe too good…

"Have you remembered a lot?" she asked.

He squeezed her fingers. "Enough." And he smiled, a rueful sort of smile that had her heart aching for him.

And she couldn't tell—did he mean that he'd remembered "enough"? Or that he'd said "enough" on the subject and didn't want to talk about it anymore?

Out across the water, the gulls cried to each other.

"Ell." With the hand that wasn't holding hers, he touched her cheek, the pad of his index finger catching a few windblown strands of hair, guiding them back behind the curve of her ear. She felt that touch like a brand, a line of heat seared into her skin. "In the past few weeks, I've remembered a lot about this town, about my family here. About my life here."

"A good life, you said…"

"It was, yeah."

"I'm…" Her throat clutched. She gave a sharp cough to clear it. "I'm glad."

"Hey…"

"Hmm?"

"You're not going to start bawling on me, are you?"

With a sniffle and a shake of her head, she blinked the moisture away. "Not a chance, Mc-Neill."

"Good, then." Tugging on her hand, he turned for the hotel. "Let's go in."

In their suite, he said he had messages to catch up on. She probably ought to check her correspondence, too. Plus, it was almost nine now—meaning midnight in Manhattan.

She covered a yawn. "I think jet lag may be catching up with me." And they had a big day tomorrow.

"Breakfast in the dining room?"

"Done." She retreated to her room, where she stared at the turned-back bed and muttered to herself, "Forget work."

A few minutes later, in comfy sleep shorts and a worn T-shirt, she climbed between the covers and turned off the lamp.

Ella dreamed of Lake Thunderbird, in Norman, Oklahoma. In the dream, she was a little girl, still living in Norman with her parents, who adored her, in a small, one-story brick house. Her mom and dad loved their boat, the *Sweet Home*. Ella loved it, too.

In the dream, aboard the *Sweet Home*, they drifted on the shifting waters of the lake. Just the three of them, her mom in the galley, making sandwiches, her dad at the wheel. Her child self sat aft, watching clouds gather over the water, knowing that before long, the rain would start. Rain often brought thunder and lightning. Any minute now, her dad would turn the boat for the safety of the dock.

It was an old dream, a good dream. And most times, the dream stayed good and they made it safely to shore, the same as they always had in real life.

Well, except for that one time. The time the storm came so quickly, pouncing on them out of nowhere, like some wild animal, the sky cracking open with streaks of lightning and booms of angry thunder.

When it finally ended, there was dead calm. Ella floated in her lifejacket, completely alone, crying for her mom and dad and getting only silence in reply.

Tonight, the dream took the bad direction. Lightning lit up the sky, and her mother's voice cried to her, desperate and terrified...

She had no idea what woke her.

One moment she sat on the *Sweet Home* staring up as her mother screamed her name and lighting split the sky—the next her eyes popped open on her shadowed bedroom at the Isabel Inn. She lay there on her back, gazing up at the ceiling, straining her ears for the slightest sound.

Nothing.

She glanced at the blue numerals on the bedside clock—1:01 on Friday morning, and her mouth felt so dry.

Leaving the light off, she threw back the covers, swung her feet to the rug and padded to the bathroom. A glass of tap water later, she returned to the bed.

Before she could reach the comfort of the covers, she heard, faintly, a strangled sort of cry, followed by a rough shout of, "No!"

Ian's voice.

Had someone broken into the suite? Was Ian fighting off an attacker?

Her heart roared in her ears as her mind raced. Should she rush to help him however she could? Call the front desk?

And beyond her bedroom door now? Only silence. Her pulse roaring in her ears, she glanced around the dark room, looking for a makeshift weapon.

Seriously, where could a girl get a sturdy, column-style table lamp when she needed one? The two that flanked her bed had fat glass bases, so unwieldy for self-defense.

On tiptoe, her breath shuddering in and out, she crept to the door, carefully disengaged the lock and pulled it inward.

Dead quiet. In the slanting shafts of illumination from the deck and landscape lights outside, the living area sat silent—and apparently undisturbed.

She heard a low moan. It came from beyond the partway-open door to Ian's room. No sounds of a struggle, though.

On tiptoe, she crossed the living area and peeked in there, saw someone in the bed—Ian, no doubt. As she stared, he groaned again and turned over. She could see his face well enough then to note the signs of distress—eyebrows crunched together, mouth turned down.

So then. A nightmare.

She had them, too—in fact, she'd been having the nightmare she hated most when Ian's shout woke her.

As she debated whether to wake him, he rolled over again and then again. Tossing and turning, he moaned in protest at whatever was happening inside his head.

She couldn't just leave. "Ian…"

He moaned some more and then gruffly shouted, "No!" again.

"Ian, wake up. Ian!"

He just kept rolling around. And then he was kicking and punching. The covers couldn't hold him. He shoved them away. In nothing but a pair of boxer briefs, he went on wrestling with some invisible foe.

"Ian…" She approached the bed, all too aware that she risked getting punched or kicked in the face. "Ian, come on. You need to wake up." She bent too close and then made the mistake of touching the hard bulge of his shoulder.

In the blink of an eye, he grabbed her arm, yanked her down on top of him and then rolled her under him.

"Ian!" She shouted it right in his face.

"Ungh!" His head reared back.

She knew with absolute certainty that he would headbutt her. "Ian, stop!"

He flinched—and then, at last, his eyes blinked open. "What…? Ella?"

They stared at each other. She dared to draw a slow, shaky breath. "You were having a nightmare."

"I don't… My God, Ell. I'm sorry…" He rolled away.

They lay on their backs, side by side, panting as though they'd just run a marathon.

And then he reached over and turned on the

lamp. As she blinked against the sudden brightness, he flopped back on the pillow.

"You okay?" he asked after a moment.

She rolled her head his way. He had one muscular forearm thrown across his eyes. His big chest, glistening with a faint sheen of sweat and crisscrossed with the remnants of pale, faded scars from the long-ago bear attack, expanded and contracted with each heavy breath.

"I'm good. Although, for a minute there, I had zero doubt you would headbutt me."

He turned his face her way again. He looked so tired. "I don't think I would've. But what do I know? Ell. I mean it. I really am sorry."

"Hey." She gave him a smile and waited for the corners of that gorgeous mouth to tip up in answer. "No harm done." She should get up and go.

But she didn't.

He rolled toward her and tucked his hands under his head, the position so boyish, somehow.

She rolled to face him. "Your nightmare just now. Was it the bear attack?"

He punched at the pillow, getting it the way he wanted it, then laying his tousled head back down. His eyes were indigo, a starless night. "Yeah. But it's not a coherent sort of dream, just terror and random images. No logical sequence. Claws and teeth coming at me, blood on snow."

"How awful."

He seemed to be studying her face. Finally, he said, "I must've been loud, to wake you up all the way in your room."

"There was a shout or two. At first, I thought maybe someone had broken in and attacked you."

He watched her so closely, his gaze moving over her face with slow care. Such a beautiful man. And such a pity she couldn't let herself hope for more than friendship with him. He quirked an eyebrow. "You came to save me?"

That made her laugh. "Yeah. Clearly, I need to sign up for that self-defense class I keep meaning to take."

"You're amazing."

"So true."

His gaze held hers. He lifted his hand. Light as a breath, he touched her hair. "And so beautiful."

Her heartbeat had picked up again. It echoed in her ears. "What are you doing, Ian?"

He guided a hank of hair back over her shoulder. "Bad idea, huh?"

Agree with the man, she commanded herself. *Tell him not to be foolish. Tell him that yes, absolutely, it's a bad, bad idea.* But her mouth opened, and she heard herself say softly, intimately, "You never made a move before."

"You're too important to me." He traced a line

down the center of her nose, leaving a trail of longing, a sizzle of sweet heat.

And she needed to call him on his crap. "I'm too important, you just said."

"That's right. You are."

"And yet, tonight, you want to pretend that I'm not?"

His forehead crinkled with a frown. "Didn't I just say it's not wise?"

"But you're doing it, anyway."

His breathing changed, his dilated pupils sharpening, a muscle twitching at his jaw. "You're right. I'm messed up tonight and not thinking clearly. You need to get up and go."

She did no such thing. "Not yet."

He groaned. "Ell. Come on. You're killing me here."

"I need you to tell me why. Why tonight, of all nights, do you want to change the rules?"

"Ell…"

"Just tell me why, Ian. That's what I need to know."

He glared at her—but then, with a hard huff of breath, he gave it up. "Because I'm all screwed up over whatever's going to happen tomorrow. I don't know these people. And yet I'm supposed to call them my family."

"You're going to be fine," she promised, though she had no way to know that for certain.

"Right." He didn't sound one bit convinced. "But there's more."

"I'm not following. More of what?"

"More reasons to want you tonight."

Pleasure tingled through her, a shower of happy sparks. Was she a total fool? Apparently so.

He went on, "I can't stop remembering what happened before we went to dinner, when I barged in on you in your black thong and satin bra, looking all kinds of smoking hot…"

More sparks. And a fizzy-champagne feeling in her tummy, just to hear him say he'd seen her as a desirable woman—desirable enough that she tempted him to take chances with their longtime friendship, with their partnership at Patch&Pebble.

She shouldn't feel happy about that. Lying here bantering with him in this intimate way posed as much of a risk for her as it did for him.

She should rise from this bed and go back to her own room.

Instead, she did more of what she shouldn't do. She teased him, "Kind of did you in, huh, me in my little satin thong?"

"Definitely did me in." His voice was a low growl. "Now I know that about you, Ell."

"That I wear underwear?"

His index finger cradled her chin, and he used the pad of his thumb to brush back and forth across her lips, causing all manner of havoc, striking sparks in her belly, sending shivers skating over her skin. "Such a smart mouth on you. And no. Not that you wear underwear. It's that you're all smooth and willowy underneath your clothes. That you're Ell, my friend. My partner in the company. But you're also a beautiful woman. It's a side of you I never let myself see before. And tonight was a bad night—until I woke up and found you here in bed underneath me."

His eyes were so dark. Turbulent. Yearning. They echoed the feelings that churned down inside her. They made her burn for something she should never let happen.

So foolish, to consider staying right here in this bed with him, to imagine letting herself give in to temptation.

Having sex with Ian…

She had to be out of her mind to make that kind of mistake.

And yet, she did want it—want *him*.

So what if he would never love her? It was the middle of the night on the far side of the country. Just her and Ian.

In his bed.

Why shouldn't she give him tonight—why shouldn't she take tonight for herself?

He leaned in, until they shared her pillow and his forehead met hers. He smelled of sandalwood and clean sweat, and her longing went fathoms deep.

To hold him. Be with him. For this one night.

"Ell," he whispered, his breath warm against her skin. "You need to say it. You need to just tell me no, or…"

"What?"

"Or say yes."

Her body ached for him. But her one absolute rule just might save her from herself. "You have condoms?" She loved her daughter more than her life. But a second unplanned pregnancy—or a surprise STD, for that matter? Not going to happen. "I'm on the pill, but…"

"…no method is foolproof," he finished for her as he tipped up her chin again. Lightning forked through her. "Protection on all fronts. I demand that, too, which is why I always have condoms. After all, I might meet an incredibly sexy brunette in a black thong who shows up in my bedroom to save me from the demons inside my head."

So much for that excuse to back out. She shouldn't be so thrilled at his answer. "Good."

"One more thing."

"What now?" Had he come to his senses and changed his mind? If so, she should be grateful.

But she wouldn't be. Not in the least.

He said, "You need to promise you won't let this come between us—as friends and at work. You need to be sure. It's just for tonight. You know who I am, Ell. I'm not going to wake up tomorrow and be someone different. Something got broken in me before Glynis found me. I don't care for hookups with random women, so I date. But it never lasts, and I doubt it ever will. I get bored—or that's what I tell myself. It's not that, really. I shut down is what I do. I shut down and I just want whoever she is this time gone."

Say no. Get up. Get out of here. The voice of reason in her head just kept getting fainter.

He said, "I want you so bad right now, but I'm not going to change. Remember my history. I'm not that guy, not someone any woman ought to pin her hopes on."

She almost laughed. "You think I don't know you? Please. After all these years?"

"So you're saying…?"

"No worries. I get it." She did get it. It hurt. But the truth did that sometimes. "I agree. It would be tonight and only tonight. And then we go back to being Ian and Ella, good friends and colleagues."

"That's right." He waited. The silence echoed

until he prompted, "Say it, then. Plain and simple. Yes or no?"

Say no, she reminded herself once more. The risks to their longtime friendship and to their partnership at work were too great. She could not take the chance—but she wanted him, and he wanted her. And this moment between them would never come again.

"Yes."

Chapter Five

Ian rolled away from her and stood.

Hardly believing she'd decided to do this, Ella canted up on her elbow and watched his broad, sculpted back, his rock-hard buttocks beneath the boxer briefs, as he walked away from her. His open suitcase sat on the rack in the corner. She watched him bend to take the little packets from a pocket.

He came back to her, a portrait in male grace, his legs thick with muscle, dusted with dark gold hair, one powerful thigh scored with faded scars—claw marks. The large, clear bulge at the front of his briefs had her catching her upper lip between her teeth and slowly biting down on it.

Dropping three condoms on the nightstand, he eased the briefs over his hardness and stepped out of them, letting them fall to the rug by the bed. His erection, thick and long, in scale with the rest of his body, stood up proud and ready.

"You should see your eyes." His grin stretched slowly as he got on the bed with her. "Dark. Soft. Wide."

He stretched out beside her, his warm hand slipping under her hair to cradle her nape as he brought his mouth to hers.

A kiss. Their first ever. Who knew this could happen?

Her own breathy moan echoed in her head as his lips worked their dark magic. Every inch of her softened. Her heart beat a hungry, deep rhythm and moisture gathered between her legs, wetting the cotton crotch of her sleep shorts.

With one hand, he fisted her hair as he held her in place for his mouth. With the other, he touched her, his fingers brushing her throat, closing on it, and then skating downward, over her collarbones and the top of her chest, between her breasts. Her pulse pounded harder as his palm lingered there. Could he feel her heart, the way it beat so hard and deep?

His hand glided lower as he kept on kissing her. He took her tongue, sucking it into the warm cave of his mouth, sliding his around it, groaning low as he tasted her. She moaned in answer.

And then he cupped a breast through her T-shirt, squeezing it hard enough to create a thrilling ache, one that skirted deliciously close to pain—so good. So right. He caught her hard nipple between his thumb and forefinger, pinching it, rolling it. She lifted her chest for him, moaning, eager for more.

His hand skated on down, taking the hem of her shirt, yanking it up, baring her breasts so he could fondle them with nothing in the way as he guided her over onto her back. Letting go of her mouth, he covered a breast, sucking it past his lips, flicking the nipple with his tongue until she was panting his name, holding him hard and tight against her.

She said things, encouraging things, needful things, punctuating them with "Yes," followed by "Oh, please..."

He pulled away. Her eyes fluttered open. His were midnight blue, full of magic and heat.

"Lift your arms."

She obeyed. Grabbing the shirt now wadded up above her breasts, he yanked it higher, over her face. The crewneck caught on her chin. She giggled. But then he gave another tug and off it came.

He tossed it over his shoulder. "There you are." He smiled at her—an intent, predatory sort of smile.

And then he took her mouth again. She kissed him back, a kiss so deep, their tongues twining together, so hungry and wild.

His fingers ventured lower. He slipped them under the waistband of her sleep shorts, touching her intimately.

It felt so good. She let out a pleasured cry.

"You're so wet, Ell. Wet for me…" His low growl of approval echoed in her head as he went on kissing her endlessly, his fingers sliding in her wetness, entering her, pulling out to rub along her eager sex and then to push at her shorts.

"Off," he muttered. "Out of the way…"

She helped him push the shorts down, kicking them off with one foot as she shoved at them with the other.

"Naked," he said, the word a dark promise whispered into her open mouth. "So good. You feel so good…" His fingers opened her, filled her—one and then another and then a third finger, too.

And then he was rolling, pulling her over him to straddle him, getting hold of her bottom with both big hands and guiding her up to her knees.

"Headboard," he commanded.

Tufted and bolted to the wall, the headboard seemed a bad bet for bracing herself. Still, she managed to grab the top of it and slip her fingers in behind it enough that she could hold on tight.

He pulled her throbbing center down onto his face.

Oh. My. Goodness. Ian knew what to do with that perfect mouth of his. He buried his tongue in her, used his chin and even his teeth. She threw back her head and screamed at the ceiling.

"Be good, Ell," he chided from down between her legs. "Someone will sic the manager on us…"

"Okay," she panted. "I will…" The rest was nothing but nonsense syllables as he feasted on her like a starving man at a royal banquet.

It didn't take long. She lit up like a string of firecrackers on the Fourth of July, biting her lip to hold her cries of ecstasy to a reasonable volume. Really, she'd had no idea that a climax he'd so quickly stirred could last such a very long time.

Hers went on and on, and he stayed with her through it, somehow knowing when to ease off and when to latch on tight again.

When the last spark had faded and there was only a shimmer and a quiver and a glow, she sank to her butt on his chest with a long sigh.

He grinned up at her, his face wet from cheek to chin from what he'd done to her. "Ell. Look at you. Flushed and satisfied, hair all over the place, breathing so hard. It's a good look. A great look. Get down here." He rearranged her on top of him, lifting her hips and guiding them lower, so she straddled him, his erection tucked against her sex, her upper body on his chest.

"You're a mess," she said, laughing, sliding her butt onto his washboard stomach, sitting up again. Grabbing her T-shirt, which had somehow ended up right there beside them on the bed, she wadded it up and wiped his face with it.

He licked his lips. "Delicious."

"Yeah, well." She pitched the T-shirt over the side of the bed. "The receiving end was nothing short of spectacular."

He reached up with both hands, pulling her closer. Forking his fingers into her hair at either temple, he combed through the long strands and then wrapped a big hank of it around his right palm. "Come down here." His gravelly voice sent heat streaking along every nerve ending. "Not done with you yet. Not by a long shot." He pulled her down.

Their lips met.

And it started all over again.

His hands touched her everywhere. His skilled mouth conjured more magic. When he rose above her and reached for a condom, she stared up into those beautiful eyes of his and wondered how they'd gotten here—the two of them, after all these years, in bed together, eager and naked, no holds barred.

He rolled the condom down his thick length.

"Ell," he said as he covered her.

"Yes, Ian. Now…" She wrapped her arms and legs around him good and tight.

He came into her in one hard, hungry thrust, stretching her open, big enough to hurt her—but in the best sense of the word. She groaned at the feel of him as he started to move.

Whatever happened, whatever tonight did to them, to what they'd built together in the past nine years, so be it. Right now, joined to him in the most elemental way, she had zero regrets. He kissed her, deep and long and perfectly, as their bodies moved together, hard and fast and hungry.

Her climax barreled toward her—until he slowed down.

Groaning in protest, she slapped at his arm, grabbing on, digging her nails in a little. "I was almost there…"

"Patience." He gave a low laugh and bit the side of her neck as he kept right on moving, taking his time, pulling all the way out until she knew she would lose him—but then sliding right back in, so slow and so deep, like waves in the ocean, a rolling, endless internal caress.

Again, she rose toward the peak, a slower, more thrilling, all-encompassing rise. The pulse of her arousal expanded through her. Her body flared and burned, the pleasure molten, all-encompassing.

And then she was coming, a shudder rippling all through her, across her skin and deeper, down into her bones. It lasted so long, flaring and then flagging, only to start again, climbing higher than before.

As she hit the peak, he rolled them, taking the bottom position, grabbing her hips and yanking her down onto him, getting deeper than ever, though that hardly seemed possible.

When she collapsed on top of him, he rolled again, claiming the dominant position once more. She held on, staring up at him, dazed and so satisfied, as he drove in for the last time and threw his head back with a groan that seemed to come from the very core of him.

When she woke, she felt disoriented at first and didn't know where she was.

Warm, strong arms held her. She felt safe. Cared for.

Slowly, she opened her eyes.

It all came back.

Ian's arms. Ian's bed. He'd had a nightmare and she came to check on him. Things got interesting from there.

It felt so good, being held by him. He smelled

cool and dark, like deep woods. Peering through
the dimness at his sleeping face, she grinned.

Sex with Ian. Amazing.

And it must be late.

She snuggled in again and shut her eyes, but
sleep didn't come.

As the seconds ticked by, she grew uncomfortable. After all, they'd agreed on just this one night.
It seemed safer, wiser, to get out of here before
he woke.

She stirred and pushed gently at his warm, rock-
hard chest. At first, he didn't budge. But when she
pushed a second time, he rolled onto his back.

Carefully, so as not to wake him, she slid out
from under the blankets and eased her feet to the
rug. She got lucky and found her sleep shorts and
wrinkled tee in a wad a few inches from her toes.

Scooping them up, she headed for the door, which
stood open on the central room. Slipping through,
she silently pulled the door shut behind her.

When she emerged from her room at eight the
next morning, Ian sat on the sofa with his laptop
open on the coffee table in front of him. Dressed
in tan pants and a dark blue shirt, he looked so
handsome it made her heart hurt. Glancing up, he
smiled at her, a warm, gorgeous smile that caused

an ache in her solar plexus—desire, apprehension and a wave of sadness, all mixed up together.

"Ready?" she asked, forcing her lips to lift at the corners.

He shut the laptop and rose. "Lead on."

She grabbed her shoulder bag, and they went to the dining room.

"You seem quiet," she remarked—quietly—once the server had poured them coffee and left them alone.

"Big day," he replied.

Her mouth felt dry. She sipped her coffee, hated how uncomfortable she felt and wondered if she should bring up the elephant at the table or if maybe he would.

Oh, God. Would they just sit here, eating their salmon eggs Benedict, pretending that nothing had happened last night?

She sipped more coffee. "It's good," she said, and it was. Hand roasted locally using the highest quality coffee beans, their server had told them.

He sipped, too, and made a low sound of agreement.

Ugh. She and Ian had never had a shortage of things to say to each other. Until now.

Last night had been amazing. But this?

Awkward didn't begin to cover it.

She did what people do when they don't know what to say—focused on her surroundings.

The dining room had windows all around. She stared out at the overcast morning, at the endless expanse of ocean beyond the mist-shrouded beach.

Another couple sat at the next table over— young, early twenties at most. The guy had full sleeves of ink down both lean arms. The girl wore her pink hair in a pixie cut. She had piercings in her nose and lower lip.

The two sat side by side, whispering to each other. A romantic trip to the coast, no doubt. The guy pulled the girl closer, and they shared a slow kiss. When they took a break from their PDA to sip coffee, they kept their bodies canted toward each other, shoulders touching.

Watching them made her wistful. To be that young and that much in love…

She heard the clink of Ian's cup against his saucer and shifted her glance to him as he leaned toward her across the snow-white tablecloth. "Looks like those two had a good night."

"Young love. Nothing like it."

His gaze held hers. "Maybe. Speaking just for myself, though, I had a *great* night." He said it softly. Intimately. Her sad feelings evaporated, and her heart seemed to expand with sheer happiness. And he wasn't finished. "It started out bad. But then you came in to save me, and everything got exponentially better."

She reminded herself not to get carried away here. They'd had sex. He'd enjoyed it a lot. So had she. End of story. "Wow. Exponentially, huh?"

He gave her a slow nod, his gaze holding hers captive as he asked gruffly, "Did some idiot say it would just be one night?"

"That's right." Somehow, she kept her voice cool, relaxed. "Sure was great while it lasted."

Their server appeared with the food. She chattered about wild-caught coho salmon and house-baked English muffins. A moment after she left, she came zipping right back to refill their coffee cups.

"What else can I bring you?" she chirped.

"We're good for now," Ian replied.

"All right then. I'll leave you to it." And finally, she did.

The minute she trotted off, Ian said, "We're here for three more nights." He took a bite of eggs, salmon and muffin. After he swallowed, he set down his fork. "Be a shame to waste them."

Three more nights. She couldn't wait.

Did that make her a fool? When this trip ended, then what?

Wrong questions, she chided herself. She wanted him, and he'd made it thrillingly clear he wanted her right back. They had three nights, just the two of them, on the far side of America, sharing the same suite. Why not make the most of it? For tonight and the two nights that followed, she would do something just for the sheer pleasure it brought.

And the future could damn well look after itself.

"Ell."

"Hmm?"

"Will you consider it?" Dear Lord, the way he looked at her—both tender and tentative.

Yes, she thought. She answered more carefully, "Yes. I will, um, consider it."

One bronze eyebrow lifted. She knew he would press her for a definite answer. But in the end, he only gave her a slow, panty-melting smile and said, "A man can't ask for more."

They ate in silence for a bit. The food was excellent, and now she had tonight to look forward to.

Maybe.

If she didn't get cold feet. If *he* didn't suddenly remember all the reasons having her in his bed could mess with their friendship and screw up their professional relationship.

Right now, they needed to focus on the reason they'd come to Oregon.

Ian had something important to do.

She dared to ask again, "Are you going to call one of your brothers?"

"No need."

She opened her mouth to object.

He went on before she got a word out, "There's a family business a few miles outside town, Valentine Logging. It's on the docks in Warrenton, a short drive from here. Two of my brothers, Daniel and Connor, run the place. We'll head up there after breakfast."

Ian tried to think about good things—like Ella, naked.

Ella naked was the best thing that had happened to him in a long time. He wanted to see her that way again—the sooner the better. Tonight, definitely.

No, she hadn't exactly said yes to that. Yet. But he intended to be at his most convincing once he had her alone in the suite again.

No, he'd never in his wildest dreams planned to put a move on her. He'd meant it when he said she mattered too much to him to take that kind of chance with what they had together.

However, too late now.

He'd blown it. The result had been fantastic—which meant he couldn't wait to blow it again. They had three days left here at the Isabel Inn. He wanted to spend every moment of today and Saturday and Sunday alone with Ella in their suite.

Unfortunately, they hadn't come all the way to Oregon so that he could get Ella into bed.

They'd come so that he could meet the Bravos.

He felt he *should* meet the Bravos.

But did he *want* to meet the Bravos?

Hell, no.

He just wanted to take Ella back to the suite and make love to her all day.

Failing that, he longed to toss their suitcases in the rental car and head for Portland. He could call Audrey on the way, tell her to find them a flight that would get them out of Oregon, stat.

Ella watched him too closely—the way she always did. "Breathe," she said gently. "It's going to be fine."

Of course it was. No big deal. Meet the long-lost family. Piece of cake.

The cheerful waitress brought the bill. He added a large tip and charged it to the room.

Too soon after that, he and Ella climbed in the rented SUV and headed for Warrenton. The drive up the coast took a mere twenty minutes.

The morning mist had burned off, and the sun shone bright when he pulled the Lexus to a stop in front of a barnlike building with a long porch in front, steps going up on either side and a sign above the entrance: Valentine Logging.

Ella said something, but his mind was spinning and he didn't really hear her actual words.

He answered with a nod and, "Let's do this," as he yanked the handle to open his door.

After that, everything had a dreamlike quality to it. In a dream, with Ella at his side, he floated up the wooden stairs, across the deck-like porch and through the door that led into Valentine Logging.

They entered a front office. Nothing fancy— some guest chairs, a table, a middle-aged woman with a kind face behind a desk near an inner door.

The woman rose. "Hey. I'm Midge. What can I do for you?"

"I would like to speak with Daniel Bravo."

"Sure. D'you have an appointment?"

"I don't, no."

"Fair enough. Just give me your name, then, and why you're here."

His throat felt tight. He coughed into his hand to clear it. "I'm Ian McNeill. As to why…" Words completely failed him. He stood there with his mouth half-open and no idea how to go on.

This shouldn't be all that difficult. What was wrong with him? He needed to snap out of it.

Ella came to his rescue. "It's a personal matter concerning the Bravo family."

He'd been grateful for Ella more than once in his life—but never as grateful as right now. Somehow, he managed to shut his mouth. Ella brushed a hand down his arm, a touch meant to reassure. He grabbed her fingers, wove his between them and held on good and tight.

Midge said, "Just have a seat. I'll be right back." She disappeared into the hallway beyond the inner door.

Ella squeezed his hand. "Holding up okay?"

He made a sound—a scoff with a side of absolute terror. "Don't get on me for not calling first."

"Me, get on you? Never."

"Ha. Right."

Midge returned. "Come on back."

He was glad he hadn't sat down. At this moment, he doubted he could have made his rubbery legs take him from sitting to upright. Stiffly, holding on to Ella for dear life, he followed Midge into the hallway. Halfway along on the right, a door stood open.

"Here you go." With a bright smile and a firm nod, Midge turned and headed back the way they'd come.

"Come on in," a man said from inside. Ian caught his first glimpse of the man. Dirty-blond hair, blue eyes—a paler blue than Ian's. Square jaw, broad shoulders. He could be Ian's brother.

Because he was.

Ian pulled his hand from Ella's and guided her in ahead of him. As usual, she understood. He needed her to speak first.

Like the reception area out front, Daniel Bravo's office was simple. Functional. A sitting area, a large desk, a window behind the desk with a view of the Columbia River. Ian took it all in before making himself look at Daniel again.

"I'm Daniel Bravo," he said to Ella and offered his hand.

Ella shook it, gave Daniel her name and stepped aside. "This is Ian McNeill."

"Ian." Daniel seemed nonplussed, but he played along, offering his hand. "Hey."

Ian reached out and took it. They shook and let go. He needed to speak. No more putting it off. He opened his mouth. Hallelujah! Words came out. "I'm, um, finding I don't know exactly how to do this."

Daniel frowned, a look of concern. "Are you all right?"

"Not really…"

"Have a seat." He gestured at the sofa and chairs to Ian's left.

"Uh, no. No sitting. Not yet."

Daniel seemed at a loss as to how to reply to that. "Well. All right. Is there anything I can—"

"No," Ian cut him off, raising a hand, palm out. "Wait."

Daniel cleared his throat. "Okay…"

Ian pushed more words out. "Eighteen years ago, I was adopted from a Russian orphanage by a woman named Glynis McNeill. I was believed to be about ten when Glynis adopted me. At the time, I had no memory of my early life. She took me back to America, gave me her name and brought me up as her own."

From about the moment that Ian had said the word *Russian*, Daniel's face changed. His eyes went blank, a distant, glacial blue. The warm color leached from his tan skin. "Finn. Oh, my God. Finn?" He reached out.

Ian blinked. Was he getting a hug? *Not ready for that.* But his reflexes were nonexistent.

Daniel Bravo wrapped him in thick lumberjack arms. "I knew it," he whispered, the words sandpaper-rough in Ian's ear. "There was something about you. When you walked in here, I knew you." He took Ian by the arms and stood back. "Alive. By God. Alive all this time—Connor! Connor, get in here!"

Ian blinked at him. This all felt…impossible. Unreal. Bizarre.

Another man, clearly a brother, came and stood in the doorway. "What? Did somebody die?" He had darker hair and a leaner build than either Daniel or Ian, but still, the family resemblance was unmistakable.

"I… I've brought proof," Ian heard himself announce, and he whipped out a memory stick. "It's on here. I've been remembering, lately. I hired an investigator. He compiled an extensive file." He shoved it at Daniel, who stared at it, not taking it, until Ian added, "Just, you know, give it a look whenever you're ready."

"Yeah, okay. Will do." With a numb sort of nod, Daniel took it and stuck it in his pants pocket.

Still in the doorway, Connor Bravo asked Daniel, "What's going on?" Daniel glanced at his brother—well, more like stared, glassy-eyed. "Daniel," Connor demanded, "what the hell just happened?"

"It's Finn, damn it," growled Daniel. "Connor, just look at him. It's Finn…"

Connor's gaze swung to Ian. He stared, looking sucker punched. "Finn? What the…?" And then he swore under his breath. "Right. I see it. Finn. My God."

A few seconds later, Ian found himself submitting to a second brotherly embrace. Connor clapped him on the back, exclaiming, "Damn it. I can't believe it. But you're right, Daniel. Just seeing his face, you can tell. It's so obvious…"

When Connor finally let him go, Ian turned to find Ella. She stepped right up and took his arm. He clapped a hand over hers so she couldn't get away.

Connor said, "Come on, sit over here."

Moving in a living dream, he went where Ella guided him. Taking one end of the sofa, he pulled her down to sit by him, good and close so he could grab her, keep her from going if she tried to get up without him.

Daniel offered scotch. It wasn't even ten in the morning, but he and Connor nodded. Only Ella took a pass.

For a while, they talked. It was almost bearable. He gave them the short version of his life so far, explaining a little more about his adoptive mother and the company he'd inherited from her. He spoke of the bear attack all those years ago, and how he still had no idea how he'd traveled all the way from where he'd wandered off near Irkutsk to the hospital in Krasnoyarsk. They agreed on DNA tests. An ancient uncle named Percy Valentine, whom Ian vaguely recalled from the memories he was slowly reclaiming and from the PI's report, would arrange those. Percy had been the one in charge of the search for him over the last twenty years. Connor and Daniel spoke in hushed tones about that.

"It's doubtful, then, that we ever would have

found you," said Daniel, looking grim. "The search for you was extensive, but I don't think it ranged as far away as you ended up."

He explained about his refusal to talk until after Glynis had brought him safely to New York. "I don't think anyone in the hospital or the orphanage where they sent me knew I was American. There were a lot of kids in that orphanage. None of the staff had the time to coax information from some messed-up, scarred kid who didn't talk."

Ian counted the minutes until he and Ella could go. His brothers seemed like good men, but his brain was on overload. He needed to get out, get some space. Process this crap.

Connor asked how long he and Ella had been together.

Ella took that on with an easy smile. "We've been friends since Glynis hired me as an intern at Patch&Pebble. That was nine years ago now."

"Ah," said Connor, apparently readjusting his view of her from romantic interest to good friend.

When Ian, pulling Ella up with him, rose to go, Daniel put up a hand. "Hold on. We need phone numbers and an address, so we can reach you."

"It's all on that stick I gave you."

"Great," said Connor. "But humor us." He whipped out a phone. "Both of you. Send your-

selves a text." Unlocking the device, he handed
it to Ian.

Ian sent the message. His own phone chimed
in his pocket. He passed Connor's phone to Ella,
and she did the same.

Daniel laughed. "Thank you. Now, no matter
what happens, we know how to reach you. Where
are you staying?"

"The Isabel Inn."

"Good choice." Connor clearly approved. "How
long do we have you here in town?"

Have him? What did that mean? How much
time would they expect him to spend with them,
hanging out with them or whatever?

Yeah, he knew that he'd be called on to meet the
rest of the Bravos, but right now all he could think
about was getting away, decompressing, finding
his way past the unreality of having brothers and
sisters, a whole family lost to him completely since
he was eight—both physically and inside his head.

Ella prompted, "Ian…"

He remembered he was supposed to answer
Connor's question. "We're flying back to New
York on Monday."

Daniel let out a relieved-sounding sigh. "Good.
At least we have a few days to get to know you
a little."

Connor said, "Starting tonight."

"Right," Daniel agreed. "Any chance you remember the house where you lived before the ill-fated trip to Russia?"

"I do... On a hill, forest all around, a big backyard, grass and swings, a jungle gym. People in town called it the Bravo house."

"That's it," said Daniel. "I still live in that same house on Rhinehart Hill with my wife and kids. And I'm calling a family dinner tonight. You can see the rest of your brothers and sisters. They're not going to believe it, that you're here at last."

Connor added, "And Aunt Daffy and Uncle Percy are well into their eighties now."

Daniel nodded. "We'll have to take special care telling them, break the news gently."

"Yeah," Connor said. "It's a good shock, but a shock nonetheless."

Daniel nodded again. "I'm betting we can get everyone up at the house for this..."

"No doubt," Connor agreed. "You couldn't keep them away if you tried." He turned to Ian. "Plus, when Daniel calls a family dinner, everybody shows. That's how he brought us up after Mom and Dad died—attendance required at dinner every Sunday *and* any night Daniel decided we all ought to be there. He was a pain in the ass as a father figure."

"I raised you up right." Daniel said it with pride.

"Harper lives in Portland now, but I'm guessing she'll get here no matter what." Ian remembered Harper, eighth born, as a blonde sprite of five or so. She and Hailey, born ten months before her, had been inseparable. Daniel went on, "And right now, luck's with us and Madison's in town."

Ian had no memory of anyone named Madison in the family. "I don't remember a Madison."

Daniel laughed. "That's another long story. Madison Delaney was born Aislinn. The two were switched shortly after birth."

"Hold on," said Ian. "Madison *Delaney*, you said, like the actress?"

"Not *like* the actress. Madison *is* the actress." Daniel beamed with brotherly pride. "That's right, our sister is a bona fide movie star. But don't tell anyone. It's a family secret. Madison likes her privacy."

"Uh, so what you're saying is that Madison is genetically a Bravo and that the Aislinn *I* remember…"

"…is our sister, same as always. Just not by blood. It's a mind-bender, I know. And a great story, but one for another time."

Connor had his phone out again. Both Ian's and Ella's phones chimed. "I just sent you both Daniel's address and phone number." Ian already had them.

But before he could say so, Daniel announced,

"Let's say six thirty. Up at my house, the Bravo house."

Connor put in, "We'll get everyone together—wives, husbands, fiancés and kids included. Uncle Percy and Aunt Daffy, too."

"Just come." Daniel clapped him on the shoulder. "I know this has to be seriously overwhelming. But you'll get used to us." Daniel's eyes were wet. He blinked the moisture away and aimed a giant smile at Ian. "Man, I cannot tell you. I always believed this would happen, but sometimes I doubted."

"We all did," Connor said gruffly.

"But now you're here. It's real," said Daniel. "And it's so damn good to have you home at last."

Chapter Six

Ella walked out of Valentine Logging with Ian clutching her hand so hard, she almost feared he would snap a bone.

He let her go so they could get into the Lexus.

She hooked her seat belt and gasped when he backed out fast from the space, slamming into Drive and speeding out of the graveled lot like something really bad chased after them.

"Are you okay?"

"Fine." Staring hard out the windshield, he hit the gas, his mouth a hard line.

"Ian, come on. You are not fine."

Dead silence from his side of the car—and

when he turned onto the Coast Highway, he went even faster.

"Ian, you're going to get a ticket if you don't slow down."

He sent her a seething look, but at least he put his foot on the brake and slowed to the speed limit.

"Are we going back to the hotel?" she asked.

For that, he granted her a sharp nod and a gruff, "That's right."

She gave up and let the rest of the ride go by in silence.

At the inn, he parked in the lot and got out so fast, she wondered if maybe his seat had caught fire. He headed straight for the lobby and from there to the suite. She followed, kind of wishing she had somewhere else to go.

In their room, he shut the door too hard and turned to her. "I'm sorry," he said through clenched teeth.

She stared up into his haunted eyes. The visit to Valentine Logging had thrilled his long-lost brothers. Ian, though? Not so much. "Are you going to talk to me?"

He took her by the upper arms in a too-firm grip. She couldn't decide if he thought she needed steadying—or he was holding on for dear life. "I can't do this."

"You just did. I know it wasn't easy for you. But objectively, it went great."

"Objectively?" he snarled. "Ella, what does that even mean?"

"It means that your brothers were so happy to see you, that the rest of the family can't wait to get to know you, that they seemed to me like good people, the kind of men who'll have your back no matter what happens. It means you didn't lose your only family when Glynis died. You've got a bunch of brothers and sisters who never gave up on finding you someday—not to mention an ancient great-aunt and great-uncle who've been searching for you all this time." What she wouldn't give to suddenly discover she had a big, loving family somewhere in this world, a family that couldn't wait to meet her, to bring her into the fold.

Ian refused to see the situation the way she did. He muttered, "I don't know these people. They're like ghosts to me, vague memories, more and more of them, all this stuff coming back to me, filling up my head. I remember them all, but mostly, those memories feel like they belong to someone else."

When they got home to New York, she would start working on him to see his old therapist or find someone new to talk to. But right now, she needed to figure out a way to settle the man down.

"I need to go," he said.

"Go where?"

"Home." He released her and headed for his bedroom. "Pack," he said over his shoulder. "I'll call Audrey on the way to Portland. She can get us a flight."

Ella remained by the door where he'd left her as she tried to decide what to do next. He would regret running away, but outright resistance at this juncture would be futile.

She could hear him in the bedroom, pacing, see him each time he went by the open door—from the bathroom to his suitcase, to the chair in the corner—gathering up his things, stuffing them in the bag.

Slowly, she approached the doorway to his room. When she got there, she leaned against the door frame.

He glanced up from his suitcase and scowled at her. "What'd I say? Come on, Ell. You need to pack."

She gave him a smile—a serene one, she hoped. "I will."

"Well, then…?"

"First, though, I think we could both use a nice walk on the beach."

His scowl deepened. "Don't try to redirect my attention. We're going. As soon as possible. You need to pack."

"I get it." She held out her hand. "A walk on the beach. Please?"

For a moment, she knew she'd lose him. He'd return to his frantic packing.

But then he let out a slow breath and grumbled, "I know what you're doing."

She kept her hand out and waited, holding his unhappy gaze.

Finally, he came to her, took the hand she offered, guided it behind her and pulled her in close.

With a sigh of relief, she let her head rest on his hard chest.

His free hand touched her hair at the crown of her head. Skimming a finger down over her cheek, he lifted her chin. "I don't deserve a friend like you."

"Hmm. You have a valid point. Because yeah. I'm pretty great—and you, my friend, need your feet in the sand."

They used the set of wooden stairs off the back deck and then took the second, longer set down to the beach.

It was a little before eleven, and the sky had cleared to a powder blue. They took off their shoes, rolled their cuffs and walked to the water's edge, where they turned and walked south, their footprints shining in the wet sand, vanishing as the fingers of each wave slid in and rolled away. After they'd gone maybe half a mile, Ella thought he seemed calmer.

Up ahead, a little girl and a boy who looked a bit older built a lopsided sandcastle twenty feet from the water. Ian took Ella's hand and led her closer to where the children squatted over their creation, patting at sand, the girl with her own small hands, the boy with a bright-colored shovel.

"I should call Abby," he said.

She nodded. "About four thirty's a good time, that's seven thirty there. She'll be home at her dad's. They should be done with dinner by then."

He tugged on her hand and they continued down the beach until they reached a headland where erosion had created a row of sea stacks marching down to the water's edge. One of the stacks not far from the waterline made a bench-like seat. They dropped their shoes in the sand, perched on the stack side by side and stared out over the constantly shifting water.

"I keep thinking I can't do this," he said, his eyes on the horizon.

"That's natural."

"It doesn't *feel* natural."

"So maybe *natural* was the wrong word. I'm guessing it's overwhelming for you. I mean, I feel kind of overwhelmed myself, and it's not even my family. But you didn't come all this way *not* to meet them."

"Do there *have* to be so many of them, though?"

She leaned his way and nudged him with her shoulder. "You're going to get through this. And once you do, you'll be glad you stuck it out."

He put his arm around her. She rested her head on his shoulder.

"Thanks, Ell, for coming with." She felt his breath against her hair and thrilled to the gentle pressure of his lips on the top of her head.

We're friends, she reminded herself.

Friends, and she needed to remember that. Friendship and great sex, nothing more going on here.

A half hour later, they climbed the stairs to the deck off the living area of their suite. A faucet by the glass door had a short hose attached to it. They rinsed their sandy feet before they went inside.

The moment she shut the door, he pulled her close.

Her shoes hit the floor and his followed right after as his beautiful mouth came down on hers. She gave herself up to it—to his kiss, to his big arms holding her so hard and tight.

When he lifted his head, she teased, "I'm not having sex with you unless you promise we're going up to your brother's house for dinner tonight and we're not leaving Oregon until Monday, as planned."

"That's blackmail." He dipped his head and caught her lower lip between his teeth, biting down just enough to make her moan.

Carefully, she pulled back to look in his eyes. "That hurt."

"You didn't *sound* hurt."

"Okay, fine. It was a good kind of hurt—and as for your blackmail remark, it's not blackmail if it's for your own good."

He tried to pull her close again.

She braced her palms against his rock-hard pecs and resisted. "Say yes. Say we'll go to dinner at Daniel's tonight and we'll stay in Oregon until Monday."

"How come you're so pushy? And why have you always been that way?"

"I get things done." She put a hand to her ear. "And that didn't exactly sound like a yes."

He grumbled, "Like I said, pushy."

"I'll be right here with you. All the way. Promise."

"Damn right you will."

"Say it, Ian."

"Yes." He growled the word and framed her face between his big, warm hands. She breathed in the scent of him—sandalwood, with a hint of the ocean after their walk. And man. All man. "And you bet your gorgeous ass you'll be here with me. There's no way I'm getting through this without you. Now kiss me and let me take you to bed. I need to work off some tension, and I need to do that with you."

"Whatever you want, Ian."

"Say that without smirking, Ella."

Lifting on her bare toes, she wrapped her hand around his nape and yanked him down for a kiss.

In his bed, an hour later, after he'd done all manner of wonderful things to her very willing naked body, he canted up on an elbow and lazily combed his fingers through her hair, spreading it out on the white pillow in a dark, wavy fan. "I think I've got a thing for your hair." He picked up a lock and brought it to his face. "Smells like coconut."

"It's called shampoo."

He chuckled, bent close and whispered in her ear, "Your stomach just growled."

"Yeah, 'cause you keep having sex with me instead of getting me some lunch."

"We can have a picnic basket sent over from the dining room."

"Ah. I like it. A picnic lunch in bed."

"Done." He braced up on an elbow, reached

across her for the hotel phone and called room service. When he hung up, he gazed down at her so tenderly. "Food will arrive at the door in about twenty minutes. We should hurry."

"Hurry to do what?"

"Here. Let me show you…" His mouth met hers as he peeled back the covers.

Nineteen minutes later when the food arrived, she was just catching her breath.

"Don't move from this bed," he commanded.

"Not a problem." She pushed her tangled hair out of her eyes and pulled the sheet up to cover her bare breasts.

As for Ian, he got up, pulled on his pants and headed for the living area.

Their picnic was fun. They sat on the tangled bed and ate sandwiches on freshly baked sourdough bread with chips and pickles—and chocolate chip cookies for dessert.

Ian really liked the cookies, so much so that he distracted her with a kiss as he snatched one of hers.

They wrestled for it, which meant cookie crumbs got everywhere.

They made love again, anyway.

At four thirty, he grabbed his phone and called Abby. Ella lay back on the crumb-strewn sheets and listened to him talking with her daughter, acting like the second dad everyone always accused him of being.

He laughed at something Abby had said—and it happened. Right then, something twisted inside her at the full, easy sound of that laugh.

Ella tried to throw up an internal wall of denial.

But it didn't really work.

It seemed more and more possible that Ian's bitchy ex-girlfriend had gotten it right: Ella loved Ian.

And not just as her very good friend.

He caught her eye and winked at her as Abby said something on the other end of the call.

How could she have let this happen?

More important—how could she make it stop?

Not by continuing to fall into bed with him, that was for sure.

Would that help, though, to call a halt to this while-we're-in-Oregon sexfest they'd decided to indulge in?

No! cried her foolish heart.

Because who cared if it would help her get over him? She didn't want to call a halt to this magic between them. She wanted every moment in his bed that she could get.

She wanted to play this out to the inevitable end, the one he'd warned her about last night. The end where he got bored, shut down and wanted her gone.

He watched her as he talked to Abby, sudden questions in his eyes. Had he seen something in her expression that worried him? He tipped his head to the side, mouthed, "You okay?"

She remembered—he'd winked at her, hadn't he?

With a grin, she winked back.

His expression relaxed. Now she envied him his absolute belief that he would never fall for anyone, that his heart was locked up tight, safe from breaking.

Silently, she called herself all kinds of fool.

Crap on a cracker. No question about it. She teetered on the edge with him. Maybe she hadn't quite fallen in love with him.

Or maybe she just refused to admit it had already happened.

But somehow, it all felt inevitable now. One more step.

And over she would go…

Chapter Seven

The Bravo house, a gorgeous three-story Colonial built at the turn of the twentieth century, stood above a wide, green sweep of lawn. The long, deep front porch invited everyone, guests and family alike, to have a seat, get comfortable, enjoy a tall iced tea on a hot day or maybe some cocoa on a cold winter's night.

Ian recognized the house immediately. It looked very much as it had in his newly recovered memories of the place—from the outside, anyway. Inside, many of the rooms had been updated, with a now-modern kitchen and new fixtures throughout.

When he and Ella arrived, the place was already

packed with his newfound family. Everywhere he turned, another familiar face smiled at him, most of them with blue eyes full of hope and joy.

They surrounded him. He thought he would suffocate under the force of their sheer happiness at the sight of him. As soon as he finished dealing with one of them, a new one came at him. He hugged them all.

Strangely, he found he recognized them, though most of them had yet to reach their teen years when he wandered off that snowy path near Irkutsk, never to see any of them again. Until now—on this cool, clear evening in May, two decades later, when they were all grown up, with husbands and wives and kids of their own.

Even Gracie, the baby of the family, four years old when he'd disappeared, had grown into a gorgeous young woman with an infectious laugh. His youngest sister had a job teaching history at Valentine Bay High and a fiancé she clearly adored. When she got married in June, she would have twin stepdaughters, too. Gracie had said yes to Connor's best friend, Dante Santangelo, of all people. It was a match that Ian never would have predicted. Gracie was a ray of sunshine. The way Ian remembered it, even as a kid, Dante had been a brooding, grim, too-serious sort of guy. Not so much anymore, though. Every time Dante looked at Gracie, he lit up from the inside.

Somehow, Ian got through all the introductions, the endless hugs and exclamations of wonder and excitement that he'd "come home" at last.

He didn't feel at home, not in the least. He felt awkward and uncomfortable and tried hard not to show it. They were good people, this family he'd forgotten for twenty years. He didn't want to hurt or insult them with the uncomfortable truth that, while he did recognize them, did know a lot about each of them as children, he didn't feel any true connection with a single one of them.

He felt like a phantom limb. Not really *there*, yet the family he'd been born into still considered him an actual, physical part of the family experience they shared.

Only the old people, the brother and sister octogenarians, Percy and Daffodil Valentine, seemed to have any clue of how he really felt. Percy spoke to him of the years they'd spent trying to find him, the dead ends they'd pursued, the promising leads that had come to nothing. Daffy treated him with care, gently patting his arm with her wrinkled, spotted hand, encouraging him to "take good care" of himself, to "give himself time to adjust"—whatever that meant.

Even the children seemed glad to see him.

Two-and-a-half-year-old Marie, Daniel and Keely's daughter, toddled right up to him and held up her arms. "Finn. Hug."

He resisted the urge to inform her that his name was not Finn and hadn't been for twenty years. Instead, he bent, scooped her up and submitted to her wrapping her chubby arms around his neck and planting a slobbery kiss on his cheek, after which she announced, "Wuv you." For that he'd managed a smile, to which she responded, "Down, now."

He set her on the floor next to the family basset hound, Maisey Fae, and she tottered off, the dog right behind her.

For him, the evening dragged on forever. Without Ella's help, he never would have made it through. If not for her, he would have run down the sloping front walk, jumped in the Lexus and burned rubber getting the hell out of there.

Ella didn't hover, but she stayed in sight. He only had to glance over and make eye contact with her. A minute later, she would appear at his side. He would feel for her hand. She would give it, slipping her fingers in his, gazing up at him with an easy smile. Her hand in his grounded him. Her touch said she understood, she had his back, she wouldn't vanish when he needed her.

Her smile somehow promised that everything would turn out right.

A couple of hours crawled by. He got through the meal and a brief one-on-one with each of his siblings save Aislinn—and Madison, the movie star, the blood sister he'd never met until tonight, the one who'd been switched with the Aislinn he remembered as his sister from all those years ago.

The few moments with Matthias had been the hardest. Matt had a wife now, Sabra, whom he clearly adored, and a newborn son, Adam, named after Sabra's deceased dad. Matt seemed tense. Ian sympathized. He felt the same, not about Matt specifically, but about all of it. About being here in Oregon, about dealing with all these people he'd finally remembered but didn't feel much actual connection to.

Ian sensed that Matt blamed himself for what had happened that long-ago day when the boy, Finn, had wandered away from the rest of the family. But in their brief conversation, Matt never broached the subject and Ian didn't really want to get into it, anyway. He did have the urge, though, to reassure Matt, to explain that by the time he'd spotted the small, white creature off the path in the snow, his grouchy older brother had been the last thing on his mind.

The right moment to say all that never exactly presented itself, so Ian just let it go.

And by then, he'd started seeing the light at

the end of the tunnel in terms of this excruciating evening. He began planning his escape. He just needed to say a quick thank-you to Daniel and Keely, grab Ella, and get out of there.

About then, Aislinn and Madison appeared on either side of him.

Madison—who should have been Aislinn—took his hand. Talk about bizarre. Hadn't she just won an Oscar a month or two ago? How many movies had he seen her in? Several. Never would he have guessed that America's darling would turn out to be his sister.

She had that Bravo look, though, golden hair and the blue eyes to go with it—also, a belly out to here. She and her husband, Sten Larson, expected their first child any day now.

"Come outside to the porch with us," said Madison.

"Just for a few minutes," added Aislinn, a petite woman with dark eyes and hair. Ironically enough, Aislinn looked like a movie star, too. Maybe Audrey Hepburn, or one of those French actresses with their pretty, big-eyed, delicate faces.

The two women guided him through the entry hall and out the front door. They were on the porch before he thought to object or shoot Ella one of his frantic, get-over-here-and-save-my-sorry-ass looks.

"Let's sit down, shall we?" said Aislinn. It wasn't really a question. They took him to a row of cushioned wicker chairs near one end of the long, deep porch and pulled him down into the center one. The two of them settled in the chairs to either side of his, flanking him, same as before.

"So how are you holding up?" asked Aislinn.

"Holding up? Good. Fine."

Those enormous dark eyes called him a liar. Her words were gentle, though. "You're in better shape than I was, then."

"Excuse me?"

"When I found out I wasn't really me, after all."

"Well, of course you're you," he argued, annoyed that she would say such a thing.

"Yeah, but I didn't feel like me when I found out that the woman I knew as my mother hadn't given birth to me, that I was no blood relation to my dad, whom I adored. That another woman had carried me inside her body and my birth father had switched me the night I was born, changed my life completely, in order not to have to acknowledge me. At first, it made me feel I was less than before. But over time, I've come to see that I really am still a Bravo—and I'm also the child of a secret affair between a woman I was never destined to meet and a man I had never liked in the least."

Madison chuckled, a rich and husky sound.

America's darling was famous for her laugh. "I was mostly just in denial after I found out. And when I did finally reach out to the family, I didn't even call first."

Now he felt defensive. "You mean, same as I did, showing up unannounced at Valentine Logging today, is that what you're getting at?"

"Finn," said Aislinn in a soothing tone. "It's not a criticism. We're only trying to say that we understand a little of what you must be going through."

"My name is Ian." He said it too fast—and much too harshly.

"Yes, of course, Ian," said Aislinn, her voice so calm, full of understanding. "I'm sorry."

Now he kind of hated himself. Aislinn only wanted to make him feel better, and he'd jumped all over her. "No, *I'm* sorry. I shouldn't get on you. That's how you knew me, as Finn."

Madison laughed again—a pained sound this time. "Believe it or not, we dragged you out here to reassure you that we understand a little of what you're going through. We know it's not easy, finding out that who you thought you were isn't the whole story—and no, your situation is not the same as ours, but there are certain similarities. We get how hard it is, we really do."

Aislinn added wryly, "Too bad we're just making it worse."

Before he could figure out what to say next, the front door opened, and Ella stepped out.

Had he ever been so relieved to see anyone? Doubtful. He jumped up and went to her as Matthias came out behind her.

Ella gazed up at him, a frown between her brows. "Are we interrupting?"

"Of course not," said Aislinn.

Madison added, "We were just trying to be helpful—too bad we failed miserably."

Even Ian chuckled at that. "Not true." It was a flat-out lie. He didn't feel the least helped by what had just transpired, but Madison and Aislinn had the best of intentions. He refused to give them any more grief for making an effort with him. "And really, we should get going." No, they shouldn't. They should stick around, spend more time with this family he'd just found. But he couldn't. He only wanted out of there—and the sooner the better, as far as he was concerned. "I'll just run in and thank Daniel and Keely."

"No need," said Madison.

"You sure?" He should go in and say goodbye properly. But then somebody else would probably try to get him talking...

"Go," said Aislinn. "It's obvious you've had enough Bravo family togetherness for one night.

We'll thank Daniel for you. It's not a problem, I promise you."

"All right, then." He took Ella's hand and felt instantly better.

But then Matt said, "One more thing…"

Irrational dread crawling up the back of his neck, Ian turned to the last familiar face he'd seen before he veered off that snowy path twenty years ago and his life changed forever. "Sure." Somehow, he managed to make the word sound friendly.

"Daniel says you're here through Sunday?"

"Leaving early Monday morning, yes."

"So we were thinking tomorrow we could make it a day, just the Bravo brothers—you, me, Daniel, Connor and Liam. Liam's got a new boat. We'll take it out, the five of us."

Stuck on a boat with four virtual strangers who happened to be his brothers. He didn't want to go.

But Ella squeezed his hand. "Sounds great." She turned those big eyes on him. Those eyes said, *You need to do it. This is what you're here for.*

Did she have to be so damn right? "Thanks, I would like that," he said, not liking it in the least.

Matt looked relieved. "Wonderful. We'll text you the time and place to meet."

"I've got an idea." Aislinn grinned at Madison. "While the Bravo brothers are out on the boat, the rest of us ought to get together, whoever can make it. We'll grill some steaks out at Wild River." Aislinn lived with her husband, Jax, up near Astoria at his ranch, Wild River.

Madison rubbed her giant stomach. "Absolutely—Ella, you in?"

"Yes." Ella sent the sisters her glowing smile. "I'm so there." She looked honestly pleased at the invitation. In fact, she'd seemed to enjoy the whole evening. She should bottle that enthusiasm and share it with him.

"Good." Madison nodded her approval. "I'm guessing Karin will want to come." Karin was Liam's wife—and Sten's sister. The Bravos were a study in complex family relationships. Ian could barely keep them all straight. "We'll make the calls, get it all worked out. And we'll pick you up, Ella."

Ella beamed. "Wonderful. Connor has my number. Text me everything I need to know."

As Ian pulled her down the steps and along the walk to the car, she gave the three on the porch one last wave. He walked faster. The quicker they got away, the less likely some random Bravo would find a reason to call them back.

Ian said nothing on the return trip to the inn. Ella didn't mind. He seemed pretty stressed, and usually, when Ian felt stressed, it worked out better simply to leave the man alone.

If he needed to talk about it, he would. If not, she had a feeling there would be lots of manly sharing tomorrow on Liam's new boat. Ian would get more than he'd ever wanted of meaningful conversation then. For now, a little peace and quiet seemed the best way to go.

They entered their suite at a few minutes after nine. Would he want to be alone tonight?

Most likely.

That made her sad. Now that she'd thrown caution and good sense to the wind and slept with him, she didn't want to miss her chance to do it again. At breakfast, he'd asked her to consider sharing more nights—three nights, to be specific, until they returned to New York.

She wanted those nights.

But what she wanted didn't come first, not now. This trip wasn't about her. After an evening with all the relatives he hadn't seen in twenty years, he probably needed to be left alone to rest and recuperate. The exhaustion in his eyes said he required time to recover from all the family togetherness.

As he shut the door to the outer hallway and she flicked on one of the sitting room lamps, their phones buzzed, one right after the other. He pulled his from his pocket as she did the same.

He held his phone up, screen out. "All the information I ever needed about hanging with my brothers tomorrow on Liam's boat."

"And mine's from Aislinn. They'll be here to pick me up at eleven. I should wear something I can ride a horse in, and if I don't have boots, Aislinn thinks she has some that will work for me." She widened her eyes. "Horseback riding is not my best event. I'm going to need the slow, sweet, *old* horse."

"I'm sure Aislinn can arrange for that." He put his phone away.

They regarded each other across the distance from the sofa to the door. She thought about last night and this afternoon, about kissing him, about all the lovely things he'd done to her body.

And then she put those thoughts away. "All right, then. I think I'll take a long bath and try to get a good night's sleep." She turned for the open door to her room.

He moved silently. One moment he stood by the door and the next, he was right behind her. "Hey."

Excitement quivered through her. "Hmm?"

He stepped in even closer. Havoc erupted within her as he eased her hair away from her neck, his warm finger brushing her nape, sending sparks of sensation flaring across her skin. "Are you having second thoughts, Ell?" His voice was soft yet rough, a whisper of sandpaper in her ear.

"Um, not exactly." Her own voice sounded strange to her—young and hesitant and so very serious.

"But you're going to your room alone anyway?"

With a careful sigh, she let herself lean back against him. He felt so warm. So solid and strong. "After all the togetherness at Daniel's house, I thought maybe you would need a little time to yourself."

Now he put both hands on her, one on each shoulder. His thumbs traced a burning path on either side of her throat—down and then up and then down again. "What I need is another night with you."

A lovely shiver went through her. "More than you need time alone?"

He laughed then, a low sound, both rough and tender. "Hell, yes."

Anticipation filling her belly with butterflies, she turned to look up into his waiting eyes. "Well, then yes, please. I would love another night with you."

He stared down at her for the longest time.

"What?" she demanded.

"For a moment there, I just knew that you would

pull away, go through that door and shut it behind you."

She laughed. Because he wanted her and she
wanted him and no matter what, tonight would be
fabulous. Okay, fine. Just maybe she'd made the big
mistake of falling in love with him. So what? People
gave their hearts all the time. Sometimes it didn't
work out. Once they returned home, she would just
have to learn to get over him, to move on. "It did
occur to me that maybe we shouldn't…"

He cut her off with a finger to her lips. "Not.
Another. Word—except yes. I'll take a yes."

She went on tiptoe and whispered in his ear.
"Yes."

"Right answer." He bent just long enough to
scoop her high in his arms.

Ella woke very late, naked in Ian's bed.

He'd thrown an arm across her upper chest, and
one big leg rested on her thighs.

Yes, it had been touch-and-go at Daniel's. But
boy, did things get good later. She might possibly have beard burn on her face and inner thighs.
Also, muscles she'd forgotten she had ached in the
loveliest sort of way.

Beard burn and muscle aches had never felt so
good.

Now came the big question. Should she ease

out from under the warm weight of his hold and go back to her own room?

She felt a little unsure about the idea of facing daylight in his bed—or more specifically, waking up in daylight beside him. Why that seemed a bridge too far, she couldn't really say.

However, yesterday morning, when she'd emerged from her room to find him on his laptop in the sitting area, he'd said nothing about the way she'd left his bed during the night. Could she assume that he approved of her leaving before morning?

It seemed very *Ian* to want a woman in his bed but then to prefer not to wake up beside her— and really, that was just sad. She frowned into the darkness.

Get over yourself, Haralson. You knew who he was when you climbed in his bed.

Yes, she'd have a price to pay for this stolen fling with her boss and good friend.

And what about the whole love question?

At some point, she'd have to face that head-on, too.

But she'd made a conscious decision to enjoy this time with him. She needed to stop second-guessing every little thing, needed to give herself completely to loving every minute of the few nights they would have together.

"Don't even think about it." His sleep-rough voice interrupted her silent debate with herself.

She hardly had to move at all to press her forehead to his. "I didn't know you were awake."

"You woke me up," he whisper-grumbled.

"How? I didn't say a word or move a muscle."

"Yeah, but you're thinking of going back to your room, aren't you?"

She almost giggled, which was nothing short of ridiculous. She'd never been the giggly type. Until now, apparently. "Okay, yeah. Let's call it an internal dialogue, a silent discussion of the pros and cons of leaving versus staying here with you."

"The way I understand it, you need two people to have a dialogue."

"Of course you would believe that. You're a man."

His arm tightened across her chest as he pressed his lower leg against the outside of her knee, pulling her closer. "There are no pros to leaving my room."

"Sure there are."

"Name them."

"In my room, I get the bed all to myself."

"That's one—and not a particularly good one. Stay."

"Hmm." She kissed the space between his eyebrows. "I admit, I'm tempted."

He nuzzled closer, catching her chin between his teeth, biting down gently and then laying a light trail of kisses up over her cheek to her ear, where he whispered, "I think I need to up my game."

"Nobody's stopping you."

He kissed her. And then he rolled her under him and kissed her some more.

After the third kiss, he lifted his head and met her gaze through the shadows. "So then. Staying or going?"

"I have no idea what you're talking about. Kiss me again…"

In the morning, Ian woke to find Ella in the bed beside him.

What a great moment—opening his eyes and finding her there, her hair all over the place, her lips slightly parted as she snored softly.

Cutest thing he'd ever seen. Made him hard, too.

So he reached out, pulled her close and showed her how happy he was to see her. Sex with his best friend had turned out to be something of a revelation. Who knew his good buddy Ella would be amazing in bed?

Certainly not him. How could he have known? Up till Thursday night, he'd never let himself think of her that way.

But as of now, well, he couldn't help thinking

that barging in on Ella in her sexy bra and tiny thong had been a great move, after all. Talk about seeing a woman in a whole new light—and then he'd gotten lucky. She'd said yes to him. Now he could touch her and hold her and make her moan his name.

The disorientation and confusion he experienced whenever he had to deal with his newfound family aside, this trip to the Pacific Northwest had turned out to be one hell of a wonderful time—the best time he'd had in a long while. He intended to love every minute of this thing with her. It would end much too soon.

Tonight and tomorrow just plain weren't long enough.

Already, he found himself imagining ways to convince her they should continue together like this after they got home.

But he wouldn't. They would cut it clean then, as they'd agreed.

And no, he couldn't predict how things would go between them when it was over. They might have a rough patch as they dealt with going back to friends and colleagues only.

But one way or another, he knew they would make it work. He had faith in him and Ella, as a team.

Chapter Eight

After breakfast, back in the suite, Ian wanted to drag Ella straight to his bed. They had a little time before he had to meet his brothers.

But they had Abby to consider.

They video chatted with her on his laptop. The kid wanted to know all about the Bravos. She said she couldn't wait to meet them. She wished she'd made the trip with them, that she could go on the boat with Ian and his brothers—and she wanted to spend a day on horseback at Wild River Ranch, too.

He felt uncomfortable listening to her go on about tagging along the next time he flew out to

Oregon. Because thinking about returning? Right now, he couldn't say for certain that he would get through *this* visit without losing his shit.

No way he wanted to imagine coming back.

Why would he?

He'd severed his connection to the Bravos and this town, severed it by necessity when Siberia swallowed him whole. Somewhere between the bear attack, the grim horror of the hospital and the misery of the orphanage, he'd let the Bravos go in order to survive.

He got it now—the pain of losing his family, of his complete aloneness in a strange land where no one spoke words he could understand, had been unbearable. So he'd recreated himself as the scarred, mute boy with no history and no family— a boy who felt nothing, who only survived.

And then Glynis had come. He'd known hope for the first time he could remember. And when she took him home with her, he'd recreated himself a second time, as her son.

So what if a few old memories of his life as Finn Bravo had finally come back to him? Reclaimed memories didn't suddenly make him a grown-up version of his childhood self. He'd come here to face the past, yeah. He hated it, but he felt driven to do it, anyway. And then he would be done with it.

On Monday, he and Ella would go home.

End of story. Back to real life.

Abby wheedled, "I'm thinking we should visit at Christmastime, you know? We could all three—you, me and Mom—go to Oregon together. Not for Christmas Day or anything, but sometime during my Christmas vacation. Like as soon as I get off school. That would work great. I've never seen the Pacific Ocean. It's about time I did."

"It's doubtful that will happen," he said carefully, reluctant as always to say no to her outright.

"But *maybe*?" Abby twinkled at him, showing off the cute dimples in her round cheeks. "Just think about it, Ian. It could be so much fun."

Ella came to his rescue with a single word. "Abigail." She said it gently, but Abby always got the message when her mother used her full name.

The dimples faded, but Abby's smile never wavered. "Okay, then. We can talk about it some other time, I guess…"

When they wrapped it up a few minutes later, it was time for him to go meet the Bravo brothers.

He hesitated at the door. Madison wouldn't arrive to pick up Ella for another hour or so. "I hate to leave you here alone."

"Why?" Ella, looking very country in snug jeans and a plaid button-up, had followed him to the little square of entry hallway. "Even if for some reason the visit to Wild River gets canceled, I'm hardly going to suffer while hanging at the beach in our luxury suite. And they do have a spa here, you know? I could get myself a hot rock massage and a fresh mani-pedi."

He couldn't keep his hands off her. Reaching out, he eased his fingers under the satiny fall of her hair and wrapped them around the nape of her neck. "Now I'm jealous."

"Of what?"

"Whoever gets to put their hands on you, gets to give you a massage and paint your toenails. I'm surprisingly good at massage, and I wouldn't mind polishing those pretty toes for you. Maybe we should both just stay here." He pulled her closer, until she was right up against him, so slim and soft and flexible, but wearing way too many clothes. With his free hand, he toyed with the top button on her shirt.

She wrapped her fingers around his and gently pushed them away. "You didn't come all the way across the country to hang out in the room and paint my toenails for me."

He made use of the hand still curled around her nape to ease her in nice and close to him again. Conveniently, she tipped her head back a little, bringing her sweet mouth within a couple of inches of his.

"All right then," he bargained, "forget the massage and pedicure. Concentrate on you and me and the two big beds in this suite. We haven't tried out your bed yet. We need to do that—and come to think of it, who needs a bed? We could make use of the sofa or maybe that club chair over there."

"I think you've become obsessed with sex."

"I have, yes. I need it. But within specific parameters."

"Wow. You've got parameters now?"

"Yeah. I need a lot of sex, and it needs to be with you." He dipped his head enough to brush his lips across hers. "You complaining?"

"I most definitely am not."

He took a longer kiss the second time.

She let out a soft sigh, and he really did consider blowing off the Bravos and doing something a lot more fun.

But then she gave him a gentle shove. "You've got somewhere you need to be. Go meet your brothers."

Five minutes later, he was behind the wheel, heading north on 101.

Liam Bravo had texted Ian directions to West Basin Marina in the Port of Astoria, where Liam docked his boat.

Ian parked his car in the marina lot and found Connor waiting for him at the end of the specified dock. As they climbed aboard the thirty-four-foot cruiser, Ian saw that he was the last to arrive. Great-Uncle Percy had come, too.

Once out on the water, they passed under the Astoria-Megler Bridge that connected Oregon to Washington State. Drinking local craft beer, with Liam at the helm, they soared up the wide Columbia. Ian enjoyed the spectacular views and felt grateful that none of his brothers or the ancient great-uncle tried to get him talking about anything too uncomfortable—like life in a Russian orphanage or how it had been for him not remembering his family of origin for most of his life so far. Percy had brought the DNA kits. He took cheek swabs from Daniel and Ian—swabbing more Bravos wasn't necessary. The whole family had been tested when they found out that Aislinn and Madison were switched at birth.

The results of this test, Percy promised, would come through by the middle of next week.

The middle of next week...

By then, Ian and Ella would be home in New York. Not that it really mattered to the Bravos. They all considered the test nothing more than a formality. They just *knew*, they all said, that he was the brother they'd lost so long ago.

He envied them their trust, the way they so effortlessly accepted him as one of theirs. And he wished he could be more like them—yeah, he knew them, recognized them as the people in his newly recovered memories. But they had no such proof that he told the truth. He could be scamming them, looking for some kind of payoff, for all they knew.

That made him grateful for the ease of DNA testing. By Tuesday, if any of them harbored secret doubts about the truth of his claim, they could let them go.

And he could move on. He had no expectations to get close to them, and he hoped none of them decided they ought to visit him in Manhattan.

In the early afternoon, they docked at a small marina on the Washington side of the river near a pretty little country town. A five-minute walk from the boat slip took them to a tree-shaded, parklike area at the river's edge.

Ian helped haul the folding chairs Liam kept stowed on the boat. Connor and Matthias had taken charge of the food. They'd packed four big picnic baskets full of sausages and cheeses, smoked salmon, crackers and artisan breads. Also on offer, more local beer and some Oregon pinot noir.

Everyone helped to lay it all out on a picnic table and they sat around sipping their drinks, enjoying the food. The talk remained casual—for a while.

Then old Uncle Percy asked about Glynis. Ian told them the story of how she came to the orphanage for a baby and ended up taking home the mute boy with all the ugly scars.

He explained how she'd died trying to screw in a lightbulb. "She was always so independent. Whatever little job needed doing, her first response was, 'I can do that myself.'"

"You miss her very much," said Percy.

"Every day. Her father died when she was ten and she spent the rest of her growing-up years in the system, but she never seemed damaged by that. She had boyfriends. Lots of them, right up until the end, though she never got married or had kids—except me. Nothing could dampen her enthusiasm for life. She was always upbeat, ready to take on the world."

His description of Glynis seemed to open the floodgates. Every brother had a question. Ian got it. Even if he felt a certain distance from them, they considered him *theirs*, somehow. He ended up telling them a sanitized version of life in the orphanage and what he remembered of his encounter with the bear.

Liam passed him another beer. "Still no clue how you ended up so far from Irkutsk?"

He screwed off the top. Since he'd talked to Ella about this a week ago, more memories had come to him, mostly at night during weird, disjointed dreams. "I have a vague memory that someone picked me up on a road after I wandered away from the family. I'm fairly sure that was before the bear attacked me. I flagged a truck down, I think. No way I could have flagged a ride after the bear got through with me. It's not clear to me, not any of what happened before I woke up in the hospital. All I've got are random flashes—a ride in a rattletrap truck, hiding in a barn somewhere, setting out on foot again, hungry but too scared to approach anyone. I remember deep woods, this strange silence—and the bear coming at me out of nowhere…"

And he'd said way too much. Shaking his head, he took a long pull off that fresh beer.

The men raised their drinks high.

"To you, Ian," said Daniel.

A murmur of agreement went up.

After that, he made a point to ask questions—about who went to college where, how they met their wives. He got them talking about their children, all of whom had been at Daniel's the night before. People loved to talk about their kids. Most of the brothers' children were babies. But Liam, who had a twenty-month-old son with his wife, Karin, also had two stepkids, a boy and a girl. Ian encouraged him to go on about the brilliant stepson's latest science project. The stepdaughter, Coco, sounded a lot like Abby. All the brothers agreed that Coco could outtalk a politician on Election Day and charm the most hardened of hearts.

Mostly, for the rest of the afternoon, during the boat ride farther upriver before Liam finally turned them around and headed back the way they'd come, Ian took care not to let too much lag occur in the conversation. He steered the talk to subjects other than himself and he did it skillfully, from years of practice. Talking about himself made him feel weak, unprotected.

Better not to go there.

In the meantime, at Wild River Ranch on the Youngs River ten miles south of Astoria, Ella had a great time with the Bravo sisters. She met Aislinn's huge, fluffy German angora rabbits, Bunbun and Luna, who lived on the enclosed porch of the ranch house. Bunbun came right to her, fluffy ears twitching. Aislinn had carrot tops to tempt him. He ate them straight from Ella's hand.

As promised, Aislinn produced a pair of sturdy rawhide boots for Ella to wear. Burt, the ranch foreman, gave her the gentlest gelding in the stable for a horseback tour of the ranch. Burt's border collie, Ace, joined them. The dog happily ran alongside them, circling back to take up the rear whenever one of the sisters activated his herding instincts by lagging too far behind the others.

They got back to the ranch house in the late afternoon. The Bravo sisters' husbands had fired up the grill. In the shade of a couple of giant bigleaf maple trees, they ate thick steaks and marinated chicken and so many sides Ella couldn't possibly do justice to them all. She settled on potato salad, corn on the cob, and artichoke and tomato panzanella. It was all delicious. She ate more than she should have and would have gone back for more if she hadn't been so full.

The early-May weather was lovely—sunny, but not too hot, with a light breeze. The men cleared off the meal and left Ella and Ian's sisters under the trees with pitchers of excellent margaritas to share.

"Who has all the kids today?" Ella asked. "I'm guessing they're not on the boat with the guys."

"You guessed right," said Madison. "Keely, Sabra, Aly and Karin—" she rattled off the names of the Bravo brothers' wives "—took all the cousins to the beach. Grandpa Otto and Aunt Daffy are pitching in there, too." Ella felt reasonably certain that Grandpa Otto was Karin and Sten's father. With so much family around, she found it quite the challenge to keep all the relationships straight.

"That way, we get to have you all to ourselves and the guys get Ian." Patting her enormous belly,

Madison raised her glass of iced strawberry-leaf tea in a toast before taking a sip.

Ella eyed her sideways. "To do what, exactly?"

"To get to know you, of course," Hailey, born seventh of the siblings, replied with a big grin. "Us girls get to pump you for juicy information and the guys get a little quality time with their long-lost brother."

Ella could picture it all too clearly—Ian, alone on a boat with the brothers he'd just met. She hoped he was getting through the experience without too much anxiety. "Ian's a private sort of man."

More than one Bravo sister chuckled. Aislinn said, "We noticed that."

Ella continued, "I've worked with him for almost a decade. He considers me his best friend, but sometimes I wonder if *I* even know him." As the words came out of her mouth, she suspected she'd said too much. She should go easy on the margaritas. But Aislinn stood beside her with the pitcher, and she automatically offered her glass for a refill.

"We're just glad you showed up on a weekend." Harper, born ten months after Hailey, had the trademark wheat-blond hair and blue eyes of all the sisters, save Aislinn. "Weekdays can be crazy, with the kids and the jobs." Harper and her husband, Linc, lived in Portland with his little niece and nephew. Linc had taken custody of the two children when his sister and her husband died in a plane crash over a year before. "It's nice to have more than one day with you guys, nice to get time with you alone, Ella, to get to know all the good stuff, about you and Ian and the two of you together."

Warmth curled through Ella, that the Bravo sisters wanted to get to know her better—but then she wondered why, exactly? She was no long-lost sibling.

She sat up straighter in her lounge chair. "Wait a minute." Sweeping out a hand around the circle of women, she accused, "You all think that Ian and I are a couple, don't you? Like dating. You think we're dating?"

Gracie scoffed. "Dating? I don't know if that's the word I would've used."

"Yeah," agreed Hailey. "You two are way past dating."

"Together." Aislinn gave a firm nod. "That's a good word. You two are clearly together."

"Wait, what?" It felt all wrong to let them assume such a thing. Ian wouldn't like it, and she… Well, she needed to keep her head on straight vis-à-vis the situation with Ian. "No, Ian and I are not *together*, not in the way that you mean. We're *friends*. And we work together—we do that very well together, as a matter of fact. We have an excellent working relationship. We are best friends who work together. That's the only kind of *together* we are."

Except for the great sex we're currently having, she couldn't help mentally confessing. Because, fine. Okay, there was that. But only until they returned to New York.

And why did the thought that the great sex would come to an abrupt forever end on Monday morning make her feel so ridiculously sad?

"You look so sad all of a sudden." Gracie leaned close and briefly clasped Ella's arm, after which she asked softly, "How long have you been in love with him?"

Ella stifled a gasp as she flashed back to that day at Manhattan General, to Lucinda in her red-soled shoes, tossing her long blond curls, accusing... *Everyone knows you're in love with him. It's pathetic.*

Apparently, Lucinda was right. *And Marisol*, Ella grudgingly added. *Let us not forget Marisol.* And now, even here in Oregon, all the way on the other side of the continent, Ian's long-lost baby sister knew. And just by looking at her, apparently. Just by seeing her with Ian.

Ella drank the rest of her margarita in one long swallow. "Not touching that one."

Gracie wouldn't stop. "Are you saying he doesn't know how you feel?" she asked, incredulous, as Ella envisioned herself jumping up and running off screaming. Did everyone think she carried a torch for Ian?

Aislinn said, "Gracie." When Gracie glanced over, Aislinn shook her head.

Gracie groaned. "What's wrong with my saying it? It's not like it's a bad thing. And it's so totally obvious that he's in love with her, too."

Ian *loved* her? For a moment, Ella's heart felt light as a moonbeam.

But no. Ian didn't do love. Ella had always known that—and if she hadn't known, he'd said it right to her face in the darkest hours of Friday morning, before they'd made love for the first time. Gracie had only misread Ian's signals. She thought she saw romantic love, but she was wrong. She saw the respect and affection Ella and Ian had for each other—that, and maybe a hint of the sexual tension currently zapping back and forth between them. Gracie saw all that and assumed it meant more than it did.

"Aw, Ella," Gracie said gently.

Ella hardly had time to set down her drink before the youngest Bravo sister leaped from her chair, grabbed Ella's hand and pulled her up into a hug.

"You'll work it out," Gracie whispered in her ear.

Ella enjoyed the hug and whispered back, "I hope so. I really do."

Ian got through the remainder of the afternoon with his brothers well enough, he thought. After those few touch-and-go moments when he'd said more than he should have about what had gone down twenty years ago in Russia, he'd managed to keep the conversation from straying in that direction again.

Both Daniel and Connor brought up future visits—that they would come to him in New York and that he would return to Valentine Bay to spend time with the family. He kept his replies to that line of questioning vague, managing not to make any commitments either way.

But he probably should have known he wouldn't get away clean. As they docked in Astoria, Liam brought up Hailey's wedding. She and her fiancé, Roman Marek, would be married on the last Saturday of the month.

"Check your calendar," said Daniel. "We would all love it if you could make it for that…"

Ian played along. What else could he do? He clapped his oldest brother on the shoulder and said he'd get back to them about it.

Uncle Percy promised that the DNA results

would go out to everyone by Wednesday at the latest. Liam thanked the old guy and said good-bye to his brothers.

It was almost six when he finally climbed in the Lexus and headed back to the Isabel Inn, where he found Ella sitting on the sofa, channel surfing, still wearing the jeans and plaid shirt she'd put on that morning for her day at the ranch.

So cute. She'd drawn her bare feet up onto the cushions and caught her tongue between her teeth as she concentrated on the screen.

Just the sight of her made everything better. The knots of tension at the back of his neck and in his shoulders from a day of avoiding too much focus on the past melted away.

She'd piled all that gorgeous hair up into a top-knot. He wanted to grab her and drag her straight to his room, where he would peel off that shirt, take down those jeans and undo her topknot. He couldn't wait to get up close and personal with those long, sexy legs and small, sensitive breasts.

He tossed his Yankees cap on the table. "When did you get back?"

"Madison dropped me off about fifteen min-utes ago." She turned off the big screen and set the remote on the stack of coffee table books. "You want to go eat?"

"I'll go with you if you're hungry, but we pretty much ate all day long. And there was beer. Lots of beer."

She laughed. "I hear you. Let's skip dinner, then. You should have seen the pile of steak and chicken I put away—no beer, though. But there might have been one too many margaritas."

"Did you ride a horse?"

"Damn straight."

"Ella, the cowgirl." He sat down beside her and shucked off his Docksiders. "I wish I'd seen that."

"Missed your chance. It's so sad…" She made a frowny face—and those delicate lips of hers? They cried out for his kiss.

"C'mere." He hooked an arm across her shoulders and pulled her against him, taking her mouth and wrapping her up good and tight in his hold. She tasted so good—both sweet and tart. And she smelled like coconut and a field of clover.

When she pulled away, he reached over and tugged on that topknot.

"Hey!" She slapped at him playfully as her hair came undone, the dark waves cascading down over her shoulders.

"Beautiful," he said, and stuck his nose in it, breathing in deep.

She whacked him again, this time with the back

of her hand. "You're kind of a hair pervert, you know that?"

He scoffed. "There's no such thing as a hair pervert."

"Yes, there is. Look it up. It's a person who is overly obsessed with someone's hair. I think they used your picture as part of the definition."

He sniffed her hair. Because it smelled so good. "You're sure about that?"

"Beyond the faintest shadow of a doubt."

"All right, then." He might just as well own it. "Yes, I am obsessed with your hair and damn proud of it, too." He levered backward, pulling her down on top of him as he stretched out across the cushions.

She braced her hands on either side of him and craned back to fake a glare at him. "Let me go. I need a shower."

"No, you don't." Her unbound hair brushed his chest and tickled his neck. He got a hank of it and brought it to his face. "You smell amazing."

"No doubt about it. You're a bad man, a hair pervert."

He eased his fingers up under all that wonderful hair and cradled the back of her head so he could bring her mouth to his again. When only a whisper of space separated them, he suggested, "Let me show you just how bad I am…"

* * *

By the time they moved from the sofa to his bed, Ian felt good about everything. Life was amazing and he wanted Ella in his arms all night and all day tomorrow. He needed not to waste a moment. They had an agreement and the agreement had a deadline. He intended to honor it.

Already, he hated Monday. It would come much too soon.

He decided not to think about that, to focus on right now—which was spectacular.

He pulled her down to the mattress and made love to her a second time. Slowly. Savoring every sigh he wrung from her, every moan, every sharp, indrawn breath.

At a little before nine, they both needed fuel. He called room service and ordered one of their fancy pizzas. When it came, he pulled on a pair of sweats and answered the door.

Back in the bedroom, he found her sitting cross-legged on the bed wearing his shirt.

"Sparkling water?" he asked. At her nod, he handed her the pizza and returned to the main room to get the waters from the snack fridge.

"You look good in my shirt," he said as he joined her on the bed.

She grinned. "Royal blue. It's my color."

"Naked is still better."

"Treat me right. You might get lucky again to-night." Ella devoured her first slice in silence, but when she started on the second, she asked, "So how did it go today with your brothers?"

He knocked back a long swallow of sparkling water and considered what kind of answer to give her. With Ella, honesty seemed the wisest course. She tended to see right through him, anyway, when he tried to fake it. Just saying he didn't want to talk about it wouldn't work. If he didn't want to talk about it, that meant something had gone wrong and she would want to know what.

She might leave him alone about it for now. But eventually, she would circle back around to finding out whatever troubled him. She considered that her job as his friend.

Picking a slice of locally crafted pepperoni off her pizza, she popped it into her mouth. "That bad, huh?"

He shook himself. "No, not at all. They were great."

"But?"

One way or another, he would be sharing. Might as well get it over with. "Percy asked me what Glynis was like. I started telling him, and some-how I found myself babbling about my fragmented memories of how I ended up in a hospital in Kras-noyarsk."

"And there's something wrong with your talking to your brothers about what happened in Russia?"

"Not wrong, just…"

Just what? He had no idea what. He hardly knew where to go from here. But she looked at him so hopefully, eager to listen to his crap, to help him any way she could.

He made himself continue. "I mean, come on. It's clear that they're good people, the Bravos. And yes, I remember them now. I know that they're my family, biologically speaking. But I've had eighteen years of being Ian McNeill now. That's who I really am. Finn Bravo doesn't exist anymore."

She had that look, like she wanted to say something but wasn't sure she should.

"Just say it," he grumbled.

"I don't see why you have to deny the boy you were, that's all. You *are* Ian McNeill. But you started out as Finn Bravo. In that sense, Finn Bravo is part of you, too."

He wanted to grab her and shake her and somehow *make* her see. "He's not. He's gone—and as for my brothers and sisters, I never missed them, not in all this time. And now, it's like this is a big deal to them, but they're just strangers to me. I don't feel what they seem to feel, that sense of connection, or whatever."

They sat cross-legged on the bed, face-to-face.

She dropped her pizza crust on the tray between them and put her hand on his knee, a touch he knew she meant to ground him, reassure him.

Too bad it only made him feel more disconnected than ever. "I don't get it, what they feel. That's all. They act like they care so much about me, and they don't even know me."

She watched him so closely. That was the miracle of Ella. She had so much heart and she saw things other people didn't. He knew the exact moment she understood that he didn't want to be touched right now.

Slowly, she withdrew her hand. "I don't pretend to have answers for you—but I *can* say that I'm sure the reason your brothers seem to care is because they *do* care."

"Ell." He gave a laugh with no humor in it. "I agree. I think they *do* care. I just don't know how to deal with that—with love, you know? I don't 'get' love." Her sweet mouth twisted. He knew that look. He accused, "I can tell by your face that you don't believe me."

"Well, yeah. You're right. I don't. Because I know you. I know that you *do* feel love. You understand it. You give it. You loved Glynis and you still miss her so much."

"Glynis was different."

"Different than what?"

"Different than anyone else for me. She found me. She *saved* me. I became Ian McNeill because of her. I owe her everything."

"And you loved her. You still do. You honor her memory. You always will—and what about Abby? Are you actually going to try to tell me that you don't love Abby?"

"Of course I love Abby. What's not to love? She's smart and fun and bighearted. And she's already got a mom and a dad and a stepmom. Everybody jokes that I'm her other dad, but really, she's just a great kid—somebody else's kid. I'm not on the front lines for her the way you are, the way Philip is."

Ella's mouth had drawn down at the corners. "Ian, I don't even know what to say to you when you get like this."

He frowned back at her. At the same time, he thought how lucky he was to have a friend like her. He went ahead and said it. "And I love *you*, Ella."

He couldn't read her expression now. What did she feel? "I know you do," she said, then added softly, her tone just a little bit flat, "And I love you."

"We're friends," he said. "I care for you. But that's not the same as finding the one person for you, getting married and building a family together, the way all my newfound brothers and sisters seem to have done. I just don't get all that. I don't get the forever thing, that coupled-up thing, and I don't get the family thing. It's like a language I don't speak, one that's nothing but gibberish to me."

Ella stared at him. He had no idea what she might be thinking.

But he did have a scary feeling that he'd hurt her somehow, that she would jump from the bed and storm out the way all his ex-girlfriends had, that he'd pushed her too far. That she'd reached a hard limit with him and his inability to give what other normal, less screwed-up people not only gave, but needed themselves.

He was going to lose her friendship because he couldn't give her more than three days in Oregon. He knew it absolutely, then.

He would lose Ella—maybe not today. Maybe not next week.

But eventually, it would happen.

He would lose her, and when he did, he had no idea what he would do without her—and whoa!

Hold on just a minute.

No. Uh-uh. Not going to happen. Ella was far too reasonable and levelheaded to let this hot, temporary thing between them do permanent damage to what really mattered—their longtime friendship.

When the sexy times were over, they would still

have their friendship, still be a team at Patch&Pebble.
He could never lose her.

She wouldn't let that happen.

And he would not allow it.

Chapter Nine

This is not news, Ella sternly reminded herself. Ian had issues, and those issues wouldn't be resolved in this one painful heart-to-heart tonight.

She wished she didn't feel so miserable suddenly, but she couldn't help thinking that she'd only set herself up for misery when she'd said yes to this while-we're-in-Oregon fling.

She'd asked for trouble, and she would get it.

Could a guy make it any clearer that falling in love with him would bring a woman nothing but heartache? If she had any sense, she would end this thing with him now. Get up off this bed, go back to her own room and firmly shut the door.

Because, seriously, what had she thought would happen? Every touch of his hand, every thrilling brush of his lips to hers, brought her just that much closer to admitting what she'd tried for weeks now to deny.

Love. The word whispered through her mind, taunting her.

Yeah. She was a fool not to get out of here immediately.

However...

Except for this awful conversation that she herself had pushed him to engage in, this visit to Oregon had been nothing short of stellar.

While helping him deal with his newfound family, she'd had an amazing time with him, a fantasy weekend, a romantic, sexy getaway with a gorgeous man who knew his way around a woman's body.

And that brought her to the big question. Exactly how many fantasy weekends had she enjoyed in her life?

Answer: one. *This* one.

She'd spent a whole bunch of years looking for something she'd yet to find—love and forever with the right man, a family to call her own. Great sex just for fun had never been something she would allow herself to indulge in.

Even way back in high school, when she and Philip had made their fateful agreement, the purpose had been to learn about sex in the interest of being reasonably good at it when the right person came along. They'd married only to appease his parents and, when the time came, they'd gone through with their sworn promise to each other and gotten a divorce.

After the divorce, she'd always made sure she felt at least a hint of possibility that a guy might be her lifetime match before she would even go out with him. She'd had four sexual partners, total—Ian and Philip, and two other men. Both of those other men had wanted what she wanted: love and forever, with the right person. Neither of those relationships had gone all the way to a walk down the aisle.

And none of the others—including Philip—could come within miles of Ian sexually.

She had to be realistic. She'd reached the big three-oh without finding the one for her. She might never find that special man, the one who not only lit her up like a five-alarm fire but also couldn't wait to spend the rest of his life at her side.

At least now she knew how it felt to burn for the touch of a certain special someone—and to know that when he *did* touch her, he would see to it that she went up in flames.

Whatever happened next, at least she could finally say that she'd made love with a man who thoroughly satisfied her—repeatedly so, each time better than the time before.

No. Ella did not want this fling with Ian to end prematurely. She still had the rest of tonight and tomorrow to enjoy this beautiful, messed-up man. Time enough for regrets when they got home, time enough to pick up the pieces and figure out what came next.

"You're pissed at me," he said bleakly. "Aren't you?"

"Hmm." She pretended to have to think the question over. "Nope. Not pissed. Not in the least."

He tipped his head to the side, studying her, looking as though he didn't know quite what to make of her. "You're lying, right?"

"No, Ian. I am not lying. I'm not pissed. And as far as what's going on between you and your brothers and sisters, there's nothing wrong with how you feel. It's all new to you, what's happening this weekend. Be patient with yourself. The more you get to know them, the easier it will be to feel love for them."

He pursed up those lips that she couldn't wait to kiss again. "You assume that I *plan* to get to know them."

She gave a one-shouldered shrug. "I do, yes. I think you *will* get to know them. You just need the time to go about it in your own way."

"You're wrong."

She sucked in a calming breath and let it out slowly. "Ian. I have no desire to argue with you. I really don't. You'll figure it out is all I'm saying. Just give yourself a little space to get used to all the things that have happened over the past couple of weeks. The parts of your life that have been lost to you for two decades have come back to you. Nobody expects you to deal with all this instantly. Give yourself a break, why don't you?"

He made a face—something midway between a frown and a scowl. "You're too understanding, you know that?"

She snort-laughed. "So I've been told."

He let his chin drop and stared down at their half-eaten pizza.

"Go ahead," she whisper-teased, "have another slice. You know you want it."

He picked one up and stuck the end in his mouth, his blue eyes locked on hers as he chewed and swallowed. "I thought for a minute there that you would get up and leave."

"Nope. Still here."

"I wouldn't have blamed you. I'm a pain in the ass."

"Yeah, you kind of are."

"How'd I get so lucky to have you for a friend?"

"Life is full of great mysteries."

"Thanks." He took another bite, his brow crinkled in a frown.

She couldn't stop herself from asking for clarification, "And do you mean that thanks sincerely or with sarcasm?"

"Sincerely, Ell. I am completely sincere."

"So then, thanks for all the amazing advice, you mean?"

"Yeah, and all the ledges you seem to keep talking me down from—and especially for coming with. I couldn't do this without you."

"You're welcome." She drank the last of her sparkling water and turned to set the can on the nightstand. "What now?"

A slow, bad-boy grin spread over that too-handsome face. "I'm going to finish this slice and then get to work convincing you that you really need to take off my shirt."

Ian couldn't remember ever having as much fun with a woman as he'd had with Ella this weekend—in bed, and out of it, too. He'd always had a good time with Ell. But getting naked with her had somehow taken the fun to a whole new level.

That night and the next morning when he woke up beside her, he couldn't help thinking that the weekend wouldn't be enough. He needed more nights with Ella in his bed. They should talk about that.

But why waste a moment of their final day at the Isabel Inn renegotiating their sexual relationship?

Later for that. Today, he just wanted to enjoy every minute with her.

Sunday morning, they used two more condoms before breakfast. While using the second one, she screamed his name loud enough that he had to cover her mouth for fear the front desk would call and demand that they keep the noise down.

A little later, over French toast in the dining room, they discussed ways they might spend their final day in Oregon.

She asked, "Anything feel...incomplete?"

Leave it to Ella to ask the deep questions. "What does that even mean?"

"With your siblings? Anything you want to clear up with one of them, or *say* to one of them?"

"Wait." He set down the slice of bacon he'd almost stuck in his mouth. "You're asking if I need to spend more time with one of the Bravos before we fly home?"

"Yes, I am. Meeting your long-lost family, that's what you're here for. If there's any unfinished business, why not deal with it now?"

Unfinished business...

The two words, which had suddenly grown sharp edges, bounced around in his brain.

He thought of Matthias, of the look on Matt's face when they spoke up at Daniel's house during the big reunion dinner Friday night, of the feeling he'd had that Matt blamed himself for what had happened the day that Finn Bravo wandered away from his family and didn't come back until twenty years later.

Yeah. He probably should spend some time with Matt.

He didn't want to, though. He wanted a whole day with Ella, just the two of them. Before they had to return to their real lives, before he needed to figure out if he could stand to go back to being just friends again so soon—not to mention, whether she would even be open to the idea of continuing their arrangement for a while.

He feared she wouldn't. He'd gotten unbelievably lucky to get these few days with her this way.

And that made every minute they had together today even more important.

The way he saw it, if Matt had needed to talk about what went down all those years ago, wouldn't he have brought it up Friday night—or yesterday, for that matter?

"No." He picked up the slice of bacon he'd

dropped and popped it in his mouth. As soon as he'd swallowed it, he added, "I've got no unfinished business with any of the Bravos. I'm good."

Her eyes said she didn't believe him. But she let it go. "There's a rack of brochures at the front desk. We can pick the best local attractions and play tourist for a day."

"As long as we put aside plenty of time to be naked, I'm fine with that."

She sipped her coffee. "Lately, you seem a little obsessed with sex, don't you think?"

"Along with being a hair pervert?"

"Yeah, that, too. Maybe you should get help."

"I don't need help. I just need more time in bed with you."

She dragged a final bite of French toast in the puddle of marionberry syrup still on her plate. "Okay, then. You got it. We'll see the sights."

"And have the sex."

She groaned around the bite of French toast. "You're gross."

"Eat your bacon, too. You're going to need the energy when I get you alone back in the room."

Ian's phone chimed with a text as they walked to the room. They paused in the hallway and he checked the message, his gut kind of sinking at the inevitability of the moment as he saw who it was. "Matt wants to talk to me."

Ella didn't seem the least surprised. "He lives up by Astoria, right? Are you going to meet him at his farm?"

"Actually, he's here. In the parking lot." Ian stuck the phone back in his pocket.

"Perfect. I'll grab my purse and get scarce. You guys can have the suite to yourselves." She started walking again.

He caught her arm and pulled her back. "Hold on. What are *you* going to do?"

She gave an airy wave. "Don't worry about me. I'll walk on the beach or see what's on offer at the spa—and don't forget you did sign me up to drive the Lexus. Give me the keys. I'll grab a brochure and check out downtown Valentine Bay or whatever. It's not a big deal. You can just text me when Matt leaves."

"I'm sure it won't be long." The shorter the better, as far as he was concerned.

Now she turned fully toward him. Her soft hand brushed his cheek. "Take your time. I mean it." She lifted that mouth he couldn't get enough of, and they shared a quick kiss. Her lips tasted of rich coffee and sweet, tart berries.

He let her go reluctantly.

* * *

A few minutes later, Ella left him alone in the suite.

Too soon, the tap came at the door. He answered and found himself looking into blue eyes a lot like his own. They were about the same height and build, him and Matt. Same dark gold hair, too. Stepping back, Ian signaled his brother inside.

Matt stuck his hands in the pockets of his field jacket and stayed on the threshold. "Thanks for seeing me."

"No thanks needed. It's good," he lied outright, "for us to get a chance to talk alone."

"Ella?"

"She took the keys to the rental car. No doubt she's about to go wild in the streets of Valentine Bay."

That brought a reluctant smirk from Matt. "I'll bet."

They stood there, still as matching statues on either side of the door, staring at each other. Finally, Ian said, "You planning on coming in?"

Matt stared at him, a stare full of pain and something else. Guilt, maybe? He still had his hands in his jacket pockets. "I was thinking maybe a walk down on the beach…"

* * *

Ian put on a light jacket and ushered Matt through the sitting area and out to the deck.

Neither of them spoke as they went down to the cliff and from there took the second, longer set of stairs to the sand. Once on the beach, Ian slipped off his shoes and socks. Matt headed for the ocean in his heavy, lace-up boots.

At the water's edge, they turned south toward the headland, the same way Ian and Ella had gone Friday morning, when she'd talked him out of running away. Matt remained silent as they walked. Fine with Ian. Meaningless chatter didn't thrill him in the least.

The bench-like sea stack Ian remembered remained clear of the water. He and Matt sat there, just as he and Ella had done.

Matt stared off toward the distant horizon for a while. Ian felt no urge to start yakking. He figured Matt would start talking when he was damn good and ready.

And he did, turning his head toward Ian, giving him another wry sort of smile. "You used to be a talker."

He remembered, but he kept his mouth shut and gave his brother a nod of encouragement.

Matt took his silence exactly as Ian had meant him to—as a cue to go on. "Everything was a big thrill to you. And everything that thrilled you, you talked about. Incessantly. The day you disappeared, I was pissed off. I was fourteen and way too cool to be traipsing around Russia with the family. I wanted to be home in Valentine Bay with my buds like any normal teenage boy..." Matt's voice trailed off. He stared out at the ocean again.

After a minute or two, he went on, "We took a day trip on dog sleds from Irkutsk. You disappeared when we stopped for lunch. The way it happened, I went off across the snow on my own, wanting to be left alone to sulk. You followed me, chattering away a mile minute, as you always did. I turned on you. I yelled at you to shut the hell up. I think I scared you, freaked you out. Because after that, I never heard another sound from you. I turned my back on you and started walking again. Not once did I check on you, not even a single, quick glance over my shoulder. Not for way too long.

"Eventually, your silence started nagging at me. I did look back. You weren't there. I shrugged it off, assuming you'd rejoined the others. By the time I trudged back to the sleds to get something to eat, you'd been gone for maybe half an hour..." He fell silent again.

Ian waited him out.

Finally, Matt said, "The mushers knew how to

track. They should have been able to find you. But somehow, you'd vanished into thin air." He faced Ian again and said flatly, "So yeah. It was me. My fault. Everything that happened to you, all that you lost. All that you suffered. I did that to you because I was a spoiled, thoughtless boy without the sense God gave a goat."

Ian shook his head.

Matt glared. "What's that? What does that *mean*?"

"It means no, you didn't do it to me."

Now Matt did look pissed. "I was there. I know what happened."

"So was I. And I do, too. I don't remember everything, but I remember that day. I remember how it happened."

"Then you remember it wrong. I yelled at you. I told you to stop talking. And you did."

"Yeah. I remember that. I remember why you got on my case, how I babbled away about wanting a husky and talking Mom into getting me one. I remember you yelling at me—and I remember shutting up, trudging along behind you, thinking bad thoughts about you for a few minutes, maybe five, tops. But I got over it. I wasn't mad anymore when I wandered off."

Matt muttered, "You're just trying to make me feel better."

"I'm just trying to tell you that it wasn't your fault. I didn't wander off because you were mean to me. I saw a white chipmunk and followed it."

"A white...?"

"They're native to Siberia. Look it up. When the chipmunk got away from me, I heard a rustling in the underbrush. I ran to check that out—and found exactly nothing. From there, I spotted a quail, I think. I ran after it. I saw something glitter in the snow, but when I got to it, there was nothing. It went on like that. I was eight in a strange land, eight and curious—and fearless, too. Up till then, nobody had ever hurt me. As a rule, I could talk my way out of just about anything."

"Yeah," Matt agreed wryly. "Mom and Dad always claimed they never played favorites. But somehow, you always managed to get them to let you do just about whatever you wanted to do."

"Exactly. Curious, fearless and dangerously overconfident. I was chasing after nothing, living this big adventure inside my own head. It was probably an hour, at least, from the time I veered off the trail behind you until I started to realize I didn't have a clue where I'd wandered off to."

Matt wasn't buying. "It was my job to keep track of you."

"You went for a walk by yourself. Nobody told you to watch me. Before Mom let me take off after you, she gave me instructions to stay with you. I put on my most serious, well-behaved face and promised I would stick right by you. It's no more on you what happened than it is on me."

They both fell silent. Ian enjoyed the sound of the waves, thinking that this conversation had made him feel closer to Matt, more immediately connected to the childhood he'd only recently begun to recall. He thought about what Ella had said the night before, how as time went on, he would grow to care about these people who had turned out to be his family. Sitting here on the sea stack next to Matt, watching the gulls over the water as the morning fog thinned and the day started to warm up, Ian could almost understand what Ella had been trying to get through to him.

When they started back toward the inn, Matt said, "I just wanted to tell you how sorry I am, to let you know that I screwed up in a big way and I never really forgave myself for what happened that day."

Ian hardly knew how to answer him. "I get it, why you feel that way. If you need my forgiveness, it's yours, man. Whatever makes it better for you. I don't blame you, though. I never did. Because it wasn't your fault."

A humorless chuckle escaped the man beside

him. "I thought you'd only recently started remembering what happened."

"A couple of weeks ago, yeah—so you're right. For two weeks, I haven't blamed you. For the last couple of decades, I didn't have a clue what happened, anyway."

When they got back up the stairs to the cliffs above the beach, Ian asked, "Want coffee? We can go to the dining room."

Matt followed him through the suite and down the outside hallways to the round restaurant at the center of the inn. They had coffee and talked some more—about the farm where Matt lived with his wife and baby son, about his job as a game warden. He said he liked working outdoors, not being tied to a desk.

"So...you and Ella?" Matt asked when the server had refilled their cups for the second time. As Ian tried to decide how exactly to answer the not-quite question, Matt added carefully, "You two seem close."

Ian shrugged. "We are. She started at Patch&-Pebble nine years ago, when she was still at NYU. We've been friends almost since her first day as an intern. Her daughter, Abby, and I are close, too. Abby's something special. She's eleven now."

Matt eyed him sideways. "I know it's none of

my damn business, but I gotta say it. Just friends? Not really buying that one."

Ian made a bad joke of it. "Didn't I just say she's eleven?"

Matt scoffed. "You know I'm not talking about the daughter."

Ian wanted to insist, *We are just friends.*

However, there was no *just* about what he had with Ella. She mattered to him in a big way.

As for having her in his bed, nothing compared. He felt far from ready to give that up, though the more he thought about it, the more he knew he needed to stick with the original plan.

No matter how much he craved her, he had to face facts. Ella wanted love and forever, and he simply didn't.

Nothing good could come of continuing this way. Too many things could go wrong.

Not that Matt needed to hear any of that.

"Truth is, Ell's my *best* friend. I don't know what I would do without her."

Matt shook his head. "It's strange, you know? I want to give you some good advice because you're my little brother. But on the other hand, you're also Ian, and I've only known you since Friday."

"Let me be succinct. Don't."

Matt threw back his head and let out a laugh. "Now how did I know you were going to say that?"

* * *

Surprise, surprise. The shops in the Valentine Bay Historic District didn't open until eleven on Sundays.

But Ella got lucky, because the Valentine Bay Sunday Market, which claimed a couple of streets and a big parking lot not far from the Valentine Bay Theatre, opened at nine. Ella browsed the booths that sold everything from wine to flowers to cute wooden birdhouses and chain-saw art. The food options were endless and the atmosphere nothing short of festive.

She bought some pretty beaded silver bookmarks and a handmade bracelet for Abby. The bookmarks really charmed her, so she went back and purchased several more for Chloe and her girls, for Marisol and Charlotte, and for the girls at the office, too. An hour passed. She enjoyed herself, chatting up the booth owners, accepting business cards from half of them.

After she wandered out of the market, she ended up strolling down Manzanita Avenue, stopping to look in shop windows, thinking that Ian's visit with Matthias must have gone well. More than two hours had passed since she left the inn. No way Ian would put up with anyone for two hours unless he considered the time well spent.

She stood outside Valentine Bay Books, window shopping the reading options, thinking that the store might open before Ian called to say Matthias had left, when her phone pinged with a text.

From Ian.

Where are you? Come back now.

She laughed as she read it. The text was so very Ian. He wanted her back there, and he wanted her there now.

And oh, did she want to be there. With him.

Standing at the bookstore window, she started to text him back, to give him a little grief for his extreme curtness, when her fingers stopped working and she almost dropped the phone.

Because...

She couldn't wait to get back to him.

She couldn't wait to be near him.

Inside the cage of her chest, her heart went crazy. It ached. It pounded. It soared.

All her denials fell away. All her reasons why this couldn't happen to her, why she had more sense than that...it all just went up in smoke. All her excuses, her maybe-nots, her vows that no way would she be that foolish...

They all deserted her.

She couldn't lie to herself any longer.

That bitch Lucinda had it right. Her dear friend Marisol had told her the truth.

For the first time in her life, Ella knew what it felt like to be hopelessly in love.

She, Ella Haralson, who damn well ought to know better, had fallen in love with Ian McNeill.

Chapter Ten

"Focus," she muttered under her breath.

And how pitiful was that?

Now she was talking to herself.

Ell? You there?

"Answer him. You need to answer him…"

Swiftly, she thumbed out the simplest response.
On my way.

As she made the short drive back to the inn, her
every nerve humming, her heart full of yearning
and her mind a bowl of mush, she somehow managed to come to a decision.

She would play it by ear.

They had till tomorrow morning as temporary lovers. After that, as per their agreement, they once more became Ian and Ella, good buddies and colleagues.

With maybe some overlap tomorrow, during the drive to PDX and the flight back home…

She turned into the parking lot at the Isabel Inn and nosed the Lexus into a space not far from their suite. Shifting into Park and switching off the engine, she flopped back against the seat and let out a groan at the headliner.

Overlap? Seriously? As if they might sneak in a quickie on the road or in the air?

Mush. No doubt about it. Love had turned her perfectly functioning brain to pure goo.

Today and tonight. That would be all. Done. Finished. End of story.

Tomorrow, they would once again become Ella and Ian, just good friends.

Unless, the voice of her braver self whispered in her ear—unless she grew a pair and asked for more.

That could bring crushing disappointment with a dash of pure humiliation—and who did she think she was kidding? Not *could*. Uh-uh.

Asking for more most likely *would* get her the answer Ian gave to all his girlfriends: no.

Ian McNeill was not, nor had he ever been, open to more with a woman. He'd made that so very clear with every girlfriend he'd ever had in all the years she'd known him. And if his actions weren't enough to convince her, what about his warnings before he first took her in his arms? *I get bored,* he'd said. *I shut down, and I just want whoever she is this time gone.*

She winced at the thought of being *whoever she is this time.* She couldn't bear that, to watch him turn away, to hear him say he felt nothing and he wanted her to leave.

And yet...

How could she expect to claim the love she longed for if she couldn't even step up and tell the man what she felt in her heart?

Nothing ventured, as the old saying went.

"Think about it. Just give yourself some time and think about it," she whispered at the windshield.

Because yeah. She was talking to herself again.

Gathering her bags of Sunday Market finds off the passenger seat, she left the car and headed for the room. At the door to the suite, she waved her key card at the PIN pad. As the green light came on, Ian pulled the door open from the inside.

"There you are." He grabbed her arm and wrapped her up in his arms, crushing her bags of goodies between them.

She laughed up at him, thinking how beautiful he was, knowing she couldn't do it, couldn't ask him for more. She already knew his answer, and she just couldn't bear to hear it.

So she teased, "You must be glad to see me." She could feel the evidence of his happiness pressing, hard and ready, against her belly.

"You have no idea." And he kissed her. A long one, deep and wet, with serious tongue. The bags dropped to the floor right there by the door. Ian eased her purse off her shoulder. It followed the bags, hitting the tile with a loud plop.

And then he grabbed her hand and pulled her to his bedroom.

They fell across the bed, tearing at each other's clothes as they went down, both of them achieving complete nakedness in record time. He had the condom out of the wrapper and rolled on his hard length so fast, she hardly knew he'd done it.

But then she looked down between their bodies and saw him wrapped and ready. "Come here."

She pulled him close, twining her legs around him good and tight, moaning in bliss as he filled her.

"So good," he whispered against her parted lips.

"Yes" was the only word she knew.

They moved together, chasing completion, almost rolling off the mattress at one point, laughing about it, laughter that caught on deep, hungry groans.

So what if she would never have more from him? This, right this minute, her arms and legs wrapped tightly around him as he moved within her...

It wasn't love for him. She knew that. It wouldn't last past tomorrow morning.

But from now until then, she would cherish every moment.

There would be time later to cry over what she'd never have with him, time to deal with her own cowardice at the prospect of showing him her heart.

In the late afternoon, they put on minimal clothing and ordered a picnic-basket lunch from the dining room. Spreading the picnic blanket on the living area rug, they sat cross-legged on either side of the blanket to enjoy the feast. As they ate, Ian explained how it had turned out with Matt.

"It's good, I think," she said when he'd finished

the story. "Really good. I mean, it sounds like he was pretty messed over by your disappearance, and you got a chance to help him see what happened through your eyes, to realize he wasn't at fault." She high-fived him.

He laughed. "Only you give high fives for a good conversation."

"It's obvious to me that Matt needed to hear what you had to say. I think you took a crushing weight off his shoulders."

"Well, not completely. I think he still feels it all could have gone differently if he'd just kept an eye on me."

"Yeah, but you showed him that *you* don't blame him. That matters, Ian. That's important, and I'm so glad you were able to say that to him."

He reached across their living-room picnic to guide a lock of hair behind her ear. "What would I do without you?" He bent close and kissed her.

I love you. You're the one for me. There'll never be anyone else like you, Ian...

The words begged to be said. And she almost let them out.

But then he kissed her again, and she focused on that, on right now, on every moment they had left to be lovers three thousand miles from home in this gorgeous little town where he'd been born.

* * *

All the rest of that afternoon and into the evening, Ian couldn't stop thinking about changing the rules and extending this mind-blowing thing between them, taking it on home, playing it out all the way.

But that path would too likely only lead to trouble.

And he couldn't afford the risk—not with Ella. She meant too much to him. If it got messy when it ended, he would never forgive himself.

He never should have started this.

And yet, he couldn't make himself regret a single moment.

He just needed to let it end as planned. And he would—tomorrow when they headed home.

Their flight, with one stop in Minneapolis–St Paul, would leave Portland at eight fifteen in the morning, so they would need to get going well before dawn.

He didn't sleep well. And when she turned over at 3:00 a.m. and he saw her eyes flutter open, he reached for her. She went into his arms one more time. He made it last, memorizing every sigh, every naughty word and throaty moan. He drank in the feel of her all around him, taking him, owning him. He'd never been owned before, probably never would be again.

He reassured himself it was okay, that he could let her go, that he would still have her the way he always had—as his best friend.

Sometimes a man had to measure the risk, see the danger ahead and pull back from the brink.

At least that's what he told himself as they packed up to leave at a little past four.

Chapter Eleven

During the trip home, Ella tried hard to believe they could go back to what they'd had before.

But trying hard couldn't make them effortlessly best friends again. She reassured herself that eventually, they would get there. Eventually, her heart would stop aching.

Ian spent most of the flight on his laptop as she pretended to deal with messages on her phone. Later, she put on her sleep mask, turned her head to the window and closed her eyes. She slept fitfully. Beside her, he said nothing. When she gave up trying to sleep, the silence between them continued.

They had a car waiting at JFK. It took an hour and a half to get to her place. When the driver finally stopped across the street from her building, Ian started to get out to help her with her bags.

"Stay there," she said quickly, as the driver got out to take her bags from the trunk. "I can manage, no problem."

"Ell, I don't mind—"

"Of course you don't, but it's almost eight at night. I know you want to get home." He had a beautiful two-thousand-square-foot loft in Tribeca, even closer to the office than her co-op.

"Come on, it's ten minutes to my place. I'll help you upstairs first."

"Don't be silly. I've got it."

He looked at her so strangely. "What's the matter?"

"Nothing." She put on a too-big smile. "See you tomorrow."

"Ell…" He seemed not to know how to continue.

And she didn't want him to continue, anyway. Sheesh. They reminded her of that ancient, depressing Simon and Garfunkel song that her aunt Clara used to love, all "dangling conversation" and "superficial sighs."

"Tomorrow," she repeated unnecessarily and shut the door before he could say anything else.

At the rear of the car, she thanked the driver and tucked a twenty into his hand.

Footsteps pounded on the hardwood floor inside as she let herself in her apartment door.

"Mom!" Abby, dimples on full display, came racing at her down the long hall from the living area. "Surprise!" She threw herself at Ella.

With the door open and her bags waiting behind her, Ella spread her arms to gather her daughter in. They hugged each other tight. Ella breathed in the scent of Prada Candy, Abby's favorite perfume, and felt a little better about everything. If she couldn't have the man she loved, at least she had Abby to come home to.

Ella took her by her slender shoulders and held her away. "You're here all alone?"

Abby nodded. "We saw when your flight landed. Dad walked me over here. I was only here like ten minutes before you came."

"But I thought you were staying at your dad's tonight."

"I was, but Dad said it was okay to come on over."

"Of course it's okay. It's more than okay. I'm glad you're here."

"Good. 'Cause I couldn't wait to see you—where's Ian?" Abby craned her head around Ella to peer out the open door to the hallway. "Is he coming up?"

Just the mention of his name caused a tightness in Ella's chest. But she kept her smile in place. "He went on home."

Abby caught both her hands. "Well, come on. Let's get your suitcases in. Did you eat?"

Ella almost burst out crying—partly in mourning for her too-brief love affair with Ian. But also for happiness, that she had a beautiful, thoughtful daughter who loved her. The teen years loomed ahead, and things would no doubt get rocky. But right now, Abby was a total sweetheart, and Ella felt like she'd hit the jackpot as a mom.

"Mom," Abby prompted. "I asked if you ate?"

"I had something on the plane."

"Okay. You can make some coffee or tea or whatever and tell me all about Ian's long-lost family and Valentine Bay."

Ian's loft had big windows. A lot of them.

That evening, he unpacked quickly, poured himself a whiskey and stood between the sofa and a giant potted umbrella tree to stare out at Lower Manhattan.

His place had never felt so big and empty.

Like some lovesick clown, he missed Ella already. She could've at least let him help her with her suitcases, let him come up for a few minutes. They could've had a drink, talked a little.

Even if he couldn't put his hands all over her, he'd always liked talking to her. They'd never had a shortage of things to say—not until today, anyway.

She'd hardly looked at him during their flights or during the stopover at MSP. And when she did look at him, she either smiled too wide or quickly glanced away.

Things would get better, though, he told himself. He just needed to give it time, and they would get back to their familiar, comfortable relationship.

Except...

Well, he still wanted her.

He wanted her a lot. Getting back to BFF status with her wouldn't help him with the wanting.

Not in the least.

That night, he didn't get a whole lot of sleep. More than once, he drifted off and woke up soon after. He lay there awake in the dark for way too long, wishing he had Ella in the bed beside him.

Tuesday came eventually. And it could've been worse—or so he told himself. He had meetings all day, which kept his mind occupied.

Unfortunately, a couple of those meetings included the COO who had kept him awake half the night. At least twice in both meetings she attended, he completely lost track of the topic, let alone what might have been decided. He nodded a lot and said, "That works," way too many times.

His gaze wouldn't stop straying her way. Today, she had all that amazing coffee-colored hair piled up in a loose knot at the top of her head. Little tendrils of the silky stuff had escaped. They kissed her temples and curled loosely down the nape of her neck.

He longed to get up and take the chair next to her, to lean in close, smell her perfect scent of coconut and spice, spear his fingers in that topknot, make it give way so he could wrap his hand around a giant hank of it. Once he had a good grip on all that silky hair, he would pull her good and close, take her mouth and not let go...

Yeah. He had no idea what had transpired in the meetings they had together. Yet somehow, he got through the day.

That night, he had drinks with two bachelor friends he'd known since they all went to Columbia together. They met up at a West Village tavern for burgers and beers. The place was packed with good-looking people, half of them female. More than one pretty woman came by their booth to chat.

His friends had fun. Neither went home alone. With a little bit of effort, Ian could have hooked up with someone new.

But that just felt all wrong. Hookups had never been his style. If he suddenly decided to go home with a stranger, it wouldn't be because he enjoyed that sort of thing.

Uh-uh. He would do it to try to get past how much he still wanted Ella.

As if such a move would even work. He knew ahead of time that it wouldn't. He would just end up feeling like crap about it—inviting some unknown woman home, using her to keep himself from knocking on Ella's door.

No unknown woman could distract him from what he wanted.

His needs were specific. All his fantasies involved Ella.

Why couldn't he stop thinking of her?

Easy. They'd had three days together. No way could that be called long enough for him.

He needed more. He needed the thing between them to play itself out. He needed dates with her, weekend getaways, a real relationship for as long as it lasted.

Too bad that, even inside his head, what he needed sounded selfish and completely unfair to Ella.

What did she need with him "for as long as it lasted"?

Really, she seemed to have moved on already.

She certainly hadn't expressed any interest in bringing their sexual relationship home with them from Oregon.

No. Asking for more just wouldn't cut it.

He needed to get over her.

And he would. He had to accept, though, that getting over her might take a while, because he'd lost her too soon, before he was ready.

But one way or another, this feeling of needing her, of longing to touch her, to kiss her, to hold her...

Eventually, the longing and needing would go away.

He only had to wait it out.

Wednesday, in a secure email, he received the DNA results Uncle Percy had arranged for. The results held no surprises. Daniel Bravo was his brother. And that made it official—he had a whole bunch of family in Valentine Bay.

Five minutes after he read those results, at a little after noon Eastern time, the calls started. He heard from every one of his siblings in Oregon—beginning with Madison the movie star, who sounded tired but happy. Madison explained that at 6:43 a.m. Pacific time, she'd given birth to a seven-pound, ten-ounce baby girl. Madison and

Sten had named the little one Evelyn Daffodil, after Sten's mother and Aunt Daffy.

"Of course, we're calling her Evie already," Madison added with obvious pride.

"It's a beautiful name," said Ian, feeling oddly bewildered. For so much of his life, he'd had only Glynis. Now he had brothers and sisters and nieces and nephews, so many he had trouble keeping them all straight.

He'd barely hung up from Madison when Daniel called. Matt called while Ian was still on with Daniel, so Ian called him back as soon as he and Daniel said goodbye.

"Hello, little brother," said Matt. "It's hardly a surprise that you're a Bravo, but it's fun welcoming you to the family all over again. We're all really hoping you can make it for Hailey's wedding at the end of the month—and as long as we're talking weddings, there's also Gracie and Dante's wedding in mid-June. It's a lot to ask, we know. But think about maybe flying out for both."

Ian stifled a groan. Both Daniel and Madison had mentioned Hailey's wedding. Ian had said both times that he would try. Now he had Gracie's big day to think about, too? He said it again, "I'll see what I can do."

"Can't ask for more."

Ian's phone lit up with a call from Connor. He

said goodbye to Matt and got on the line with his second-born brother.

By the time every one of his siblings—*and* Percy *and* Daffodil—had expressed their joy and excitement at the news that wasn't really news to anyone, Ian felt relief that all the calls had finally been made.

He also felt a little, well, happy. The Bravos were good people. And as usual, Ella had gotten it right.

He'd always considered himself content not knowing where he'd started out, always told himself that he'd gotten everything that really mattered when Glynis adopted him, that she was all the family he'd ever needed.

But the mystery of his past had always haunted him, no matter how hard he'd tried to deny that it did.

He had a feeling some of the holes in his memory would never fill in. It felt good, though, to know that Finn Bravo had started out his life loved and cared for. That he'd *mattered* to his family, that they'd looked for him and never stopped.

And slowly, as he got over the shock of their very existence, he found he had good feelings when he thought of them, a certain gladness that they existed, that they really seemed to want to include him in their family events whenever possible.

Yeah.

Ella was right. In time, he could definitely get used to having a big family.

He went to her office and found the door wide open. She stood beside her desk, typing something on her phone, looking amazing in a soft white shirt and pink pencil skirt, sky-high nude heels on her slender feet.

"Hey." He tapped on the door frame.

She looked up. For a moment, they simply stared at each other. He imagined himself crossing the threshold, kicking the door shut as he entered, marching straight to her, grabbing her close and crashing his hungry mouth down on hers.

In real life, he stayed right where he was.

She set the phone down and smiled—a forced smile. "Hey."

He leaned in the doorway and drank in the sight of her—right here at Patch&Pebble, a single wall between his office and hers. So close.

And yet a million miles away.

"I got my DNA results a little while ago," he said.

As he rambled on about all the calls from Oregon, her face relaxed a little and her forced smile turned real. "I'm so glad, Ian. You're fortunate to have such a wonderful family."

"Yeah," he said quietly. "I wanted to tell you that I'm starting to see what you meant, about how it would take time, but I would slowly realize how good it is to know them, to start to see them as an important part of my life."

She gave him a slow nod—of acknowledgment, of understanding.

But then he suggested, "Want to run out for some lunch? How about that place around the corner we both like?"

She was already shaking her head, that invisible wall between them going up again, cutting him off from her. "Samar's ordered takeout." Samar was her assistant. "I've got a video conference with Production."

He felt so bad—exiled, displaced. Banished.

From Ell, of all people. He'd lost his best friend when he took her to bed. He could kick his own ass for his own total foolishness. And yet, at the same time, he knew damn well that given the chance, he would do it—do *her*—all over again.

In a heartbeat if she would let him.

Right then, he despised himself. He'd lost his best friend for a weekend fling.

All the good family feeling of a minute ago deserted him, left him empty, lurking in her doorway, with nothing else to say.

"Fair enough. I'll leave you to it." And he turned and started walking, marching right past his office, headed for the elevator. As he passed Audrey's desk, he said, "Back in an hour."

His assistant smiled and then frowned. He just kept walking, his mind lost in Ella, wishing…

But it didn't matter what he wished, now did it?

He needed to get over wanting her. And then, eventually, he would have his friend back. The old ease and companionship would be his again.

He refused to consider that it might go any other way.

Thursday, Ella had lunch with Marisol—a lunch during which she promised herself she would *not* bring up the subject of Ian.

They met at a small Italian restaurant they both liked on Ninth Avenue, where they served wine by the glass and delicious prosciutto and mozzarella sandwiches.

Marisol breezed in, her cloud of natural curls bouncing, her dewy amber skin aglow. "Love the gorgeous bookmarks," she said. Ella had given them to Abby to give to Charlotte. "Thank you," Marisol said as soon as they had their wine.

"I'm so glad you like them. They have a great

little farmers market there in Valentine Bay. The chain-saw art alone left me breathless. I mean, a life-size, anatomically correct bull moose? It almost killed me not to bring that one home."

"And yet somehow, you restrained yourself?" Marisol teased.

"I did, yes."

Marisol allowed only a few seconds to elapse before demanding, "Oregon with Ian, huh? How did it go?"

Her chest too tight and her heart heavy, Ella turned her wineglass by the stem. "I take it Abby's been talking."

"She's eleven. Of course she's been talking. When I picked the girls up from hip-hop class Friday, she chattered the whole way to Philip's about Ian's newfound family. Then Monday, after tap class, she said you and Ian were coming home that night."

"Yeah. The trip was pretty tough for Ian…" Quickly, she filled her friend in on the parts of Ian's story that Marisol hadn't already heard.

Their sandwiches came. When the waitress left, Marisol kept after her. "But what about you? Wasn't it tough on *you*, to be there alone with him, supporting him as a friend, given the way that you feel?"

"The way that I *feel*?" Ella couldn't resist playing dumb on the love question. After all, she'd yet to admit to anyone but herself how she really felt about her friend and boss. "I have no idea what you're talking about."

"Oh, yes you do. Don't be coy. Be strong. Be true."

Should she keep her big mouth shut?

Hard yes on that.

But then again, she pretty much always told Marisol everything, and she did need to talk to a friend about this…

Marisol took a big gulp of wine. "Okay. I can't take it. Something happened. Tell. Me. Everything."

"Well, as I said, Ian was pretty tense the whole trip out there. Thursday night, he had a nightmare about the past. He cried out in his sleep. I went into his room to see if I could help. After I woke him up, we started talking…"

"And talking wasn't all that happened, right?"

Slowly, Ella nodded. "I stayed with him all night. The next day we came to an agreement to be together, to be lovers, but just for the time in Oregon."

"A fling."

"Yeah."

"And then?"

"It was beautiful. I loved every minute of it.

And by Sunday, I realized that you and that harpy Lucinda were right."

Marisol smirked. "You did it. You admitted you're in love with him."

"Could you not look so smug?"

Marisol waved her hand, long fingers spread, in a circle in front of her own face. "This is not my smug look. This look means 'It's about time.'"

With a hard sigh, Ella picked up her wine and downed a fortifying sip. She set the glass down firmly. "Yeah. I'm in love with him. I realize that now."

"Good. So then…what happened next?"

"Next? We kept the agreement. It's over. We came home."

"Oh, baby…" Marisol reached across their little table. Ella met her halfway, and they laced their fingers together. Marisol gave her a reassuring squeeze before they let go. She asked gently, "So then it went badly, when you told him that you love him?"

Ella had just picked up her sandwich for another bite. She set it back down.

And Marisol *knew*. She accused, "You haven't told him."

Ella stared glumly at her sandwich. "Are you *trying* to ruin my appetite?"

"Let me phrase that as a question. Have you told Ian that you love him?"

"I've thought about it. A lot."

Her friend reached for her hand again. She gave it. They leaned across the table, fingers intertwined.

Marisol said, "Sweetheart, you have to tell him."

"No, I don't."

"Oh, honey…" Marisol shook her curly head.

"It won't do any good. He doesn't want a relationship, ever. He said something shuts down in him after he's with someone for a while. He says he's just not going there. He says that love, marriage and all that are never going to happen for him."

"A lot of men say that—women, too—until they meet someone who makes them change their mind."

"I'll bet Jacob never said that. Your husband adored you at first sight. And the way you've always told it, you felt the same for him. So I'm asking you, what men? What women?"

"You just made my point. Jacob and I were right for each other, and we were fortunate that we both knew it from the start. Not everybody is like that. It takes some people longer to come to grips with their love. But they have to stay open to making it work. They have to be brave and up-front about what they want with the person they love—and you're not behaving bravely, Ella. You're not being up-front. You are evading."

"Gee, Mari. Tell me what you *really* think."

"I think you should tell him how you feel."

"I know you do. But you're not me. It was a simple thing for you, with Jacob, for both of you. You just now admitted that. With Ian, I'm fighting a losing battle."

"Uh-uh. Not true. Not necessarily—but okay, say you're right. Say Ian is the only guy in Manhattan who swears he'll never fall in love and settle down and means it. That doesn't change the fact that you need to tell the man you're in love with him. You need to do it for yourself, so that you will know you pulled out all the stops. That you put your whole heart in it, that he knows exactly what you want from him. How he takes it, what he does in response, that isn't the main issue."

"Maybe not to you. You're not the one who gets to face the rejection."

"You can't be sure he'll turn you down until you tell him what you want."

"Easy for you to say."

"You're right. It *is* easy for me to say. And I never said it would be easy for *you* to do. I said that you *need* to do it. You need to stand up for your heart and tell the man you're in love with him."

For Ian, the hits just kept coming—Ella-wise, anyway.

Not only was she missing from his bed now, she'd gone AWOL from their friendship, as well. From the moment they got in the car to head for the airport on Monday, she'd been distant with him.

She spoke to him only when necessary. If he walked into the break room, she walked back out again. On Friday, he tried harder to get her alone, to get her to talk to him, to look him in the eyes.

Really, would it kill her to give him a damn smile?

She had to walk by the open door of his office to get to hers. Friday morning, he watched for her.

Ten minutes after she zipped by, he went to her. At least she'd left her door ajar again. She sat behind her desk typing something on her MacBook.

He tapped on the door frame, just the way he had on Wednesday. "Got a minute?"

Her smile came fast—a cool smile that matched the distant expression on her beautiful face. "Sure. Come on in."

He shut the door behind him.

She bit her upper lip. He wished she'd let him do that.

But she wouldn't. Because that part of their relationship was through.

The rest of what they had, though? What about that? Didn't years of friendship matter? The more he thought about it, the less he liked her putting up a wall between them. So what if they'd had a hot weekend together? Why should that mean he had to lose her as his friend?

"What's up?" she asked him—not impatiently, exactly. But she had a vibe, that *how can I help you so you can leave?* vibe.

He forged ahead with an unnecessary question about the upcoming product launch of Woodrow the warthog.

"Sounds good to me," she said when he stopped talking. She was still smiling. Her big brown eyes asked, *Anything else?*

We weren't supposed to lose our friendship because we had sex, but it looks like we have. He should just say it, just ask her, *Have we lost our friendship?* But she looked so…unwelcoming.

Maybe if he got her out of the office. In a nonwork setting, they could talk honestly and frankly—about the fling, the end of the fling, what was going on with her now, all of it. "You free tonight?"

Something flashed in her eyes. It looked like panic. "No. Really. I have, um, stuff."

"Stuff?"

She threw her hands up, outright impatient now. "You know, *things* that I, uh, I need to do."

It was too much. He bent at the waist, braced his hands on her desk, leaned into her space and said quietly, "We need to talk. You know we do."

Two bright spots of color rode high on her soft cheeks, and her mouth drove him crazy. He almost lunged forward and claimed it with his. "Ian, I just don't—"

"Please. Let me come to your place. Or you come to mine. Go to lunch with me, whatever works for you."

She stared at him, stricken. And then she gulped. "Um. Okay."

He waited for her to name the place and time. When she just continued to stare, he did it for her. "Is Abby at her dad's for the weekend?"

She hard-swallowed again. "Yes."

"Your co-op, then. I'll be there at nine tomorrow morning."

Ella managed to avoid Ian for the rest of the workday.

At home, she felt desperate and lonely and wished Abby was there. Five times that evening, she almost called Ian and asked him not to come.

But no. He had a point. They needed to talk about this.

She needed to do what Marisol had challenged her to do—tell him she loved him and take it from there.

In bed, sleeping proved impossible. She spent half the night on her laptop watching decade-old episodes of *How I Met Your Mother* and *Scrubs*, shows she'd seen too many times already. Something about their familiarity soothed her somehow.

By 6:00 a.m., she couldn't stay in bed a minute longer. She got up, showered and dressed and then started cleaning things to keep busy. She dusted shelves and vacuumed rugs, and by seven thirty, she felt grubby and sweaty.

So she showered and changed clothes again. Piling her hair up in a casual knot, she refused to allow herself to spend more than ten minutes on minimal makeup. Marisol's advice kept playing in her brain on an endless loop.

...you need to tell the man you're in love with him. You need to do it for yourself, so that you will know you pulled out all the stops. That you put your whole heart in it, that he knows exactly what you want from him...

It sounded so good inside her head.

But the little girl from Oklahoma who'd lost her parents and suddenly found herself in an Upper

East Side apartment with an aunt who only took her out of duty—that unwanted little girl was still inside her, the same way the little boy torn from his family and lost in Siberia still lived inside Ian.

How could she and Ian ever get to love and forever together when he'd made it so clear that he would never even try?

They wrote songs and made movies about that, didn't they? How two people filled each other's gaps, fixed each other's broken places.

But movies and songs, they were just fantasies. In real life, it hurt so bad to be the one that nobody wanted. In real life, a woman could work on her confidence, make herself step up, put in the effort and time for her degree. She could divorce the nice guy and good friend she'd married at his parents' insistence—divorce him so that both of them could find the love of a lifetime. A woman could get a great job in a growing company, raise a beautiful, smart, kindhearted daughter, all while holding out for the one man, the *right* man.

And then, when said woman finally realized she'd found the man for her, it wouldn't matter. Not in the least. Because she'd chosen a man who didn't want a forever with anyone.

A long chain of obscene words scrolled through her brain.

It was all just so wrong.

She didn't want to be brave and strong and determined, damn it. Not about this.

Couldn't a man's love be the one thing in all her life that came easy? Couldn't the man she wanted be sure and strong in his heart? Couldn't her man be the one to say it first, the one to coax her along, to make the impassioned promises that they would work it out, that everything would be all right?

She stood at the window in the living area, staring blindly through the glass at the back of the Chelsea Hotel, thinking how she'd spent her life picking up the pieces, doing what she had to do to build a decent future. Thinking about how love had to go both ways, and with Ian, that would not be happening.

The more she stewed on it all, the more she wanted to pitch a toddler-worthy tantrum, maybe break a few dishes. She wanted to throw the window open, lean out with her hands on the sill and howl in frustration. Longed to scream out her hurt and anger loud enough that they would hear her cry all the way to the Hudson Yards.

The intercom buzzed. Ian had arrived.

And she was furious.

She marched to the door, buzzed him up and then stood there, waiting, every nerve in her body vibrating with frustration, until he knocked.

Ripping off the chain and slamming back the dead bolt, she yanked the door wide.

And there he stood, every woman's dream of male perfection, with his sexy blue eyes and thick, wavy hair, his broad shoulders and deep chest, that strangely compelling facial scar. He held a cardboard tray with coffees from the place up the street, a bakery bag dangling from one big hand.

They stared at each other. He looked vaguely alarmed at the sight of her. "Why are you mad?" he asked. Because of course, he knew her so very well.

He could know her a little less and unconditionally adore her a lot more. That would totally work for her.

"I'm fine," she said and ushered him in.

He followed her to the kitchen, where he set down the bag and coffees and turned to peer at her through narrowed eyes. "*Fine* is not a good word. Not when you have that expression on your face."

Violent urges quivered through her. She really needed to chill. So what if she loved him and he couldn't—or simply wouldn't—love her?

She'd always been the most reasonable person in any room.

Where had all her levelheadedness gone?

"I brought you a latte, one Splenda," he offered cautiously, like a zookeeper throwing fresh fish to a hunger-mad polar bear. "And a bagel, cream cheese and strawberry jam on the side, just the way you like it."

"Thank you." She gestured at the dining table behind them. "So...you want to sit?"

"Great." He said it kind of hopefully—but with an edge of desperation.

She reminded herself that he was trying. That he cared about her. That he clearly didn't want to lose her as a friend. Or as his COO.

She took the bakery bag and he took the coffees. He sat facing the window. She sat in the chair just around the corner from him, with a view of the bright room's brick accent wall and bookcases full of personal mementos, her favorite books and her daughter's, too.

She removed the lid from her latte and had a sip. "So good. Thanks."

He almost smiled as he sipped from his own cup.

A terrible thought occurred to her as she unwrapped her bagel.

Had he come here to tell her he couldn't work with her anymore?

The very idea had her fury escalating again. Seriously? The nerve of him if he did that. She did an amazing job for him, and she loved Patch&Pebble. They were a great team.

Or they always had been.

Possibly not so much this past week. He'd seemed a little distracted. And to be perfectly honest, she had been, too.

Her anger settled to a simmer. She felt marginally calmer.

It occurred to her then that changing jobs might be the answer for this problem she had. Having to see him every day—well, it was awful. She might get over him more easily if she didn't see him at all.

And it wasn't as if she lacked options. More than one other company had sent headhunters her way with excellent offers. And Ian paid her a top salary, with generous bonuses. She had a nice nest egg to tide her over should that become necessary.

It made her sad, though, to think of leaving the company. She'd never wanted a change. She loved her job and everything about it—or she had until recently.

And even if she left Patch&Pebble, she would probably still have to see him now and then. He and Abby shared a strong bond. He cared for Abby as much as he could care for anyone—so no, he wouldn't want to lose what he had with Abby. And it would hurt Abby if he vanished from her life.

But Ella could cope with occasionally having to see him for her daughter's sake. Dealing with him for a few minutes now and then wouldn't be near the hell she currently lived in, having to work with him every day.

"Something wrong with the bagel?" he asked.

She yanked her shoulders back and stared straight at him.

He said in a cautious tone, "You unwrapped it and then you just sat there, staring at it…"

She glanced down at the bagel, unwrapped, her hands on the table to either side of it, the little tubs of jam and cream cheese nearby.

So what if she'd only stared at it? She had bigger things on her mind than a bagel.

"It's fine," she replied through clenched teeth.

He muttered, "There's that word again."

She took the bagel by the corner of the open wrapper and pulled it out of her way. Then she braced her forearms on the table, folded her hands between them and stared him straight in the eye. "Listen. Can we just get down to whatever it is you wanted to talk about?"

He jerked up straight in his chair. It took her a moment to realize he looked absolutely terrified.

And just like that, in an instant, her fury at him melted away. Because she loved him, damn it. She couldn't stand being around him now. It hurt too much. But neither could she bear seeing him upset.

She ached to reach across the distance between

them, put her hand on his, ask him coaxingly, *What is it? What's wrong? How can I help?*

Somehow, she kept her hands to herself. Sucking in a deep breath to settle her churning emotions, she suggested softly, "Whatever it is, why don't you just tell me, just say it? I'll help in any way I can."

He glanced down at his untouched coffee and from there, out the window. Finally, he looked at her again. "I don't want it to be over with us," he said in a low, pained growl.

Her heart slammed against her rib cage, soaring, aching for him, expanding with hope. That he still wanted her.

That just maybe it wasn't over for him any more than it was for her.

She just needed to do it, like Marisol said. Just open her mouth and say that she loved him…

He said slowly, with care and intensity and passion, "I think we made a mistake, putting an artificial ending on it. I want to be with you, Ell. So much. For as long as it lasts."

As long as it lasts…

She drew in a slow breath and let it out with care.

No. Just no.

That wasn't good enough—oh, but that look in his eyes. It said so much more than his words.

That look said he wanted her, needed her, the same as she needed him. That he couldn't stop thinking about her, longing for her, reaching for her in the night…

And finding nothing but emptiness.

She stared into those beautiful eyes—and realized her throat had locked up tight from the pain and turbulence inside her. She swallowed, hard, to relax it.

And she made herself say what *she* needed from *him*. "You would have to agree to be open to, um, more."

More?

Oh, God. Could she be any wimpier?

"More?" He echoed the word, gruff and gentle at once—and wary now. He took her meaning. And he didn't feel the least comfortable with it.

Say it. Just get the damn words out. I love you, Ian. Do you—could you—love me, too? "Ian, come on, we've been friends forever. You know what I want. I want love and I want marriage. What happened in Oregon was beautiful. But I can't *not* be me. I can't go on with you unless you're willing to try to, um, be with me permanently."

Be with me permanently? Dear Lord have mercy. Had she really just said that?

Pathetic. Oh, yeah. That shrew Lucinda so had her pegged.

As for the handsome man around the corner of the table from her...

Silence. A long, awful stretch of endless, word-less seconds. He had that look, the one that spoke of regret and all the things he simply couldn't give her.

Finally, he said what she already knew he was thinking. "Ell. That would never work out."

She scoffed, softly. "In other words, no. You will never want to make it forever with me."

"You know me, Ell."

"Oh, yes, I do. And you know me." She stood, her heart twisting inside her chest, for what he re-fused to give. For the fact that she was losing him without ever having had him in the first place. "You really need to go, Ian."

"Yeah." He got up, too. Carefully, he pushed in his chair before he turned for the door.

She remained standing at the table, staring after him until he vanished down the hallway. A moment later, she heard the door click shut behind him.

Ella understood then. She knew what she had to do.

After reengaging the dead bolt and the chain, she got out her laptop and sent him an email.

From Ell's place Ian went straight to his gym. He stayed for three hours, lifting weights, working up a serious sweat on the elliptical machine, trying to burn off his misery and frustration. It didn't help much.

After a shower and lunch at a diner near the gym, he almost went back to his place. But the idea of sitting alone in his apartment wishing he were someone else so he could have Ella?

No, thanks.

He ended up walking to Battery Park and staring at the Hudson, then wandering around some more, taking the F train to Brooklyn Heights for no reason at all other than he needed to keep moving. He walked down to Cobble Hill and then up and down Court Street for a while before he finally got back on the subway and went home.

His apartment felt every bit as empty and lifeless as he'd known it would. He wandered from window to window, thinking about going out and getting drunk off his ass, knowing it was pointless. Getting plowed would only earn him a hangover.

It would take time, he kept telling himself. This obsession he had with his best friend would end eventually. They would get back to who they used to be together. His life would feel bearable again. He just had to wait it out.

And maybe stop acting like some hopeless, lovesick fool in the meantime. That wouldn't hurt.

Man up and stop dragging around like the world had come to an end.

Yeah. He would do that—buck up, get over himself.

Soon. Very soon...

He went to bed late and couldn't sleep. In the morning, he checked messages—and started to smile when he found an email Ella had sent yesterday, right after he left her co-op.

His smile died half formed as he read.

Ian,
Just a heads-up. Given the situation between us, I think it would be best if I left Patch&Pebble. I don't want to put you in a bind, so I'm happy to stay on for a few weeks to help train my replacement. I will visit HR to give my formal notice on Monday, so please let me know beforehand how long you'll need me to stay.
All best,
Ella

Through an enormous and heroic effort of will, he did not throw his laptop out the nearest window. Instead, for several minutes, he just sat there, fuming, debating the wisdom of going straight to her place all over again—this time to inform her that he would not accept her resignation.

Somehow, he quelled that wild impulse and replied reasonably and calmly to her email instead.

Ella,
You love your job. You've always sworn you would never work anywhere else. There's no reason to leave. Tell me you'll give it more thought before you make such an extreme decision.
Yours,
Ian

He hit Send and tried to concentrate on his other mail, though mostly he just stared at the far wall and considered whether he should go out for breakfast. It took about fifteen minutes for her reply to appear.

Ian,
I don't need to think about it. I've made up my mind. It's time for me to move on.

That did it. Enough of this email crap.

He grabbed his phone and called her.

She answered on the first ring. "Ian, it's what I want. You aren't going to change my mind. I'm happy to make it a smooth transition, but you need to tell me how long you'll—"

"Why, Ell? Just, honestly, why?"

She scoffed. "Please. You know why. We have to deal with reality."

"And that is?"

"It's no good between us now, okay?"

"*Okay?* What the hell? No, Ella. It's not okay. None of this is okay."

"I'm sorry you're upset about this, Ian, but—"

"You're damn right I'm upset. I get that you don't want to go on with me, that what happened in Oregon is as far as you're willing to go with me. I understand that. But eventually, things will get better. There's no reason to quit a job you love because we had a thing once for a few days."

"You're wrong."

"Ella, if you'd just—"

"No. Uh-uh. We never should have had a *thing*, as you call it. It was a bad idea for us to get into bed together. I never should have slept with you, but now that I have, I can't work with you. Not anymore."

"That makes no sense to me."

"Ian, it makes perfect sense."

"We can deal with your issues, whatever they are. You just need to tell me what's really bothering you. We'll work it out. We'll move on. As a team."

Dead silence on her end.

"Ella. Are you there?"

"I am, yes. And you're not listening to me. I am leaving Patch&Pebble. You need to hire someone else."

He couldn't let her do that. "No way. You're irreplaceable."

She scoff-laughed at that. "Please. I'm good, not irreplaceable. You'll find someone just as good. And since you seem so reluctant to decide how long you need me—"

"How can I decide that? I don't want you to go."

"But I am going. And since you won't name a date certain for my departure, I will do it for you. Three weeks and I am gone."

"Ella…" He struggled to find the words, the perfect words that would make her see that she really didn't want to quit.

She didn't wait for him to find those words. "I have to hang up now. Bye." The line went dead.

He started to call her back again, but sanity won out.

She meant it. She wanted out, and he couldn't stop her from going. Somehow, he would need to learn to live with that.

Ella was leaving Patch&Pebble.

And he had lost his best friend.

Chapter Twelve

Monday morning first thing, Ella turned in her formal resignation. And then she went to the morning meeting, dealt with a couple of crises in Minneapolis and touched base with the head of sales. David, their CFO, knocked on her door at noon.

"Lunch, Ella," he said. "Let's go. I'm buying." David had been at the company almost as long as Ella. She read his intention just from the look on his face.

"I'm leaving," she informed him. "I really am. You won't talk me out of it."

"Maybe not. But look at it this way—it's a free lunch, am I right?"

They went to a brasserie a couple of blocks away. David said how much everyone would miss her and he hoped she might consider changing her mind. She made it clear that her mind was made up.

"Well, I'm probably speaking out of turn," he said. "So shoot me. If you do change your mind, just be sure to let Ian know. You can always come back. You know that, right?"

"Did he ask you to say this?"

David chuckled. "I'm guessing you won't buy my act if I ask who you mean by 'he'?"

"I'm not coming back, period. Full stop."

"Aha. Say no more. You've made yourself perfectly clear."

"Good."

"Let's check out the dessert menu, shall we? I've heard the chocolate roulade is the stuff of dreams."

That afternoon, Ella arrived at the dance studio just as Abby and Charlotte's tap class ended. They rode the subway together, got off at Charlotte's stop and walked her to her building. From there, Ella and Abby walked the few blocks home. It was a perfect New York City evening, a few clouds drifting by way up there above the tops of the buildings, the temperature mild with a hint of a breeze. Ella focused on enjoying the moment, on clearing her mind of longing and sadness.

She'd decided to move on, and she'd made the right choice. It might take a while, but in time she would get over Ian. She had to. She saw no other option. What else could she do when the one she loved insisted he could never love her in return?

At home, Abby tossed a salad and heated garlic bread while Ella put together a simple pasta dish with sausage and marinara.

Abby seemed fine. She chattered about her day and got stars in her eyes over the Yankees home game Ian would take her to this coming Saturday against their century-long rivals, the Red Sox. Ella made the right noises in all the right places. She felt sure Abby had no idea that things had changed between Ella and Ian. Maybe she would get lucky—Abby would keep her own relationship with Ian and would never have to know that her mom's friendship with Ian had crashed and burned.

You just keep thinking that, scoffed a sour voice in her head.

Her daughter was no fool. Abby would figure it out even if no one ever told her the truth outright.

As soon as she found out that Ella had quit her job, Abby would know something had gone terribly wrong.

Ella's brilliant solution to that dilemma?

Put it off.

And she did, for three more days. By Thursday, she knew she had to get it over with. What if Ian said something on Saturday and she hadn't prepared Abby first?

No. She had to tell her daughter before Ian picked her up for the game. Either that or get Ian to agree not to mention anything about it.

But to get Ian to help her out with evading this issue she ought to just face, she would have to have a private conversation with him, one in which she asked for what could only be called a favor. She didn't feel comfortable asking Ian for favors, not the way things stood now.

And anyway, she avoided Ian as much as possible at work. He seemed to avoid her, too. They'd come to that. Putting up with each other. Both of them waiting out the time until they no longer had to deal with each other in any way, day to day.

No one at the office had said a word about her replacement. As far as she knew, they hadn't even started looking for anyone.

Not that it should matter to her. She would help however she could if asked. Otherwise, she just needed to get through the days until her last one.

Thinking of the mystery employee who would eventually take her place reminded her sharply that she needed to dust off her résumé. But she had enough money to get by for a while without much of a hit to her savings. A few weeks off wouldn't hurt her. She and Abby might go someplace tropical, take a little vacation, a break from real life.

Thursday night during dinner she spent several dreamy minutes picturing herself on a golden beach shaded by palm trees, at some luxurious resort where they offered any number of fun activities for the kids, while for sad, lovelorn single moms, they kept the umbrella drinks coming 24/7.

Abby said, "You're acting strange, Mom. You keep staring out the window, and when I ask you a question, you don't even hear me, and then I have to ask again before you give me an answer."

Realizing she couldn't put it off any longer, Ella said, "As a matter of fact, I am a little preoccupied, honey."

"Why?"

"I've decided on a career change. Two weeks from tomorrow will be my last day at Patch&Pebble."

Abby's mouth formed a large O. She blinked twice, after which she cried, "But you love your job. Why are you leaving?"

Busted. Clearly, she should have given this conversation careful forethought. However, too late now. She tried for an upbeat tone. "I just realized I'm ready for a change, you know?"

"No, Mom. I *don't* know." For a second or two, Ella braced for tears or accusations—or both. But then Abby drew a slow breath and tried to be calm. Ella loved her so much in that moment—loved both her passion and her true goodness of heart. "But, um, where will you be working now?"

"I'm not sure yet. I'm thinking of taking some time off. I'm thinking that as soon as school's out, you and I might take a little vacation."

"Yeah, but, Mom, I don't get it. What happened? Is something wrong? It does seem like something's been bothering you."

"Um, ahem. Well, of course it is a big change."

"Then why are you doing it? And wait a minute." Abby set down her fork. "Ian can't be happy about this. Is Ian okay?"

"Ian is fine."

Her daughter peered at her, brown eyes doubtful. "I can't see him being happy that you're leaving him."

Ella winced before she could stop herself. "Honey, I'm not *leaving* Ian. Not at all." Had her face turned red? That happened sometimes when she told a fib. She'd just never been all that good at lying—not that she'd lied just now.

She hadn't. Not exactly, anyway...

Abby's mouth had pinched up.

Guilt and misery flooded through Ella. Being

a mom? Hardest damn thing ever. How could she explain this to Abby honestly without saying way more than she should?

An eleven-year-old didn't need to know the gory details of a too-brief love affair gone sour. Especially not when the ex-lovers in question were her mother and the guy everyone called her second dad—the guy she'd known for years as her mother's best friend. To Abby, what went on between her mother and Ian had never gone beyond friendship. And the way Ella saw it, Abby never needed to know what had happened in Oregon.

Lord. It had been so much simpler when she and Philip had divorced. At two, Abby had taken the end of her parents' marriage in stride. She'd been too young to ask questions anyway, and Ella and Philip had never been at odds. Their relationship to each other had remained essentially the same— that of good friends with a daughter to raise.

Abby asked, "How many times have you said how much you love being part of creating the toys kids all over the world can't wait to call their own—and you also love working with Ian. Why would you ever give up what you love?"

Because I'm in love with Ian and he's not in love with me. Ella pressed her lips together to keep the bald truth from getting out.

She couldn't share that with Abby, couldn't take

the chance of damaging Abby's relationship with her second dad.

At the same time, Ella needed to help her daughter make sense of all this.

Ella decided to go with the truth, just easy on the TMI. "Ian understands that I need to try something new. He's not happy about it, but he accepts that it's what I need to do."

Abby groaned. "Why do you need to do it, Mom? I mean, really. Why are you leaving the job that you love?"

"I already explained why. I need a change."

"But *why*?"

Ella hadn't heard that many "whys" in a row from Abby's mouth in years. Her little girl had outgrown the "why" phase at the age of five. But now she sensed that her mom had held back a good portion of the story, and the "whys" wouldn't stop.

Having a smart, sensitive, perceptive daughter had a downside. Who knew?

Abby scowled. "Wait a minute. Is this Ian's fault?"

"It's my decision. Don't blame Ian. I mean that, Abigail."

"You didn't answer my question."

I got nothing. How pitiful is that? "Sometimes things just don't work out in life."

"What things?"

Ella knocked back a big gulp of ice water. "Eat your dinner. It's getting cold."

"Mom. What things?"

"That's all I want to say right now. I'm sorry if I'm disappointing you, but I have no more to tell you, except that everything will work out just fine. I've had a lot of offers from other companies over the years. I will reach out and get something new—interesting work that will pay the bills and challenge me. You and Ian will go on as always. He loves you very much and so do I, and that is never going to change." As those words left her lips, she recognized them as words parents might say to their children when they'd decided to divorce—and not amicably. This was nothing like the friendly, mutually agreed-upon divorce she and Philip had so carefully planned and executed nine years ago.

Ella and Ian had been so close—for so long now. Even closer than she and her first best friend, Philip. She'd honestly believed that nothing could ever destroy their friendship, that what they had was strong, deep and lasting. That they would always be there for each other no matter what, be each other's refuge, each other's sounding board, the one to count on, the one to call when it all went wrong.

She should never, ever have gotten into bed with him.

Except, well…

No.

She couldn't bring herself to regret their weekend in Oregon. For a few beautiful days and nights, they'd had it all, together.

She'd never had it all before.

At least now she could say she knew what it meant to love a man completely, head to toe, inside out, heart and soul. She would hold on to that now, when things felt so bleak and sad and empty.

"Oh, Mom…" Abby's big eyes looked misty, and her shoulders had drooped.

"Sweetheart, don't be sad. Please. It's a good thing. You'll see."

"Mom…" Abby got up and came to her.

Ella stood. They wrapped their arms around each other. Tears burned behind Ella's eyes, too. She blinked them back and held her daughter tight. "I love you. So much," she whispered.

"Oh, Mom. I love you, too…"

Ella framed her daughter's face with cherishing hands and smoothed her brown hair away from her freckled cheeks. "So then. We're good?"

Abby nodded. "Yeah."

Ella nodded back. "Well, all right. We should eat then, before it gets cold."

* * *

The Yankees played the Sox at two thirty that Saturday.

Ian used his car service to ferry him and Abby back and forth to Yankee Stadium. He picked her up at Philip's place, which worked out great—he didn't have to see Ella, didn't have to pretend for Abby's sake that nothing had changed.

Not that he had a clue what Ella might have told Abby. For a week now, he and Ella had only spoken when they needed to at work. He hated it—that she seemed to want nothing to do with him.

At the same time, he found himself waiting for her to come to her senses and realize that quitting the company would never really happen. He just knew she would come around and decide to stay on—aka, plan B, as he'd come to think of it. In plan B, she stayed at the company and slowly, over time, they worked their way back around to being best friends again.

As for plan A? He'd given up on plan A, in which they could continue as lovers until the hot thing between them wore itself out. He looked back on that now as his own deluded fantasy.

Wisely, Ella had nixed plan A right from the gate. He should have known she would never settle for that. Ella had it all going on. Someday she would get what she wanted with a very lucky man.

Not that he could stand to think of her with someone else. His jealousy of some guy she hadn't even met yet made him kind of want to punch himself in the face for being an idiot. He could have had a chance with her. All he had to do was ask for it.

But he'd already hurt her. If it didn't work out—which it most likely wouldn't, given all the ways he could possibly screw it up—she would only get hurt again. He couldn't bear to do that to her a second time.

And plan C? That was her plan, a very bad plan. The one where she left the company and their friendship ended for good.

Never going to happen. She would see the light about that eventually. And when she did, she would still have her job. Because he refused to start looking for her replacement. She didn't need replacing. Plan B would work out in the end. Ella wasn't going anywhere.

He glanced over at the cute kid in the back seat next to him. She had on her Yankees hat and her #45 jersey. "You're kind of quiet," he said—and then wished he hadn't. She might tell him why, and he might not like what she said.

But she only gave him a smile and replied, "Just thinking."

At least he had sense enough not to ask what. "Written any good books lately?"

That got her going. She started in about her latest literary creation. "I'm writing one now about a girl my age that nobody will listen to—well, it's not really that they don't listen. It's that when she talks, *she* can hear her words, but nobody else can."

"So at the end, do they finally hear her?"

Abby tipped her head to the side. Beneath the bill of her hat, he could see she wore a thoughtful frown. "Hmm. I'm not sure yet. Still working on that."

The floodgates seemed to open from there. She talked nonstop to the stadium and all the way to their seats. He listened to her voice, enjoyed her animated descriptions of things going on at school and the hip-hop class recital she expected him to attend in early June.

The game turned out to be a nail-biter, but the Yankees came through four to three.

Never once during the whole afternoon had she mentioned her mother. It bothered him a lot. He had Ella on the brain these days, and he should be grateful Abby didn't have a bunch of questions about her mother's decision to change jobs or…

Well, or whatever. No good could come of him and Abby discussing what might be going on with Ella.

It nagged at him the whole afternoon, though. How much did Abby know about him and Ella, about her leaving Patch&Pebble? He couldn't get answers from Abby without asking the questions. And asking the questions would most likely only end up making him wish he'd kept his damn mouth shut.

"Actually, Ian, we've been sitting all day," she said, so calm and thoughtful, like someone much older than eleven. "How about a walk? The High Line is nice, and it's close to my dad's."

He let the driver go, and they strolled the elevated paths of what used to be a freight rail line, ending up descending to a tree-shaded circle of benches around a pair of spray showers—two seal sculptures, one bright red, the other bold yellow. The seals sprayed mist to cool the air and give kids a little fun on a hot day. Abby dropped to a bench and patted the space beside her.

His butt had no sooner hit the seat than she turned to him, her freckled face sweetly serious, no dimples in sight. "I think we need to talk about my mom, Ian."

He gulped. Set up by a smart little eleven-year-old. He should have known this was coming. "Uh, sure. What's going on?"

Abby wore her patient look. She was like her mother that way, several steps ahead of him too much of the time. "I don't know, really. That's why I'm asking you. She loves her job, but she's quitting. Why?"

"Ah," he said, for lack of actual words as he mentally scrambled for the right thing to say to her.

"It just makes no sense to me, Ian."

"Well, what did she tell you?"

"That she's ready for a change and that you're not happy about her leaving but that you understand. What does that mean, Ian? What do you *understand*?"

The kid was too smart by half. And what the hell *did* Ella mean, anyway? He damn well did not *understand*. Not in the least.

Plus, he reminded himself, Ella would never leave Patch&Pebble, he felt sure of it. Plan B would win out. Just see if it didn't.

But however it went down in the end, Abby needed reassurance now. "Your mom is right. I don't know how I'll get along without her." That sounded good, didn't it? Plus, it was true. He *couldn't* get along without her, and he wouldn't have to when it all shook out.

Plan B. No doubt.

But he couldn't tell Abby about plan B, so he went with what her mother had told her. "It's your mom's choice. It's what she feels she needs right now. And no matter what happens, everything stays the same as far as you and me. You need me, you call me. I'll be at your hip-hop recital, down front and center. Nothing will change, Abby. I promise you that."

Abby still didn't show him even a hint of a dimple. Her big eyes remained way too serious, trained right on him. "That's not what I asked you, Ian. I asked you *why* my mom decided to quit her job suddenly?"

He stared in her eyes and felt hopeless. Hopeless and pissed off at everything in general. *Keep calm*, he ordered himself. *Don't lose it over this.* Abby needed comfort and reassurance, not his crap raining down on her.

But Abby's big brown eyes, expectant and trusting and frustrated, too—those eyes of hers combined with how much he missed her mother…

It all got to him.

It wrecked him.

His best friend had turned her back on him when he only wanted to protect her from his inability to be what she needed in a man.

He threw up both hands. "How the hell should I know? What can I say to you? It's what she wants. Ask *her. She's* the one who's leaving…" *Me.*

Somehow, he kept himself from saying that last, damning word. But not saying it didn't make it any less true. If Ella left, it would be him she was leaving.

Because she needed more than he knew how to give her. He had too many broken parts inside his heart. And he'd yet to figure out how to put them all back together. The broken parts kept him from getting on with his life in the important ways—like loving the right woman and starting a family.

The broken parts held him back from letting Ella know how much she mattered to him. He didn't want Ella to go. But she *would* go. And he was just blowing smoke up his own ass, pinning his hopes on plan B.

He needed to find a way to step up for Ella. If he didn't, plan C would happen. All his ridiculous denials to the contrary, she would go and stay gone. Forever.

At some point, it would be too late for them—for Ella and him. He needed to figure out how to pull it together before she left him behind.

Beside him, Abby seemed not the least bothered by his irrational outburst. Gently, she patted his hand. "It's okay, Ian. I'm not mad at you. But I would really like it if you would talk to my mom and make her feel better. Communication matters. It really, really does."

And from there, she launched into one of her stories about a book she'd just read wherein two smart young girls learned to open up to each other about what was bothering them.

"So that's what you need to do, Ian. Be honest and truthful, really *talk* with my mom."

What could he say to her? "It's good advice, Abby. Thank you."

"Don't just thank me. Do it."

When she looked up at him like that, with all the trust in the world shining in her eyes, what else could he say but "I will."

Sunday, Hailey called. A take-charge kind of woman, his sister got right to the point. "I'm putting the pressure on, Ian. My wedding is next Saturday. If at all possible, I want you there. We *all* want you there, all your brothers and sisters who have been missing you for twenty years. Will you please come?"

He opened his mouth to make excuses—and then realized he had nothing planned for next weekend. No mystery how things would end up if he stayed home. He would mope around his apartment, staring out the windows, thinking about Ella, feeling time slipping away from him. Every day, every hour, every freaking minute only brought him closer to losing forever what he wanted most but somehow couldn't let himself have.

Or maybe he'd already lost Ella completely and just hadn't allowed himself to admit it yet.

Whatever the reality of the situation, it sucked sitting home brooding about it.

"Ian. Did you just hang up on me?"

"I'm still here."

"Well? Will you come to my wedding, please?"

"Sure," he replied before he could think of all the reasons he had no interest in flying across the country for the wedding of a sister he barely knew.

A moment of silence, then, "Terrific. Everyone will be so happy to see you."

He couldn't help chuckling. "You're so determined."

"And damn proud of it, too. Bring Ella. And I want to meet Abby, so think about including her, too."

"Don't push your luck." He said it jokingly. But he wasn't kidding, not really.

"Fine. Just Ella, then."

"I'll see what I can do." Which would be nothing, but he didn't feel like going into all that, so he let his bossy little sister believe whatever she wanted to believe.

"Great. Did you get the invitation I sent?"

"Yes, I did."

"So you've got all the deets—and you know, there's plenty of room at our house for both you and Ella. Stay with us, why don't you? There's a whole separate suite, your own kitchen and separate entrance included, on the bottom floor." She lived with her fiancé, Roman Marek, and his toddler son, Theo.

"Thanks for the offer. I might take you up on it." No, he wouldn't. He needed his own space, and he didn't want to get down in the weeds with her about that.

"Just let me know—and I hope you can make the rehearsal dinner Friday evening…"

"I'll try." Would he? He just might. And that he might shocked the hell out of him. "And I got all the information you sent about that, too."

She stopped pushing, but she didn't say goodbye. For the next ten minutes, she provided updates on every little thing that had happened in Valentine Bay since he'd left two weeks before. He listened to her chatter and realized he kind of enjoyed listening to her. He might even kind of *miss* her—along with all his other siblings on the far side of the USA and their wives and husbands and cute little kids.

Yeah, Ella had predicted that would happen, that he would start to care for them, over time. He hadn't believed her. Plus, "over time" implied a long while, didn't it? It hadn't taken long at all.

Didn't matter, the whole caring thing. He'd decided to go. A weekend away would help keep his mind off Ella and her imminent departure from his company and his life.

He chartered a jet for the trip, a ridiculous extravagance for one person. But he could afford it. Nonstop flights at his convenience to and from the small airport just outside Valentine Bay made it all so much easier.

At three on Friday afternoon, he checked into his bare-bones room at a motel several blocks from the beach. The Isabel Inn and everywhere else in town had been booked for the weekend.

Didn't matter. A bed was a bed.

At five, he arrived at the old theater in the Valentine Bay Historic District where Hailey and Roman would say "I do." Hailey directed community productions in the theater. Roman had put his talents to work renovating the building, strictly adhering to its original structure and design. In the note Hailey had sent him along with the wedding and rehearsal invitations, she'd explained that the old theater had brought her and Roman together, so they'd decided to get married in it.

Half the family was already there. He got a lot of hugs and claps on the back just for showing up. They really did all seem glad to see him. And for the first time since Ella gave him her notice, he felt marginally less alone.

Both Hailey and Daniel asked after Ella. Ian said she couldn't make it. His brother and sister expressed regret at not seeing her and left it at that. He ended up sitting in the second row with a toddler in his lap—along with the others who weren't taking part in the ceremony.

After the brief rehearsal, they filed out into the lobby, where a catered dinner was served on white-clothed tables between the wide Tuscan pillars that held up the ceiling. He sat at a table with Matt, Liam and their families.

The speeches went on forever, mostly humorous ones about Hailey and Roman, who had both grown up in town, though Roman had moved away years ago. Last fall, he'd returned with his little son, Theo. Roman and Hailey had butted heads over the future of the theater. Sparks had started flying and hadn't stopped since.

Ian found he enjoyed the kids a lot—especially Liam's eight-year-old stepdaughter, Coco, who regaled him with stories of her performances in the *Festival of Fall Revue* and another big production titled *Christmas on Carmel Street*. "We put on the shows right here at the Valentine Bay Theater, Uncle Ian," Coco explained.

Next up would be the Medieval Faire, Coco

said. Hailey would be running that, too, this summer in a local park.

The evening kind of flew by. Ian thought about Ella constantly; good thoughts—how much she would have enjoyed this, his lost family, found at last. All of them together, celebrating Hailey and Roman and their new life as a married couple.

After the dinner, he let Daniel talk him into driving up to the Bravo house.

Surprise, surprise. His brothers drove up there, too. Daniel broke out the good scotch and the men sat on the big front porch in the mild late-May evening, sharing family stories until far into the night. Nobody asked him a single uncomfortable question. They let him be.

At two in the morning, having downed a couple more scotches than he should have, he accepted Daniel's offer of a bed for the night. He dropped right off to sleep in the downstairs bedroom off the kitchen, with the window to the backyard halfway open, letting in the cool night air and the smell of evergreens.

His dreams were vivid, real.

Good dreams. True dreams, because they were memories of his childhood in this very house. In those dreams, his past flooded back into him, filling the empty spaces in his mind. In his heart.

He'd given up this family once. There had

seemed no other choice at the time. He'd had to forget them, forget the past, in order to go on without them, to survive in a brutal land. But he woke on Saturday morning knowing he belonged to them again, as they to him.

He shared breakfast in the kitchen with Daniel, Keely, the four-and-a-half-year-old twins named Jake and Frannie, and the littlest one, Marie. Then he hung out with them, not returning to the motel until he needed to shower and change for the wedding.

At three that afternoon, Hailey married Roman on the stage at the theater that had brought them together. It was short and sweet and simple. Hailey, gorgeous in a white lace gown, had all her sisters for bridesmaids and her stepson, Theo, not quite two, as the ring bearer. Roman's mom, Sasha Marek Holland, kept the little one on track. Patrick Holland, the groom's stepfather, stood up as Roman's best man.

After the ceremony, horns honking, cans clattering behind Roman's Lamborghini, they caravanned out to Sweetheart Cove, where Liam and Madison and their families had side-by-side houses right on the beach. They'd put up party tents for the reception.

It was quite a party, too, with a big dance floor assembled not far from the shore and a six-piece band that played well into the night. When Madison and Sten urged Ian to stay over at their place, he didn't even argue, just stretched out on the guest room bed and dropped right off to sleep.

Sunday morning, Ian joined them all for a family breakfast at Madison's—Liam, Karin and their three kids, and Madison, Sten and their new baby, Evelyn Daffodil. Like yesterday up at Daniel's, Ian didn't want to leave.

And no one seemed to expect him to. He spent an hour shooting the breeze with Sten and Karin's dad, Otto. Later, he took a long walk on the beach with Madison, who said that she'd left acting behind and put her Bel Air mansion on the market. She and Sten and baby Evelyn would make their permanent home right here at Sweetheart Cove in Valentine Bay.

Matt showed up in the late afternoon. He said he was hoping Ian might stay over tomorrow, Memorial Day, maybe come on up to the farm on the outskirts of Astoria, where he lived with his wife and baby son.

Ian couldn't say yes fast enough. Matt followed him to the motel so he could check out and then led the way to the farm, where Ian shared dinner with Matt and his wife and the older couple who worked with them raising goats and sheep, fields of flowers, and produce they sold at farm stands, and to restaurants and local markets.

They stayed up late, just Ian and Matt in the company of Matt's sweet-natured, three-legged Siberian husky, Zoya, playing *Grand Theft Auto 5*, catching up on the past twenty years. An hour or so before they called it a night, Matt asked about Ella.

Ian told the truth. "She wants a real relationship. I'm not that guy."

"You might surprise yourself. With the right woman, anything's possible." Matt launched into the story of how he'd met Sabra seven years ago when she broke into his isolated cabin in Clatsop State Forest seeking shelter from a bad storm. "Took us four years to get on the same page at the same time. But in the end, here we are."

Ian said, "That's a great story."

Matt grinned. "And it has a moral, too. Never count love out. Eventually, you'll make it work." He fake-punched Ian on the shoulder. "Grab your controller, little brother. Let's play. I'm the mood to whup your ass."

Ian stayed until after dinner the next day. When Matt and Sabra walked him out to his rental car, they both urged him to come back soon. He found himself saying he would do that.

And meaning it, too.

His plane was waiting at Valentine Bay Executive Airport when he arrived. He slept through the flight, which took most of the night. At his loft, he left his suitcase in the foyer and went to the nearest window to watch the sunrise.

When daylight filled the space, he made himself coffee and breakfast. With a full stomach, he headed for the master bath to clean up.

At eight, he called Audrey to let her know he was taking the day off. "Can you clear my calendar?"

"Of course."

"Thanks, Audrey. You're a treasure."

"I certainly am. Jet-lagged?"

He wasn't, not really. He felt ready for anything. But he supposed jet lag would do for an excuse. "Yeah, I need the day."

She kept him on the phone for a while with the thousand and one problems she'd been saving up for him since Thursday. He listened, answered her questions, agreed with her solutions to all the issues she could solve herself and gave her instructions for everything else.

It was after nine when she finally let him go. He unpacked his suitcase, put everything away and called the car service. Fifteen minutes later, he ducked into the cool, dark interior of the town car.

And twenty-five minutes after that, he entered the Central Park Zoo.

Bypassing the tropic zone, he strode by the seals and the snow monkeys, headed straight for the bear habitat, where he found Betty and Veronica napping on the rocks.

He stood at the viewing screen in the gray light of the overcast day, staring at the two giant, oblivious bears, waiting for the panic to set in. It was a long wait.

And yet a strangely pleasant one. Women pushing strollers and a few random couples went by. More than one group of tourists observed the bears, each group with a guide to explain about Veronica and Betty and their individual journeys from the wild west to the Central Park Zoo.

The bears kept yawning, rolling over, making lazy growling noises, seeming completely satisfied not to do much more than lie there, easy and content in their giant, open-air cage.

Finally, one of them—Betty, he was fairly sure, the one with the blonder hair on her head—rolled into the stream below their resting spot on the rocks. She landed, then rolled again to get her giant paws under her. Sitting up in the water, she threw her head back and let out a mighty roar, displaying her long, sharp canines meant for ripping and those jagged rows of incisors that could cut to bits what the canines had ripped.

It should have happened right then, at the sight

of that wide-open mouth filled with so many flesh-tearing teeth. That should have triggered him.

But it didn't.

Betty shut her mouth and rolled to her back again. She wriggled a little, enjoying the water, and then set about climbing back up on the rocks.

Just a big, shaggy bear in the Central Park Zoo, lumbering about on the ledges well below him in the bear habitat, unable to reach him, no matter how hard she might have tried. Betty couldn't harm him—Veronica, either.

Just bears in the zoo.

And he was no longer a scared, lost little boy.

He knew where he came from and how he had gotten there. He knew who his people were—on both coasts. In the deepest sense, he belonged.

Belonged to the family of his early childhood, the family in Oregon who had never given up trying to find him. He belonged to Glynis, the mother who had found him, lost and unspeaking, alone in a strange land, the woman who had taken him home, healed him in every way she could, given him a good life. And when she died too soon and way too suddenly, she had left him prospering, with a bright future ahead.

But most of all, he belonged to Ella. And he had for years now, though he'd let his fears and his scars—the scars inside that no one could see—

keep him from knowing who she really was to him, keep him from admitting all that she meant. For too long, he'd let what had happened to him as a lost child hold him back.

Not anymore.

He needed to show her that he was finally ready for her—for all she had to give.

If only she hadn't turned her back on him for good.

If only she would give him one more chance…

Chapter Thirteen

Ella had schooled herself.

The lesson was simple: don't think about Ian.

Don't wonder where he went when his office remained empty all day Friday. Don't just happen to drop by Audrey's desk and ask her casually where the boss had gone.

All Friday, she kept herself from getting anywhere near Audrey. Even when Marisol had to back out on their usual Friday lunch and she ended up alone at her desk with takeout tom yum goong and Thai iced tea, Ella never let her weaker self take control.

But late Friday afternoon, she got her answer

anyway, when she heard her assistant, Samar, and Audrey chatting in the break room.

"Oregon, huh?" Samar asked.

"That's right. He's got family there, did you know?"

"I heard, yeah."

"One of his sisters is getting married this weekend…"

Although she had nothing to smile about where Ian was concerned, Ella felt a happy grin spread across her face. Hailey's wedding. He'd actually flown out there for it.

She should have guessed.

But she hadn't. He'd seemed absolutely determined that he would never go back to Oregon, been so cold and confident about it that she'd begun to believe he meant what he said.

And yet, within a few weeks of that first visit, he'd flown back.

Ella wished she could've gone with him. She would have loved seeing Hailey get married in that old theater where she and Roman had met. Maybe she could have dropped by Wild River Ranch to visit Aislinn Bravo Winter's giant, fluffy rabbits, or maybe hung out with Keely, the twins and little Marie up at the Bravo house.

So sue her. Since it had all blown up in her face

with Ian, she'd let her envy of all he could have that he'd just turned his back on get to her a little.

Or maybe a lot.

Yeah, he'd had a rough go of it. But other people suffered, too, in life. Since ending it with Ian and giving her notice at work, she'd spent too many late nights after Abby went to bed sitting on the sofa in the dark, scowling at cable television and obsessing over the thousand and one ways Ian didn't appreciate all that he had.

At least he seemed to have finally seen the light that when you had a family like the Bravos, you didn't just go meet them and then never go near them again.

"Way to go, Ian," she muttered angrily under her breath, tiptoeing away from the break room so that neither Audrey nor Samar would know she'd eavesdropped on their conversation like some brokenhearted fool.

Which reminded her.

Clearly, she needed to get herself schooled all over again.

She needed to get over Ian once and for all.

And she was. She would.

Ian who?

Never heard of the guy.

In a week, she would leave Patch&Pebble for good. That would help. She would only ever have to see him again now and then if he happened to pick up Abby at her place. Mostly, Ian and Abby got together on the weekends, and most weekends Abby stayed at Philip's.

So big yay on that. As soon as she left the company, Ella might go for months without seeing his gorgeous face.

The long weekend crawled by, with Abby upstate. She'd gone camping with Philip, Chloe and the girls. Ella did some shopping. She cleaned the apartment and constantly reminded herself how she ought to dust off her résumé, update her LinkedIn profile and contact those headhunters. She tried not to wonder about Ian's trip to Oregon, not to picture all the smiling Bravos and Hailey in her wedding gown.

Philip dropped Abby off at six Monday night. Ella hugged her tight, breathed in her scent of insect repellent and dust—and felt better about everything, to have her daughter home again.

Tuesday morning, Ian remained absent from work. Had he stayed on in Oregon? Ella ached to know. But she made herself avoid the break room and keep well clear of Audrey's desk.

Marisol called her at eleven. "Charlotte's missing her bestie after the long weekend." Their tap class Monday had been canceled due to the holiday. "Okay with you if I have them over here at our place? They can hang out and have dinner, maybe even do a little studying. I can get her home by eight."

"Thanks. She'll love that."

"Good, then. We're set. And I've been missing you, too. Sorry I couldn't make our lunch Friday. It's been forever since we got together. Any chance you could steal an hour away today?"

They met at a Greek place they both liked.

Ella had taken just one bite of her gyro when Marisol said, "Charlotte reports that Abby told her that you quit Patch&Pebble."

"I did, yeah."

"You love that job, Ella."

She set down her sandwich. "I need to move on."

"Did you tell him how you feel?"

Ella tried not to wince. Okay, she hadn't, not exactly. But she didn't want to get into all that. Not now. "It's a long story. Can we save it for some future lunch, please—like, maybe a hundred years from now?"

Marisol stuck her fork upright in her salad, shoved back her chair and stalked around to Ella's side of the table. "Get up here." She grabbed Ella's hand and pulled her into her arms. "Hold on tight," Marisol commanded.

Sob-laughing, Ella hugged her friend good and hard.

"It's all going to work out," Marisol promised in her ear.

Ella didn't really believe her, but she agreed with her, anyway.

The rest of the day at the office? Four hours that took half a lifetime to go by. Nobody in the break room gossiped about Ian's current whereabouts, so she remained in the dark on that score.

At five o'clock she got out of there. Twenty minutes later, she let herself in her front door—and felt immediately at loose ends, with Abby at Charlotte's and a dinner alone to look forward to.

She'd just engaged the dead bolt and put the chain on the door when someone knocked on it. Probably one of her neighbors in the building.

But you never knew. Some creep could have slipped in downstairs behind her and followed her up. To be safe, she checked the peephole and got the shock of her life.

Ian?

Oh, God. She'd lost it. Now she was seeing him when no way he could be here.

She squinted through the tiny glass again.

Still Ian.

Her knees went to rubber. She turned, flopped back against the door and took slow breaths, waiting for...

What?

She had no idea.

He knocked again. "Ell, come on. I know you're in there. I followed you up."

That stiffened her spine. He had a nerve and a half, scaring her like that.

Whirling, she slid back the dead bolt, took off the chain and pulled the door open. "What are you doing here?" she demanded through clenched teeth.

He fell back a step. "I need to talk to you."

"Why?"

Cautiously, he tried to peer around her shoulder. "Is Abby here?"

"She's having dinner at Charlotte's."

"Good," he said quietly. "That's good. I was hoping to get a few minutes alone, you and me."

"What for?"

He just stood there, in perfectly tailored gray slacks and a crisp blue button-up, looking effortlessly hunky, with those thick, muscular shoulders and that jaw carved from granite beneath just the right dusting of scruff. "God," he said, sounding downright reverent. "You look good, Ell. I've missed looking at you." He stared at her so…longingly?

No. That couldn't be. Ian McNeill didn't *do* longing. "Ian?" she asked in a tiny voice.

"Yeah?"

"What's going on?"

He looked at her like he could just eat her right up. "Let me in? Please?"

She moved back and gestured him forward. He filled up her doorway and then he was inside, stepping past her, bringing his beloved scent of sandalwood and new-mown grass. She shut the door and indicated the far end of the hallway and the living area beyond.

He led the way. She followed numbly behind him, feeling strangely disembodied, like she'd landed in an alternate universe where nothing was as she knew it to be.

In the main room, she sucked in a shuddery breath and asked again, "What is it?"

"Ell. Damn it. I..."

She put up a hand. He fell silent.

They stared at each other some more.

And it came to her. This was her chance, to step up. To say it. To get it right out there, no matter what happened next, to override the lonely little orphaned girl inside her, to be strong and speak her truth out proudly. "Ian, I've been a coward."

"What?" He blinked and his head jerked back, like she'd slapped him in the face. And then he closed the few feet of distance between them and put his big hands on her, clasping her upper arms, holding her gaze, so sure and steady, those blue eyes full of heat and intention. "No, you're not.

No way. You're brave, Ell. The bravest, strongest person I know."

She lifted her right hand, brought it up between them and pressed her fingers to his warm lips, felt his breath flow down her palm. "I never said it. I need to say it." Her throat clutched and her eyes burned with hot moisture. But she didn't let the rising tears stop her. "I love you, Ian. I'm *in* love with you. I think I have been for at least four or five years now. I never even had a clue of it until that day in the hospital last month, when Lucinda said it right to my face. She said that everybody knew I was in love with you. She said I was pathetic."

His mouth had dropped open. "Say it again."

A smile trembled across her lips as she gently nudged his chin. "You're gaping."

"Damn straight. Say it again."

"That Lucinda said I was pathetic?"

He scowled. "Forget Lucinda. Just say it."

She sucked in a slow breath and told the truth. "I love you, Ian McNeill. I'm *in* love with you."

And he said, "That's good, Ell." His hands strayed upward, big, warm palms skating over her shoulders, up the sides of her throat until he framed her face.

She gazed into those unforgettable eyes of his and wished with all her heart never to have to look away. "Yeah?"

He nodded. "Yeah. I can't tell you *how* good. Because, Ella Ryan Haralson, I love you, too. So much. For such a long time, years of knowing you and not realizing what we had, what we were always meant to be. Tell me there's still a chance for me—for us. Tell me you haven't given up on me yet."

Her vision blurred. She had to blink the tears away. "I tried to give up on you."

He kissed her, a sweet brush of his mouth across hers. "I can't blame you. All these years. I've been such an ass."

"Yeah." She sniffled. "You *have* been an ass, so thickheaded. All wounded and unwilling."

"It took finding my family and thinking I had lost you to get me to open my eyes and see what's been right in front of me all this time—it's you, Ell. You're the one. You're *my* one. My only one..."

She could not survive another second without her mouth pressed to his. Surging up, she wrapped her arms around his neck and claimed his lips.

"Ell..." He groaned.

And then he kissed her.

And then, his mouth still locked to hers, he lifted her. She jumped up, wrapping her arms around him, sparing a second for gratefulness that she'd worn a flared skirt so she could wrap her legs around him, too. One of her shoes fell off and clattered to the floor. She kicked the other off to join it.

He held her tight, kissing her endlessly as he strode back down the hall to the first door, her bedroom. Carrying her in there, he turned and sat on the bed, still cradling her close in his lap, her ankles hooked behind his back.

The kiss continued, so deep, so hungry, for the longest time. She reveled in it, rocking against him, feeling how much he wanted her and wanting him right back, for now.

And forever...

Her mind could barely encompass the wonder of that—Ian and Ella, now and forever...

He caught her face in his hands again. "Look at me, Ell."

"Hmm?" She gazed up at him, her vision only slightly blurred by happy tears.

"This," he said, long fingers combing back into her hair. "Us. I'm talking forever, Ell. I'm talking you and me and Abby—maybe more kids if that's how it works out. I'm talking a lifetime. Could you do that, Ell? Would you take that chance with me?"

She pressed her palm to his lean cheek. "Funny you should ask. I was just thinking..."

"What? Say it. You're killing me here."

She laughed for sheer joy, pushed him back across the bed and got her legs folded under her, one on either side of him. Bracing her hands on the mattress, she got right down in his face. "I was just thinking that forever with you is what I want, what I've hardly dared to dream of."

"Ell…" He lifted his head off the mattress enough to kiss her again, a soft kiss, a kiss of promise, reverent and slow. "So that's a yes, then?" He growled the question against her lips.

"A yes, absolutely."

"I'll be yours, you'll be mine."

"As it should be, for today, for tomorrow, for all our lives." And she claimed his mouth with hers.

For a while, they didn't need words. They undressed each other and celebrated their union with more slow kisses, with long, lingering sighs and, ultimately, deep and mutual satisfaction.

In time, they got up. He put on his pants and she wore his shirt—and then they stood by the bed, looking at each other, barefoot, half-dressed with messy hair.

They both started laughing.

And he asked, "When, exactly, is Abby getting home?"

"Around eight."

He grabbed his flashy watch off the nightstand. "Forty-five minutes. I know she'll be happy, seeing us together…"

Ella snickered. "Yeah. But maybe we need *not* to look like we just crawled out of my bed."

He pulled her close and kissed her deeply. "Agreed."

So she gave him back his shirt and he put it on. She dressed in jeans and a knit top. They stood in her bathroom, side by side, combing their hair, grinning at each other in the mirror like a couple of naughty kids with delicious secrets no outsider could ever share.

And she thought, *This. A lifetime of this. Us, side by side, sharing the bathroom mirror. This is what it's all about, the dream I thought I would never get to live...*

But she'd conquered her fear and so had he. And that finally made it possible for them to reach for each other.

They ordered takeout. Once the delivery guy had come and gone, Ella locked up, but with the chain off so that Abby could let herself in. Over dumplings and Szechuan pork, Ian shared all the details of his recent trip to Oregon, including the rehearsal dinner, Hailey's wedding and reception, and his visits to the Bravo house, Sweetheart Cove and Berry Bog Farm.

"And you were right," he added. "I don't know how it happened, exactly, but I feel that I'm part of them now, one of the family."

"Because you are, very much so. We should go back again soon, take Abby this time."

"Gracie's getting married next," he said. "Soon. In a week and a half, to be exact. But we can make it. I'll charter a jet."

"Whoa. That's extravagant."

"What's money for except to spend on things you really want to do? And I've been thinking…"

"Tell me. Everything."

"It's just that there's something I failed to do." She frowned at him. "Can't think what…"

He pushed back his chair. She gazed up at him, still puzzled.

But then he knelt at her side and took her hand. "Ella, I love you. You're everything to me. Will you make me the happiest man on earth and agree to marry me, to be my wife?"

"Ian…" Her eyes got all misty again. "Yes. Absolutely. I love you, too, and I can't wait to marry you." She bent and kissed him, taking her time about it, tasting Szechuan sauce and thinking that from now on, Chinese food would remind her of this perfect evening when she and Ian became so much more than just friends.

A moment later, as Ian sat back down in his chair and picked up his chopsticks, they heard Abby at the door, the key in the lock, the dead bolt sliding back, the sound of the door opening, shutting, the clinking of the locking process all over again.

And then Abby's rapid footsteps approaching down the hall. "Mom, I'm…" She stopped stock-still where the hallway opened into the living area. "Ian?" She shook her head, blinking, as though not quite believing what she saw.

And then, with a happy cry, she ran to him. He rose, opening his arms just in time for her to throw herself against him. Wrapping her arms around his waist, she squeezed good and tight.

When she looked up at him, she asked, "Are we all back together again?"

He stroked her straight brown hair, skated a finger down the bridge of her nose. "Yes, we are. Very much back together, more together than ever before." He glanced at Ella then, love and their future shining in his eyes.

"I knew it." With her arms still around him, Abby managed to jump up and down. "The minute I saw you guys just now, I knew that everything would be all right." She glanced over her shoulder and beamed at Ella. "You're keeping your job, right?"

Ian answered first, his gaze holding Ella's. "God, I hope so. I haven't hired anyone. I haven't even considered anyone. I just didn't want you to go."

Abby demanded, "Mom?"

Ella confessed, "I haven't been looking, either. Guess I'll just have to stay on at Patch&Pebble."

"I knew it!" crowed Abby. "You could never leave, and Ian couldn't let you go." She glanced up at him for confirmation.

"I can't speak for your mother," he said. "But you're right, Abby. I never want her to go."

"Then it's settled," declared Ella, rising, stepping closer to the two most important people in her world. "I'm staying." She and Ian gazed at each other, a long look, one that promised so much—all the days and nights to come.

Abby let go of Ian and pulled back a fraction. She eyed him and then Ella, and then she asked cautiously, "Are you guys...getting married?"

Ella nodded at Ian.

His smile got wider. "As a matter of fact, we are. Your mother has just agreed to be my wife."

Abby gasped. She stacked both hands on her chest. "My heart is beating so fast. You guys, I'm so happy." She hooked an arm around Ella and then one around Ian and side hugged them both, beaming up at them with a proud gleam in her eye. "You've been *communicating*, haven't you?"

"We have," Ian readily agreed. Ella felt a blush coming on from the way he looked at her. She knew he was thinking of the two of them, all wrapped up together in her bed, saying so much without uttering a word.

"A family, that's us." Abby's eyes shone so bright. She beamed up at Ian. "You're my second dad for real now. Just think about that."

"It's a good day," said Ian.

"The best day," agreed Ella, leaning toward him for a quick, sweet kiss.

Epilogue

The three of them—Ian, Ella and Abby—flew to Oregon ten days later for Gracie's wedding. Abby loved Valentine Bay and wanted to come back often. And they did come back, returning for two weeks that summer and then for five days during Abby's Christmas break.

Ella and Ian decided they wanted a place all their own to start their new life together. They bought a rooftop apartment in Chelsea, not far from Ella's co-op, which they sold, along with his loft in Tribeca. Their new place was large and full of light. Abby loved it, plus, she stayed close to her school and her dad, stepmom and little sisters, and her best friend Charlotte's apartment, too.

As for their wedding, Ella and Ian decided to get married in Oregon, on the Fourth of July of the following year. Ian chartered a jet and flew all their New York friends and family to Valentine Bay for the celebration.

He and Ella said their vows in the backyard up at the Bravo house. Ella had Abby for her maid of honor. Marisol, Chloe and Charlotte attended her, as well. Matt stood up as Ian's best man, with their three other brothers and Philip stepping up as groomsmen, too.

The reception took place on the beach under white canopies at Sweetheart Cove. Champagne flowed freely and they had music and dancing, the same as at Hailey's wedding the year before.

After dark, the town fireworks display lit up the sky out over the ocean. The band took a break for that. They all listened to the music broadcast by a local radio station to go with the pulsing lights high above. Sten, Madison's husband, had rigged up a couple of giant outdoor speakers and they blasted them out over the sand. Katy Perry sang "Firework" and the sky blazed bright with every color of the rainbow, the lights shooting high and falling to the ocean in a shower of sparks.

While everyone stared up at the bursts of fire high in the sky, Ian's bride took his hand and pressed it to her belly.

More than a little stunned, he stared into those fine dark eyes of hers, hardly daring to believe. "For real?" he asked gruffly. After all, he had everything. "A baby, too?"

She nodded, so beautiful in her filmy white dress, her hair down on her shoulders, tossed a little by the night wind the way he liked it best. "In early March, I think."

He pulled her close and wrapped his arms good and tight around her. They shared a slow kiss as more streams of light shot skyward.

"I never thought I would make it back," he said, still holding her close, his mouth a breath from hers. "Never thought I would find all I lost so long ago."

"But you did, Ian." She lifted enough to kiss him again, a quick kiss, sweet and true, a kiss of love, of belonging. "You found your way home."

"Home to you." His voice sounded ragged to his own ears, rough with all the big emotions, the ones that make a man ache in the best sort of way. "I love you, Ell."

"I love *you*. And I am so glad you made it home—to the family you thought you'd lost. And at last, to me."

* * * * *

MILLS & BOON

Coming next month

THE PRINCESS AND THE REBEL BILLIONAIRE
Sophie Pembroke

Isabella had to admit to herself that she was just postponing the inevitable. She had the whole rest of the week here in this glorious villa, beside this beautiful lake, with Matteo. Not making the most of it would be a terrible waste.

Throwing open the doors to the shared balcony that joined their bedrooms, Isabella let the morning air rush in, and felt her own breath rush out.

Once again, Matteo was already sitting at the table on the balcony. There were shadows under his eyes that suggested his sleep might have been as disturbed as her own. But he looked up as she appeared, and a slow smile spread across his face at the sight of her, making him look instantly younger. More free.

Was he remembering that moment last night, too? The one when he'd been close enough for her to kiss, if she'd moved her head just ever-so-slightly? Was he thinking about the suggestion he'd made to her?

The smirk on his face suggested he probably was.

"Good morning," he said, his voice low and warm. "Sleep well?"

She took her seat. "Like a baby." It wasn't a lie. Babies were notoriously bad sleepers, weren't they?

"Me too." The smirk hadn't gone anywhere. "So, how are we going to spend our second day in secluded paradise? Chess? Poker?"

He was teasing her now, but she didn't rise to it. Instead, she looked out over the lake, the balcony suddenly claustrophobic, despite all the fresh air. This villa was huge, and she knew that if she asked for space Matteo would give it to her. He wasn't the kind of man to press where he wasn't wanted, she could tell that already from the way he'd backed off last night after the merest suggestion of more.

The problem was, she wasn't at all sure she wanted him to keep backing off. But she wasn't certain enough to let him in, either.

She wanted him; she wasn't lying to herself about that anymore. But it was so against The Rules. And beyond anything she'd let herself want for so long—ever since Nate. The desire she felt for Matteo…it was overwhelming, and terrifying.

And it felt amazing, all the same.

She stared out over the water and the mountains in the distance. The June air was warm and welcoming, but the breeze from the water kept things fresh in the shady trees that surrounded the villa.

She didn't want to be trapped inside today—otherwise, this villa was no better than the palace in Augusta that she'd escaped from.

Maybe she wasn't ready to take the risk of letting Matteo in quite yet. But perhaps she could take the tiny risk of letting herself out. Just a little bit.

One small first step towards where she was almost ready to admit she really wanted to go.

To bed, with Matteo.

Isabella placed her empty coffee cup down on her saucer. "I'm going for a walk, down by the lake," she said, before she could change her mind. That would give her time and space to keep figuring out what she wanted from this week. Time away from the allure of Matteo's smile, or those green eyes that pulled her in whenever she caught them.

Matteo grinned. "Great! I'll come with you."

Continue reading
THE PRINCESS AND THE REBEL BILLIONAIRE
Sophie Pembroke

Available next month
www.millsandboon.co.uk

Copyright © 2021 Sophie Pembroke

COMING SOON!

We really hope you enjoyed reading this book.
If you're looking for more romance, be sure to
head to the shops when new books are
available on

Thursday 13th
May

To see which titles are coming soon, please visit
millsandboon.co.uk/nextmonth

MILLS & BOON

LET'S TALK
Romance

For exclusive extracts, competitions
and special offers, find us online:

 facebook.com/millsandboon

 @MillsandBoon

 @MillsandBoonUK

Get in touch on 01413 063232

For all the latest titles coming soon, visit
millsandboon.co.uk/nextmonth

WANT EVEN MORE
ROMANCE?
SUBSCRIBE AND SAVE TODAY!

'Mills & Boon books, the perfect way to escape for an hour or so.'

MISS W. DYER

'Excellent service, promptly delivered and very good subscription choices.'

MISS A. PEARSON

'You get fantastic special offers and the chance to get books before they hit the shops.'

MRS V. HALL

Visit millsandboon.co.uk/Subscribe
and save on brand new books.

MILLS & BOON
A ROMANCE FOR EVERY READER

- **FREE** delivery direct to your door

- **EXCLUSIVE** offers every month

- **SAVE** up to 25% on pre-paid subscriptions

SUBSCRIBE AND SAVE

millsandboon.co.uk/Subscribe

MILLS & BOON

THE HEART OF ROMANCE

A ROMANCE FOR EVERY READER

ODERN

Prepare to be swept off your feet by sophisticated, sexy and seductive heroes, in some of the world's most glamourous and romantic locations, where power and passion collide.

STORICAL

Escape with historical heroes from time gone by. Whether your passion is for wicked Regency Rakes, muscled Vikings or rugged Highlanders, awaken the romance of the past.

EDICAL

Set your pulse racing with dedicated, delectable doctors in the high-pressure world of medicine, where emotions run high and passion, comfort and love are the best medicine.

rue Love

Celebrate true love with tender stories of heartfelt romance, from the rush of falling in love to the joy a new baby can bring, and a focus on the emotional heart of a relationship.

Desire

Indulge in secrets and scandal, intense drama and plenty of sizzling hot action with powerful and passionate heroes who have it all: wealth, status, good looks…everything but the right woman.

EROES

Experience all the excitement of a gripping thriller, with an intense romance at its heart. Resourceful, true-to-life women and strong, fearless men face danger and desire - a killer combination!

To see which titles are coming soon, please visit

millsandboon.co.uk/nextmonth

JOIN US ON SOCIAL MEDIA!

Stay up to date with our latest releases, author
news and gossip, special offers and discounts, and
all the behind-the-scenes action
from Mills & Boon...

 millsandboon

 millsandboonuk

 millsandboon

It might just be true love...

Unlimited access to all your
favourite Mills & Boon romances!

Start your free trial now

We Love Romance
with MILLS & BOON

Available at
weloveromance.com

GET YOUR ROMANCE FIX!

MILLS & BOON
— *blog* —

Get the latest romance news, exclusive author interviews, story extracts and much more!

blog.millsandboon.co.uk

MILLS & BOON

HISTORICAL

Awaken the romance of the past

Escape with historical heroes from time gone by. Whether your passion is for wicked Regency Rakes, muscled Viking warriors or rugged Highlanders, indulge your fantasies and awaken the romance of the past.

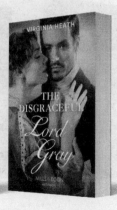

Historical stories published every month, find them all at:

millsandboon.co.uk/Historical

MILLS & BOON

HEROES

At Your Service

Experience all the excitement of a gripping thriller, with an intense romance at its heart. Resourceful, true-to-life women and strong, fearless men face danger and desire - a killer combination!

Eight Heroes stories published every month, find them all

millsandboon.co.uk/Heroes

MILLS & BOON
MEDICAL
Pulse-Racing Passion

Set your pulse racing with dedicated, delectable doctors in the high-pressure world of medicine, where emotions run high and passion, comfort and love are the best medicine.

ght Medical stories published every month, find them all at:

millsandboon.co.uk

OUT NOW!

A Royal Declaration

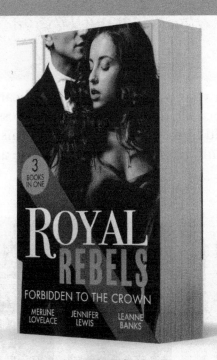

Available at
millsandboon.co.uk

MILLS & BOON

OUT NOW!

Here comes the bride…

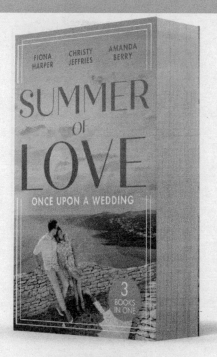

Available at
millsandboon.co.uk

MILLS & BOON

OUT NOW!

The royal treatment

3 BOOKS IN ONE

ROYALLY
Ever After

LYNNE GRAHAM | CARA COLTER | A.C. ARTHUR

Available at
millsandboon.co.uk

MILLS & BOON